Second Coming
Christian Apocalyptic Horror

John James Minster

DEDICATION

With all my heart, soul, and mind to the carpenter.

CONTENTS

ACKNOWLEDGMENTS

Egregious thanks to spooky artist, Stephanie Jamison, for acting as first reader of Second Coming, and for then hand-painting the magnificent original cover art. Her use of light never ceases to arrest the imagination. Equal thanks to the greatest editor, Nicolette Cavallaro, whose brilliant eyes see every word as a criminal suspect, resulting in multiple convictions and capital executions. To Means Smith, Jr. of Philadelphia, who argued with me daily for one entire year and pointed The Way, back in 1985. To God, for the seventy-seven chances. To my readers: welcome to my nightmares, happy to share, with love. Stay spooky!

First Flood

Mesmerized by the dark, swollen sky birthing an impossible volume of hard-falling rain, Gabriel Thomas stared east out of the South Elementary School third-grade homeroom window. His blond scalp itched from lice. *Too much togetherness is a dreadful thing,* he thought. Hypnotized by the steady percussion of large droplets smashing against glass and roof, his melancholy thoughts drifted home. He missed his mom and dad something fierce. In this emergency July session, the governor and legislature for once in agreement ordered every Pennsylvanian to shelter in place until the storm abated. This was the thirty-eighth day of a non-stop deluge with a ferocity never recorded, save for an old story dating back four-and-a-half millennia about a man and his boat filled with animals in pairs. Similar storms engulfed every continent.

Dear Santa, for Christmas in July please bring me a neck that doesn't hurt. Gabriel ached all over from awkward and uncomfortable sleep on the gym's wrestling mat. Despite daily showers in the locker room, the tangy stink of mildew, a moist, musty, pungent scent like old logs rotting in a swamp clung to the same clothes he had worn now for weeks. He along with five hundred students and fifty adult employees had learned what it meant to shelter-in-place under a ceaseless downpour while rebreathing the same uncirculated indoor air, close, and sticky.

This day, he swooned and rested there, like a small river creature dreamily estivating the summer away in cool mud. *This is not good, not good,* his mind looped as he gazed out at a muddy ditch under a scud of black clouds that could not be any thicker. A pervasive sense of disquiet and dread descended on him like an oppressive malodorous fog, which clamped his mood like frozen vice grips.

Every day he watched the flood progress. Memories of sunlight seemed to him as alien and untenable as waking dreams. The Perkiomen Creek had overflowed its banks weeks ago. Last week, dank sodden fields started to disappear under a newly formed river of mud, gradually swallowed by its merciless flow. Today its banks lapped at the school's brick exterior walls.

Gabriel loved to daydream, following whimsical thoughts wherever they wanted to carry him. He dreamed of building his own terrifying robot protector made from spare parts in his dad's basement. He had almost no idea of its mechanics, but the mechanized monster appeared finished in his mind, so it was time to decide on its name. *Minotaur,* he decided.

That was the moment his mind became invaded by thoughts not his own. It surprised him. He sat up straight and inhaled deeply. He blinked and thought he had spotted pinpoints of red and white light exploding behind closed lids, so he closed them and kept them shut. The effect persisted. *Am I going crazy? Is this what being insane feels like?*

The thought of going crazy did not frighten him—quite the contrary. *God…I…feel…so…*strong! He struggled to identify this new sensation: golden white warmth; heightened senses; logic. Clarity and critical thinking expanded from dirty narrow trails to high-speed superhighways. A hot injection of wisdom that he perceived as good, and cool waves of knowledge, especially of the nature of evil, infused him with an indomitable sense of confidence. Feelings of invincibility and power flooded his core. He glanced down. *Is heatless light exploding from my chest? Feels like it. Why can't I see it?* He tingled from scalp to soles. At this moment it was as if his brain itself had eyes, and for the very first time his eyes had been opened. They took in not only the world, but the universe.

If this had not been a waking dream he would have fought to remain asleep and prolong this disruptive, pleasantly surreal fugue for as long as possible. Senses of hearing and smell had become more acute. Gabriel felt energized like never before yet blanketed in peaceful serenity. *What a rush! God speaks to me! Thank you Lord for these gifts. Please use me however you will. I am yours.*

From a vague place he heard his name spoken. He heard it a third time like a persistent morning alarm clock. It pulled him from his dream-like reverie back to the here and now.

"Mr. Thomas," boomed Mr. McGonigal, who bullied students in health and gym classes when not acting as Gabriel's homeroom teacher. "Do not force me to demand your attention a fourth time.

Gabriel tore his gaze from the window to face the front. "Sorry, what did you want?"

Safely ensconced behind his throne of power McGonigal, all six-foot-one, hundred-sixty pounds of him towered menacingly over his third-grade loco parentis charges. He walked from behind his desk and stood in front of it. Gabriel's gaze focused on the crooked half-Windsor knot in McGonigal's hideous, long-obsolete cellulose cravat. McGonigal tilted his long scarecrow arms with elbows down, palms facing up. "Mr. Thomas, I asked the class a question and called upon you to answer it. So, what is the answer?" Every one of the thirty students recognized the smirk and tone from their most despised of all teachers. It meant he had singled out today's scapegoat for his hateful rage. This midday was Gabriel Thomas's turn.

"My mind was on new information. Please repeat the question."

McGonigal paused and stared for effect. Then: "Although it goes against my policy to repeat a question for rude children insulting me by withholding their rapt attention, since you asked so politely, I will give you one final opportunity. If you answer the question correctly, I will not send you to the principal's office for misconduct. Ready? Paying attention this time? Here goes: where did General Washington spend the winter of 1777? Come up and write the answer on the blackboard."

Gabriel Thomas stood. He did not look at his classmates nor did he acknowledge the comic book caricature of the overbearing sadistic teacher. He felt every eye in the room trained on him. He sensed empathy and sympathy from students, while others, the class bullies, no doubt, were spoiling for his humiliation. *I could care less what they think of me*, he thought. *God has elected me. I will obey only him, now.*

Gabriel walked to the blackboard. From the grooved aluminum tray his fingers found the largest unbroken piece of white chalk. He pressed the chalk against the slate. What happened next defied rational explanation. He reproduced the name, Valley Forge, in perfect Chancery Italic calligraphy, a difficult enough achievement for an experienced adult Augustinian brother or Catholic monk using calligraphy dip pens and ink. An eight-year-old using chalk on a blackboard had broken new ground in human history. Bullies stared, slack jawed. One girl applauded; with few exceptions, so then did they all. McGonigal's thin-lipped mouth clamped into a straight bloodless line.

"Any other brain-buster questions for me, McGonigal? How about we solve linear algebra or discrete math problems? I know! Let us have a little academic competition, just we two." Gabriel's face was a picture of cool-headed confidence.

"Tell you what," Gabriel continued. "If you can answer one question from me, I'll tell everyone that you're the smartest teacher in the school. Also, I will obey State law and remain here. If you cannot answer the question directly, I am gone. Ready? Here goes: Old Testament prophets wrote that The Christ is the distant progeny of King David. How then does David in the Spirit call him 'Lord'? For he says: 'The Lord said to my Lord, 'Sit at my right hand until I put your enemies under your feet.' So, if David calls him 'Lord,' how then can the Christ be a descendant of King David?"

McGonigal stood with fists balled and his pasty white face flushed to a dark crimson, taut lips peeled into a snarl which revealed yellow-tinged smoker's teeth. He jabbed his right index finger at Gabriel's desk. "Sit down, Mr. Thomas."

Gabriel replied, "I don't think so, McGonigal."

Turning to face his astonished classmates, he pointed at the analog wall clock. "Time reveals all things, reduces all things. The time is now for me to leave. I have no idea where I am going. I do not see the road ahead of me. I cannot know for certain where it will end. Nor do I really know myself, and the fact that I *believe* I am following God's will does not mean that I am doing so. But I believe that the desire to please him does in fact please him. Simply put: if you follow me, you are really following Yeshua, the Christ, whom I obey. He promises you will have life and have it abundantly. Or you may remain here in this clammy, dewy tomb, staring straight ahead at chalked runes of little import. You can choose fear, and the prolongation of the inevitable. In the dead grave of night, you can pray for quick and merciful deaths. As you so choose."

The children had never heard adult words spoken with authority coming from someone their own age. Gabriel Thomas marched to the classroom door, assured and purposeful. He turned the knob, opened the door, and walked out. A part of his brain listened for the automatic door-close hinge that would have ended in a bang, which he never heard. He smiled. A boy held the door open from outside, allowing sixteen more classmates to file out. Gabriel heard vain threats from the teacher, then finally the banging of the door. He glanced back only once, and counted seventeen followers, ranging in height from forty-seven to fifty-four inches. Gabriel led the diminutive procession down hallways. He ignored demands and threats from both McGonigal and administrators for him and his followers to stop in their tracks.

Passing through the school lobby and out the front doors, Gabriel, and his procession of nine girls and eight boys stood in the pelting rain, warm and stinging. Eighteen children were drenched to their underwear in fewer than sixty seconds. The group surveyed the front lawn of the school for the first time in almost one month. The only sound Gabriel heard was the burble and whoosh of water currents and cannonade rain.

Then came the high-pitched screams.

In stony silence, Gabriel beheld men wearing local fire company black logo tees, firefighter hats, and fluorescent green safety vests standing before a disturbing and surreal sight: a new river flowed in the exact spot where school buses had last dropped them off. The water's edge was fewer than ten yards away. As the torrent rolled past north-to-south at a record-breaking sixty-two-hundred cubic feet per second, the men held long poles with gaff tips. Working in pairs, they pulled dead bodies from the currents. Behind them, corpses were stacked as neatly as possible like macabre cords of firewood. The noisome stench of putrefaction radiated from piles of decomposing human meat. Kids shrieked; others stared in shock. Eight vomited.

Gabriel barely noticed the kids and their reactions. He focused on the men who at first failed to notice eighteen short spectators standing behind them. The firefighters did not acknowledge the kids until they heard the alarmed shrieks, retching, and school administrators who just then burst outside shouting. Altogether as one, the firefighters turned to stare back at them. Gabriel's newly attuned senses picked up a very strange aura from these men. *Predator prey is the new world order. There is no mercy in nature. As they feel the end of the food supply upon them, moral compasses not grounded in Christ eroding away drop by drop. The hearts and thoughts of men are turning evil.*

The apocalyptic storm was not the only sign and symptom of forces beyond the terra coming down fast and hard on humankind. Now Gabriel knew with certainty. *Society is falling apart fast. The prince of this world, Satan, has ascended to his throne.*

Then he heard his own voice speaking within him, though unlike anything he had ever heard, like a supernatural version of himself. He heard it plainly: *North.* That was all. One word. Cub scouting had given him an accurate awareness of compass point directions. Without hesitation or warning, he turned his back to the bizarre scene and led his companions north in a double-time march.

Shaking off extreme fear and horror, in a panic, each of the seventeen kids became forced to decide on the spot either to obey the brusque commands of the administrators or follow Gabriel. They chose to follow Gabriel. An indefinable quality Gabriel possessed infused them and drew them to him like moths banging against parking lot lamps on summer nights. The children would never be able to explain why they wanted to follow him any more than moths know why they so ardently seek light.

As Gabriel walked, he mused over the differences between cool blue intellect and red-hot emotions. *Feelings are irrational and defy explanation*, he thought, *though they have their use, I suppose. Lord, I promise I shall strive always to be rational; mind first, feelings last.*

The kids trotted after Gabriel until they caught up. None drew too close or felt worthy to walk beside him. Something like awe held their tongues. Each wanted to complain of anxiety, discomfort, fears, and grief for the loss of the only lives they had known, of a predictable world they had only barely begun to understand, but none dared to break Gabriel's intense concentration.

Pounding staccato rain made it impossible to hear their footfalls. Gabriel did not turn. Somehow he knew they were there. Purposefully he marched. He calculated that the main road affronting the school, Seventh Avenue, lie submerged beneath a thirty-foot-deep river of mud, dead animals, and drowned humans. Momentarily he thought of home. In winter months when all the leaves were down, through a coppice of trees behind the farm across the Avenue, he could see his parents' house from the school. He wondered if they might be all right.

The inner voice returned. *Everyone you love is gone. Do not grieve. For your sake, God saved them. They will not face Judgement, and one day you will join them in Paradise.*

Reality seized his soul. *My home is underwater. My parents are dead. My cat and dog are dead; there is a chance they joined the bodies stacked in front of the school. More likely they drowned in the deluge days ago. By now they are floating in the Schuylkill River or emptied into the Delaware River; or they float in the Atlantic Ocean, food for awful sea creatures.*

Grief and self-pity smacked him hard. His pace slowed. Hot salty tears commingled with rain on his face, grief for a childhood lost and for a predictable future which God obliterated in the blink of an eye. The confidence and singular purpose that had saturated his entire being in the classroom weakened. *Lift these feelings from me, Lord, I beg you.*

Just then he felt something like an embrace, just like when he would fall and skin his knees and his mother would cradle his head against her warm chest until his sobbing ebbed. He felt a warmth, an internal hug of sorts. He could not pinpoint it, but eagerly he welcomed it.

Again, he heard the voice. *I knew you before the womb. Take courage, Gabriel.*

Tears ceased. Heightened confidence quickly reinfused like an intravenous stimulant push. He thought of the new river to his left, which seemed to originate from elevations to the northwest. To the east, Perkiomen Creek now qualified as a bona fide river. *Extremely dangerous. Which means that Seventh Avenue and portions of Gravel Pike must be underwater, which is our sole path north.*

He picked his way across residential lawns and dense thickets of trees and pucker brush. The other kids mimicked his every move. A quarter hour later, Gabriel gazed upon the partially submerged intersection of Gravel Pike running north-south, with Route 113 heading east. Slogging through waist-deep water, he led the way forward through the intersection until his feet stood on clear asphalt. He stopped.

The sick-sweet bouquet of rotting human flesh had not followed him. *Thank you Lord for that small kindness.* He faced north along a barren and deeply puddled Gravel Pike. To his right, the Perkiomen Creek, which normally burbled along in serene silence roared along like Flatiron Mountain springtime melt rapids into the Colorado River. He spotted the occasionally floating body, entire large uprooted sturdy trees, and pieces of homes carried along at breakneck speed by the fierce currents. The natural western bank, now a mere twenty feet to their right, lay submerged under deep, fast-moving water. He knew that soon, all of Gravel Pike would disappear under the currents. Gabriel expected no end to the torrential rain. *We need to hurry…keep ahead of it.*

He started walking again at double-time pace; the others fell in behind him. Suddenly he stopped. He listened not only with his ears, but also with every attuned fiber of his new, improved senses. He closed his eyes in a kind of rapture. *No voice this time. Why am I seeing the image of a tree?* He looked right and saw nothing. On the left, he saw it: a very dense, mature Norway spruce, not native to the area, planted half a century ago on the front lawn of a residential homeowner attempting to block traffic noises from Gravel Pike. *Exactly matches the image in my mind.*

He walked and stood under the tree. Leaping as high as his short legs would allow his hands found purchase on the lowest limb. He swung his legs until his sneakers connected with the mottled, rough, green lichen-tinged trunk bark. This afforded him the leverage needed to loop his left leg over the lower limb. There he sat and made eye contact with each of the seventeen.

"Climb as high as you can. Flatten yourselves against a sturdy bough. Make yourselves invisible and silent. No whispering, not even a cough. Do this, and you shall live," said the voice in his head that sounded like his own voice, though this voice was not conjured willingly from any conscious thought.

Using boughs and branches as a ladder, monkey-like, he ascended fifty-five feet up. He assessed the boughs above and decided they were too thin to support his weight. He stopped climbing and shimmied along his chosen bough until he stopped five feet out from the trunk. He made himself as comfortable as possible. *I love the smell of fresh pine sap. Never knew how much until now.*

One of the girls followed, imitating Gabriel's jump moves to attain a seat on the first bough. A boy, Drake Childers, went next, climbing to the next highest level, but he stopped. He watched as a tiny girl, Jordan Stockley, struggled impossibly. She was too small to jump high enough. Wordlessly he descended, draped himself over the lowest bough, caught her hands, and pulled her up to a seated position. Jordan smiled at Drake, husky blue eyes and long lashes batting a thank-you to him. He grinned, felt warm all over, energized. He allowed Jordan to climb ahead of him in case she slipped on the rain-slicked boughs. In turn, all but six of the group made it up the tree to a minimum height of fifty feet, which made it impossible to see them from below.

Three girls and three boys stood on the soggy ground. They stared up. None were able to spot any of their classmates hidden inside the branches.

"This is stupid!" Gabriel heard one of the boys yelling.

"You're not the boss of me, Gabriel!" yelled another.

"People are dying, and you want to climb a tree? Are we on a playground?"

Gabriel heard three girls arguing. His 'passenger,' as he now thought of the stranger inside him, one with its own thoughts yet who spoke to him using his own voice, perceived their emotions. *Frustration. Indignance. Insubordination. Resentment.* A cacophony radiated up from ground level. *Six followers have taken an adversarial stance against me.*

He sensed the voice returning, his yet not his. *It is not you whom they hate. It is I.*

The twelve in the tree heard men's voices. Gabriel perceived waves of pure evil. Now he understood the purpose of the tree image vision: the tree meant deliverance from this impending threat.

What followed changed each one of them. Tortured high-pitched shrieks and wails, high and undulating. Unnatural screams of mortal desperation. Panic and fear beyond all measure. Terror that forever breaks people. Fright and physical agony from which no heart, no soul, and no mortal body could ever recover.

Gabriel received mental images of the carnage, forever embedded in his mind. A pile of clothing. Girl's and boy's bloody underwear strewn about the woods. More blood in great quantities pooled with rainwater onto long-ago-fallen leaves. Adult male teeth, tobacco-stained, injury-blackened, or missing. Blood in beards. Chewing jaws. Sardonic laughter, a terrible noise, like a clockwork crow winding down. Axes and large knives dripping with gore.

Blissfully shielded from eye-witnessing the sickening destruction of their six classmates, eyes frozen open from shock, all Gabriel and his eleven remaining followers could do was endure it in silence.

High and Dry

North said the voice. Gabriel felt determined to obey it blindly. He would permit nothing to stand between him and it. He and the eleven remaining followers had spent a full hour hiding up inside the Norway spruce. Agonized sounds from somewhere further inside a wooded patch to the south of them had subsided over thirty-minutes ago. Gabriel now fully relied on his newfound senses and the inner voice of his spiritual guide, his 'passenger.'

"Everybody down!" he yelled. All were in descent beneath him when he shimmied backwards to the trunk and reversed course.

"What happened to the six kids who didn't climb the tree with us, Gabriel?" Jordan asked in her mouselike, tremulous voice. More than anything she needed a hug. Gabriel's eyes met hers only briefly. Surprised at seeing the cold, adult-like intensity of his gaze, Jordan took one step back away from him.

When Gabriel's sneakers mushed into the muddy ground, he looked around and recognized artifacts from his classmates. Two sneakers and tufts of wet hair darkened with blood. "Nothing good," he answered.

"What kind of monsters would do this to kids?" asked Drake.

Gabriel closed his eyes. After a time, he spoke. "Ordinary men once who banned God from their hearts. Now they believe the world has changed; that they can make up their own laws and rules as they go. The reality is this: nothing has changed. Nothing ever does. What kind of monsters are they; you ask? The dead kind, as they will soon learn."

Giving the blood-baptized assault zone a respectfully wide birth, Gabriel walked until again he stood on Gravel Pike. Raindrops pelted his eyes as he chanced a quick look up at the merciless sky. The sense of urgency returned. Heading due north he slogged through waist-high and knee-deep areas of Route 29 which slowed his pace a little. He thought of the sun, how he had not seen it in over a month. *Is it even still there?* He quickened his pace.

"I'm hungry!" one of the girls announced. Gabriel turned on her, his face a mask of emotionally distant disinterest.

"Shh! Here," whispered Jordan. She handed the girl a protein bar fished out from one of her backpack pockets. "Not another word! You want to end up like those others?" Immediately the little dark-haired girl began to sob quietly. Jordan placed her arm around the girl's shoulder and gave her an encouraging shake. In a whisper, "Everything will be all right. Gabriel knows stuff. No clue how, but he does. There is a strength in him, like older men have; like he's an adult stuck in a kid's body, or something. In class, Gabriel said we will have life and have it abundantly; I believe him.

He will get us to someplace safe and dry, where there's food."

The little brunette brightened a little. She offered Jordan a wan smile. "Thanks for the bar."

After a little more than an hour of walking and, at one point, swimming past a submerged tavern, the group had come to an intersection. Gabriel stopped to listen. Immediately he turned right walking now on East Park Avenue. He walked until the raging Perkiomen Creek made forward progress impossible. He felt a complete loss of what to do or where to go next. To swim across meant certain death. *East* urged the voice.

East Park Avenue led to a traffic bridge that had crossed the creek before the Flood; now he saw the bridge swallowed under the Perkiomen's rapids, rendering it useless. To the left, a walking trail led to another submerged bridge built across the Perkiomen strictly for foot traffic, its high, curved steel arches still visible above the raging currents like green camel humps. *These would have been the top of the structure, ten feet above the heads of pedestrians. The steel arches are the only bits of the bridge not submerged. Must be sturdy to survive the currents. Thank you, Lord, for sparing this bridge.*

Gabriel did not receive any mental images or internal voice. To continue on an eastern heading required crossing the Perkiomen at some point which, as far as he could tell, meant using one of these hearty humps. It felt right. He slogged through muddy water until he grasped the exposed steel arch.

Only six inches wide.

Squatting, he pressed his muddy left sneaker to the right-most steel arch and balanced carefully, gripping the smooth steel edges, then lifted up his right foot onto it. Progress forward was slow-going but do-able. He inched forward, feet and hands in contact with the cold slippery steel, trying to ignore the rushing water a foot below him. *If I slip and fall in, it is game over.* As if in cosmic confirmation, a rancid body cruised inches beneath him. Gabriel came face to face with a moldering, nauseating horror. One rubber-band eye lolled from its socket, skeleton teeth grinned up at him, waxy yellow fingers sloughing skin that still clung in spots, not already reduced to bright white bone. *Pffew! The stench. Worse than a dead skunk smashed and baking on an August roadside.* Despite terrifying experiences no eight-year-old comes equipped to endure, Gabriel Thomas felt no fear. He was intent on the task assigned to him.

He forced his body forward another half a foot. He slid his hands, then slid one foot forward at a time. Carefully he found footing, one behind the other, back arched uncomfortably making it a challenge to breathe. The steel beam arch which inclined up made the task increasingly more difficult. All he wanted to do was stand up and huff in deep breaths. *Do not stand up. Do it and you are dead.*

After ten minutes of progress, Gabriel passed the apex and felt the arch begin to curve downward. Cautiously he lowered his right leg through the calmer edge of the water and found solid ground. He stood on terra firma, arms spread. He faced the others watching him from the opposite bank.

"I'll wait here until the last of you makes it across," he shouted above the rain and roaring creek. "Jordan, have the girl you fed go next, then you follow closely behind her. Drake, you come last. Since you are the strongest and most athletic of us all, you get to be anchor. Make sure the eight others all go in turn. Drake: I trust you to choose the order. Now! Get moving!"

Jordan felt puzzled. *There is no way Gabriel could have seen me slip the girl a protein bar. He had his back to me. How did he know?* She shrugged it off but made a mental note to ask Gabriel about it later. Jordan grabbed the girl's hand and led her through the mildly churning water. She watched the girl form a camel-hump, having established a firm handhold and sure footing. Encouraged by Jordan behind and Gabriel ahead, though the girl was the physically weakest of the band she made it across in less time than Gabriel had taken, setting a new time standard. *Good balance*, Gabriel thought. When the girl stood next to him, he asked, "What's your name?"

"Nicole Mensch. Nikki."

"Good work, Nicole Mensch. Your sense of balance may come in useful someday." She grinned like a child on Christmas morning.

Gabriel and Nicole stood together watching as ten kids crossed the beam, until finally Drake walked across, arms out for balance. At one heart-pounding point he slipped a little and nearly plunged into the maelstrom of death-water. He banged his knee hard against the steel but regained balance and stood. Gabriel could not help noticing Drake was thickly muscled for an eight-year-old.

When at last Drake stood next to Gabriel, he grinned. "Almost didn't make it."

Gabriel said, "If anyone has the physical strength to survive the current and swim to shore, it would be you. I think that someday, among us you will be the most difficult man for our enemies to kill. You will be the granite foundation of our Church." Drake appeared dumbfounded. All he could think of doing was nod.

Gabriel marched forward to the east. He led them steeply upward. *Seems like a muddy mountain run-off now, but once this might have been the Perkiomen Trail,* he thought.

The gradient increased with every step. Drake followed directly behind him limping a little, favoring his sore knee. "Gabriel, is it okay to talk?"

"I sense no immediate danger. What is it?" he answered.

"How did you know? To leave the school, I mean. And to climb the tree just before those bad men came out of nowhere and took our classmates. About which direction to go, and where we are gonna end up."

Gabriel shrugged, "I really could not tell you. All I know is that we will have a lifetime together to seek answers. To grow and learn far more than we would have in school. Time will reveal all things to us. Now let me ask you a question. Do you believe in God? In Jesus and the prophets and the Elect?"

Drake did not immediately respond. Then: "Your eyes see further than ours. You see more than I do. If you are not some sorta prophet of God, I will eat my sneakers. Yes, Gabriel. Totally. Whatever you believe is what I believe."

They walked in silence for the next ten minutes. The forest canopy and understory shielded them from the worst of the pounding rain. Drake broke the silence. "If you're the prophet, Gabriel, what does that make us: disciples?"

"Not sure yet exactly what I am," said Gabriel. "What I know is this: together we are the Elect, whom God himself elected to walk in his ways and die in his service."

Turning around, Drake shouted, "Hey guys! Gabriel says we're the Elect! We're a team now and that's gonna be our team's name. The Elect!" Ten voices cheered.

Gabriel stopped when the trail emptied out onto a paved road. Everyone pressed up behind Drake, huffing air, completely winded from an endless ascent up a mud-slicked steep grade. They yawned and opened their mouths wide to pop the pressure bubbles in their ears caused by the elevation change. Gabriel had his back to them. None could see his closed eyes. His stony silence went on like this for minutes.

Snapping-to from a silent reverie, Gabriel turned right and walked along the crumbling asphalt that was Spring Mount Road. *At least it is downhill*, he thought.

On the right they recognized a ski lift mounted above a grass-covered slope running parallel to the road. They saw peculiar-looking contraptions anchored down the slope at regular intervals. "What are those?" Jordan asked.

"Snowmaking machines," said Nikki. Dad used to take me here snow tubing."

High steel poles with stadium lights on top stood at regular intervals. At the bottom of the slope, a lovely ski chalet came into view. There stood a barn, and other structures: one a two-story tower-like affair with a second-story wood deck. This held Gabriel's focus. *Why am I drawn to this one?*

Closer now to the chalet, he studied it: white, with cross gable roofing and steep rooflines in front with an 'A' shaped entranceway, exterior walls covered with a veneer of stucco and decorative faux timbers in the American Tudor Revival style. But again, his eye felt drawn to the tower.

"*Home*," advised the inner voice.

Gabriel walked across the unlined asphalt parking lot for a hundred yards until he reached the chalet. He tried the glass door. Locked. He walked to the metal side door service entrance. Locked. A small window next to the metal door, the sill about five feet above ground, appeared promising. The group had formed a semi-circle behind him. Over his shoulder he said, "Drake. Please give me a boost."

Gabriel flattened his hands against the rough white stucco. Drake made a firm cup of his hands. Gabriel placed his right foot into the cup and pushed himself up, balancing with his hands against the wall. He climbed to the window. Peering through its greasy glass he saw a kitchen. Someone had left the window open two inches. *To vent cooking smoke and bring fresh air to the kitchen staff,* he thought.

The window was ancient. Nothing about its opening-closing operation worked smoothly. Struggling, Gabriel managed to apply sufficient upward pressure to raise it all the way open. He did not believe he could easily fit through the opening.

He stepped down. "Thank you, Drake. Wait here. I need you to do it again but not with me." Turning to the eleven, he pointed at Jordan's little friend, Nicole. She pointed at herself; eyebrows raised. Gabriel nodded. He made the 'come closer' signal with his pointer finger. Hesitantly, she walked closer. Gabriel sensed her unease. He smiled and reached out his right hand. "Nicole, we need you."

Weakly she shook his hand. He gave her hand two succinct pumps then laid his left hand over top. His smile widened. "Nicole is such a pretty name. I hope you don't mind if I call you that. May I?"

She smiled brightly. "No!"

"No, you don't mind? Or no, you prefer Nikki?"

"Please, I wish everyone would call me Nicole. It sounds less childish. Besides, Nikki could be a boy's name, too."

"Eww, boys!" he joked. She giggled. He released her hand and put on a more serious expression. "Well, Nicole, the team needs you. I need you. If I ask you to do something important for me, will you do it?"

Mesmerized by hypnotic eyes, she nodded. "Yes. Whatever you need me to do, I will do."

She wondered: *What is it about him? Like, the nicest grown-up ever trapped inside a boy's body. I trust him completely.*

"Nicole, I want you to do exactly what I just did. Step into Drake's hands, climb up, but then I need you to squirm your way through that little window. You are the perfect size for this mission, and you have the best balance. Can you manage it?"

She looked up at the window. Drake was already bending over forming the foothold with his hands. She nodded at Gabriel. He smiled. She climbed. It was easy for her, lithe and strong. She wriggled all the way inside. Once her feet hit the ground, Gabriel stood under the window.

"Nicole, can you see daylight from the front doors?"

He heard her walking. Voice muted, "Yes! I see the doors."

"I noticed both glass doors have metal knobs used to lock and unlock them from inside. Go and unlock them." He walked back around to the doors and found Nicole holding one of them open for him. Shaking hands felt natural to her now; she reached out and he shook her hand hard, five pumps, in the most intimate expression of gratitude Gabriel could muster. Having never hugged a girl in his life, though he wanted to right then, he felt that doing this would somehow be inappropriate. They exchanged smiles. Ten others came around the building; Nicole held the door open until all twelve Elect reconvened inside.

The charming scene within drew all eyes to a big circular fireplace for gathering, topped by a large, cowled vent. Padded benches sat fixed atop an unpainted concrete floor. Dark wood walls; serving counter; games for kids; racks of books and magazines: *It will do*, Gabriel thought. He walked to the kitchen and found the water running cold. He held his mouth under the flow, and decided water had never tasted so clean, cold, fresh. *Natural well water.* He wiped his mouth on his sleeve, then joined the others in the main gathering area. "Drake. Please walk down to that hockey rink area. Count the number of livable structures you find on these grounds, beginning down there. I will inspect the two-story building beside the barnlike structure. I need to pray. Meet me here in twenty."

"Got it," Drake said, heading outside. "Um, Gabriel, are you sure the owners won't mind us breaking in and taking over their property?"

"Quite sure. From today until forevermore, welcome to the Church of the Elect."

As Drake jogged away to complete his mission, Gabriel made eye contact with the remaining ten. "Please make yourselves comfortable. I noticed a big meat tenderizing hammer in the kitchen. Put a towel over the snack machine and soda machine glass before shattering them with the hammer. Have a snack and a Coke. You need energy. The rest of the day will be physically demanding."

In a barn-shaped structure, Gabriel found exactly the tool he needed, a heavy crowbar. He took it and walked to the two-story building. He popped the door lock and entered. Daylight barely made a dent in the gloom. Ahead, a fireplace. To the left, stairs. He climbed them. He found the deck, walked outside, and sat down cross-legged in the pouring rain.

Gabriel prayed.

Twenty minutes later, a drenched Drake found Gabriel back in the chalet and gave him a report. "Twelve total buildings including your two-story: each one livable. Each has insulated walls except for the barn. I saw scads of inner tubes used on the ski slope we can use to make mattresses. Tons of clothing racks and cold-weather gear. Skis, of course, and decent bicycles. Four-wheeled carts with tractors and lawn equipment. I counted two pick-up trucks and a van, and also eleven mega-fun-looking four-wheelers with big gasoline and diesel tanks for those things. Someone stacked cords of firewood five times my height. Hanging from hooks on a wall are big handsaws and fourteen chain saws. Power is out everywhere. There is a huge diesel generator big enough to power the whole place. My dad has—had—a small one. Gigantic loudspeakers on the same poles as the stadium lights."

Gabriel nodded. "Once I've settled into my two-story tower and we restore electricity, I'll want the microphone and power switch cabled from here over to my tower." He walked behind the service counter, found the microphone under the ledge, and held it up for Drake to see. "Former staff use it for announcements to crowds. One day, I will need it for similar reasons."

He motioned for everyone to approach the service desk. They stood in a semi-circle. "I will teach you everything needed for survival here. This is our home, now. Rain will continue to fall. Everything below will become lost to floodwaters which will not reach us up here on the mountain. We will live."

"What about our families?" asked Jordan.

Gabriel frowned. "We must accept that our families sleep in the Lord, and we will rejoin with them in the Resurrection. We are a new family, now. We are the Elect family who walk in the Lord's way. Do not cry. We have no time for grief. We have work to do now."

Murmuring. Shuffling. Drake interrupted the silence. "What do we do next?"

"Go in the kitchen. Each of you take a knife. Break into teams. Continue walking down the road. You will find deserted homes. Enter like I showed you: safely. Do not injure yourselves. Fill your backpacks with anything edible you find, especially canned goods and fruit. But the priority right now is guns and ammo. Look in every drawer and closet. Look in the basements, under beds, and open every drawer. Bring back every gun and all the ammo you find before sundown. A rifle with a scope would be best. I alone will manage security, but I need the proper tools. Go now and get them for me."

"Are we in danger, Gabriel?" Nicole said, with a body shiver.

"Life is a struggle. Know that God is with us. We are losing daylight. Tonight, you will all sleep in here." He pointed at another boy. "What is your name?"

"Paul."

"Drake, before you go, pair up with Paul. See if you two can fire up the generator. I need all those bright lights on tonight."

"The evil men who took our classmates are out there still, looking for us, aren't they?"

"Yes, Jordan," Gabriel answered, "bad men are coming. And when they see the lights they will become drawn here like bugs to a flame. I will end the threat. No more questions…GO!"

The God Vulcan

Twenty years had passed since the First Flood had driven eighteen Pennsylvania school children out into the rain. It had been one year since the Second Flood's waters had receded. A thousand miles south of Spring Mountain and Gabriel's Church of the Elect: in Birmingham, Alabama, Burl 'Booker' Bailey laid upon a pad he had lugged up the stairs to the outdoor observation deck of the Vulcan statue. He stared up into the blameless blue sky, ceramic and cloudless. Occasionally he jotted story ideas into a spiral-bound notebook.

Booker loved to write. Since age five, he continually authored stories to entertain himself. He figured that, having reached the wise old age of seventeen, he was easily the absolute best writer in the world. At least the best out of the small pool of people he knew. Apart from Cleon and Jayla, his parents, he knew absolutely no one.

This morning, he overslept. *What was that dream? So good! I never wanted it to end. A green mountain up north. So many people my age! Everyone was so happy and shiny. So free. And peaceful. Love glowed upon every face like warm stars. The smiling man with yellow hair gazing down upon us like a strong loving father, or like a shepherd. The people call him Gabriel. He wants me in his Church. Walk north, Booker. Walk soon.*

Fully conscious, aloud Booker said, "I so want to have this same dream again tonight." Now he laid in bed attempting to do math in his head. Math always sharpened his mind awake better than anything else.

The world population when my parents were in grade school, what did they tell me again? Seven-point-nine billion, I think. They said the First Flood had wiped out ninety-nine percent of all people on earth, leaving only one percent. That would leave 790,000 people. Last year's Second Flood they guessed had taken fifty percent of people who survived the First Flood, which leaves 395,000 people on earth. So, if half are female, that leaves…197,500 chicks for me to love. So why can't I find even one? Black or brown girl? Great! White girl? Asian? Redhead? Fine-fine. Native? Inuit? Polynesian? Fabulous! Short hair-long hair, fat-skinny, older-younger hey—beggars can't be choosers. Dear Lord, I ask nothing of you. But if you care to send to me the love of my life, I promise to be extra grateful. Just sayin.'

Booker bounced out of bed, used the bathroom, brushed then flossed. *Food. I need food.* Separately his parents had been rummaging through ransacked and flood-damaged Birmingham left in ruins ever since waters from the First Flood had receded. The story of their union looped in his head daily, like a prayer. They had met this way:

Cleon Bailey, twenty years old, not quite five-foot-eight at a skinny weight of one-thirty-five, was filling a gym bag with canned goods inside the ruins of the Piggly Wiggly in Homewood, a suburb of Birmingham, located on the other side of Red Mountain due south of the city center. Cleon heard a scream. He ran out, looked left, saw three large, bearded biker-type older white males outside the CVS tearing the clothing off a petite little teenaged Black girl. He ran straight toward them.

They stopped; Cleon stopped. They sized him up; a loud burst of laughter erupted at his expense. Ignoring Cleon, they returned to their attempted rape mission. Though Cleon did not appear threatening, the men could not have known about his high-school football quarterback fame before the First Flood. Reaching into his sack, he grabbed a can of peas. Winding up, he threw a perfect pitch at one of the men, thrown with no less force than a baseball bat against the back of the man's head. It mashed against the man's cervical spine and compressed critical nerves. The man simply crumpled unconscious face-down on the wet asphalt.

This arrested the attention of the other two rapists. They watched Cleon's second pitch hit another directly in the larynx; the man fell to his knees, holding his throat. The last man standing charged toward Cleon like an enraged bull. Winding up, Cleon released a can of corn straight against the bridge of the man's nose. His face exploded in blood. He fell to his knees. Cleon walked until he stood before the kneeling man. "Rapist redneck muthufucka." Whipping the bag of cans in a circle to gain kinetic energy, he aimed at and connected with the man's head. Male pattern baldness widely displayed the deep gash with white exposed bone. The man fell face down, semi-conscious, whimpering.

Checking pulses, he found that the man whose airway he had crushed was dead. Cleon checked the first man he had knocked down. Dead. The man whose head he had split was still breathing. He placed his bootheel over the man's neck and applied his full weight until the man breathed no longer.

Fists balled, breathing heavily, Cleon stood back attempting to process his first killing of fellow human beings. Minutes later he snapped-to and walked to the girl. Looking up, she thought she saw light framing Cleon's face.

"Angel," she had said.

He smiled. "Hi, the name's Cleon. Your name is Angel?"

She smiled. "No, yours is. You saved me, Cleon. My name is Jayla." She reached up. He took her hand and pulled her to standing. *Light as a feather,* he thought. Standing on her toes, she leaned in and kissed his mouth. "Take me with you, Cleon. My family is dead. I'm all alone."

"I didn't save you," he said, pointing at the uniquely thick gold rope chain he had worn around his neck since childhood so that, as he grew, it had become impossible to remove it without a cutting tool. He held out the small gold cross and glanced down at it. "He saved us both. And yes, same here, Jayla: the last Bailey. My family's dead and I too am alone. You can come if you want and help me stock the Vulcan Museum. I live there, high in the statue tower which is completely safe from floods. I welded steel over the museum doors which were mostly glass. Little by little I have collected damned near a lifetime supply of food for one person. The day is still young. Help me fill up with more food, then come home with me. I promise to keep you safe. How does that sound?"

This morning, Booker could not help recalling the story that Cleon and Jayla had told him a thousand times until he started rolling his eyes, sick and tired of hearing it. Mentally replaying the story this morning made him cry. With a heavy heart, he wiped his face with his thin, bare brown forearm, then walked to the room assigned as the pantry stocked floor to ceiling with canned goods. The Vulcan statue stood fifty-six-feet tall from toe to spear point, upon a one-hundred-twenty-four-foot pedestal rising a hundred-and-eighty-feet. It weighed over a hundred-thousand pounds, the largest cast iron statue in the world and the largest metal statue ever made in the United States. Vulcan Park atop Red Mountain, with over a thousand feet of elevation, was the only home Booker Bailey had ever known. He had only left its iron-clad safety one time.

He opened a can of refried beans, stirred the contents with a spoon and started eating. He decided that this would be the last meal he would ever eat trapped alone in the iron prison. His mind created a list of items to pack into a knapsack after breakfast. He thought of which footwear would be best. He found Pennsylvania's Spring Mountain in his map atlas and resolved to go there no matter what. *The Applachian Trail seems the most direct route*, he thought.

At every meal, he thought of Cleon and Jayla. Especially Jayla. Oh, how she loved her little Booker. He had authored stories of high adventure for her to read to him at bedtime, tales where the three Baileys conquered and subdued the Golgoths, and rebuilt a kind, loving world. As always when finishing a meal from the larder his parents had collected, he thought of the fateful night when he had left the compound for his one-and-only venture-out. The night that his parents had not returned from their daily foraging venture.

That morning before they had left the safety and security of Vulcan, Cleon had warned Booker about the Golgoths. "Everything has consequences, son, you know that. Small actions create big ripples in the fabric of the unseen universe. Do not even think about them or say the name aloud."

"But dad, you said the Golgoths—I mean the savage cannibal tribe—rest by day and do all their hunting at night. Why can't I leave Red Mountain and come gathering with you and mom one morning?" he had asked.

Seeing his son's sad brown eyes, Cleon's face had grown grim. As though he struggled between telling the whole truth, or a watered-down version to spare Booker nightmares. Booker had noticed the eye-to-eye exchange between husband and wife. "Viruses and bacteria," said Jayla. "Son, you have been holed-up here your entire life. You have zero natural immunities. You are like a sponge. Even a tiny cut on your skin out there could let teeny-tiny critters inside your blood which can eat you alive and kill you faster from the inside than cannibals would. Now, I have a box of antibiotics in storage, but after twenty years, who can say any of it is still effective?"

"Anti-bi…"

Cleon had bent to place a kiss on Booker's nappy scalp. "We only have old medicine. You have our whole hearts, son. Sorry to say, until things change out there," he said, with a sweeping gesture to suggest the whole of Red Mountain: "this is your entire world. Thanks be to almighty God in Heaven that we three are alive, all together, and healthy."

Six days a week, Cleon and Jayla left the mountain at nine sharp. From there, they would hike southwest along the Vulcan Trail, foraging. To walk north would bring them to the former cultural hub of Birmingham, Five Points South, which was much closer to Red Mountain, however it is where the area tribe of Golgoths had made their camp. Cleon and Jayla made certain to conclude their canned goods foraging by three each afternoon, well before sundown. They would never risk spraining an ankle and slowly walking back to base so close to nightfall.

By ten minutes past three on the day Jayla and Cleon disappeared, Booker had started to have a bad feeling. By half past three he was half out of his mind. By four, hoping to spot them, he had ascended the statue stairs; he stood upon the steel platform using binoculars to scan multiple drowned cities in the dying light. At quarter past four he was kneeling, praying, sobbing.

By half past four he had made his decision to violate the prime directive hammered into his head since birth. Grabbing the largest kitchen knife from the wooden block near the pantry, battling back waves of deeply ingrained guilt, he unlocked the heavy steel-reinforced doors and, taking a deep breath, he closed the doors behind him. He guessed from the orange sun in the west that he had an hour of usable daylight.

He walked to the Vulcan Trail parking lot, the point of embarkation and trail head. About to hike south he stopped, transfixed. Tentatively he stepped closer to the object, a silk scarf with African patterns on the water-cracked asphalt. He knew that there could only be one of these. It belonged to Jayla. Next to it, dark red drops. He had little experience with blood, only enough to recognize what it was, and the keen intelligence to connect the blood dots with the scarf that once adorned his beloved mother's neck.

My Lord God, sweet Jesus. Please tell me this is not really happening.

The blood trail continued north every five feet, then no more. Fear rose like magma in his gut threatening to erupt. He could not swallow. Richard Arrington Junior Boulevard stretched ahead of him. On this, the blood trail ended, but he knew the road led to Twentieth Street—a straight shot into the dreaded Five Points, the Golgoth Nest, as Cleon had once labeled it. Booker tried again to swallow; like trying to choke down a golf ball. He felt terror seep into the chambers of his heart, founded in warnings drummed into him since forever. Every fiber of his body urged him to run back to the safety of Vulcan.

But a force more powerful than fear infused him with courage, emboldened him forward. *This might be a one-way trip. But I must go. I love them so much. I need them. God would want me to rescue them.*

Ten minutes later he stood on Twentieth Street: where a black void occupied both sides of the street that had once teemed with people, reduced now to piles of residue that decades prior were homes, now crumbled to their foundations. He realized his remaining daylight estimate had been wrong, for now he walked where shadows grew and multiplied in their twilight dance of death. Stars provided just enough light for him to see shapes: rubble; darker areas that were water-filled potholes; and rusting vehicles strewn about the road.

Ten minutes later, dim flickers and tendrils of firelight reflected in filthy glass still framed in the upper floors of tall buildings ahead in the distance. He caught whiffs of something unusual wafting in the air, like a distant cousin to the canned pork Jayla had heated on the wood stove so many times. He did not like it.

Human-like sounds, not words, reached his ears. Rhythmic thumping. *Somebody is beating a drum.* He liked this even less.

His mind's eye saw Golgoths hiding in each shadow and in every building's doorway, like figures cut from white construction paper glued into onyx backgrounds. Inconceivable monsters, hungry, livid—waited inside every rusted-out vehicle to explode out and feed upon his healthy, sanguine flesh. Trying not to breathe loudly, he stepped lightly but with purpose. Fear had made ten minutes feel like hours, his sense of passing time askant.

From the middle of the street where he stood, he could clearly see the bonfire reflected in the glass of a building on the left: The Original Pancake House. He had no idea who the Pancake People may have been. *A tribe that went extinct after the First Flood, along with most every other tribe and this was their house.* For a moment he paused to look down at his body. *Yep, camouflaged. I blend into the shadows. Thank you, Lord Jesus, for my Black skin, and for these dark clothes. Amen.*

Shadowy building doorways had unnerved him up to this point; now, standing in the middle of Twentieth Street, he felt like a chicken in a wolf's den. It was time, he decided, to embrace the dark, to let the shadows swallow him. He crept slowly behind the Pancake House and navigated the rubble strewn Twentieth Alley. He crossed over Eleventh Avenue South, walked east, and made a horseshoe move that brought him around again to Twentieth. Hiding in the dark doorway of Little Italy's Pizza and Pints, he sat, pressed into the corner. *I hope to God I am invisible.*

Golgoths. Naked men, a bright white substance painted onto bare flesh from head to feet. *Fifty? A hundred of them*—he wondered. Now he knew from where the sounds had come.

Rarely did Booker remember good dreams, but he never forgot the dark ones, which he considered bad omens, portents, cawing death crows flitting through his night mind. He fought to push those away, to bar the mental door against them. At half a year past seventeen years, he could recall lucid dreams from age seven with clarity. Fifty yards before him was the strangest scene he had ever witnessed, ghastly and terrible, more potent than his worst nightmares.

The bonfire climbed high from a source in the middle of the square between Magnolia Avenue and Eleventh. In quivering light thrown by the flames, he noticed that the street was not asphalt, but rather a clay red color with yellow lines painted in pedestrian crosswalks. Golgoths had made it impossible for Booker to see the full bonfire. He could only see flames licking up higher than their heads illuminating the red-colored square.

One of the Golgoths a hulking, tall, overly muscled male arose suddenly from the hoard, standing with the fire behind him, his head and trunk visible behind the rest. Woven into the big Golgoth's white-painted dreadlocks, Booker saw white bones. Around the bare neck hung a necklace of human ears: multiple ears seemed desiccated and old; others appeared fresher. He thought that even at this distance he could see dried blood splats in relief against white-painted skin.

And then it spoke. "Hostis Dei, laudamus te."

Booker had taught himself English to a level well beyond his parents, simply by reading every word of the thousands of books they had recovered between the First and Second Floods, soggy but serviceable. Cleon had tried to talk him out of tackling Latin books. "It's a dead language, son," he had said.

"But dad, isn't every language but English now dead to us, also?"

He had stared at the Latin Vulgate Bible, comparing it word for word to the English version, and thus learned to read Latin. But it had never been a spoken language in his orbit. He could only guess the pronunciations.

The gargantuan Golgoth repeated the words, and now Booker was certain it was Latin. "Hostis Dei, laudamus te."

Enemy of God, we praise you.

Affording Booker his first clear look at the bonfire, huge pallid arms slowly parted, dividing the revelers into two opposing lines. He had seen images of fountains in books. He deduced that this circle once held water. Inside were metal sculptures of creatures. He counted five frogs arranged in a pentagram: a dog with a kid goat on its back; a wolf; and a rabbit on the back of a tortoise. A grotesque central figure of a human with an infernal goat's head, appeared to read from a book to the amphibian-animal audience gathered around it.

Satanic scene, he thought.

But then he glimpsed two human forms strapped with thick ropes, one on each flank of the metal devil-goat. Naked, ankles fixed to the goat thing's neck, arms hanging limply below. The crotches were nothing but mangled gore, both bodies split open from pudenda to ribcages, hollowed out, brown skins blistering over the bonfire. *Hip curvature: one is female, though who can tell from those crotches. Eviscerated so completely even the breasts are gone. Roasting meat. What I smelled was not pork.*

Booker threw up in his mouth a little but then choked it down. He squinted at the Golgoth who repeatedly bellowed "Hostis Dei, laudamus te." He tried to focus on the victim's faces. *Who were they?* A metal goat prevented him from identifying a single facial feature, or anything at all below their necks. He glimpsed something against the male corpse's skin.

Cleon's chain.

Hell's full horror obliterated every atom of Booker as shock and terror seized and momentarily paralyzed him. He could not move; he could not think. He passed out for six minutes. When he regained consciousness, he sobbed in silence. *They mutilated and cooked my parents for food.* He felt the scream boiling up from deep inside. *Can people who go insane ever recover back to sanity? The fact that I ask this question means that my mind still works.* He felt the claws of Hell shredding his gray matter into gory mush. One lone emotion ruled his every neuron: revenge. *These demons stole everything from me.*

He stood, ready to die. He visualized his hands ripping the eyeballs out of each Golgoth, saw his fingernails digging in and shredding exposed genitals. Muscles coiled, he nearly sprung forward.

A rush of soothing warmth, his father's strong arm around his shoulder, his mother's warm hands firmly cupped both cheeks. He stopped.

Stay calm, son. Grieve later. You must survive. God has need of you in his Church on the green mountain.

In a state of shock, trancelike, Booker swayed on unsteady legs, bowels hot and crampy, nauseated like never before. Unendurable pain in both eyes and ears; his temples throbbed; he saw spots before his eyes and flashing lights; and his vision had degraded to blurred ripples like opened eyes underwater looking up to the surface.

The Golgoths appeared transfixed by the fire. *But even animal monsters have peripheral vision.* Attempting to become one with the walls and glass, slowly he reversed course, holding his back flat against the outer walls of the pizza place, then against the Thai restaurant, making himself into the dark shadow he had feared along the way here. He crossed Eleventh out of their sightline. He walked briskly along Twentieth Alley, this time taking it a block further to Thirteenth, then jogged east at a normal pace back to Twentieth Street South. Crying as he ran, eventually he made his way home.

Cold Mountain

Forty-five hours had elapsed after Booker Bailey searched the Vulcan Museum for a compass, flashlight, knife, and solar charger. He packed them in a knapsack along with his road atlas and started hiking north to Amicalola Falls in Dawsonville, Georgia—the Southern Terminus of the Appalachian trail. Booker felt a sudden wave of homesickness that was unexpected and almost sickening in its force, but the green mountain of his dreams, a real Christian Church with people his own age gradually enabled him to push down the feelings and dispel them altogether. *The Trail*, he thought. *It is really real. The Trail that leads to the last Church community on earth. The Trail that leads to an authentic miracle of God: the prophet; like those of old except fresh and new for the times.*

Three hundred miles north of Booker, a mountain man named Marshall Langar turned up his face to the remorseless mid-morning sunshine. He tasted the air and scratched at his sand-colored beard. He had spent a rare night in his dead parents' cabin, angrier than ever before. The bunk of his youth had been no match for his now six-foot-four-inch, two-hundred twenty-five-pound adult body. "Oof." He stretched to loosen body aches fostered by the ridiculous two-sizes too small sleeping arrangement, also to clear mental fog.

He walked until he stood outside the entrance of the cozy, rough-hewn log cabin, illuminated by candles and kerosene lanterns, with heat, cooking, hot water, and refrigeration made possible by liquid propane gas. Inside this cabin, his common-law wife lay sleeping upon a comfortable foam bed covered with clean linens and warm Hudson Bay wool blankets. After his enormous self-restraint had worn mica-thin, last night he had grabbed his pillow along with the key to his parents' cabin and walked out on her.

God, I sure could use a little guidance lately, he thought. He wished at least that his dad could be here to give him a bit of sage life coaching. At an elevation of sixty-four hundred feet, at that moment he stood higher than any surviving human in the State of Tennessee. "Behold, the only world I have ever known," he muttered, taking in the vista.

Marshall grew up strong and tall, crammed with his parents inside one of the LeConte Lodge cabins. After they died, no longer able to bear living among the artifacts of his beloved parents, Marshall locked up their cabin, considering it a shrine of sorts. He had fixed up one of the other guest cabins and moved into the highest one in the eastern United States, situated on an open glade just below the summit of Mount LeConte. His entire life consisted of spectacular views of the Smoky Mountains.

Marshall buried his mother beside his father. He was seventeen when his father had died from a rabid raccoon bite. Months after, his mother had slipped on a mossy boulder and fallen down a craggy ravine; a hard landing had snapped her petite neck like the driest twig.

LeConte Lodge encompassed all the cabins and was accessible only by hiking. No road led up to the Lodge. Marshall had at his disposal five hiking trails from LeConte Lodge down the mountain, ranging in length from five to nine miles. The shortest trip down the mountain was the five-mile Alum Cave Trail; instead, he would push a wheelbarrow along Rainbow Falls Trail downhill seven miles, then another flat two-and-a-half miles along Cherokee Orchard Road into the flood-wasted town of Gatlinburg, for foraging. This morning as he stood alone outside their cabin looking in, he reflected on the years between the afternoon he found her years ago while foraging, and the disaster that was last night. After diffident sex, he and Delilah had fought. Or, if he were being candid, she had laid into him for no reason or provocation.

One midday six years prior, just after burying his mother, Marshall plunked down a heavy steel propane tank into the wheelbarrow tray with a loud bang. From inside a nearby pharmacy, he heard a scream. He had never met other people apart from his parents. Heart pounding, he ran toward the sound. He found the glass double doors locked. Shoulder forwards he ran at the door until he rammed the middle metallic strip at full force. He felt it give a little. He hit it again and felt more give. *Third time's a charm*, he had thought, and it was: the heavy lock bent, and the doors swung inward. He stepped inside, looked around, but saw no one.

"Hello? Anybody in here? I heard a scream. Here to help."

He heard high-pitched sobbing and walked toward the source. In the candy bar aisle, he first laid eyes on the most exquisitely wonderful vision of his life. A young girl, with dirty bare legs and feet which extended into the aisle; the back of her summer dress leaned against the denuded bottom rows labeled for candy items. Bright blonde tresses spilled around her dirty face. Trails of tears had cleared bright paths through dust and filth like termite trails down her filthy pale cheeks. Tensed to run she looked up at him, hands flat against the low-pile commercial carpeting.

"Um, hi. My name's Marshall Langar. What's y'all's name? Everythin' okay?"

Sniffling, she shook her head. "Delilah Owens."

"Delilah's a real pretty name. How old are y'all, Delilah? I turned seventeen this year. Where d'y'all live?"

"Thirteen. My parents are Byron and Dixie Owens. We live in a hunters cabin on a mountain about a four-hour-walk away."

"Where are they now, y'all's parents? How 'bout we go find 'em 'n get y'all home," he said.

The crying grew to a frenzy. He dropped to his knees beside her, his eyes never leaving hers. She managed to choke out, "Yesterday we were here gathering supplies. The Golgoth white monsters are supposed to come out only at night. My parents pushed a grocery cart outside. We have a horse and a wagon. The horse pulls the wagon. They were loading the wagon with supplies when…"

"Golgoths took 'em during daylight?"

She nodded. "They always told me the monsters only come out at night. I watched through the glass door from in here."

He reached out slowly so as not to spook her. She gazed at him through hot tears. With the back of his left forefinger, gently he wiped under her eye. "Truly I am so sorry this all happened to y'all, Delilah. I lost both my parents too." He pointed. "I live way-way up in Mount LeConte. There's an open cabin with y'all's name on it. Would y'all wanna come live up on the mountain under my protection?"

Her emerald-green eyes studied his brown eyes. When he smiled, the corners of his eyes crinkled. She noticed that his teeth were straight and very white. With a child's innate sense of goodness or badness living inside people, she trusted him. She nodded.

Last night, sounds of her vomiting had reached him from a distance and pulled him from a recurring dream still fresh in his mind. Light and uneasy sleep returned him to the exact same green mountain as before in this recurring dream. *So bizarre*, he thought, and shook himself awake. *Guess I'm up for the day now, thanks to the vomitin' soundtrack.*

In the dream, he had stood on a vastly different mountain, one far shorter and lower, a mere foothill compared to Mount LeConte. *The trees there are different from trees here. Mount Spring, maybe? Yep, that'd be its name, I think. Nothin' 'bout it compares to the grandeur of the Smokies, yet Mount Spring is better in every way. Filled with people my own age, smilin' and couples playin' with babies and infants. Wild animals there ain't afraid 'a humans. Bears and deer amblin' about the perfectly even grass within arm's reach 'a people. Here in this place, love is greater than human emotion. Love radiates from every livin' creature. Round rocks break the water in the clear stream runnin' under a covered bridge with open wood plank sides and Y-beam roof supports. I seen young lovers kissin' under it. Love lives here, a force more powerful than the sun, radiatin' warmth to all 'a God's creatures without exception.*

A man robed in white linen stands alone higher up the mountain. An aura of golden light surrounds him. A large carved wooden crucifix hangs behind 'im. He reaches out his right arm, palm upturned, and stares at me. He mouths the words, "Come north. Join us, Marshall. You belong here. The Lord has need of you."

He rarely recalled dreams upon awakening and only fragments at that; last night's dream seemed more like a memory of an actual event, clear in every way. He walked to the iron pitcher pump beside the cabin he shared with Delilah, worked the handle, and held his face under the flow, swallowing. The squeaking of the simple machine must have awakened her.

Nineteen, now five-foot-eleven in bare feet yet so thin that her ribs showed, Delilah supported herself inside the open cabin doorway, wearing a halter top, white granny panties, and nothing else. Her long blonde hair was a bird's nest in a hurricane. Marshall dried his face on his sleeve, and out of the corner of his eye he spotted her. He stood at attention, muscular arms hanging down, hands opening and closing. He refused to be the first to speak. Her words and body language the night prior had deeply offended him. He felt that nothing short of her apology could make things right. He studied her features and body language. *What am I seein?' Defiance; unrepentance; emotions darker still. Great, just swell. This outta be a long, bad day.*

Delilah had slept away the morning in the cabin. Pregnancy had been causing her to lose sleep at night. She had spent time with medical books his parents had tucked away in the storage cabin. He had believed her when she said nausea, insomnia, and bad dreams were normal side-effects of pregnancy, though he did not think to research it. Last night had been dramatically different. All night long she had retched violently, screaming out incoherent words commingled with profanities. Looking at her now, despite her vile expression, he felt pity. He swallowed his pride and asked, "Bad night, D?"

Her tiny breasts had barely swelled; her hard, flat stomach appeared unchanged, at least not to him. "Marshall, I told you last night, I'm not bringing a child into this awful world," she said.

He pretend-smiled. "I think you are, D. Nothin' so much y'all can do about it now, is there? If God didn't want us to have a child it never woulda' happened."

Delilah pumped both middle fingers at the sky. "Here's to your God, Marshall! That imposter is nothing but a myth your parents told you to make you sleep better at night, along with a devil to blame for accidents and mistakes. Do you really think your loving, personal God would send two Floods, destroying mostly everything it created? That your God would let mutants kill and eat my parents? It is all just bullshit, Marshall. This life," she said, making a sweeping motion with her reedy arm, "all of it, including you. Everything I see is all bullshit."

Marshall's stomach rolled back and forth like a wine cork in a river. His head was suddenly an iron cannon ball that had learned how to sweat. Anger boiled up fixed and fast. Fists balled, he closed the twenty or so paces quickly until he stood two feet away. "God is bullshit? I am bullshit? Our baby is bullshit?"

She nodded. "Not our baby, your baby. It's dying, Marshall. Already dead."

"*What?*" His lips felt curiously cold.

"I remembered something from the medical books. That the fruits and roots of May Apples are an anti-parasitic. That thing growing inside me is a dark and malignant parasite. Last night I ate six of the May Apple's yellow fruits and a quarter inch of root. More than that would have killed me along with the parasite. It made me extremely sick all night, and I saw things: hallucinations; visions; whatever. These things were not real, even though seen with my eyes wide open and my body awake. The leader and blessed prophet of the Golgoths, Hostis Dei called me to him, to a place named Valley of The Forge. He is the closest thing we have to a real god. Nothing like your bullshit God with his pallid, incompetent Son who voluntarily got himself nailed to a tree. How weak and stupid is that? Hostis Dei and his Golgoths rule the world. He embodies true power. In my visions he wants me…calls to me to become his queen. Great daydream, considering how rotten I felt."

For a moment, Marshall wanted to punch her face until his fist came out the back. "Y'all poisoned our baby, Delilah? Y'all killed an angel 'a God?" Tears filled his eyes, salty and scalding. Delilah, I…" His body went limp.

"Look Marshall. Don't think that I don't appreciate everything you've done for me: I do. But you and I, well, we're not exactly on the same page, are we? You and your storybook God and his miracle-worker Son. The humble and meek shall inherit the earth. Bullshit, Marshall. The earth belongs to the strong. It's called the Law of the Jungle, or natural selection. Your body is strong, but your spirit is too soft. You are a weak man."

Marshall wept. "Y'all's right. I am weak." All he could do was mourn. Grieve for a future that suddenly he realized could never be. His heart felt cleaved in two. He felt physical pain behind his ribs, acid stomach like it might drop out his bottom, and burning in his bowels, crampy-hot and painful.

"I think you should leave. Today," she decided. "As in, right now."

He looked up finally and met her eyes. "I saved y'all's *life*, Delilah! Those monsters woulda' eaten y'all in a day if I hadn't come along. I brought y'all here to my family's home and took y'all in; I kept y'all clean, dressed, fed, safe, and warm. I ain't never asked for nothin' back. Three months ago, it was *y'all* who initiated a sexual relationship; *y'all* who told me that y'all loved me. It was all *y'all's doin,*' Delilah. Everythin' I done for years now has all been for y'all. And this is how y'all repay me? By murderin' my baby and tellin' me to leave *my* home?"

She nodded. "You don't own the mountain. Your parents just took it over. Now I'm taking it over. Goodbye, Marshall. Thanks again. Now go."

He shook his head; looked at his feet; and toed the gravel. He remained like that for over two minutes. *Dear Lord, I am all used up. Do what y'all will with me.*

She stared. He stood; eyes closed. All at once his posture changed.

Energy and purpose flowed through him. He snapped his head up and looked at her with eyes like searchlights; a half-smile froze on his lips. He turned and walked back to the cabin of his parents and his childhood. He went inside and left the door open. Twenty minutes later he emerged wearing a full-size backpack loaded with a hunting slingshot and bag of marbles; honing oil and whet stone; rope; a wire saw and pocket chainsaw; flint and steel for starting fires; a waterproof tarp; and plastic bottles of bug repellent. To the base of the backpack's light, aluminum frame he had strapped a bedroll and sleeping pad. He strapped two long machete knives in leather sheaths against the backpack, crisscross with handles up for easy reach. He walked to the storage cabin and emerged wearing a sturdy pair of laced waterproof walking boots. He topped off the backpack with food and bottled water and slipped his arms through the padded chest-shoulder straps. *About forty-five pounds*, he guessed. In reality it weighed slightly over sixty-five.

Praying in silence he knelt in front of his parents' cabin. "Our Father in Heaven. Thank y'all for Jesus Christ, y'all's Son, for my salvation, and for all the blessins' y'all give me: none of which I deserve. Please accept my child into y'all's Kingdom. I know that he or she will see y'all's face. Please keep my parents for y'all's self. Forgive Delilah her trespasses, for she knows not what she does. I pray, wash over me with y'all's Spirit without limit, to guide and protect me; and when the trail ends that somehow I might serve y'all. Use me, Lord: for I am y'all's to command in all things. If givin' y'all my life benefits the Kingdom—take it. I don't want it no more. Got no use fer' it. Y'all's will be done; never mine. In the name of y'all's Son, Jesus Christ, I pray. Amen."

Marshall rose up. He would not look back at Delilah, at the cabin, or out across the vista that had served as home since birth. Shaking the dust from his boots at the entire scene, he turned, and walked north toward the Trillium Gap Trail. This trail he had never taken. His parents had always told him it leads to nothing of value, but only to danger. He had briefly reviewed the trail atlas before stuffing it into the knapsack. Trillium would lead him to a main artery, Route 321, heading east. At the end he would find the Appalachian Trail at Spivey Gap, North Carolina, the capillary that would lead him to the Mountain of Springs in his dreams.

"Thank y'all, Lord, for y'all's Holy Spirit. I believe he has made his home in me."

He stuffed the map into a knapsack pocket and decided not to use it. "The Spirit will guide my way."

His feet knew where to walk. Somehow, like migrating birds, they just knew. He walked and talked with his God, sometimes silently, sometimes aloud, unaware of any difference between the two.

Team Antebellum

Arabella Pendleman accompanied by her best friend since childhood, Tatum Winters, twenty-two, celebrated the morning of her twenty-first birthday outdoors at the Georgia resort and spa's terrace and pavilion. Each had consumed one entire bottle of Riesling wine from the resort's cellar. Together they reflected on life, taking a renewed look at the breathtaking mountain views they had known since their lives started here shortly after the First Flood. From the safety of their mountain stronghold at over twenty-one-hundred feet, they had watched the Second Flood waters swell high then recede, leaving destruction in their wake. This made them sad, but living above it all, stocked with a lifetime's worth of canned food, liquid propane gas for heating, cooking, hot showers, and hot tub baths, abated their grief.

"My parents surely chose well when they took this place over," said Arabella. "Safe, secure, comfortable. Everything we will ever need or want is here."

Tatum uncorked a third bottle of Riesling and poured each a fine crystal glass of it. "Not everything." She finished her glass in three gulps and refilled it.

"Dad told me if you take a drink before ten in the morning, you're an alcoholic."

Tatum giggled, blowing a stray lock of short, thick, straight deep brown hair away from her cobalt blue eyes. "That's us. Just a couple of drunken sluts are we, my friend." She raised her glass. "Happy birthday to you, Bella. The most aptly named human being in all history."

Arabella snickered drunkenly. "Tatum my love, I know you want to. You keep your hair close-cropped like a boy, keep your little tits pressed down tight like you have none at all. Believe me I get it. But for the billionth time, hear me now believe me later: it ain't ever gonna happen ya little bisexual bitch. I don't pray to my dad's terrible God who doesn't exist. But if I did, I'd pray for a big strapping man to have his way with me ten times a day."

"You wish. Orange-headed bitch."

Arabella laughed hard. "I always thought that being a redhead made me a freak, kinda. Confession: I've always envied that you quickly tan up in summer. Me, I burn. Me and el sol parted ways at birth. I feel paler than a damned Golgoth."

Tatum grinned. "The Lezbo and the Orange-Headed Goth. Ain't we a pair."

"Maybe you could convince Aliyah or Dodie to submit to a bit of bushwhacking."

Choking on a sip of wine, Tatum coughed, laughed, and cleared her throat. "The Bible-bangers? Our own little God Squad? Hah! Fat chance. I do think Aliyah Freedman is one super-hot little number, though. I like the way she moves."

"Ew! Out of the two you prefer the negro?"

Tatum smiled. "I've read that once you go Black you never go back."

"Ewwwwww! Gross."

"Oh right. I almost forgot. You're a direct descendant of plantation owners. Racism lives in your mutant red genes."

"Damned right it does. Sorry that I, a mere mortal, cannot be as progressive and worldly as you."

Tatum drained her glass and belched loudly. Arabella made a disgusted face. "If you really believed that, Arabella, never could we have become so close. The fact is, you believe you are of a higher caste than I, than all of us. Southern royalty. Entitled little snobby bitch, you."

"Oh, am I, now? Watch how wrong you are," said Arabella. She snatched away the bottle and refilled Tatum's glass. "I live to serve. If the pedestal upon which I have placed you were any higher, my neck would freeze gazing up at it all day." Both giggled. "On my birthday, I propose a toast to you, Tatum Winters. To the baddest ass of them all. I salute you."

Wine-soaked brains failed to register approaching footfalls. A dull surprise registered on both their faces when Aliyah and Dodie crashed their terrace birthday party.

"Arabella, Tatum. We came here to tell you something important," said Aliyah, voice anxious.

Both Arabella and Tatum looked up and glanced at each other, more curious than alarmed. They stayed like that for twenty seconds. Surprise turned to irritation. Arabella, who had only spoken to the 'darkie' when necessary, directed her narrowed eyes at Dodie. "What is it? What is so goddamned important that couldn't wait 'til after my birthday?"

Dodie's face showed no emotion. "You don't believe in God, so why petition him to damn us?"

"Pfft. Flick-off, Dolores. What do you want?"

Dodie bristled. All understood it deeply irritated her to use her full given name, which she hated. She glanced at Aliyah, who nodded. "Aliyah and I are leaving the mountain today."

Arabella took a sip of wine. "Well. Bye."

"For good, Arabella."

Her eyes opened wide. "What do you mean? This is your home, Dodie. My dad risked everything to bring you up here."

Dodie nodded. "Yes, he did. Apart from our dads Grady Pendleman was the bravest man we ever knew. Aliyah and I would be dead if he hadn't rescued us when our parents left us in the Baptist Church belltower and led the Golgoths away from us. The same monsters that took them almost took

Grady, but he fought them off, loaded us into his backpack and bicycled us here. The few times Golgoths found the road leading here: Grady shot them all. Thanks to him, long ago they stopped trying. Golgoth skeletons litter the road, causing the live ones to believe this mountain is evil," she said, words rushing out of her at breakneck speed. "No thanks to you. You'd be dead too without Grady. All of us would be dead. Only you would try laying a stupid guilt trip."

"Yes, he did, even me," Aliyah added. "Even though he had a serious problem with Black people, he rescued me. I can forgive his racist wiring."

Arabella drained her glass. "I forgive your absence of gratitude and lack of humility. But you and your dark little friend are defective defectors."

Dodie chuckled at the irony. "Your dad walked in the ways of the Lord to the very end, died peacefully in his sleep, and went to his reward in Heaven. Leaving the four of us here alone. For how long are we going to hide? Staying here is not living a full life in the Lord. We are not walking in his way. We were meant to serve husbands, raise children. Be fruitful and multiply…"

"Hah! That'll be the day," said Tatum.

Dodie refused to be dissuaded. "We need to find other likeminded people."

Arabella drained her glass. "Dodie, have you ever considered that we might be it? We four, and the Golgoths, and that's all? I mean, two global floods, mass starvation, animals and crops gone, too. No, up here is not an exciting life, but it's a life. I long for the company of others, too. But there is nothing out there beyond these mountains. The only thing awaiting us is a horrible, torturous death."

"Correction, birthday girl," said Tatum. "Your father told you something once that time you threatened to run away from home."

Through soggy miles of alcohol-fogged synapses, an old memory burbled up. "Ah. Yes, Tates. Yes, he did. I remember now. Go ahead, tell them."

"He said that Golgoths have two uses for females: rape and food. The Golgoths keep them pregnant. They pump puppies until they are too old to conceive. Then Golgoths tie them up; hack off an arm; then cook and eat it. Then a leg. Then the other arm and other leg. So far, the poor bitches are still alive. They drag out the dismemberment to make the food last across weeks of meals. When all four limbs are gone, they gut them alive and cook whatever usable flesh is left. Did I miss anything, Bells?"

Arabella shook her head. "Nope, I remember it all, now. I guess my brain had formed a sort of callus around the memory of that fight with dad, but thanks to you, Tates, it's all coming back now in lurid, living color. Which, Dodie, is why you are nuts to want to leave here. Again, it's not much of a life here, but we're alive. Out there?" she said, panning the horizon and knocking over her wine glass. "Death or worse awaits. You must think I and Tatum are crazy if you think we would even consider leaving."

"No wait, Arabella," said Tatum. She looked at Aliyah and Dodie. "I have a question for you two. Who told you that there are people out there like us, not Golgoths or their victims? And where are they?"

"God told us," Aliyah answered.

Dodie nodded. She could tell from the expressions on the faces of the two avowed atheists that Aliyah's proclamation, so delivered, just did more harm than good. "Do either of you remember your dreams?" Dodie asked.

Tatum glanced at Arabella. "I do," Tatum said. "Sometimes."

"And do you ever dream the same dream more than once?"

Tatum nodded. "Sometimes, especially lately."

Dodie looked at Aliyah. "So do we," said Dodie. "Both of us dream the exact same dream every single night without exception. Our dream is of a mountain up north filled with lots of people our own age. It is safe and loving there. People there are given in marriage all the time; have babies; and walk in the Lord's path. Beautiful people of all races living simply and cleanly forming families, building cabins, and moving into them. They all live together on a rich green mountain. This is what Aliyah meant. Only God could give us both the exact same vision every night, Tatum. So what's in your dream?"

"I see lots of log cabins, too," said Tatum. "And a man with hair lighter than yours, Dodie."

"Yes! The golden-haired man! We're being called there, Tatum, and so are you! Come with us, you two!" Dodie said.

"You did *not* have the same dream as Alliyah and Dodie did, Tates; c'mon, be real. And you know we'd all be dead in no time. That would be a big fat no from me. What say you, Tates?"

Tatum sat in quiet reflection. "I'm never going to meet anybody here, and it's driving me nuts. Sometimes I think it would be better to die than to live like this for the next half a century."

Arabella jumped to standing. She jabbed her finger at Tatum's head. "Are you nuts?

Tatum nodded. "Yes, Bells. I do believe that I am." Looking at Dodie and Aliyah, she said, "I can't prove or disprove the existence of your God. Pretty much resigned to the fact that this world, and all the garbage in it, just happens. There is no magic. There is no great Intelligent Designer and no personal God like in your Bible. He'd have to be one broke-assed designer to make this awful world. But whatever. Three of us having the same dream is…well. It can't be a coincidence. It's a kind of magic," she said. "Okay. I'm in. When do we leave?" She sensed Arabella's angry stare.

Dodie smiled. Aliyah clapped. Dodie responded. "Now, today. Let's go pack knapsacks full of essentials. God will keep us safe and guide our path. But let's go help ourselves to stuff."

"My stuff!" Arabella screeched.

Dodie smiled patiently. "Your dad took over this place after the First Flood. Before that, the ownership deed, framed and nailed to the administrative office wall shows that all of this legally belonged to a hospitality company. It was never Grady's to own, which means the stuff here belongs to whomever lives here. They called it 'adverse possession.' While you were reading comic books I was reading history and whatever Georgia law books I could find to better understand the world before the Floods. Squatters can be considered the lawful owners of a property after living in it for twenty continuous years without the owner trying to evict them. This means everything here belongs to all of us, Arabella, not only to you."

"Fine. Go to your deaths, then. To Hell with all of you. Happy birthday to me." Turning her back to her friends, Arabella righted her wine glass, refilled it, and gulped it down.

While organizing their knapsacks, Tatum interrupted the discussion about survival tactics. "How do you propose to convey us to this mythical mountain, oh dearest Dodie?"

Reaching into the front pocket of her backpack, Dodie withdrew an old Rand-McNally Road atlas. She tapped it to her head, then against her heart. "God shows me the way. But since you have no faith, feel free to follow me, and follow this," she said, and tossed the booklet to Tatum.

Tatum opened a page to Georgia and found their current location in Young Harris. "All bridges surely got destroyed in the Floods. Highways will be crawling with Golgoths on the hunt for walkers. They may be monsters, but they aren't stupid. They'll consider major roads just as they do city centers: ripe hunting grounds."

"We're not taking major roads," said Aliyah. "We are going to walk northeast until we get to Sams Gap, North Carolina, where we'll hook up with the Appalachian Trial. I saw myself in a dream walking on a clear path through woods; the Trail must be that path. People before the First Flood used to hike its full length for something fun to do, for adventure, and to challenge themselves. Not expecting to spot too many Golgoths hanging out along its length. There's nothing in it for them. People use roads, especially main arteries. Golgoths set traps on roads for walkers. That is exactly what Grady told us, and we all saw the skeletons.

"But you're right, Tates," said Dodie. "Surely some bridges spanning bogs, creeks, rivers, streams, and swamps got severely damaged by the Floods. We should each lug along a lightweight two-person inflatable kayak, a paddle, a plastic foot-pump, and repair kits. I saw shelves of them down in storage along with fishing gear. Pre-Flood people used to paddle around in the kayaks for fun. Come down with me, you two. Let's bring up water transportation and anything we find that's lightweight and useful."

"Make that four." All three turned in the direction of the sound. Arabella stood in the doorway, long auburn locks hanging down, covering her eyes. "Changed my mind. I'd be too scared here all by myself."

"Well tie my face to the side of a hog and roll me in the mud. If it ain't the Grandy Lady Antebellum herself," said Tatum, smiling. "Glad you could make it, bestie. Thought you might change your mind," she said, and pointed to a spare but empty knapsack. "We were just headed down to the pool to get kayaks, plus you'll need to pick out a giant pair of rubber boots that'll fit those size-eleven, big, smelly clodhoppers of yours, dearest. Also, you'll be loading your own pack. Chop-chop, no time to waste. You're playing catch-up."

Arabella whispered into Tatum's ear, "God is guiding her way? Seriously, is that her plan? You do realize that's completely insane. Our lives, Tates. That's what she's playing with. We each only get one of those."

Tatum half-closed her eyes. Lightly she twitched Arabella's hand. "Relax, hon. I have a road atlas. God exists, or he doesn't. Think of it: twins finish each other's sentences, and, when separated, they hear each other's thoughts. Scientific fact. I must believe there is something to these recurring identical dreams. People are not able to communicate via an ethereal Coconut Telegraph. This suggests to me that God is real. Just maybe there *is* magic in the world. Who knows? But we need to find people, Bella, and if we don't then we can always reverse course and come back here to grow old and die lonely and miserable and low risk, just how you like it. Okay?"

Arabella stood erect and shook her head. She glanced at the other two, then at Tatum. After two full minutes had elapsed, finally, she nodded.

"Okay then," she said. "We're a team of four. Dodie, by all means, please lead on."

Multiples of Three

Spoggs Reichert, top general of the Golgoth tribe knocked on the heavy wood door. The sound echoed hollowly. He knew that despite his master's allegiance and his high rank, to walk inside without knocking, or to show the slightest measure of disrespect, or bring unwelcome news in which he played some part, would lead Hostis Dei—the Lord Master; prophet of the one true moon god, Hubal; the supreme leader of every Golgoth—to make a very painful and public example of him. He listened, and wondered what that might be.

The Lord-Master will not kill me over it. Public flogging. Branding. Chopping off one finger.

His mind drifted back to the day when a fellow member of the Golgoth top command, General Gode, had gotten himself caught inside Gode's cabin fondling one of the Lord Master's breeders. It had happened one summer between the First and Second Floods; he could not recall which. As punishment for insubordination, which amounted to high treason in the tribe, the Lord Master had a Saint Andrew's Cross built and strapped to the base of the fifty-foot granite obelisk across the road, so that thousands of rank-and-file Golgoths, under orders to witness the conducting of the sentence while standing in the grassy field, would each be compelled to enjoy an unobstructed view of the Cross.

General Gode was marched by force to the cross, every trace of his white warpaint scrubbed from his naked body like any other breeder or filthy human cattle. The Lord Master, holding his bullhorn, had said to the thousands, "Behold the awful price of treason! General Gode touched a breeder. His man-parts led him to this grievous sin. Therefore, to spare his life eternal and his illustrious rank of honor, I hereby pronounce sentence: nullification. The breeder he molested must execute the sentence. If she fails, immediately she will be transferred to the cattle pen for processing and consumption. Breeder," he said. A nude, white-painted young woman knelt before him. The Lord Master reached out his left hand holding a sharp Karambit knife. "Carry out General Gode's sentence."

Standing outside the chapel now in view of the obelisk, listening for any sign of the Lord Master, Reichert recalled Gode's terrified screams and agonized high pitch wailing. *As if it happened yesterday.*

Just then Reichert heard steps approaching behind the door. It creaked on its never-oiled hinges; the heavy door swung inward.

"Spoggs," said Hostis Dei. "What is it?" All were forbidden to use his name, Hostis Dei, in his presence. Only his title, Lord Master, or a derivation of it would be accepted, under penalty of pain.

Reichert lowered his head subordinately. Only briefly did he glimpse the hairless, white-painted genitals of the Lord Master. In stark contrast fresh blood dripped from the penis, enormous even when flaccid. Spoggs would not look above the Lord Master's neck at the white-painted hairless head, at the hypnotic lash-less black eyes, at the supercilious lips pulled away into what seemed a permanent snarl that revealed yellow teeth filed into sharp points. The blue eyes were too much for Reichert to take. Only once had he ever looked directly at them: unsettling, preternaturally glittering with mirthless cheer, an ecstasy of terror. The piquant, vinegary bouquet of decomposing meat and sex hung about Hostis Dei like a bad omen.

Years earlier Spoggs had decided never to look into the Lord Master's eyes again if it could be avoided without giving offense. Bioluminescent eyes bloated and cheesy, an imitation of fire, of moonlight refracting through blue glacial ice. These were eyes that grew larger or seemed to. Looking into them was like looking into Saltstraumen maelstroms: icy cold, ancient, and immeasurably deep. Spoggs sensed that if he were to plumb their revolting depths he might never crawl back to the surface. Or that doing so might come across as implied disloyalty. But worst of all, the Lord Master would read his most private thoughts, which at times like this flirted with the tantalizing concept of army desertion. A conversation with the Lord Master might then very well end before it even began. Or worse. Usually, Spoggs felt safest staring at the silver crescent moon hanging between thick white pectorals from a leather lanyard around the Lord Master's neck.

A cold comber of fear washed over Spoggs Reichert at every meeting with their anointed leader, earthly prophet of the most high, the moon god, Hubal. "When he grins at you, all the blood in your body falls into a dead swoon, leaving your flesh cold and gray," he once heard another general whisper at a bonfire. "Afterwards you feel done-in. Your lips are blue and numb. Your butthole puckers up." Which is why the other generals, though envious of Reichert's ascendant positional power, seemed mostly content to step back and let him handle all face-to-face meetings with the Lord Master, due to the fear Hostis Dei inspires in every member of the tribe.

Then there were the dreams, or rather nightmares. Even sleep offered Spoggs no respite from the leader's black and dangerous sphere of influence. Hostis Dei dominated his waking mind and usually his unconscious dreaming mind. Nightmares dispelled any notion that this man felt anything gentle. The monstrous eyes haunting his subconscious disclosed nothing humane dwelling behind them.

Spoggs hated the core command given to all Golgoths that, using whatever simple tools they had available from tweezers to pliers to clamshells, each must pull out every body hair from head to toe, including the nostrils, from his own body.

"Lord-Master, forgive my intrusion. I have received word from our spies that Gabriel's numbers have swelled to over sixty thousand. Furthermore, the Elect are felling hickory, ash, red oak, and acacia trees, and tearing up railroad tracks. M' Lord, we deduce they mean to process the steel and wood into cutting and stabbing weapons."

Without pause, "How many spears and swords do we have in the armory?"

Spoggs felt no small measure of relief at that moment. Staying ahead of the Lord-Master, anticipating his questions, and securing accurate information before being asked was, he recognized, the main reason why he was rarely reprimanded or threatened.

"Seventy-five thousand of each, m' Lord."

"By now you should well know that I do not suffer numbers indivisible by three."

Spoggs nodded curtly. "Seventy-eight thousand it shall be. I will take care of it, m' Lord."

"Of course you will, Spoggs. Is that the whole of your report?"

"No, m' Lord. As you commanded, I have dispatched messengers to the northern and southern colonies."

"Over land?"

Spoggs shook his head. "No, m' Lord. Overland would take weeks. I sent them south to Delaware to embark using our sailing craft. This will cut the time in half. Messengers bearing your orders are dispatched and will deliver them before your deadline."

"Precisely what command did you send with our messengers?"

"All must make their way to Valley Forge. Along the way invert the daily cycle. Rest at night, cover all paved roadways by day. Hunt walkers; keep whatever you kill. Capture and force-march all breeders here unmolested."

The thickly muscled left arm of Hostis Dei shot out: a pallid hand clamped the throat of Spoggs so tightly that he gagged; his eyes bulged in surprise. Silently he plead for his life.

"Spoggs, one of my breeders claims she was molested."

Spoggs was thirty seconds away from losing consciousness. His lips moved in response. "I will investigate, m' Lord. Let me punish the accused."

Hostis Dei smiled, a cold, horrid rictus that travelled up his face like rising damp. He released his grip and gently patted the right cheek of his Number One. "I can always count on you, Spoggs. How inadequately may I reward your unflinching loyalty?" he said, black eyes a vacuum. Spoggs felt that somehow Hostis Dei had probed straight into his innermost thoughts and desires. "Ah. I see. Yes of course, and why not? Does this not benefit both of us?"

Spoggs often failed to recognize trick questions and suffered for it. Today, he refused to underestimate the dark leader's craft and cozening. Self-preservation guided his politically correct response. "I benefit only when you benefit, m' Lord. So mote it be."

Hostis Dei threw back his head and roared with sneering laughter, which boomed and echoed throughout the tall Washington's Chapel structure.

"Sometimes your alacrity and quick-thinking does surprise me, Spoggs. It pleases me. When inspecting the next harvest of breeders, choose one that appeals to you. Take her to your cabin, remove every hair, and have your way with her. Put her on a leash and lead her around; publicize this gift. I want your fellow generals to know how generously I reward my most loyal. Parade her around but let no one touch her. When you grow bored of her, butcher the meat yourself. Make it last. Make a public show of your feasts by inviting the generals. When you finally butcher the living torso, bring me her heart as tribute. Make sure the others see you do it."

"Thank you, Lord-Master. You are the anointed prophet of the true god, Hubal, and you shall lead me to life eternal. I am not worthy."

"Pfft." This sound, accompanied by a dismissive hand-gesture, was Hostis Dei's signature period nailed onto the end of every alarming exchange and signaled the close of discussion.

Spoggs Reichert stood facing the now shut and deadbolted door of the chapel. He felt eyes on him. *Of course, the treacherous weasels study me, seeking the smallest flaw or weakness for them to exploit. Oh! —how they envy my position. Let them stew in their own juices. I will sit at the left hand of the Lord-Master and rule this earth for a thousand years. With m' Lord until the end of time.*

He walked to the straw-covered Breeder Pen and surveilled the filthy, naked captives caked in their own offal. One teenaged female with generous curves, olive skin, and dark, pleading eyes, held his attention. She watched in horror as Spoggs Reichert's white-painted member grew engorged; she started screaming in Spanish, a language with which he was familiar but far from fluent. He did, however, recognize the meaning of "Quiero a mi mama! Dios ayúdame!

He laughed. "Your mother can't save you, child. As for your God, well. Let's just say that he has forsaken you. He is soft: He is weak. My god is stronger. There is no one to save you. Renounce your God, and I will make your death quick and merciful. Praise Hostis Dei and the All-Father, Hubal, god of the moon. Do it not, and I promise you unendurable pain, both in this world and the next."

"No! ¡Amo a Jesus! ¡Ve al infierno, diablo!"

Strapped down Spoggs Reichert's cabin, as Isabella Albo screamed and squirmed in depilatory Hell—six-hundred miles south, Jayden Bonner took one final mental snapshot of the city skyline he had called home since birth, then cast a brief glance up at the savage gunmetal sky, the sun blaring down its indifferent furnace heat. Jayden left Nashville alone on foot heading east toward the Appalachian Trail. He carried a backpack containing food, water, and a portable telescope. Strapped to the backpack frame, a vintage Martin acoustic guitar.

Jayden had never given much thought to his body height since the only people he had ever met were his parents, both equally as long and lean. He rubbed at the stiffness in his neck and back. Forced to duck under ancient, downed power lines and dangling tree branches, today he felt too tall. He used his fingers to comb detritus out of his long, dark, greasy waves of hair. His dad had raised him to shave daily; he found the stubble on his neck irritating. *This new hobo lifestyle will require some significant adjustment.*

The last of the light had nearly gone out of the sky. Jayden stopped for the night in Cookeville, Tennessee. He figured the Golgoths would be out tonight and had vowed to walk only during daylight. It was almost dark when he broke into a building with a damaged sign, *Mumbles Inn & Suites.* He explored the fifth floor which was the highest point in town. In front of him, knowing even behind occluded window glass, opaque with grime, any moving light would be a dinner bell for Golgoths. He found a room less damaged and mildewy than the others. *Home sweet home*, he thought. Ardently he wanted to do his two favorite things: gaze at the stars and play his guitar.

He would do neither for an exceedingly long time.

He laid down hands folded behind his head and contemplated why he was here tonight instead of in his comfortable safe zone in Nashville. *Will I dream of the green mountain again tonight?*

When Jayden was a baby during the First Flood, his father had retreated with him and his mother. They usurped an unoccupied residential apartment on the forty-fifth and top floor of Nashville's 505 tower, the tallest residential building in the state. As a teenager during the Second Flood, he had watched the waters reach as high as the twentieth floor. That memory had frightened him even more than glimpses of cannibal Golgoths lurking about the streets at night. Relentless, roiling depths had swallowed everything in their paths. He had felt certain that the water would reach his floor and carry him and his parents away. Eventually, after a long time; the waters did recede, and once again he saw the decimated and dreary asphalt streets below.

His father had felt confident that Golgoths, who nested at ground level, got swept away by the "just act of God," as his parents chose to label the Second Flood. One day they went out foraging and never returned. *God must've missed a few in his sweep,* he thought, as he calmly vowed to kill every last Golgoth, if he ever mustered the gumption to leave the safety of the high-rise vault, a moral imperative he wrestled with.

Because of the promise he had made his parents, Jayden continued to obey their commandment to remain locked inside. He never ventured down to the streets. Like Booker Bailey of Birmingham, he lived off food stores his family had accumulated.

God, I miss them. Tonight as Jayden stared up into the blackness of the ruined hotel, he replayed mental scenes from his recently celebrated twenty-fourth birthday. Saw himself naked except for his sneakers holding his guitar in hand, a pique protest against his self-imposed lock-down, bursting outside through mud-caked doors; and then sitting on a public bench in the warm spring sunshine where he plucked out a new melody. Then he added lyrics to the chorus.

"You saved me
In every way
You saved me
Giving one more day
You saved me
We both know what's true
Maybe in some small way
I hope I saved you, too"

Naked and alone on that bench, he'd felt the pride of his parents beaming through from a distant plane of existence. *The former mechanical engineer and the physician's assistant had conceived and birthed a genuine bard.* He considered song verses, but then infused with energy and inspiration which he thought of as being 'in the zone,' creatively speaking—the sun went down. Demons would soon awaken and come out to feed.

Back in the apartment, he heated water on a small propane stove and gave himself a shampoo and a sponge bath. He sneezed three times in succession as he had all his life. The fresh air and stair-climbs had generated a raging appetite. He heated and inhaled two cans of pork and beans and a can of mixed fruit. "Three full cans," he said. "That boy is a pig." He treated himself to half a bottle of 1980 vintage cabernet sauvignon. More tired than he had felt in a long time, he climbed into bed. He barely got through his 'Our Father' universal Christian prayer, when the arms of Morpheus swallowed him in one quick embrace.

That was when the dreams first started. Reading psychology journals and textbooks recovered after the First Flood, Jayden self-assessed as a pure introvert since he turned inward for good company. He did not feel a dire need to be with others. Yet it was not until these dreams introduced him to a better world populated with joyful, loving, peaceful people, safe and warm in the bosom of God's Church that he felt a strong new need to socialize. The dreams were like a camera hovering over and weaving through the daily lives of happy people: cooks, carpenters, craftspeople, beekeepers, builders, candlemakers, diggers, farmers, fishermen, foragers, metal and woodworkers, machine mechanics, potters, nurses, scouts, and spies. When these people spotted him holding his telescope and guitar, every single one of them, hundreds—no, thousands—smiled at him and opened their arms to him. His sleeping spirit felt overcome by the warm, welcoming emotions there on the green mountain of springs.

He awoke from his dream to a tear-soaked pillow. When he would fall back asleep, the same dream always continued where it had left off. Now that it was happening every night, Jayden's days felt longer. Time began to draw out. He wondered if a powerful celestial force with a sadistic sense of humor had tacked more hours onto his already long, lonesome twenty-four-hour days.

Because of the dreams, finally he had started to recognize deeply buried feelings and a strong need to belong. Poignant dreams lately convinced him of being called to a purpose greater than mere day-to-day survival. His conscious, rational mind had recently faced a binary choice: live for something or die for nothing. *Walk north. Live.*

Studying maps, he had figured that the safest route, if not precisely the shortest, would be the Appalachian Trail. *Fewer Golgoths.* For a long time, he had carried hate, bitter-tasting and sharp, toward these fiends who had taken from him the only people he had ever known. For a time, hate had consumed his days and seeped into his nights. This day he felt less angry. Like a bowl of boiling water placed in a freezer, over time his white-hot magma core had chilled to solid ice.

Tonight, on a mildewy bed a day's walk from home, Jayden thought now of the Bible, a verse he remembered from Matthew. "You have heard that it was said, 'Love your neighbor and hate your enemy.' But I tell you, love your enemies and pray for those who persecute you, that you may be children of your Father in Heaven. He causes his sun to rise on the evil and the good and sends rain on the righteous and the unrighteous. If you love only those who love you, what reward is there for that? Even corrupt tax collectors do that much."

Context, he thought. *Those had been vastly different times, when the Word needed to spread, and people's enemies were their own government.*

Another Matthew verse he pondered. "Immediately after the tribulation of those days: 'The sun will be darkened, and the moon will not give its light; the stars will fall from the sky, and the powers of the heavens will be shaken.' At that time the sign of the Son of Man will appear in Heaven, and all the tribes of the earth will mourn. They will see the Son of Man coming on the clouds of Heaven, with power and great glory. And he will send out his angels with a loud trumpet call, and they will gather his elect from the four winds, from one end of the heavens to the other."

"Not one but two great Floods. Tribulation? Yes, this qualifies," Jayden whispered aloud.

He thought of Revelation. "'Behold, I am coming like a thief. Blessed is the one who remains awake and clothed, so that he will not go naked and let his shame be exposed.' And they assembled the kings in the place that in Hebrew is called Megiddo."

It gave him no satisfaction to imagine that those very ancient dots appeared to connect, symbolically at least, with dots of today, in this time. *Fitted,* he thought. The last battle before the Son returns with his angels. Satan bound for a thousand years. Christ ruling a just new world at last reconciled to its Creator. *Clearly this present epoch is not about forgiving enemies. This is all about holy war. Righteous king against Antichrist king.*

Note to self: tomorrow, find a compound bow and as many arrows as I can carry. Find the closest washed-out Walmart.

"Forgive me, Lord, if I've failed to interpret your word as you had meant it. I perceive now is the time to sell my cloak and buy a sword. I will slay every unholy Golgoth animal I find along the way. I do not know for sure if this pleases you. Though I believe that it does," he whispered.

He had walked the whole of that first day. On the morrow he would seek additional supplies and then walk for the remainder of daylight. *If I can't find weapons and supplies in Nashville, surely I will in Knoxville. It'll take me a total of six days to make the Appalachian Trail at Spivey Gap, North Carolina. Six divided by two is three. Three times two is six. Six equals three plus three. The Son died and rose again in three days...*

Jayden Bonner slid into unconsciousness thinking that three must be some kind of magic number.

Fire on the Mountain

With the fewest miles separating him from the Spivey Gap section of the Appalachian Trail, Marshall Langar arrived at the Trail first. After a lifetime spent in LeConte Lodge atop a mountain in Gatlinburg, Tennessee, every step he had taken since leaving LeConte had felt exhilarating and new. True to his faith, though he had glanced at a map before leaving and brought it, throughout the trip he had left all navigation up to the Holy Spirit, or so he had believed. He had arrived close to the Trail at a place named Sam's Gap. Looking now at the map, to make it to Spivey his original target he would need to hike another thirteen miles uphill. There was no rush. Several hours of daylight remained. He decided to find as secure a spot as he could, a place to sleep camouflaged.

Knowing the river was close meant sharing his skin with biting insects. Scratching at bug bites or poison ivy rash could easily lead to infection. *Bugs and plants could kill me with just as slow and horrible as them Golgoths.*

He walked over a mile, closer to two, when he found a narrow foot trail, dirt with no plants which intersected the Appalachian Trail, or so he thought. He hiked up a very steep foothill. *Worth a shot.* As he ascended the first twenty yards, he realized this was not a narrow foot trail worn into the earth by the constant traffic of humans or animals. *This is water erosion.* He wondered if the two Floods had created it, or simply rain runoff from a flat plain somewhere above. *Lord, show me a nice flat plain at the summit. I'm claimin' it for my bedroom tonight.*

The climb was brutal. His calves, glutes, hamstrings, and lumbar sung arias he had never before experienced. At least sixty degrees of slope. Though it felt like miles uphill, in actuality it was a hundred feet shy of a quarter mile, when at last he stood upon a flat area twenty feet wide by forty long. To Marshall's beleaguered mind, he was standing on a rock shelf attached to a precipitous rock face which soared even higher until he lost sight of it. Looking up as far as his backward-tilted head and neck would allow, he saw a low mountain of endless brown-gray rock, sparsely decorated with bent-trunked trees and bright green shrubs determined to grow in impossible solid rock spaces inhospitable to plant life. *But life finds a way*, he thought. *God is great.*

He unshouldered his knapsack and emptied the contents onto the rock shelf. He drained a bottle of water in seconds. He unfurled his camp mat and sleeping bag. After stuffing marbles into his right front pocket, sliding a wire saw into his left rear pocket; he reshouldered the empty knapsack. He palmed the slingshot and stepped over the ledge, back onto the dirt drainage path. His stomach rumbled and he thought about fresh meat for dinner.

He had only seen photographs in books and magazines of cats and dogs, cows, horses, and other domesticated animals. He had long ago concluded that the two Floods had been as unkind to these species as to humans. Aquatic life had done very well. Birds and wild animals had sought high ground and after the waters had receded, multiplied. With his slingshot he was lethal, almost never missing a target up to fifty yards out. He returned to camp ninety minutes later with two pheasants and one quail in the knapsack, along with twenty-five pounds of kindling and hardwood.

Up here, everythin's a permanent dry age, he thought. There was evidence of recent rainfall, but sun and wind had dried the organic material, especially the critical ingredient of his campfire—lichens—Old Man's Beard. He struck the flint against the steel twice and generated the sparks needed. He picked up the white fluffy material and gently blew on it until it ignited with a mini woof! sound. He dropped the flaming wad seconds before it could burn his left hand; expertly he placed tiny twigs, then slightly larger twigs, until he had a real fire. After adding larger branch sections he decapitated, gutted, and plucked all three birds. He created a makeshift spit out of a Y-shaped branch and straight green branch for a skewer, then positioned one of the pheasants over the low fire. He committed to a long, slow cook.

He knew that if he sat down, tired as he was, falling asleep while tending the fire was too real a possibility. He stood gazing out over the unfamiliar area. *Beautiful*, he thought. *Everythin' feels new.* At his back was the sheer rock face. The shadow of the mountain printed its depthless image on the ground in the day's kind, last light, the sweat of his exertions dichotomous against the cooling air now drying his skin. He stripped naked and laid his clothes out flat near the fire to dry. He paced between the ledge and the fire to keep warm, but also to stay sharp. Curls of delightfully aromatic smoke, along with savory cool air snapped him awake and made him feel optimistic about the journey ahead.

Being alone in nature exposed to dangers like never before, and feeling closer than ever to God, also created emotional distance between himself and Delilah, and from his baby she poisoned to death. *She is just a big spider who crawled into my sleepin' bag and bit me all night. Yesterday I woke up. Past the time to broom her outta my brain.* "May God have mercy on y'all's soul, Delilah," he said. For a time, her name hung there on its own like a bad hex. But then he started feeling shades brighter.

Beginnin' to feel like a fresh start. Up the trail apiece, everythin's' new.

He laid two medium pieces of wood onto the fire and gave the pheasant a turn. Back at the ledge he closed his eyes and groaned in pleasure as the scintillating cool atmosphere bathed his skin. *It'll drop to the low sixties tonight up here on this ledge. Sleepin' weather*, he thought. He imagined lying cocooned within the insulated sleeping bag. *Soon enough, Lord, your wayward son's gonna rest his weary head*, he thought.

Then he froze. Listened. Murmuring up from a distance, human voices.

Children, or adult females? Laughter. Not Golgoths. But who? He knew there were people up north as shown to him in dreams, but he had never seen any, not one in this southern region save for Delilah, the baby-murdering succubus.

Sounds grew louder. Squinting, now he could make out four young adults, three females one male. *The one with the short hair and baggy clothes gotta be male.* His breathing convulsed. *Ain't Golgoths.* In another hundred feet they would pass the end of the drainage cut. Suddenly realizing his nakedness, he stepped into now dry pants and went over the ledge so that even from this distance they could see him. He took twenty paces down the hard-packed dirt culvert.

He cupped his hands and yelled into them at top volume, "Y 'all'd better make camp soon. Golgoths are wakin' up."

The group froze wide-eyed, every ear tuned to the source of the sound. Marshall perceived their struggle to find him in the shadowy woods and at such a high elevation. "Up here! Hello? The name's Marshall Langar, from Gatlinburg. I'm hikin' to a green mountain 'a springs in Pennsylvania."

The tall female with the big chest and red hair shouted up, "How do we know you aren't with them?"

"Darlin,' if I was one of them y'all'd be trussed up like piggies by now. I could hear y'all a-comin' from half a mile away."

He could see heads turning, lips moving. Then the redhead yelled, "What are you doing up there?"

"Camp for tonight. I got dinner cookin.' Come on up. Y'all are welcome tonight to share the food and space. Safe from the Golgoths."

"What about you? Are we safe from you?"

Marshall laughed. "Hope so. If it's any help y'all need to know I'm with God. Jesus is my Lord and Savior. I don't hurt people; only Golgoths. But then they ain't really people now, are they?"

More head-tilts and murmurs. *Debatin' my offer.* Both the slim, petite blonde and the black-skinned woman immediately stepped onto the culvert and began their ascent, followed by the short-haired male. The loud redhead finally decided to follow, though she started climbing well behind the others. Marshall ran over to turn the pheasant. "Done," he said. "Came out perfect. Now that we're havin' company..." His hands trembled from excitement. He placed the cooked bird on the warm smooth stone beside the fire, then skewered the second pheasant and quail. "Wonder if they'll hear my heart poundin.' Be cool, Marshall. Be cool."

Gently he positioned the birds on spits over the fire then ran back to the ledge. He saw the group making timely progress. Now he could make out faces. The petite blonde in a vague way reminded him of Delilah as a teenager. Skinny as a rail, hardly any breasts, waist about as narrow as his thigh, her face a pretty collection of sharp angles, cheekbones, nose, chin, and her mouth was a thin straight line. Her green eyes set wide apart struck him as alert, intelligent, and kind.

He had never seen a black person in the flesh, only in images. He found her sloe, up-slanted brown eyes fascinating, along with her aquiline nose, full rubicund lips, and lithe, muscular body. As she moved through the woods with the confidence of a mountain lion her pinkish palms showed such stark contrast to her smooth, mocha skin. *Beautiful yet fierce*, he thought.

The one he thought was male appeared to him shaped like a female in the hips, moved like a female, but one with commanding extent and repose. *Oh, how wrong I was. Now* that *is a woman all right, for sure. No male could ever be this pretty.* He could not take his eyes off this one. Skin rivalling the purest ivory, the delicate outlines of the nose, harmoniously curved nostrils. *Such a sweet mouth*, he thought, momentarily lost in the magnificent turn of the short upper lip, and at the soft, voluptuous slumber of the darkly pink lower lip, cheeks that dimpled when she smiled, offering glimpses of teeth glancing back with a brilliancy almost startling. Close-cropped raven-black hair, glossy and luxuriant even in the anemic light.

Be cool, Marshall. Calm your storm good buddy...

The animal attraction he had felt for Delilah, once it took, had knocked him into an unparalleled summit of existence. When she had rejected him, he had never felt lower. The deaths of his parents had been far easier to bear because that was the natural way of things. What Delilah did was the most unnatural thing he could ever conceive. From the scared little girl in the pharmacy, she had become a friend, then the most ardent and enthusiastic lover. His common-law wife.

Last week, Delilah's inner demon had taken full control. *Succubus*, he thought, *driven by pure hatred of all things good and holy and lovin.' Snap! —just like that, she had turned on me, on our baby…discardin' our love like rank garbage. Turnt' against God.* In the eleven hours it took for him to hike from LeConte Lodge to Sams Gap, he had contemplated the spirit of pure evil, Satan, wondering if, like Delilah, the Golgoths also had become possessed by the powerful existential force with many names. *The same eldritch spirit that beguiled the men who eye witnessed supernatural healin' and raisin' 'a the dead, those who heard words of authority, backed by works far outside the realm of the known universe; the devil tricked 'em, blinded 'em into rejectin' their God's Son; deceived 'em 'til they murdered the Son of God. The same spirit of vengeance and anarchy, of pure hate that once seduced a nation into murderin' millions 'a God's chosen people.*

One question dominated his mind along the hike more than others. *Is it even possible for my heart or soul to ever rise to the spirit-liftin' ecstasy I felt drownin' in Delilah's enthusiastic, innocent affection before she had embraced, or let herself be embraced by the most sinister force in all creation?* He did not believe he would ever again allow himself to fall into another woman's gravitational orbit; to feel the irresistible pull of the carnal event horizon surrounding the black hole that was woman.

The short-haired woman ascended the culvert, her eyes fixed on Marshall. Connecting with her bright, blue eyes mere feet away suddenly caused him to speculate. As she grew closer, he looked down into the depths of her memorial eyes and thought only of them—and of her.

Each one 'a these women look pretty, at least as beautiful as Delilah. If I walk with this group, I might just be able to put Delilah and LeConte Lodge behind me for good. But that short hair. Like dad always said, "Keep your own council, Marshall. Be cool. No matter how hot things get, you keep that heart a' yours in the ice box, son." Now I think I know what he meant.

Aliyah, Arabella, Dodie, and Tatum made their way up the natural rainwater culvert and closed the distance. Dodie was the first to reach the ledge. Marshall reached out with both hands. She hesitated at first, searched his eyes, then raised both hands and allowed him to pull her up and over the big step up onto the rocky outcropping. *As light as Delilah when she was twelve.* Aliyah quickly followed. *Heavier. Stronger. This girl is solid muscle. Her hands feel a bit rough.* "Thank you!" said both in turn.

And then came the short-haired girl. Their eyes locked. Marshall felt her like a jolt through his nervous system. He caught her rapid eye-flick down at his bare chest and abdominals. He reached out both hands, caught hers, and pulled her up and over. Their eyes met. He felt her body heat. "Well thank you, sir," she said, punctuated by rapid eyelash-batting and a flirty smile. "I'm Tatum."

Sweetest voice I ever heard, he thought, her pitch a seductive, silken octave lower than the others. *Lioness.*

Two minutes later, the redhead stood at the top. Her hands found purchase on the rock. She breathed heavily. He helped her onto the ledge.

"Hi y'all, I'm Marshall," he said, and he nodded with a sweep of his arm around the full expanse of the rock shelf. "As I said, plenty 'a room for everyone. Gonna be dark in a blink. Headin' down to get more firewood. Be back in a hot minute. Y'all make yourselves at home."

"Thank you for your hospitality, Marshall Langar of Tennessee. My name is Arabella Pendleman. We all just walked here from Young Harris, Georgia. The skinny little blonde over there is Dodie Sealy. The negro—"

"What'd you just say?"

"…The Black one is Aliyah Freedman. That one over there is my boyfriend, Tatum Winters.

"Hey!" Tatum shouted in a terribly angry tone.

"Sorry, my lesbian friend who dresses like a boy," said Arabella.

Marshall's gaze lingered on Tatum. She did not look away. He'd read about lesbians, and from Paul's letter to the Romans, 'Even their women exchanged natural sexual relations for unnatural ones.' Although he knew he was doing a fair job of keeping his head, his mood tumbled a little at the possibility that Tatum might never recompense his unbridled interest. He grabbed his empty pack and dropped over the edge out of sight, pondering these things in his heart.

When Marshall wandered out of earshot, Arabella said, "Well ladies, he seems like a polite southern gentleman. Shall we stake out our spaces for the night?" Dodie immediately set down her pack near the fire, as did Aliyah, both of whom hated cold temperatures. Arabella watched as Tatum walked close to Marshall's area and set her pack down three feet away from his bedroll. Arabella acknowledged a twinge of jealousy, for she too had taken a furtive look at Marshall's rippling arms, chest, shoulders, and deeply appreciated his washboard abdominal muscles.

"Um, Tatum? That's my spot," said Arabella.

"Pffft," said Tatum, imitating her best friend's annoying body language. "Snooze-lose, girlfriend."

"You prefer beavers and bushwhackers, Tates. How about you give way to a lady who appreciates strong males."

Dodie and Aliyah smiled at each other; both had caught the silent exchange between Marshall and Tatum. Female intuition ran strong in both though neither had any experience with boys or men as a baseline. Ignoring Arabella, Tatum unfurled her bedroll and sleeping bag.

Arabella was about to protest when Marshall ascended and walked to the fire. He gave the pheasant a turn, then placed new wood onto the hot but diminishing fire. He picked up the fully cooked pheasant laid near the fire. "Not sure if y'all ever tasted fresh meat. This bird is good eatin' I promise," and with that, easily, he pulled away a leg and immediately bit into it. "Mmm mm mm." Tatum, closest to him, moved beside him. He handed her a leg. She took it.

"No, I have never had fresh meat. Only canned, and it was all incredibly old," Tatum said. She glanced toward her three fellow hikers. "None of us have. Thank you for this, Marshall." Imitating him, she bit down. Aliyah, Arabella, and Dodie studied her face. "Mmm oh my God! So good!" At that, the three converged on Tatum.

"Hang on, my friends," said Marshall. "Let me slice off breast pieces so that each of y'all gets an equal piece." He kept a folding knife clipped to his belt, which he used now to divvy up the bird. He took no more from this one. He sat back watching, delighted to see women feast on his afternoon's work. It was the first time he had ever seen such a feeding frenzy. He found all of it gratifying. He had almost put Delilah out of his thoughts.

"Can Golgoths see this fire, Marshall?" Aliyah asked.

"Not unless they use the Trail after dark. My daddy, God rest his soul taught me how to hunt, to look for signs in nature of animal traffic. I saw no evidence of large animals from the trailhead to here. Golgoths hunt roadways at night, and the roads are on the other side of this metamorphic mountain," he said, rapping the vertical stone face. "Unless they can see through mountains, we're safe."

He wondered if he came across as convincing. He made a promise to sleep lightly from here on out.

Good Vibrations

The first pheasant disappeared in fewer than five minutes. He divvied up the second pheasant and the smaller quail and handed out pieces to his new friends. They walked over to the ledge to eat while watching the bruised purple sky slip-slide into jetty black.

He started thinking of the night ahead. *Would Golgoths see the fire? Smell the smoke? They all's awake now, preparin' to hunt. Should I just let the fire go down to coals?* Tatum crept back to the fire. As she munched happily on the quail breast, she studied Marshall's eyes.

"You're worried about Golgoths smelling the fire," she whispered.

Snapped from his trance, he met her gaze. "Wow, Tatum," he whispered. "I am impressed. Y'all 'r a mind-reader. Best keep a tight lid on my thoughts."

"Oh that ship sailed hours ago, bubs." She gave him a knowing grin of triumph. In the firelight she watched him blush.

"Sorry for starin.' T'weren't my intent. You four sorta just threw me for a loop, is all. Before t'night I ain't only ever met three other people, y'all gotta understand. Not such a stretch then that already I feel very…protective of y'all. And y'all's friends, a'course."

She smiled. He had never seen anything remotely as captivating. He felt tingles all through his guts. "Uh huh. Well, let's just say it's been a coon's age since I've felt safe behind a strong man. And that man was my father."

"My father, Tates. Not yours." Despite their whispering Arabella eavesdropped, which was easy to do with the reflective rocky acoustics on the ledge.

Tatum turned toward her friend; lips drawn back in a sneer. "Grady Pendleman was my adoptive father as much as he was your blood father. Same with Dodie and Aliyah. He was father to all of us."

"Pfft," Arabella flicked her off.

Arabella had no way of knowing at this point that this dismissive sound was precisely how Hostis Dei also ended his conversations.

"I bet me 'n Grady would'a been fast friends," said Marshall. "Sounds like my pop. Earlier generations had done and seen things none of us all ever will. I don't think there could be very many 'a them pre-Flood folks left. 'Cept the ones on the mountain in my dreams, the saved ones. I believe this. Call me crazy."

Dodie stood at attention. "Marshall, are you talking about the green place with all the families, and the blond man in robes on the Mountain of Springs?"

He shifted his weight, steeled his whirling thoughts, and attempted to control his facial expressions as he looked at Dodie. "Are y'all tellin' me y'all's havin' the same dream?"

She nodded. "Most of us have."

"Pfft," said Arabella. "Magic from a higher place makes no sense."

"Nope. You are sane, Marshall. It sounds crazy for sure but it's real, which is exactly why I trust it," said Aliyah.

"Whew!" said Marshall. "Thanks for not callin' me crazy! Yes, I am here followin' my dream, that I also believe is God's will. I was safe on my mountain, but then…"

"What happened? What are you running from?" Arabella asked.

Marshall's face changed. "I don't wanna talk 'bout that place. I ain't runnin' *from* there. I'm walkin' *toward* someplace new, and a new purpose for my life: to serve God rather than only just servin' myself."

"Was it a woman you left up there on the mountain?" Arabella pried.

Marshall walked over to her, his face inches from hers. He fought to keep his tone even. "Arabella, what about 'I don't wanna to talk about it' do y'all not understand?"

Arabella took two steps back holding her hands up flat. "Whoa, down boy. Easy. I just want to know what kind of man I'm supposed to follow through the wilderness."

"A Jesus-lovin' kind a man. All y'all need ta' know 'bout me."

"You really believe in all those old fairytales?" Arabella asked.

He glowered at her. "I believe that one day: y'all and I are gonna have us a serious disagreement."

He stepped back, then walked to the ledge. He gazed down at the eerily quiet, wooded scene below, then he looked up at a coldly lustrous tapestry reminding him of reflections on a windy night lake. The moon stared back at him like a decomposing fisheye. He stood and gazed at the scene for longer than ten minutes.

Finally, he turned and said, "Y'all 'r welcome to claim this safe zone for y'all's selves. Come mornin' I'm strikin' out on my own. I'm going to bed now. When y'all wake up, I'll be gone."

"No!" Tatum shrieked. Aliyah and Dodie joined the chorus. "Absolutely not! We're stronger together! We can be a help to you, Marshall!"

"How's that?" he asked.

Tatum pointed at her pack. "How are you going to cross rivers, swamps, and waterways, Marshall? Swim? Slog through the leeches and bacteria, step on submerged sharps, die of septic poisoning? We have inflatable kayaks, and paddles. You can't forage what we have," she said. She made a show of shooting a death-stare at Arabella. "She doesn't speak for us. Never has and never will.

"Look," said Dodie. "We're all headed to the green mountain, Marshall, to join the community our dreams tell us is there. Each of us seems different or weird to one another. It's the same there on the green mountain, at least in my dreams. Individuals with unique gifts and quirks united by love for God and each other," she said. "Everyone pulls together there for the common good. Shouldn't we do the same?"

She got up and walked closer as she spoke, with Aliyah at her side, who nodded. Dodie stood before Marshall. She reached out and wrapped her tiny hands around his long thick fingers. She gazed into his eyes. "We stay together. For each other. Okay?" Aliyah gently pressed her hands over his. Marshall nodded but backed away. He returned to his ledge lookout.

Tatum walked over, close enough to whisper at a volume so light that only he could hear. "No matter what, I'm with you now, Marshall Langar."

She watched anger gradually subside behind his eyes. She perceived in him a deep hole running straight through his core. "Somebody back there hurt you bad, I see it. A deep wound that's still fresh and smarting. But I won't ever hurt you, I swear. Nor will I allow anyone else to hurt you. Just as you won't let the Golgoths take us." She reached out and squeezed his neck. "I may have only just met you, but already I trust you. I like you. I feel so healthy and normal with you. You can teach me all about your God: I want to know him, and I want to know you. Okay? Please?"

Looking down at her, he nodded. She smiled. He smiled back. Both of them felt the voltaic connection. He leaned down to her ear and whispered, "But I thought y'all like girls."

She shrugged and made a face. "Girls are all I have ever known except for Grady. I didn't really know myself. I've never met anyone like you before. Please, Marshall, show me who I am. Show me how to live right. I'm like one of those trees growing out of the rock," she said, pointing up. "Absurd, bent, crooked. I need new soil, a new planting, new light to shine on me so that I can grow straight and true. I'm meant to be someone, someplace. Take me there. Please?"

"What about y'all's leader, Arabella?"

"Oh please. I am so sick of that thundercunt." Eyebrows raised, taken aback by her profanity bomb, he pulled back to look at her. Affecting childlike innocence, she interlaced her fingers under her chin, tilted her head, and batted her eyelashes at him. He broke into raucous laughter that boomed down the mountain. He clapped both hands over his mouth.

"Shhh!" whispered Dodie.

"An' here I thought girls 'r sugar, spice, and everythin' nice, Tatum," Marshall whispered. Tatum grinned and wiggled her eyebrows at him. He stifled laughter.

Speaking in a normal tone, "Thanks, Dodie, y'all are so right about bein' quiet. Let's all go to bed. Gather round the fire a moment; I need everybody to hear this." They did. "Y'all listen up. If in the night y'all gotta relieve yourselves, there's enough moonlight and starlight to see. I'm gonna let the fire go out. The wood I've collected I'm gonna lay over there at the far edge. Look," he said, pointing. "Ain't can see over there from here. It's private. I'll make a line of wood. Don't cross it. Y'all do yer thing over there on this side of the wood. Now me, I sleep like a stone: ain't no chance 'a me seein' y'all. Don't use flashlights and be quieter than dead flies. Now," he said, looking at his bag, "Let's get ready for bed."

"Thank you for dinner, Marshall. Best meal of my life. Seriously," said Aliyah, smiling.

Arabella removed her boots. "Eww!" said Tatum. "Rancid."

"Oh, my gawd," said Dodie, pinching her nostrils. "Just so wrong."

"Like somebody spilled a jar of pickled poop," Aliyah chimed in.

"Oh, and yours don't smell?" said Arabella.

"Mine don't," said Tatum.

"Liar!" said Arabella. "Such a lying little dyke."

"They don't! Seriously! Not even a little."

Arabella stroked her chin. "Marshall, I don't trust these others. Please settle this."

"Wait. What?" he asked.

"Take off Tatum's boots. Let us know what you smell."

"Arabella, y'all leave me outta it," he said. "Settle y'all's own issues."

"It's okay, Marshall," said Tatum. She sat on his bedroll and pulled off her boots and socks. "Well? Do they?" she asked, looking up at him. He shot her a brief grin that only she could see, knelt, scooped up both bare feet and pressed his nose against them. She giggled. "Your mustache and beard are tickly!"

He turned to face Aliyah and Dodie and flicked a glance at Arabella. "Ain't no smell whatsoever. Zero." He turned back to Tatum. She averted her eyes down for a millisecond, then gazed at him, lips pursed ever so slightly. *Message received*, he thought.

"Hah!" said Tatum. "Bella my dear, I might be many uncomplimentary things, but I don't believe I have the reputation of being a liar. And: you still stink."

"Pfft. Little miss perfect. Hey Marshall—too bad she likes girls. Hands and feet are as close as you'll ever get to this one."

"Arabella, y'all outta grab some shuteye and forget all this bullyin' guff," Marshall said. He stood, reached down, and pulled Tatum to standing. "Goodnight," he said.

Tatum, still smiling, took three steps to her sleeping bag and crawled in. Marshall zipped into his. The others followed suit. Snugly swaddled in their bags across from each other, Dodie and Aliyah wished all a blessed night.

After restless minutes of tossing and turning, brute exhaustion nearly had its way. *I feel eyes on me.* In the dying firelight, he caught Tatum gazing at him, her face submerged in her sleeping bag. The two remained eye-locked until the fire made it impossible. Fatigue returned and bedded his bones. As he drifted down to sleep, Tatum's alluring eyes dominated his mind. He thought only of them, and of her.

Then he dreamed of the yellow haired man on the mountain.

"The Lord of Hosts has placed his finger upon your bosom. He has need of you. Shepherd the Elect, Marshall, until the Lord arrives."

He awoke to a three-flavor layer cake of a sunrise topping trees to the east, dark blue atop reddish orange. He knew this meant no rain would fall on them today. "Red sky in mornin,' sailors take warnin.' Red sky at night, sailor's delight." His father had taught him to read signs in the heavens, and with rare exception, this and all the rest of his dad's little sayings had proven to be accurate.

Marshall had been dreaming of the green mountain and the man with the bright yellow hair when a sound rudely pulled him out of his dream. He lay on his right side facing the forest and the trail far below, ears perked. Male voices, and something else. *A sound wave produced by a vibratin' object. A tone. What is that sound?* He had never heard music before, had only read about it. *Surroundin' air molecules excited into vibrational motion. The frequency at which these air molecules vibrate is equal to the frequency of vibration of the musical instrument. Could it be music I'm hearin?'*

He stood, goosebumps all over from the motionless, humid fifty-five-degree air. He pulled on his fleece sweatshirt and wool socks; stepped into his hiking boots; and laced them quickly. He grabbed the slingshot and pocketed marbles. He also took one of his two machetes and headed over to the ledge. Soundlessly, he slipped over.

Gravity is my friend right now, he thought. It took him less than half the time to half run-half slide down the culvert. He used his heels and butt as brakes when he was about twenty feet from the Trail. He remained seated, holding a marble inside the pouch of the slingshot.

Then he waited.

Seven minutes later, two men approached from the south. One was only an inch or two shorter than he, and was white, thin, stern, and with a focused face; with long dark wavy hair, but clean shaven. He recognized from photographs the object strapped across the man's chest: a guitar. Sticking up from the rear of his backpack was a compound hunting bow. Metal-tipped broadheads at the ends of arrow shafts protruded from knapsack side pockets.

The short man walking next to the guitar man was colored like Aliyah only darker still. His wiry black hair reclined atop his head like an exhausted black sheep. Glimpses of very white teeth, with brown eyes that were intelligent, kind, and thoughtful. Marshall decided it would be best to announce his presence before finalizing the last twenty feet of culvert to avoid any risk of surprising the two men.

"Hey y'all, good mornin!'" Marshall said.

With the quickness and surety of practice, the taller man reached up with both hands. In fewer than two seconds he had nocked an arrow, pulled back the bowstring, and pointed it directly at Marshall. This caught Marshall off-guard, but only for less than one second: Marshall, still sitting to present a smaller target reached down and loaded his slingshot, pulled back the pouch as far as the surgical rubber bands would allow and aimed for the tall man's eye.

"Whoa! Whoa! Take it easy, gentlemen," said the brown man. "Nobody here shaves his head and paints himself white! We're all on the same side, right?"

"I say good mornin' and all I get in return is an arrow pointed at me. Yes, archer-man, y'all sized me up right. I'm the world's first polite Golgoth."

"Easy, Jay! Lower your weapon! Clearly he is not one of them." The Black one looked at Marshall: "Mister, I apologize for my friend's overreaction. Please try to understand that recently, Golgoths jumped him." The taller man lowered the arrow and allowed the bowstring to relax. Marshall likewise eased the tension of his slingshot bands.

"Wow. Y'all got attacked by Golgoths and survived without a scratch? That's amazin.' I ain't never met anyone grabbed by them monsters and got away." The taller man reached up and back; effortlessly he restored both the arrow and the bow to their original positions on his backpack.

"My name is Marshall Langar, from Gatlinburg, Tennessee. We'all's walkin' north to a place we think is called Spring Mountain. Been told that a whole lotta' Flood survivors live there in a large colony."

"Who's we? Told? In a dream, perchance? Same dream every night?" asked the Black man. "Sorry, forgetting my manners: I'm Booker Bailey from Birmingham, Alabama, the handsome and smart one. The guitar-man here is Jayden Bonner, coming to you from the Mecca of music, Nashville, Tennessee. He doesn't talk a whole lot, reticent as they come, a touch introverted. Unlike the garrulous affable me. I talk way too much."

Marshall walked the final twenty feet and joined them on the trail. He extended his right hand to Booker, who took it and shook it. Then he offered his hand to Jayden. Hesitating at first, Jayden reached out and shook it. "Sorry, Marshall. Didn't mean to get your hackles up."

"Yes, Booker. Same dream every night. A bunch of us 'r havin' the dream," said Marshall.

"Bunch? There are more of you?"

Marshall nodded, narrowing his gaze on Jayden. "How'd you do it…survive the attack? Tell me, seriously. I am beyond interested."

Jayden shot Marshall an empained look. Then, "Back in Knoxville. Foraging in Walmart. I walk outside and see five Golgoths running across the parking lot toward me. I knew that if I'd gone back inside they would've never stopped until they found me. Five of them against one of me; rotten odds. So, I ran left, then left again until I saw a metal drainage pipe leading all the way up to the roof. I shimmied up the pipe. Just as I hooked my leg over the top there they were, five of them stood there staring up at me trying to figure out how they could climb the pipe while still holding their primary weapons."

"What weapons?" Marshall asked.

"Spears. So, I nocked an arrow, aimed, fired. The razor tip easily parted tissue. I had aimed for its collarbone. The razor went all the way down into it, slicing up heart, lungs, all kinds of major organs. The Golgoth dropped like a sack of meat."

"You're a cold man, Jayden," Booker interjected.

Jayden grinned. "So, I quickly repeated the shot and one more hit the pavement dead. Another Goth lobbed a spear up at me. Dumbass screamed as it released. That one I got straight through his gawping mouth. It was like a one-in-a-million shot. The arrowhead exploded out the back of his neck…smashed him back as it shredded his spine. The other two stood there staring at the gaudy arterial pumps. Gurgling and grabbing at the arrow, finally the fool dropped like a sack of flour. Blew their minds, I tell you. They didn't know what to do. Obviously shit like this never happens to these alpha King Ding-a-lings. Those last two were about to cut and run but I never gave them the chance. The one on my left I nailed through the eye, the other through the Adam's Apple."

Marshall shook his head. "Wow, Jayden. Impressive! That there is some darned good shootin'! Hey, y'all should walk with us since we all 'r headin' to the same destination. Ain't we, Booker? The place in the dream?"

Booker nodded. "Us? I only see you."

Marshall pointed up the mountain. "Me, and also the four young ladies I met last night, same as we are meetin' right now. We all camped together for the night. I found us a safe spot."

Booker and Jayden exchanged glances. Jayden spoke first. "They attacked me in broad daylight. High noon, or close to it. They got my parents during daylight."

Marshall shifted uneasily. "This goes against everythin' we got taught growin' up."

Jayden nodded. "Yessir, indeed it does. My parents said Golgoths only hunt at night. Recently I had a birthday. Came down from my safe citadel to the street to spend the day in the sunshine. I saw not one trace of them. I hiked here in daylight and never eyeballed one single Goth along the way until Walmart happened. Now I figure both times, I was just damned lucky."

"I was taught the same. Something is changing," Booker said, nodding furiously "Golgoths always hunted at night, trying to catch foragers and survivors holed up in the dark. But they got Jay's and my parents in the late afternoon. The sun wouldn't be setting for hours when they got taken. Also, I had a heluva long hike to get to Sams Point from where I started. At times I used major roads, but I walked only at night. Sometimes I walked during daylight and used trails, like this one. Sometimes from the trails way high up, I could see roads down below. Marshall, every road was lousy with Golgoths, all of them walking north in broad daylight, same as us. Never saw one along any trails or in the woods; only on highways and roads did I see them, all painted up white like ghosts, holding long spears. They carried girls and women hog-tied and dangling from long poles. Four Golgoths would set pole ends on their shoulders and walk single file to balance the weight."

"Dear Lord," said Marshall. "So them stories were all true. 'Breeders,' my dad had told me. Men and middle-aged women they butcher and eat same day. Young women they capture for breedin' before eatin' 'em. Young boys they either eat or groom into their ranks."

Jayden nodded. "Best strategy is keeping with trails until they intersect with roads, then make camp for the day and cross the roads only at night."

"Sorry to hear 'bout y'all's parents, guys, truly. May God bless and keep 'em."

Booker and Jayden both nodded. "I killed one myself," said Booker.

"Really? Y'all killed a Golgoth? Mind if I ask y'all's age?"

"I'll be eighteen soon enough."

"At seventeen y'all ghosted a Golgoth?" asked Marshall, grinning.

Booker nodded. "Uh-huh. I had crossed a road. Thought I'd heard something, so I climbed up branches high in a bush pine tree. I waited. Sure enough, a Golgoth crossed right where I'd stood, all by his lonesome. Guessing that sometimes Goths split up if they're hot on a 'game' trail, which this one clearly was, like he was tracking me, sniffing me out or something. He lost my trail under the tree. Took out my big butcher knife. Soon as he looked up, I just let my butt slide off the branch and let gravity do the rest, holding the knife straight down clamped between my legs. Got him right in his ugly mouth. Teeth all pointy like a creepy fish mouth. My mama's favorite kitchen knife came out his back below his shoulder blades. I pulled it out and wiped it clean as best I could with pine needles. I said a little prayer and dedicated the kill to my parents. Looked around, saw no more, and continued on my merry way. Now here I am."

"Well don't that just dill my pickle, Booker! And Jayden. Y'all gents are exactly what this group needs. Wait here a bit; I'll hike back up, break camp, and bring the four girls down to meet you. Will y'all wait?"

Booker and Jayden read each other's eyes but only briefly before they nodded.

All heard the loud snap of a breaking branch and spun to look in the direction. Marshall pointed at the middle of a tree. "Only just a vulture, see 'im? They eat the dead. No worries, gents, we ain't dead. Soon enough we all gonna be, but not today."

FUBAR

Spoggs Reichert knocked on the chapel door at precisely nine in the morning. He waited: then knocked again at ten past the hour; again, at twenty past; and tried knocking one last time at half past the hour. He turned and started walking back to his cabin for a refreshing round of morning sexual torture of Isabella. Reichert allowed his carnal imagination to wander and imagined her pitiful screams in that wonderful high-pitched accented voice of hers.

Just then he heard the awful grinding creak and groan of the chapel door, heralding the approach of Hostis Dei, which snapped him back from his fantasy. "Spoggs! What is it?"

Reichert's mind and body instantly grew cold, turgidity deflated like a latex balloon in the Antarctic. He dashed back to the tall door. "M' Lord, there has been an important discovery."

Eyes lambent and watchful, pectorals and flat stomach still bright white though dotted with dried red blood splatter Hostis Dei stared at him. Reichert reported: "The men found an old survivalist shelter seventeen miles to the south. They returned with a beneficial haul. Tons of preserved food and military meals-ready-to-eat. And a weapon."

White eyebrows raised, Hostis Dei responded: "What weapon?"

Spoggs nodded. "An M2A1 tripod-mounted Browning .50 caliber machine gun with a quick-change barrel for when it overheats. Shoots eight-hundred-fifty rounds per minute. You can feed ammo belts from either the left or right."

"Useless without ammunition."

"Truth. We also found shelves of ammo cans stacked floor to ceiling. Forty thousand rounds, m' Lord."

Hostis Dei clapped once. "Outstanding work, Spoggs! You shall have your reward. Go and select a breeder. As for the preserved Pre-Flood food, barter it with the other generals for their labor. Increase your power, Spoggs. You have earned it."

In Spoggs's experience, girls with Irish backgrounds lasted longest under extreme torture. He made his way from the breeder pen back to his cabin clutching the skinny arm of a sobbing strawberry-haired, green-eyed teenaged girl.

At that precise moment over one-hundred miles north of Valley Forge, Drake Childers directed his motorcycle past Sherwood Street, then traveled southeast on Pine Street in Scranton, Pennsylvania. A compact steel and wood trailer rattled behind the bike. Drake stopped in the middle of the street diagonal to the U.S. Armed Forces Reserve Center, a large two-story brick structure which appeared exactly as Gabriel described it. The two motorcyclists trailing behind him pulled up along either side. All three cut their engines at the same time. It was the first time they had spoken since leaving Spring Mountain.

The rider to his left spoke to Drake. "Gabriel was right again. If we had taken a vehicle larger than these bikes we never would have made it. I can't believe what the Floods washed onto the roadways from the Poconos. Someone's entire house! Stories to tell my grandchildren someday. This one is a doozy."

"Gabriel is always right because God speaks through him. Never again point out that he was right. Not to me. Got it?"

Eyes fell. "Got it, Drake. Sorry. I know God showed Gabriel this place in a vision."

Drake nodded. "Follow me. When we see the man with the long face, hold your hands above your head, palms open and facing forward. Keep walking and let me do all the talking. Got it?"

"Yes sir, Drake," said both. Leaning the big bikes on their kickstands; all three dismounted as one. Side-by-side they marched across the street and up the flood-cracked concrete walkway toward the front double doors of the Reserve building. Drake noted that the thick steel lattice covering the glass had been a post-Flood addition. *A do-it-yourself job*, Drake decided. When Drake and his companions were about fifty feet from the main double doorway, from the left, a single gray steel door eased open. A man with a salt-and-pepper beard nearly reaching his navel, and white hair framing his face which was longer than the beard, stood with his back against the open door. He gripped an M1 Garand rifle pointed directly at Drake's heart. As instructed by Drake, his two companions and Drake held up their hands.

"Sorry to disturb you, sir. The Lord of Hosts has need of you," Drake said, in a voice loud and clear, calm, and even. "We serve the Lord Jesus Christ, sent here by his prophet, Gabriel, who lives among us. Our community is named the Church of the Elect. Please listen to what we have to say before you kill us."

Slowly, the bearded man lowered his rifle, and raising his right hand, he motioned with his forefinger that he welcomed their approach. Together the line of three men approached at the same slow, even pace, hands still in the air. They stopped when they saw the man's right hand returning to the trigger guard of the Garand. "How many in your Church?" asked the man.

"Sir, my name is Drake Childers. These two men are with me." Drake stood looking them over from head to shoes. "We represent thousands of followers of Christ."

"Whew! Didn't think there were that many folks around no more," said the man."

Drake nodded. "Young people dream of us, feel drawn to us, and eventually find us, sometimes up to a couple thousand every month. This has been going on over the years; a good number have started families further increasing our number. We call them 'pilgrims' and they still come, bands of survivors traveling from the north, south, and west. Gabriel said the last of them are on their way now, walking here from somewhere deep down south, still weeks away; he said that if they survive, they will be the final band of outsiders to get baptized into the Elect. Sir, will you join us? Gabriel very much wants you to be a leader among us."

"Why me?" asked the old man.

"Sir, Gabriel knew you long before you two would ever possibly meet."

The young man to Drake's left stood staring with his mouth hanging open. "What the hell's the matter with you, son?" asked the bearded man. "Ain't never seen a U.S. Marine before?" The man returned his attention to Drake. "Gunnery Sergeant Patrick Powell. You can call me Gunny Powell. Or just Gunny'll do. And son, I was baptized when you weren't even a sperm in your daddy's sack yet."

Drake grinned.

"Gunny, sir, forgive me please. I'm only twenty," interrupted the young man to the left of Drake. "It's just that I have never seen an old—anyone as mature, as you."

Gunny's sharp blue eyes were deeply lined at the corners, with puffy purse-like flesh sagging beneath those eyes. He smiled. "That's right, son. I'm old: you can say it. And you're ugly. Ain't we a pair."

Drake laughed heartily as the young man flushed crimson. "Sir—I mean Gunny—I have been asked to invite you back to base and to take along with us three 120 mm M74 light mortars with a minimum of nine shells. With your permission we will drive our bikes up here for you to evaluate the size of our carts and weight capacity: because Gunny—none of us have any clue what an M74 light mortar is."

Gunny Powell laughed and extended his right hand. Drake shook a hand that felt old, cold, and rugose, like the shed skin of a snake in November.

"Save the 'sir' shit for the do-nothing college pukes shining desk chairs with their fat asses; I work for a living. Something told me this day would come," said Gunny. "Saw it in my dreams, maybe; a golden-haired man in robes looking out over a green mountain. Well? We gonna stand out here all day pulling our puds or are we gonna kick asses and take names? I gotta keep my back to this here door, 'cause once she closes we are all locked out. Permanent-like. Tell you what: get them bikes a-yours. I'll go and unlatch them two big swinging doors out front. Hain't been open in prolly half a century. You boys go find two heavy-assed stones to prop 'em open. Then all three of you can drive straight inside. Gunny Powell will take you back to storage where we keep the ordnance." He read the question on the three faces. "Ordnance is military-speak for guns, rockets, or armor."

"We? Are any others living here with you?" asked Drake.

The old face sagged. "Just me and the ghosts, ticking away the four seasons in a dry age. You're the first people I've talked to since I was at their stage of life," he said, flicking his eyes at the two twenty-year-olds. "For fifty damned years I've been talking only to God, and to my dead parents. Funny part about that is: I do all the talking. They're such great listeners that never once have they interrupted me." He laughed.

Gunny's laugh struck Drake as the saddest sound he had ever heard.

"Sir, I mean Gunny," said one of the young men. "There are thousands of Elect back home who will want to learn everything you know about the World Before, meaning Pre-Flood society, and what it feels like to be old. They'll want to touch your amazing hands. Back at Spring Mountain you'll be a huge sensation. I think the word they used back in your day was 'celebrity.' You're about to know what that feels like."

"Let me check my calendar…oh look, nothing scheduled!" Gunny said with a snort. "Sounds fairly good to me, sonny. Now go and fetch them bikes, and two heavy stones to prop open the doors."

When the four stood in the storage area, Sergeant Powell barked orders at the two as he and Drake stood back, arms folded. "Easy does it, boys. I know them bastards are heavy but trust me, ya gotta set 'em down gently."

"How heavy, exactly?" asked Drake.

"Just barely too heavy for them Harley Hogs you're driving, son. M74 light mortars ain't so light; suckers weigh two-hundred-thirty-one-and-a-half pounds, unloaded."

"What do they do?"

The sergeant smiled. "Well, there's an answer for that. I can't tell ya's why your commander needs 'em, but I can tell ya what we did with 'em in the Middle East. Each mortar requires a five-man crew to operate it. One stares into its range finder calling out to the machinist—that's the guy who aims it—giving him the exact latitude-longitude coordinates of the target, numbers which the machinist dials in to the control. These babies use high-elevation ballistic trajectories. Team communication is necessary to aim it perfectly. One millimeter off and the guy pulling the trigger will miss his target. M74s are good out to 6,400 meters, which is around 21,000 feet. It's a light-weight weapon used for infantry close support, designed for annihilation of manpower. We used 'em for destroying firing points during short-term engagements far enough back so their snipers couldn't reach us. It's the best way to defend hilly terrain where the enemy hides behind a rear slope. It opens breaches in wire barriers and clears mine fields. Demolishes lighter fortifications in a snap. Removes topsoil covers over heavy bunkers. In a nutshell, these babies are perfect for eliminating mechanized units by destroying their infantry. When down-range, and the bad guys point a

Howitzer at you, one of these shells will mangle that weapon. You just need to know how to work it."

Drake nodded.

"Is there a war going on I don't know about?" Gunny asked.

Drake shrugged. He still had no clue as to why Gabriel would want such a destructive weapon back at base. Gunny walked to the nearest little wheeled trailer. He bent and snapped the steel latch on the wooden case. He motioned with his head for the three visitors to take a look at the M74 shells inside.

Drake walked over for a peek. *Huge.* An old, repressed memory flashed to mind, of him as a little kid going through empty houses along Spring Mount Road, collecting guns and ammunition, just as Gabriel had directed. This morning, his body remembered the fear he'd felt that first night when they got the generator working, night fell, stadium lamps flickered on, designed to attract dangerous men into Gabriel's kill zone. Gabriel had perched high on his wooden deck while Drake and his fellow elementary school students hid at ground level and watched men slither into illuminated zones, then watched flashes of light from the tower, followed by loud reports. Holes suddenly opened in white chests; perfect heart shots fired by a third grader at a distance of over one-hundred yards, like opening blood faucets. These men simply crumpled, as if they were marionettes and someone had sliced their strings with a sharp scissors. Each man hit the ground before the echo from the loud shot that killed him ceased booming and reverberating throughout Spring Mountain.

That next morning, Drake loaded bodies into a golf cart, drove them back down the Trail and rolled them into the Perkiomen Creek rapids, watching the bodies taken by the currents bob and float away quickly. If nothing had cemented his loyalty to Gabriel apart from supernatural actions and words up to that point, the courage required to shoot adult men dead had been it. Whatever force had been operating inside Gabriel; a force that infused him with other-worldly confidence, decisiveness, precise knowledge, and general wisdom, had to come from someplace higher. For thirty-two years, when Gabriel called Drake to a task, not even for a second had he questioned it. He simply executed it to the best of his ability. He considered himself blessed, chosen, to serve Gabriel and his most unfathomable God.

"These are the largest bullets I have ever seen, Gunny."

Gunny snort laughed. "Son, we call these rounds, or shells. Propellant plus explosive. Heavy buggers. Given the square footage of your little trailers here, your commander, Gabriel, called it perfectly. Three shells per bike is about all that we can fit into one trip."

Drake smiled. "Gunny, I look forward to introducing you to the Prophet Gabriel. When people meet him for the first time, later they describe power radiating from him like a mini sun. He has strength. I'd die for Gabriel Thomas."

"You said the Lord of Hosts has need of me. Are you saying this Gabriel is your Lord?"

Drake smiled consolingly. He shook his head. "No, Gunny. He is something magical. A bona fide prophet of God. To follow him is to obey the Lord of Hosts."

Gunny's eyes narrowed. "I'll believe your Gabriel is a prophet of God when I see it for myself. Gonna take evidence to convince this old cynic."

Drake nodded. "And so you shall. Please go pack whatever personal belongings you need. Not food, though. The Lord provides."

Gunny returned his attention to securing the weapons. "Gents: see that box of red tie-down straps? Bring it here. I'll show you how to properly secure the munitions payload." Gunny turned back to Drake, speaking quietly. "It's eleven-thirty. We'll be on the road by noon. About them dreams I've been having lately: always I see a mountain, and a tall, blond-headed man surrounded by an aura of light. Also I see babies, tons of 'em, sitting on the grass as four-hundred-pound black bears give 'em a sniff and a lick before ambling off. Weirdest damned dreams. The same movie plays out in my head every night. Guessing that man in my dream is your prophet?"

Drake nodded.

"Drake, tell me something. To tell the whole truth, this place where we're standing is all I've known for nigh on three quarters of a century. I'm a little nervous about seeing the world beyond these grounds. Is it really tragic out there?"

Drake gave a single nod. "But not where we're going," he answered. "Our world within the world, up on the mountain, is good. We live as God originally intended for people to live. You'll wonder why you spent all those years here alone, instead of finding us there long ago and joining us. Those dreams you've been having are God's way of calling you to us. Why did you stay? I mean, with all the Pocono Mountain homes lying empty up in the higher elevations, you could've been living in far nicer places than this brick-and-mortar prison."

Drake watched a single tear spill down Gunny's wizened cheek, his mouth drawn down, trembling.

"I didn't know for sure if I was following God's will, staying here in this place. Like I said the relationship between me, and God, seems mostly one-way. It just felt like he wanted me here. Whenever I'd think about exploring the world outside of here: I'd get this empty, hollowed out feeling. Who am I to question God's divine purposes? I serve only him, and the Corps. Semper Fi; Jesus saves."

"Have the Golgoths tried to break in?"

"Naked painted white jihadis?" Drake nodded. "Ghosts, I call 'em: yes-yes. About once a year, groups of ghosts try to break in here." He walked over and demonstrated for the young men how to use the tie-downs. "Make sure the straps wrap flat underneath the trailers. When we're riding back, if I hear a single rattle, gents, I'll use these straps to hang your asses from the highest tree."

Quietly, he watched. Satisfied that the two young men were properly securing the munitions, he looked at Drake. "Come with me a moment. There's something I need to show you."

"Gunny, you'd better get packing. Twenty minutes until noon."

"What I want to show you is on the way."

Together they walked through the armory's mazy corridors, past Gunny's billet, to the end of the hallway brightened by daylight streaming in through a window. Gunny pointed outside. "What am I looking at?" Drake asked. He saw a green field bedotted with dirt mounds arranged in perfectly equidistant rows and columns.

"You're looking at graves for ghosts. Gollygoths, or whatever you called 'em."

"Oh, my dear Lord! There must be two hundred graves out there. You killed all these men?"

"Whose counting," said Gunny with a nod and a shrug. "And listen I don't need much. I pack light. But you can bet your ass I'm bringing my M1 Garand and sacks of ammo. And another thing, just thought of it. Your commander will need a handheld range finder. I know where to find one that's small enough to load into your saddlebags. We'll grab extras in case a lens in the finder breaks. They're the old kind, not battery powered."

Drake noticed Gunny's eyes watering. "Killing these men, does it weigh on your conscience?" Drake asked.

Gunny shook his head. "No sir. This species is lower than animals. I knew the Lord would call me home someday. My hour has come. It's just hard letting go, you know?"

Drake appeared puzzled. "You mean you'll miss this solitary existence?"

Gunny snorted. "Sure. Anyway, the only things I'm packing are my rifle and ammo, spare clothes, and my Bible. I killed a few dozen jihadis in the Middle East. Rotate back here and I end up killing four-times as many of my fellow citizens. Kinda fubar, don't you think?"

"Sorry, what does 'fubar' mean?"

"Fucked Up Beyond All Recognition. Military jargon."

Drake nodded. "That it is, Gunny, that it is. The entire world and even in the stars above, everything is pretty much fubar. Except that where we're going: things still make sense."

All four men stood outside in front of the armory. Using the key on the chain he lifted from around his neck, Gunny Powell locked up the double doors behind him. He handed the chained key to Drake.

Gunny stood with his back to the three, taking in one last look at the fortress he had defended for over half a century. Drake and his followers watched Gunny's left arm rise and wipe his sleeve against his face. His right snapped up in a smart salute. After a full minute, he turned to face them, eyes red.

"Well don't just stand there jerkin' yer gherkins. Fifty years and a wake-up. Time to go embrace the suck." They stared back at him blankly. He grinned. "Remind me to teach you tadpoles military jargon. It means it's time to jump into battle and get bloody."

First Step

Marshall leaped over the ledge and found Aliyah, Arabella, Dodie, and Tatum up and dressed. "Good mornin'! Did I wake y'all?"

"We heard voices. Sound carries well here. Yes, you woke us up," said Arabella.

"Pack up quick, we're movin' out. I made new friends on the Trail, mustn't keep 'em waitin.'"

"So other people really do exist," muttered Arabella.

As his eyes rested on Tatum, the words of Marshall's father bounced through his reenergized, rested mind. *Yes, dad, I'm keepin' a cool head.*

Good morning," said Tatum. She returned to gathering her gear, bent over facing away from Marshall. She glanced back at him and flashed him a quick smile. "It's not polite to stare at my butt, mister." His mouth gaped open. She laughed. "You've heard it said that women have eyes in the backs of our heads? If not, now you know."

"I wasn't starin' at your butt: I was checkin' for ticks. Lucky for y'all I didn't see none."

Snickering, she said, "Next time you should check more thoroughly. Little buggers love to hide in places that are not obvious to us."

Wearing a self-conscious smile, he struggled to reconcile the fact that his normally calm, composed, self-possessed head was no longer entirely his own; thoughts of Tatum left room in his mind for little else. He reached down and took her hand. Their eyes met. She smiled back; her nostrils flared wide as she followed his lead over the edge.

"Hey! Wait up!" yelled Aliyah. Within minutes she, Arabella and Dodie had fallen in step behind them.

"Booker Bailey from Birmingham, and Jayden Bonner from Nashville. I'd like to introduce y'all to my friends: Tatum Winters, Dodie Sealy, Aliyah Freedman, and Arabella Pendleman."

Marshall hung back studying the reactions. Tatum was the picture of cordiality. Politely she grinned and extended her hand, as would the Chairman of The Board's wife meeting majority investors, so excited was she to meet new people. Dodie's huge, excited grin and twitchy movements reminded Marshall of a kid on Christmas morning. Arabella's face was inscrutable. She gave one limp pump of her hand to Jayden. When she offered the same to Booker, she appeared as if she had just met the greeter at a leper colony.

Aliyah gave Jayden a firm handshake, then turned to behold the only other black person she had ever met. *Dear Lord, I need a man! Why must he be younger?* Her face revealed to Marshall a general curiosity about Booker, but nothing as powerful as he had felt meeting Tatum, every atom exploding within, grappling with polite societal norms of behavior and proper strategy. *Keep your head, kid. Easier said than done, I know.*

"So Jayden. You're a musician?" Dodie asked.

"Yessum. Sure am," said Jayden. His hands flew to the beautiful guitar. He thought of a difficult flamenco piece he would sometimes use to limber up his hands. Deftly his fingers danced, so rapidly that to Dodie they became a blur. He finger-picked through brief riffs, scales, and stanzas, to prove his dexterity, then a brief but explosive conclusion. Dodie jumped up and down excitedly as everyone applauded Jayden's tour de force.

"Before this journey ends, Jayden, I want your autograph. You know, like girls asked rock stars for in Pre-Flood days. So retro!"

Jayden's mouth finally upturned into the slightest of grins. He snorted. "Sure, Dodie. Maybe after you have endured a full two-hour concert performance."

"Wow! Y'all 'r good!" Marshall chimed in.

Aliyah nodded, grinning. "I've never heard music before in my life."

"I have."

"How's that, Booker?" asked Aliyah.

"My parents kept a Grammyphone at home."

"A what?" she asked.

"Well, that's what they called it, anyway. And they had piles of old vinyl records of songs. They used to wind up the Grammyphone by cranking a handle, then select a record album befitting the mood of the moment. It was a cool game they played: Cleon—that's my dad—always guessed Jayla's mood—my mom—or she would guess his. Nine times out of ten they guessed exactly the right music the other wanted to hear; that is how close they were. Me, I just enjoyed the music and watching them dance together. Often they'd pull me in to their dance. When I was little I'd stand on my dad's feet to learn his moves. By my teens I had become a fair dancer."

"Teach me?" Aliyah said.

"Um, so…" said Booker. He swallowed hard and inhaled deeply. Aliyah snickered at Booker's awkwardness around his first real girl. "Hey Jayden," said Booker, "play anything that has rhythm and a funky beat to it?"

Jayden appeared thoughtful. Then, picking hard at the strings and thumping the guitar body he launched into an old number by Rick James. Booker started to move. None of the group had ever seen or heard anything like what they heard and saw in that moment.

Booker's entire body became possessed by the music; glassine movements perfectly syncopated with the rhythmic sounds. He stopped and looked at Aliyah whose own hips and knees had started to move a little. "I'm also fluent in several languages, plus I am unequivocally the best writer alive today," said Booker.

"Smart young guy," said Aliyah.

"Also," he continued, "I watched my parents get gutted and cooked. I hiked over three-hundred-miles to get here and killed a Golgoth by hand along the way. So please don't ruminate on my age, or my stature. It would be a grievous error for you, Aliyah—for any of you—to judge a book by its cover. Isn't that so, Jay?"

Reading the younger man's undisguised emotions which seemed to him almost childlike, to lighten the heavy moment, quick strumming an E chord, Jayden said, "Introducing the one man I respect most in the world, Mister Burl 'Booker' Bailey, ladies, and gentlemen. Underestimate him at your own peril. I couldn't be prouder to walk with him."

Aliyah and Booker exchanged glances. *Please, Lord: tell me I have a real shot with her.*

"So sorry to hear about your mom and dad, Booker," Aliyah said.

Marshall interjected, "I'm proud to walk with y'all. Now, let's cover the basics. Booker, Jayden: please share the information y'all gave me with the others."

Jayden deferred to Booker, the most glib and garrulous of the two. Booker explained the time of day that Golgoths grabbed his parents, an inversion of everything they knew about Golgoths up to that point."

"Booker, what if the Golgoths who attacked your parents during daylight was just a one-off?" Aliyah asked.

Then Jayden told his story, of his noon attack in Knoxville. Booker told them about the highways and roadways, the northern migration of Golgoths. Jayden confirmed parental stories of girls and young women kept alive as breeders who were slowly butchered and eaten when no longer useful. Booker described seeing the girls trussed up to poles, getting carried north by Golgoths, as he had witnessed from trails higher up which ran parallel to roads down below.

After hearing the tale, Aliyah, Arabella, Dodie, and Tatum shuddered in alarm.

"Things 'r changin' with them," said Marshall. "Even if some hunt by daylight, at least during the day they're easier to spot; hard for glowin' white men to lay in wait and ambush us. And I don't really expect 'em to hunt along this Trail. So listen up, y'all: I know where I'm goin,' called to action by the recurrin' dream of the Spring Mountain, where I'll find life among my own kind. I think maybe ya'll will agree, the Holy Spirit of God is at work in us."

Arabella snickered. Everyone else shot her with a dismissive stare, for all but she were experiencing the identical dream.

"I believe God called us all to this Trail. I could be wrong. Y'all feel free to correct me at any point." Nobody spoke except Marshall. "So our strategy as I see it is to stick to the Appalachian Trail. We travel by day and camouflage well for our nightly rest. Golgoths are usin' roads not only for travel, but also for huntin.' It may be that there are more of us with dreams also walkin' north, out there, who got called to the Trail, too. There may be others who choose to override the subtleties of the Spirit which guided us all to this Trail; people who overthink it, because they know roads 'r more direct and faster to their destination. These will perish. To ignore the Spirit of God is to become food for Golgoths."

Marshall's expression grew hard. "Slow and steady wins the race."

Marshall perceived the anxiety coursing through all four women. "I'm sorry. We all need to face facts. The more we all know and work together, the better our chances of survival. Booker and Jayden: I was havin' the green mountain dream, with no great desire to wake from it, yet all the way up on that ledge I heard y'all comin' from a mile away. I heard y'all's voices and especially the guitar. If Goths are within five miles of that racket they'll home right in on us. Noise is a dinner bell for them. Hate to say it, because what I just heard were the finest sounds I ever heard in my entire life, we'll be safer if you strap the guitar up and forget it a while. All of us need to communicate as silently as possible. Whispers from now on." He searched every face until he saw nods of assent.

"We all have one problem; and unless y'all 'r into raw meat which I for sure ain't, we all need to find an alternative heat source for cookin.' Woodsmoke? Might as well draw a big arrow in the sky pointin' straight to us. An arrow that stinks to high Heaven. Breezes will carry the aroma of cookin' meat and announce our presence. Start thinkin' of alternatives."

Nobody spoke. Marshall nodded. "Okay, so what did that famous Chinaman say, 'A journey of a thousand miles begins with a single step.' Let's get to it. Jayden here is positively lethal with that compound bow strapped to his back. I'm ten-for-ten with my huntin' wrist slingshot. Jayden, I'll take point, if you'll watch our six."

"Our what?" Jayden asked.

"Analog clock," said Marshall. "6:00 p.m. position, means y'all 'll protect the rear. Y'all got our backs. Any Golgoths sneak up on us from behind, y'all get to shoot first until Booker and I run back and join in the fun. If I sense anythin' up front, I'll put up my hand and we'll pause until I sort it out. We can switch off periodically to keep things fresh if y'all like." Jayden nodded. "Booker, you take the middle so if there's trouble ahead or behind y'all can rush in." Booker glanced at Jayden, who nodded.

"So mote it be," said Booker.

This made Marshall smile. "The Holy Spirit of God is here to help us. I believe that in my heart. If anyone gets a bad feelin' please—do not ignore it: say somethin.' As an example, if y'all hear an unnatural movement, or even have a sense somethin' feels off, we need y'all to call it out. We'll check on it and discuss it, in whispers of course. These are dangerous times."

"Hah. One way to put it," Arabella added sourly.

"I want to walk with Jayden," Dodie announced, unabashedly.

"I'm with Marshall," said Tatum, without looking at him.

"I'd be happy to walk with Booker," said Aliyah, who flicked Booker with the briefest glance.

"Great. So what: I walk alone?" said Arabella.

"No," said Marshall. Nobody walks alone. Please understand how predatory animals operate, huntin' in prides or groups, changin' tactics but never their main strategy, which is: peel off the lone herd member. The slow one. The one who stands out. I don't know if the Floods left any reindeer, but in Nordic countries these animals used to group together and run in a crazy-lookin' vortex, tornado-like, to defend against predators like polar bears, and darn if it don't work like a charm. Safety in numbers. We gotta stick together. Arabella, stay alert and focused and in the middle, somewhere close to Booker. Pretend you left your feelins' back home. Ain't sayin' y'all 'r vulnerable or weak physically..."

"No way. I'll hang back with Dodie and Jayden. Bless your heart, Marshall Langar. Who elected you leader, anyway?"

"If the straight-jacket fits, Bells..." Tatum said.

"Eat shit and die, butch dyke!" Arabella screamed at top volume.

Marshall's fists balled. "Thank y'all, Arabella, for validatin' my very point. Y'all 'r emotionally unfit for this journey: only clear-thinkin' heads gonna survive. Look how easy 'twas for Tatum to mash y'all's buttons. How loud y'all are. Maybe best if y'all walk on back up to that mountain paradise." He broke eye contact with Arabella to scan the group. "And please, if y'all think it's better for Arabella to lead this circus raise your hand so she can step right up. I was perfectly fine all by my lonesome before y'all happened by. Just me and the Holy Spirit 'a God."

Angry at first, Arabella's face softened. "Sorry, Marshall and sorry, Tates. I'll behave."

Marshall relaxed his hands. He looked over to Tatum. Her kind, gentle face and bright, expectant eyes assuaged his anger. "Great. Now remember, stop if y'all feel anythin' that don't quite fit."

Booker pulled his atlas from a backpack pocket. He stood shuffling through pages and tracing lines with his finger. "Wait, hang on a sec, Marshall. Portable bottle-top propane camp stove with adjustable burner. Zero smoke or odor; burns clean. Wrap a tarp around and over it, it'll become a low-smoke oven."

Theatrically, Marshall stroked his beard. "I hear y'all. Unfortunately, Booker, I don't happen to have a bottle-top propane camp stove in my bag of tricks."

Booker grinned. "If you did, I might think you are some kind of prophet yourself. Our best chance of finding a propane stove that survived the Floods intact is right here," he said. He moved beside Marshall, then fingered a spot on the map. "A Walmart Supercenter. My parents used to love to forage there. These places used to sell everything."

"Y'all mind?" Marshall said. Booker let go of the road atlas. Marshall studied it, did quick math in his head. "Only twenty miles from here which, if we don't take no breaks, is only about six hours away in the direction we're headed anyway. But…" he said, tracing lines, "parts involve walkin' on roads."

"I got attacked at a Walmart in Knoxville. Goths must stake them out knowing foragers are drawn there," said Jayden.

Marshall rubbed his bearded face. "I say we stick to the Trail for as long as we can. Then, we'll find a safe place where we all can make camp. Tonight, y'all 'r just gonna have to chow down on whatever y'all packed or walk in the woods lookin' for nuts or berries. Towards dusk, Jayden and I 'r gonna hook over and hit this Walmart place. Booker, we need at least one warrior to remain behind to guard the women. Did I just hear y'all volunteer?"

Booker tried hard not to smile. "Oh yes. I volunteer," he said. He reached into his backpack front pocket, then handed the ten-inch black metal cylinder to Marshall. "Point the glassy part at your eye. Now, flick the switch forward. Here, like this," he said. Booker placed his thumb over Marshall's thumb and pushed. The bright L.E.D. flashlight beam hit Marshall square in the eyes, so bright that he yelped.

"If you can see the flashlight, Marshall, so can Golgoths. Remember that. At night, a beam that bright would be visible from space. Once you get in the building, Jayden can lead you through the flood-rubble to the back section where stuff like the camp stove and tarps should be located. My parents found this flashlight and solar charger in the Walmart about a three-hour walk from our home. Maybe just cover the lens with your hand to diffuse the light once inside."

"Tatum, y'all packed two-person kayaks with paddles, foot pumps to inflate 'em, and repair kits: that right?"

She nodded. "Each of us did."

"Do smelly feet inflate 'em faster than odorless feet?" he asked.

This comment met with Tatum's luminous cobalt-blue eyes. *Rare and radiant*, he thought. He noticed her nostrils flare; and the momentary blush on her cheeks. Aware of everyone staring at her, Tatum chose to ignore the bait.

Flirt received loud and clear, he thought. "Might there be anythin' else there of value to our mission we all should look for?" he asked.

"Tampons," said Arabella.

Booker tilted his head. "What-pons?"

Arabella rolled her eyes. "I'm coming with you two."

Marshall rubbed his temples. He heard his heart beating crazy blood deep in his ears. "I don't think that's a good idea."

"Actually, I think it's a great idea," said Tatum. "Look, we have four females here with a monthly consideration. You have no clue. We've lived together so long that our menstrual periods have synchronized." All three of her girlfriends glared at her. "I know guys, but this is reality." Turning to Marshall, she grabbed both of his hands. "Please? We need this."

Booker cleared his throat. "Well, the ladies have expressed their priorities, and we must respect that. Now for group safety: we require night vision goggles ideally one for each person along with a solar charger for each," said Booker. "Get the ones that strap onto your head, so you don't need to hold them."

"What in the Sam Hill is a night vision goggle?" Marshall asked.

"If you manage to find any, they will be useful gadgets. In the darkest night, they let you see as though it were daylight. Military used them to attack enemies at night. Night vision goggles sense tiny amounts of infrared light reflected off objects and then electrically amplify the light into glowing green images of the objects. If I stood right beside Jayden in the night, wearing these things you could tell who's who. Could come in handy, don't you think?"

Marshall nodded. "In theory, yes. Okay. We'll look for those things."

"What about tampons?" Arabella said.

"Fine. Y'all can come too," said Marshall. He looked at Tatum: she winked.

Marshall walked up to face Arabella. In a low growly tone, he said, "But this is me makin' a promise, Arabella. If y'all don't follow my orders to the letter, or become a burden and slow us down, I promise we are leavin' y'all there for the Golgoths."

"You don't like me much, do you?" she whispered.

He glowered, fists clenching and unclenching, pronounced carotid arteries pulsing.

Finally, she relented. "Deal."

Hate

Marshall with Tatum close at his right took off walking north along the trail. On his left hand and wrist he wore his powerful slingshot and a pocketful of marbles. Booker and Aliyah followed, with Arabella trailing. Nobody spoke.

Marshall's long legs set the pace for all to follow at three miles per hour that was brisk, but not strenuous. Although his head remained turned to study the rolling wooded hills to his left and the down grade to his right, scanning for game animals and potential threats; he walked straight. The Trail here smelled and sounded much like summer up in LeConte Lodge. This set him thinking about Delilah; how she murdered his baby before driving him away. He wondered if she was still up there, or if Golgoths had taken her. He wondered why he still cared.

Mostly keeping her head straight and eyes on the Trail ahead, Tatum continually stole furtive glances at his face.

"Marshall," she whispered. He looked down at her. "I just want you to know that I will never ask for more than you want to give me."

"What?" he responded. "In what context?"

On the right, they passed a white oak grove and clearing. He made quick mental notes about its suitability as a wild game hunting ground.

She paused. "Applies to anything and everything, but what I meant was, personal information. I'll never ask you any personal questions. If you want to give freely, then please know that I would rather die than share with any other person. What I mean is…"

"You mean y'all 'll keep my secrets and got my back."

She smiled. "Yes! Exactly that."

He smiled. "Didn't need to say it. I already knew."

"You're a wise old man, Marshall Langar."

Smirking, he asked, "Y'all are how old?"

"You first."

"Twenty-four."

"Hah! Old man. I'm only twenty-two."

He grinned. "If I'm a wise old man, then y'all 'r a spry little empath."

Her face grew serious. "Empath. I've been called that by my besties back there. Seriously, how do you know stuff?"

He shrugged. "For things I can't reckon on my own, the Holy Spirit 'a God shows me truth."

She thought about this. "I don't know much about these things. You can teach me?"

Unaware that he had slowed his pace a little, "Maybe," he whispered. "It's a little like tryin' to explain music to a deaf person. God the Father created the universe and everythin' in it. Inside Mary, a virgin, God planted his seed and begot an only Son, the Christ, who is also the Word of God, who was human in every way, but inside him was the power of God. The Father created a third being, a Counsellor named the Holy Spirit; this he sends to live inside people who wanna grow closer to God. It's a helpin' thing, the Holy Spirit."

"Like a guardian angel?" Tatum asked.

Marshall smiled. "God's Holy Spirit is a little more than that. It's God livin' inside us, givin' us signs, sharpenin' our consciences, guidin' us; strengthenin' us. When tempted to do wrong, the Spirit helps us walk in the Lord's path. Now, angels are real too, and helpful, but like us they are individual spirits with their own consciences created by the Father like billions 'a years ago. I do believe the Father sends 'em to help, sometimes; kinda like God's First Responders. Satan and his arch demons are fallen angels. God is spirit: the Bible says so; Christ himself said so. Angels are spirits. And," he poked her chest, "livin' in here is a spirit. All made 'a the same stuff."

"You're saying I'm an angel?" said Tatum.

Marshall giggled. "Jury's still deliberatin.' Anyway: decidin' to be ruled by God alone is a decision mixed with emotion. What I mean is, I feel the Spirit workin' in me only when I feel consumed with a deep-down ache for what's real, what's true; and God is true. The Holy Spirit gives me signs that point the way. That's how it works, Tatum Winters," he said, and gave her a straight-lipped expression and a nod.

"So God is really three distinct spirits?" she whispered.

"Mm hm, yep! Y'all got it! God is a three-in-one package," he whispered. "The Holy Trinity."

"The dreams some of us are having: are those signs?"

"Yes! Very much," Marshall said. "That is one way the Holy Spirit communicates with us, through dreams and visions. Prophesy is another. But also signs: physical signs."

"Like what?"

His eyes narrowed at her. "Tatum, God loves us. He really, really loves us. Y'all 'member what I said at the start of this journey not twenty minutes ago: report to the group any weird feelins' y'all might have? Sometimes life forks left, or right. What if we reckon to take the left path, but thinkin' 'bout goin' left makes us feel dreadful deep in our guts? That dread feelin' is a sign. Or say, before eatin' a berry from a plant I don't recognize, I spot a dyin' bird near that bush and feel a pit in my stomach for no good reason. That's a physical sign not to eat them poison berries. Signs come in different forms, but they all come from his love."

"What about our dream of the blond man on the mountain?" she asked.

"My understandin' is that this man, named Gabriel, is leader of the mountain Church of the Elect, and an authentic prophet 'a God. Dreams 'a him are a sign."

"What does that mean: a prophet?" Tatum asked.

"The Spirit—God's Holy Spirit—speaks directly to Gabriel and gives him more than signs. God the Father directly increases Gabriel's knowledge and abilities beyond what we know; communicates directly with him. Past prophets received glimpses of the future, 'cause only God the Father knows what happens in the future. He only gave Jesus glimpses of the future. Coulda' been billions 'a years ago when God set a date to judge ev'ry human spirit. That's when Jesus returns to earth, to judge the spirits of the livin' and the spirits 'a the dead, all in one day. Only the Father knows that date. Could happen soon."

"Judged for what?" she asked.

"Sin. To break one 'a his Ten Commandments is to break 'em all. And we all do. Jesus is the only human who fully kept 'em. The rest 'a us, well. We suck! We're all sinners. God is holy. He won't look upon anything unholy. Which means us; we ain't holy."

"Oh my God! So I'm going to face Judgement?"

Marshall nodded. "But not if you love his Son, Jesus Christ, who became sin and died on the cross so that if we love Jesus, that's all God the Father sees is our love for his Son. He don't look beyond our love. Deletes ev'ry sin like they ain't never happened. Then we get to spend eternity livin' as his children, safe and happy, together with those we loved here on earth…I mean those who also loved Jesus and make it to Heaven."

"Wow. I never knew any of this. Aliyah and Dodie tried talking to me about it and I just blew them off. God, I was so stupid! Marshall, you know Gabriel is a prophet from your dreams?"

Marshall nodded. "Yes, Tatum, I do. If y'all read about prophets 'a old, I see the same happenin' with Gabriel in my dreams ev'ry night. Sounds crazy but it's always the same dream, goin' into a bit more depth, showin' me a little more each time. I remember it the next mornin' until the day washes away details. I feel like I'm gettin' to know Gabriel a little better ev'ry night; and feelin' like he knows me, too. God's got his finger on the hearts of people on the green mountain; hopefully on all 'a us, too. Guess we'll find out who's who along the way," he said, wondering if Arabella shared the Spring Mountain dream, or Delilah's nightmare.

"I will ask you one personal question but only as it pertains to me."

"Okay. Shoot."

"Do my feet smell?"

He beamed at her. "A little. Yes."

"Liar! You lied to the whole group!"

"A little white lie to embarrass y'all's nasty ginger-headed friend, Arabella."

"Oh wow. So, are they foul?"

His eyes held hers. "Contrary. You smell like a raindrop." His nostrils flared and unconsciously he licked his lips. Her wide eyes blinked; cheeks blushed. He grinned. He knew now that his immeasurable passion for her might not go unrequited.

For the next twelve minutes using peripheral vision as a radar to spot danger, seven bodies robotically walked the Appalachian Trail, or as all thought of it now simply: the Trail. In silence, Marshall and Tatum continued to make brief eye contact, perfectly communicating this way.

Aliyah broke the quiet when she turned to Booker. "So, your real name is Burl?" she whispered.

He rolled his eyes. "Yes. My mother, Jayla, was half Seminole. The European-American practice is to name babies at birth. Not so in the tribes where young people earn their names. Natives believe that when you're a baby or infant you have few distinguishing personality traits. Dominant traits manifest over time. Turns out I was reading adult-level books by age five. The following year I was bored reading other people's stories and started writing my own. By age eight I wrote my first novel-length story and had mastered Latin. They started calling me Booker, and never used Burl again."

"Damn! Seriously? You were a child prodigy; a genius! A wise old man trapped in a youthful body!"

He grinned. "Thanks, but unfortunately intelligence and wisdom aren't even kissing cousins, Aliyah."

"I know what you mean, I think. Wisdom comes from experience, from trial and error. Which is why the old and the young can both think critically about the same situation—insert any example you want here—yet both arrive at vastly different conclusions about future outcomes of present decisions. Because the old person's universe of dots, with myriad ways to connect them, is so much more expansive than the smaller worlds of the young. Is that an accurate paraphrase of what you meant?"

Booker walked, unaware that his mouth hung open. He realized it and closed it.

First he said, "Wow. You gave no indication that you were such a deep thinker with an impressive vocabulary." She smiled. Then he said, "Omnia vincit amor, et nos cedamus amori. Amor est vitae essentia. Nescit amor habere modum. Si vis amari, ama."

Aliyah giggled. "Say what? What does that mean?"

"What, you don't speak Latin? Well then, I guess I just wasted my breath."

Giggling, she punched his shoulder. "Come on. Tell me! Don't make me spank you, little boy."

He grinned. "I really want you to pull my pants down right here and spank me. That would break up the monotonous miles nicely, don't you think?"

"Hmm. I should try a different approach. If you tell me, I'll let you hold my hand."

"Carrot and stick, I see, I see; okay then. I think I prefer carrots. What I said was, translated, that love conquers all things; let us yield to love. Love is the essence of life. Love does not know how to keep within bounds. If you wish to be loved—then love."

Aliyah's hand closed inside Booker's.

"Well isn't that special. Jungle love," muttered Arabella.

Booker froze. He released Aliyah's hand. Slowly he turned to face Arabella. His expression halted Arabella mid-step. Booker stepped toward her; she backed up. His face was now two feet from hers. He studied her eyes.

"You will never make it to Spring Mountain, Arabella. Call it a prophecy. Even if somehow you did make it, the Church of the Elect there would reject you, because you are of your real inamorata, the devil, and you honor him with your words," said Booker. He started to turn back to Aliyah but cast one final baleful glare at Arabella and pointed. "Know this: the next time you make a racist comment, I will personally deliver you to the Golgoths, where they will positively just eat you up. C'est vraiment appétissant. J'en ai l'eau à la bouche. La viande est très bien cuite, et tendre. Bon appétit!" He licked his lips. "Yum!"

By this point, Jayden and Dodie had closed the gap between Arabella and Booker and had stopped to witness his threat to Arabella.

"Was that French, Booker?" Jayden asked.

"Oui; yes it was." Booker had still not broken eye contact with Arabella, who appeared amused by his fury.

"What did you say to her?" Dodie asked, smiling.

Booker started to calm down. "Jayden and Dodie, my friends: do not become allured by the Irish Setter's jocund expression. I have an extraordinarily strong feeling about this: we each come into this world crying and kicking; Arabella will leave it screaming for death, but death won't come fast enough. Not until torturous agonies have twisted that charcoal briquette of her soul into something even more dark and hateful than it already is."

He broke eye contact with Arabella and looked back to Aliyah. "Sorry, I know she's your friend, but I feel no sympathy for racists and haters." He turned to Jayden and shook his head. "Arabella's heart belongs to Satan, and she walks in his ways. Golgoths *will* have her, pay attention; and I will lose precisely zero sleep over it. Call it my prophetic twinkle of the day. Okay, let's walk."

Arabella had experienced surges of anger from time to time, but nothing ever close to the spirit of hate which consumed her now more deeply with every heartbeat. Enmity coursed through her blood like a virus replicating at lightning speed. The one anti-viral medicine required to fight off an infection of the soul—love—was absent within Arabella entirely.

"What the heck was that about?" asked Dodie.

Jayden grinned and shook his head. "I think your bitchy redheaded friend, Arabella, interrupted a tender moment between Aliyah and Booker with a deeply offensive insult related to their skin color. What I gather, anyway."

"Gawd. I'm tired of apologizing for Arabella," whispered Dodie. "Each of us is our own person. From the time our eyes open in the morning until we close them at night, everything in between is a decision. Like deciding to leave the safety of the only home I have ever known, to walk a thousand miles through hostile lands in pursuit of a dream. Or deciding to love our enemies as the Lord commanded, and like I've always done with Arabella. She has spent a lifetime disparaging my God, me, my faith, my core beliefs; she hates everything I love and hold dear. God tells me I must love her, so I force myself. She decides to hate, and the consequences are entirely on her."

She met Jayden's astounded eyes. "But God never told me that I had to like her," Dodie said, and winked.

Jayden grinned. "Fabulous observations, Dodie. Is Dodie your given name or is it short for something longer, like Dorothy or duodenum or something?"

She laughed. "Duodenum? I'll kick you in your duodenum, jackass."

He grinned. "I just want to know everything about you. That's all."

She made a sly face. "Gotta give to get. Okay, I'll start first. But you must promise never to tell anyone. Everrrr…"

"Dodie, I am a subterranean bank vault of information made of concrete and steel that no human can penetrate. Whatever information you deposit therein shall remain secure. You can tell me anything. I promise never to share it with anyone."

"Okay then. My given name is Dolores Leona Sealy. Don't laugh! I see you laughing inside."

"Nonsense! I find Dolores to be quite beautiful. So beautiful, that if I had any say in the matter, I would not permit you to part with a single syllable of it."

"You're joking."

"Okay, let's examine the root of the name. Dolor means a state of great sorrow or distress. So really, your name means someone who sees the world as negative. Everything in it is evil, or rotten. Adding the 'eses to the end means that you freely accept all of this. Like a seamstress or governess except someone pasted a second 's' to the end to make it seem more sophisticated. But same meaning: you were named to be a person who deals in glumness as a way of life. Which sets you at opposition to all the happiness and joy in the world. It makes you a 'farmer of melancholy,'" he said, making air quotes.

He reveled in the comical expression of disgust taking root on her face.

"Which then makes it my job to bring you joy and happiness in this world. For the ancient root meaning of my name, Jayden, means 'thankful.' So, see? Just maybe, God put me in your path to prove whoever named you was wildly off target. That it is not only possible to be happy in the Lord, but to be abundantly joyful. Which is why I'm thankful to God for delivering you to me. My new favorite person. All kidding aside, I am very fond of your real name, Dolores. Love it!"

"Wow. I mean, just, wow. Grady, Arabella's dad who raised us had always warned us girls to be super wary of guys. He said even the dumbest, meanest dolts become Shakespeare when they smell girl pheromones on the air."

Jayden laughed. "I love this man! I hope one day to be as good a dad to my daughter as he was to you four."

"You have a daughter?"

Jayden laughed. "Futuristically speaking. I would love to have a daughter to spoil. Okay, I owe you something super-secret about myself. Ready?" he asked. She blinked and nodded. "I'm a virgin. Apart from my mother, you and your crew are the first flesh and blood women I have ever even seen."

She rolled her eyes. "All of us are virgins, genius. Apart from our real dads and Grady, you are the first men any of us have ever seen. I'll bet Booker and Marshall are virgins, too."

Jayden shook his head. "Not Marshall."

"How would you know?"

He inhaled deeply and exhaled slowly. "Only a lover could wound a man as deeply. I can see it in him. Like when my parents would argue sometimes. They wouldn't speak to one another for days. One time it was weeks. Each thought he or she was right about something. But I could see the loneliness eating them up, especially my dad. The bigger the heart, the more loving the soul, the deeper pain magnifies. That's my take on Marshall. Someone loved him and left him or died on him. But I don't think death because that is something surmountable, acceptable. Death is a natural part of the cycle of life each of us learns early to accept. No—Marshall gave his heart to another, and she ground it to bits. That's what I believe, anyway."

"Huh. You could be right."

"I think I am," Jayden whispered with a nod.

"Are you okay with him leading us?"

Jayden nodded three times. "Marshall is the oldest of us with the most experience in hunting and tracking; a real outdoorsman and survivalist. I don't doubt his survival instinct and alpha wolf 'protect the pack even if it means dying' worldview. God runs him completely, I see it because God runs me, too. Yes, I've killed Golgoths and I'm itching to kill more. I don't know if that's right or wrong in the eyes of the Lord but killing Golgoths feels right. Marshall won't kill unless he must. I'm meaner than Marshall; with me, anger always comes first. He keeps his head very cool; he is a utilitarian. I trust him to get us through this. Besides, I am way prettier than this man. God gave me all the looks and talent. Marshall—let him keep all the responsibility and risk. Everybody wins."

She giggled. "So modest! Love that about you. Not conceited or anything."

"Seriously, I have his back and everyone's. To get to you, Dolores, they'll have to go through me, first. And that won't be easy as I have so gorily demonstrated back at that Walmart. May I start calling you Dolores? Please? Pretty-please with a cherry on top?"

"Absolutely not. What does that even mean, cherry on top?"

He grinned. "Who knows. Something mom used to say. A bit of her 'old-timey' colloquial language. Idiom, I think it's called. I ate canned cherries once. Not particularly good."

She gave him her flirtiest grin. "You can, but only in private, not in front of others. To them, I'm Dodie. Only to you, I'll be Dolores," she said. She brushed his hand with hers. "You can try to make me farm less melancholy and sadness. But I'll make you work hard to sow if you want to reap smiles, buster."

"Just wish I could sing you a song. I've started composing one in my head about you. One day, if you'll let me, I'll perform it for you."

"Oh my gosh! Really? A song about me? Gimme a hint. Is it a boy crushes on a girl song?"

"Okay here are the lyrics I have so far: There once was a maiden named Dolores, with teeth like a Tyrannosaurus. She said with a grin as she wiped off her chin, 'Eating Jayden made me burp, and now for the chorus.' Sorry, that's all I have so far."

Her hand flew up to her mouth to muffle raucous, bellowing laughter. Tears ran down her cheeks. "I can't," she said through closed fingers. Booker and Aliyah glanced backward to see what was so funny. Jayden appeared straight-faced and inscrutable as always, though inside he could barely contain laughter. His eyes met Dodie's just as she looked up; he bared his teeth and champed his jaws like a giant reptile predator. This set her off again for another hundred-and-fifty feet of loud shrill laughter. She refused to look at Jayden. Booker shot Dodie the finger-on-lips 'hush!' commandment, wary of sound carrying to Golgoth ears. Jayden kept his eyes straight ahead but could see Dodie in the periphery. Every time she glanced at him, he would look down and make faces. Each made her laugh harder than the last time.

Her hand brushed his again. This time, he grabbed it. Neither let go. Until abruptly they stopped, because up ahead, Booker had frozen in place and turned back to look at them.

Booker appeared alarmed.

Minutes to Hours

Spoggs spent the entirety of the morning supervising the mounting of the Browning M2A1 .50 caliber machine gun into the bed of the Golgoth's one functioning pick-up truck. He had chosen four fellow Golgoth generals, each of whom owed him favors. First the men used a hammer and chisel and metal files to reduce sharp edges, which was a long and awkward process, to hack holes into the steel pickup truck bed. After hand-hewing the holes they lifted the M205 tripod up to the bed. The holes did not perfectly align.

Spoggs singled out one general, the one who most vigorously competed against him for his top rank, to make an example of what would happen if tasks he assigned were not completed to perfection. While three generals held down his rival, Spoggs addressed him and said: "I expect you to accept your punishment stoically." Spoggs grasped the chisel in his left hand, the hammer in his right; and with one half-strength blow he lopped off the small toe of the man's left foot. As ordered, the man grimaced and blew air between his teeth, and hyperventilated, but he did not scream, nor did he pass out.

The punished general's misaligned bolts error required another forty minutes of chiseling and filing. The remaining three generals used rusted bolts and nuts along with two fixed steel wrenches and managed to firmly secure the tripod to the bed.

This time, the devastating weapon slotted down perfectly.

"This calls for a feast which will be delayed, thanks to him," said Spoggs, pointing at the man with the bloody foot. "All of you: go get a bonfire started near my cabin. I'll be inside preparing the meat."

Roughly centered under the roof within the simple one-room wooden structure ran a thick hand-hewn roof support beam. Mounted to the middle of the beam dangled a ten-foot-long manual hand chain block hoist with a metal hook at the end of the chain. Below the chain and hook, on the floor sat a crudely built rough wooden table, three feet wide and six feet long, with sawed sections of tree along the sides of the table used as crude stools.

On top of the table lay the limbless torso of Isabella Albo, squirming like a snake, pitifully attempting to wriggle off the table, and from there perhaps slither away to freedom. Spoggs closed the door behind him. He smirked at the sight of the suffering breeder. At the sound of the closing door, Isabella looked at Spoggs and started sobbing. "No! No! No! I don't want to die!"

From his pocket he unfolded a karambit knife with a four-inch curved blade, which was shaped like a Velociraptor claw. It locked open with a resounding click. He made sure to open the knife where Isabella could see it. The site of the blade changed her even, steady sobs into a high-pitched squeal of panicked terror.

"Please, oh Lord Jesus, I'll do anything! Anything you want please… just please no more torture no mas tortura no mas no mas por favor quiero a mi mama! *I want my mama! —oh God please…*"

"Ah. My dear Isabella, you pathetic little dead woman. Have you forgotten my generous offer? Renounce your false Jesus and I will make your death quick and merciful. Praise the one true god, Hubal, god of the moon, and his earthly prophet, Hostis Dei. Remember? I promised you unendurable pain if you refuse." As he spoke, he studied her red, tear-stained face. "This is the part I like best," he said.

"Okay! I renounce Jesus and I praise your gods!"

He laughed and shook his head. "Too late! You had your chance. You just renounced your stupid God for nothing! You blasphemed your own false God and so now, supposing he were real, even *he* would reject you! The entire universe rejects you, Isabella! And so you must die two deaths: first the death of your body, then the death of your soul.

"*Nooooo!*" she screamed.

"Me, I took you in and offered you a quick death. Am I not merciful? You rejected me and my god. As a result of your foolish actions, both your God and my god will reject you. What do you suppose happens now: No afterlife? This is it, the true end of the line—your soul simply evaporates along with all your knowledge and memories? Or will you be stuck here, a ghost condemned to float around this miserable rotating rock for all eternity, who knows? You'll find out soon enough," he said. He touched the karambit blade with his thumb. "Honed to a razor's edge, my dear. How long will it take for you to die?"

Walking to her left side, he lightly scratched the blade's tip along her sides. "Here is what is going to happen, my beautiful Isabella. I am going to open your abdomen in a nice, deep, straight line. See the hook hanging above your middle?" he said and tapped it. "I will loop your guts over the hook and pull the chain attached to the hook. You get to watch yourself unravel!" He reached for two cotton swabs. "Soaked in ammonia, these go up your nose to keep you from passing out as your body goes into shock. I'm about to eviscerate you like a fish, and seal bleeding arteries and veins with this blow torch so that you won't bleed out and die. I'd roast you alive as is, but we can't have the bitter taste of bowel spoiling our roast now, can we?"

Isabella's head shook wildly. As she grappled with denial, anger, bargaining, depression, and finally acceptance, Spoggs inserted himself for the last time. "After I gut you I will tie you to a wooden ladder and slowly lower you over the hot coals prepared for you outside. Your skin will sizzle as fats heat up and burst through. I will position your head away from the coals and swab your face with cold wet towels to keep your brain from accepting your body's imminent demise and shutting down your heart. You will be in shock—can't help that—but I promise to keep you conscious. I will not permit you to pass out," he said, savoring the expression of naked terror on her face.

"From the moment my knife enters your flesh until your slow-roasted meat finally gives up the ghost, hopefully it will last about thirty minutes. The strongest girl lasted forty-five minutes. Irish girls last longest, in my experience. As you see, I have done this many times before, my beautiful Isabella, so please…feel free to start counting the minutes," he said. He paused in his exertions to steady the blade tip. "Pain turns minutes to hours. Though I bet in your case the hours will feel more like an eternity," he said with a sinister chuckle.

He positioned the sharp tip just under her xiphoid process and pressed down hard, delighting in the bittersweet music it coaxed from her throat, high tones that passed through his ears straight to his sex. He drew the blade down a straight line through her navel until her pubic bone prevented further travel. "Funny how you don't all sound exactly the same at this point," he muttered over her agonized cacophony. "It's those subtle differences that keep the slaughter of breeders interesting."

After lunch, Spoggs walked to the Washington Memorial Chapel to inform Hostis Dei that the slaughter was done. He pounded on the door. After eleven minutes, it opened. "What is it, Spoggs?" Hostis Dei was unaccustomed to daylight. Today the sun was hot and bright, forcing him to shield his eyes with his pale left hand like a salute, and squint.

"M' Lord, I am reporting that the weapon is mounted, and the first breeder you gifted to me is now working through the digestive tracks of thirty individuals, as you so ordered, m' Lord."

"I am familiar with Pre-Flood military ordnance, Spoggs. Have you ever operated a firearm of any kind?"

Searching old memories, Spoggs looked down at his leader's white-painted feet. He realized that these feet were bone white even before his house servants had painted them this morning. "Once as a boy, I fired a .22 rifle."

This met with hoarse laughter. "Then the answer is no, you have not fired a gun. If you were to fire the Browning M2A1 .50 caliber machine gun, Gabriel and his Elect would hear the explosions all these miles away. If you stand anywhere close by when firing the weapon you will lose your hearing without ear protection. I want you to drive the Browning back to where you found it: test-fire fifty rounds. Make certain the action works smoothly. Then oil every moving part. Wipe away the oil. Clean the bore using a brass or copper wire brush, and solvent. If you cannot find solvent use oil but wipe the inside clean after. Bring the weapon back and cover it.

If you let one drop of rain fall on it, I will be most displeased."

"Should I leave now m' Lord?"

He hesitated. "No, Spoggs. We have time. Do this tomorrow morning. Go now and take another breeder." He glanced down. "Do you have something for me?"

Spoggs nodded. From inside the leather pouch dangling from his left hand, he reached in and showed his master the bloody raw heart of Isabella Albo. "Thank you again, m' Lord. I am not worthy," he said, head bowed, and handed over the bag.

Spoggs hustled straight to the Breeder Pen to shop for his next house guest and found her in fewer than sixty seconds: he selected a pretty, thin, blue-eyed Caucasian barely into her teens with long blonde hair. *Irish,* he thought. *Maybe I can keep her alive for an hour and shatter all the records.*

At the same time as Spoggs Reichert dragged a young victim to his cabin nearly seven hundred miles north of the Trail hikers, hearts raced in pre-panic as Aliyah, Arabella, Booker, Dodie, and Jayden ran forward to join Marshall and Tatum up front. Marshall stood frozen in place with his hand up and finger pointing.

Booker and Jayden trained their eyes up along the direction of Marshall's finger. They saw a flat, high elevation rock ledge on Iron Mountain. Marshall judged it to be similar in square footage to the one he used as camp the prior night, although shaped differently. The mid-afternoon sun had warmed the air, but all three knew it would cool down fast in one or two hours.

Aliyah, Arabella, Dodie, and Tatum had followed Marshall, Booker, and Jayden halfway up the natural dirt drainage culvert until they stopped to rest, per Marshall's request, while the men continued up. Four women sat in silence awaiting word from the men who had reached the ledge high up.

"This'll do," whispered Marshall. "Let's stake out our spots with bedrolls and empty our knapsacks of everythin' 'cept water and weapons."

"Still want to hike to the Walmart this afternoon?" asked Jayden.

"Yessir," Marshall nodded. "Now, this map shows us all the best route is followin' TN-107. The problem y'all is that's a road. With roads come Golgoths."

"I'm up for it," said Jayden. He tapped his quiver of razor broadhead hunting arrows.

Marshall grinned. "Sure are. Love that about y'all. But Golgoths travel in packs. They call their groups 'colonies.' Fittin',' don't y'all think? Termites on two legs. We might juss git lucky and run across none. Or like y'all did, we all might-could encounter a small huntin' party. Then again, we might-could git very unlucky and run into a colony movin' north, same as us. In which case," he said, also tapping Jayden's arrow quiver, "y'all ain't got enough time to get us outta that scrape, unless y'all can fire two-three arrows with every reload."

Studying his road atlas Booker remained quiet. "Follow North Indian Creek: it's fed by smaller unnamed creeks, one of which runs right past Walmart. If you're able to walk along the banks, or in the creeks and streams…"

"Booker, great minds," Marshall said, and pulled out his own map. "Exactly what I had in mind. If we all start now and keep up a good pace we'll git there after dark. We'll find supplies, fill up our knapsacks, strap on them night vision thingies y'all described, and walk the road back to the Trail, then back up here to camp. Y'all, if we do this right we all gonna be back in our bunks by midnight."

Jayden nodded. "Sounds like a plan. What about Arabella? You did agree with her coming along to grab girly stuff, those wontons or whatever."

Marshall sighed like a bitter February wind through a grove of denuded oaks. "I only agreed to let Arabella come along 'cause Tatum begged me to. 'Sides, we don't know what them-there girlie things are or what else they might need, otherwise no way. And if we leave Arabella here with Booker, he might just cut out her hateful tongue and whip 'r with it."

Jayden snickered.

"That is a distinct possibility," muttered Booker.

"I'll git Arabella up here to empty 'r sack. Stay put, ya'll," Marshall said over his shoulder already on his way. Seven minutes later he again ascended the rock platform, this time with Arabella in tow. "Arabella, please find a spot 'n empty y'all's sack to fill it with new stuff that we'll distribute 'round."

"Fine," she said, complying.

"Okay then. Let's boogie-woogie," said Marshall.

When Marshall, Booker, Jayden, and Arabella hiked down the drainage culvert and rejoined Aliyah, Dodie, and Tatum midway down, Marshall took Tatum aside. "Take Aliyah and Dodie up to the ledge and make camp. Booker's gonna keep y'all safe. It'll get cold. Suggest y'all eat then jump right in them sacks. Stay warm. And please keep everyone quiet. I couldn't live with myself if anythin' happened to y'all while we're gone."

Tatum took his hand and squeezed it firmly. "Don't worry about us. Complete the mission, soldier. I know you will. Keep our God close."

No longer caring if anyone noticed, Marshall pressed a kiss to Tatum's forehead. "God never leaves me to face my perils alone, believe y'all me."

Marshall and Jayden, followed by Arabella, found North Indian Creek beetled in on both sides by thickly wooded understory far too dense and poison ivy-laden to navigate. For a moment, staring at the creek, Marshall and Jayden toyed with the idea of walking in the creek itself, but there were too many slimy river rocks of all sizes and shapes, and dark, deep pools along its length. All knew at least one of them would slip and get injured in the attempt; also it would be painfully slow going.

Jayden whispered the obvious. "Sorry, hoss. We need to risk TN-107. It's the only way. I have enough arrows, so no worries."

Marshall hesitated, then nodded. "But we do it my way. Not a whisper 'tween us. We stick to the shoulder of the road near the woods and keep our ears tuned like deer. If y'all hear a stick break somewhere; we dive into the woods and wait five minutes. The creek woulda' taken us four hours. Walkin' the road'll be quicker, but we budgeted four hours travel, and I don't care how much time we waste hidin' in them woods yonder. If we throw down with Golgoths more will come, guaranteed. War on the road ain't our mission. Are y'all crystal clear on this?"

Arabella nodded vigorously. Jayden gave a single nod.

As the hours wore on, the three became forced off the road three times as Marshall had described: the unmistakable cracks of dry sticks or branches made under someone or something's weight, coming from inside woods that flanked both sides of TN-107. A deer, a raccoon and a fox soon revealed themselves as harmless sources of sounds.

As the three walked west, the sinking sun and surrounding dark clouds appeared like a bucket of entrails emptied down a haunted well, dusky red and purple snakes of light. By the time they reached the Walmart in Unicoi, the entire sky had gone ebon black, and their skins crawled from electrified nerves. They walked more slowly, giving their eyes time to adjust. Bathed in cold, deceptive witchlight from constellations, along with gray and yellow from the buttery cue-ball moon rolling maverick across an obsidian sky, both Marshall and Jayden felt an eerie, novel sense of excitement deep in their guts.

They used their knapsacks to muffle the sound of breaking door glass. They listened and watched for potential Golgoths coming at them from outside. Jayden nocked an arrow. Marshall pouched a marble. There was neither movement nor sound. So all three climbed carefully through the jagged opening. The stench of mildew, mold, dust, and decay assaulted them.

Marshall held Booker's flashlight lens in his hand. Holding his breath, he thumbed it on. Arabella gasped.

Flash Deals

"Gunnery Sergeant Powell is comfortable in his new environment?" Gabriel asked Drake.

"Yes, oh yes, Gunny is wonderfully comfortable. It did not take him longer than a day to position and mount the three mortars," Drake replied. "I had to run interference to keep the entire Church away from him while he did his work. Everyone wants to know him."

Gabriel nodded. "None except for me and you eleven original Elect have experienced the company of someone advanced in age. Naturally, they are curious about aging, and the world before The Floods. Please give me a progress report."

Every member of the community knew not to disturb the meeting between Gabriel and Drake, yet nothing stopped thousands of Elect from gawking up at them as they stood together on the deck of Gabriel's two-story structure. Elect referred to the building as Gabriel's Tower, where he mostly remained alone in prayer, except for his public announcements and his New Testament readings which boomed every Sunday morning throughout the mountain via the original outdoor loudspeaker system. Otherwise, Drake functioned as his mouthpiece for all other information.

Drake paced as he spoke. "The main armaments and housing labor force is five-thousand strong, divided into six-man crews. Four-hundred-sixteen crews are erecting one hundred fully functional cabins per day. By the end of this month, we will have completed the last two thousand cabins empty and move-in ready for the last of the Elect pilgrims."

Gabriel nodded. "What of the tunnels?"

Two hundred and ten crews are excavating twenty-five hundred square feet of tunnels per day."

"What of the soil and rock?"

"From here you can see the earthwork berms growing along Spring Mount Road, but you can't see up in the woods, near the summit, and down below. Excavated rock and soil make a formidable barrier surrounding our perimeter, growing taller and steeper by the hour."

Gabriel nodded. "Are there sufficient weapons and shields?"

"One-hundred-ten crews of combined blacksmiths, textile craftspeople, and woodworkers, have stockpiled the armory with one-hundred-thirty thousand shields made from lightweight wood and covered with linen, held together with metal. As for the swords, the seven-foot-long javelins, the daggers, and the throwing axes, the same teams have completed one-hundred thousand of each," Drake said.

"What of the catapults?"

"Eighteen operational and tested. One-hundred-ten crews are finding the work moves more quickly now that they have the manufacturing processes committed to muscle memory. We will have thirty catapults in three lines of ten, at the three-hundred, one-hundred-eighty, and one-hundred-twenty-foot lines in all directions."

"Firebombs?"

"We fired six-hundred earthen jars in the kilns, sealed except for fill holes ready for cork fuses, thirty-two inches high and twenty inches in diameter, each with nine-gallon capacity. We repurposed two large copper tanks we found in the ruins of a nearby microbrewery to mix diesel fuel with salvaged Styrofoam packing material and created all the napalm needed to fill every jar and then some. Consider that task completed."

"Have them make two hundred more," said Gabriel. He watched Drake struggle to refrain from showing emotion. "Ah. You believe my preparations are extravagant."

"Never. Not once have I ever questioned your wisdom. I have heard from our spies that our fighting men will not equal Golgoth numbers even after the last of our pilgrims arrive and settle in. There will be at least fifteen thousand more of them than there are of us."

Gabriel closed his eyes and pressed his lips together. "Your eyes see only what they see, Drake. A lifetime ago before I received the Holy Spirit giving me glimpses into the future, like you, I only saw what was right in front of me, in the here and now. Oh how simple life was for me as a child. I would wish to become childlike again, but not yet. Not yet. In times like these it would be foolish of me to pray for such luxuries."

Drake's face melted. Knees trembled. "May our merciful God and his Son, Jesus, forgive my questioning spirit. Cursed be mine eyes, Gabriel."

Gabriel rose, standing a foot taller than Drake. Yellow hair hung low around his face like an energy aura. He pressed his hands against Drake's shoulders. He smiled and kissed both of Drake's darkly bearded cheeks. "God has chosen you, Drake. His love for you is endless, as is mine. Your work pleases him. After all Elect have had the chance to question Gunny about what life was like in the Pre-Flood world, this day and time next week, please bring him up here that I may speak with him."

"Thank you, Gabriel," Drake said. Turning on his heels, Drake went back inside and down the stairs. His meeting in Gabriel's Tower dominated his thoughts even through dinner. As several crew foremen jockeyed for his attention throughout the meal, feeling somewhat overwhelmed, Drake excused himself and took a walk through the covered bridge. Along the way, young Elect and their children waved to him, though he failed to notice. Tonight, he stared at the ground before him as he walked.

The battle with Hostis Dei and his Golgoth hoard had changed from a possibility to a certainty. Gabriel, characteristically cryptic who often spoke in figures, in metaphor, and in parables had, knowingly or unknowingly, revealed the future. *Gabriel wanted powerful mortars and now he wants two hundred more immolation bombs. Now we know what becomes of our peaceful community.*

Over seven hundred miles south of the Elect, in Greeneville, Tennessee, Marshall, Jayden, and Arabella surveyed the chaotic rubble in shadow ahead. Water from the two Floods had relocated every object in the Walmart Supercenter that had not been securely fixed, along with those that had been securely fixed. The square footage was daunting. Each felt defeated because there was no conceivable way this mission would require less than a full night and a full day.

Marshall whispered, "One hour inside this here Walmart. If we can't find what we're lookin' for then God didn't mean for us all to have it. Arabella, only y'all can find what the ladies need. Jayden and I know what we're after. Come with us. We'll try to find them night goggle thingies or another one of these," he said, flicking his gaze down to Booker's flashlight— "or a butane lighter. The minute we find one 'a these tools to see our way around inside this tomb, we split up; y'all go your way, me and Jayden will head to the back, like Booker and Jayden had said." Marshall saw Arabella nod.

Getting to the rear of the building proved difficult. Piles of steel shelving and formidable entanglements of bicycles to climb over, under, around, or quietly pick their way through, within a one-hour self-imposed time limit, sustained the gnawing feeling that this was proving to be a long side trip for nothing. Arabella's foot unknowingly connected with a soccer ball, which sent it jouncing in front of them. "It's okay to talk now," said Marshall. "We're far enough away from the doors."

"We are in the sporting goods section," said Jayden. "I think it would be okay for you to shine that beam around unless Golgoths can see through mountains of opaque steel. Just keep the light pointed at the floor."

Removing his hand, Marshall did exactly that. "Ain't got a clue what we're lookin' for."

"You know what binoculars look like, don't you?" asked Jayden.

"No," said Marshall. Looking at Marshall, Arabella made a condescending sound.

"Great," said Jayden. Marshall shone the beam around while Jayden reached down and began pulling up shelving to expose fallen objects underneath. "Look! I've found bows, arrows, and slingshots!" Jayden levered aside the length of shelving with significant effort. Finding the weapons infused him with renewed vigor. He quickly made a pile of bows and arrows. He added all thirty translucent plastic boxes of the thousand-count three-eighths steel ball slingshot ammo balls for Marshall. Jayden smirked.

"Excellent haul!" said Marshall.

"Arabella, please follow us with the light beam," Jayden said, and handed it to her.

"Look at what I found just lying loose on the ground," Jayden said. He stood up holding a pack of Bic lighters which he promptly pocketed.

Working together, Jayden and Marshall cleared section after section of shelving. "Well looky-there, Jayden! Darned if that don't look just like Booker's portable bottle-top propane campin' stove with an adjustable burner right beside little propane bottles. I don't know if we all gonna find night vision goggles or pom-poms, but lighters, ammo, and this here itty-bitty smokeless stove are gonna save our bacon on this journey. Score!"

"Not pom-poms: tampons, Marshall. Genius," she muttered under her breath.

"Whatever," he said. "Oh, we need this, too, to wrap around the stove for cookin.'"

Jayden examined the plastic tarp Marshall was holding. "Polyethylene is combustible. Can't use it."

"Sorry, what?" asked Marshall.

"We can't use this. It might work but it's not safe. Unless you want to risk yourself going up in flames right along with the meal while cooking, then we need to find a heavy-duty canvas drop cloth."

"Yikes. Okay." Searching, Marshall found and grabbed five, nine-by-twelve canvas cloths each sealed in its own thick plastic bag. He stuffed these against the bottom of his knapsack. He also grabbed and packed one-hundred feet of black paracord and eight folding knives.

Knowing that he was in the right area of the Walmart and determined to find night vision goggles, Jayden recruited Marshall to help excavate the shelving. Finally, they hit upon something. "These are binoculars. During the day, I'll show you how useful they are. Right now, for the long walk back to camp we need night vision. Okay, next shelf oughta do it."

Not the next shelf, or the next…but then underneath the seventh shelf, longsuffering patience nearly gone, the allotted hour ticking fast to a close, they found an enormous variety of different boxes each marked 'Night Vision.'

"Back in Pre-Flood days people exchanged currency for things," said Arabella. "Typically, the higher the price the better the quality, if that's any help."

Jayden found the box with the most numbers on the price tag. He opened it. In the battery compartment he found batteries marked lithium-AA rechargeable. "Marshall, I know Booker has a charger for his flashlight. I'm going to try on these goggles and see if they work. Regular batteries would've leaked acid and ruined it by now, but these lithium things look brand spankin' new to me. We still need solar chargers for the night vision goggle batteries. Keep looking."

Jayden found the on-off switch on the night vision goggles and the head strap in the box. He put it on his head and flipped the switch. "This thing is from another world! Hey, turn away the flashlight beam, Arabella, you're blinding me. This is unreal!"

"Well, I'll be a Jim Dandy. Hey Jayden," said Marshall, "I found a solar-powered battery charger!"

"Actually, hoss, we need eight: one for each of us plus a spare."

"Two-four-six… I got eight," said Marshall.

"Fantastic! Take the goggles, Arabella," said Jayden. He removed the goggles from his head and handed them to her. "Use these and go find your crampons."

"Tampons!"

"So you say. Now's your chance." Jayden reached into his back pocket, freed one of the Bic lighters, and thumbed it on.

"Ouch, the flame hurts my eyes!" shrieked Arabella. She turned and started walking. "These goggle things work great! It's like green daylight!"

"Careful where y'all step," said Marshall. "And be quiet! Women's stuff might be up front close to the door. Only use goggles. Don't y'all use a lighter so close to the glass."

Marshall unboxed then filled his knapsack with the bottle-top propane camp stove with two spare fuel tanks, four of the unboxed night vision goggles, and all thirty boxes of slingshot ammo balls. He hoisted the pack up onto his shoulders with a groan."

"Heavy?" asked Jayden.

"Full as a tick. Ain't much lookin' forward to a four-hour walk with the equivalent of an adult female on my back."

Jayden grinned. "I'm sure you'd much rather carry Tatum home on your back than that sack of stuff, friend."

Marshall grinned. "That obvious?"

"Oh yeah."

"Y'all and Dodie seem to be fast friends."

"She's a real bee charmer, that one." First Jayden looked for and found a length of fishing line. "Hold the lighter for me a sec," Jayden said. He used this to neatly tie together seven bows and an impossibly large bundle of arrows. Using more line he affixed the load of bows and razor head arrows to his knapsack frame.

"Hey Jayden, might that be fishin' tackle in y'all's hands?"

"Yep."

"Where'd you find it?"

He pointed. Using a lighter, Marshall followed Jayden's finger and found hooks and light line. He returned quickly. "This is fantastic! Eatin' birds and animals gets stale after a while. It'll be good to mix up the menu a bit."

Jayden unboxed the remaining four night-vision devices and seven hunting slingshots. He stuffed these into his bag along with flat plastic envelopes containing spooled bow strings. Next went the solar-powered charger. He still had room inside the knapsack; it still felt light when he hefted it. "Marshall, hand me a propane bottle and half the steel ammo boxes."

"Did I say cain't never could? I can handle it."

Jayden smiled. "I know you can, big gorilla. Teamwork makes the dream work. Let's lighten your load a little, spread it around. I'm sure Arabella will fill her knapsack. Also, do you have a whetstone and oil?"

"Back at the ledge, I do."

"Okay then I won't look for one. It would only add more weight," said Jayden.

Marshall complied, handing over one of the two spare propane bottles. "Speakin' 'a wet hens, it's been half an hour since we all seen Arabella. Gotta find her. She got brains scarce as hen's teeth. Oh wait— almost forgot," Marshall said. "Hold the lighter." He attached straps to the two unboxed goggles. "We gonna need these. Hope the batteries hold out for eight hours."

"Thanks," said Jayden. "If they don't, we'll use up the partially charged batteries in all the others and recharge 'em all tomorrow." Jayden adjusted the goggles onto Marshall's head for him. As Marshall fumbled around for a switch, Jayden grabbed Marshall's thumb and guided it to the switch.

"Well tie my face to the side of a hog and roll me in the mud—ain't this groovy! I can see! I mean yeah sure, everythins' green, but I can see! Bless Booker's French-speakin' heart: these things are dynamite!"

"Right? Pretty amazing. Okay let's find the Red Lady Antebellum, then roll. Mustn't keep the ladies waiting. Rumor has it, Dodie and Tatum require additional body heat round about now."

Marshall snickered. "Sinner. Y'all got a one-track mind. Which reminds me; hold up a sec."

Marshall dropped to one knee. "Heavenly Father, we thank y'all for this bounty tonight. Please watch over my new friends, protect 'em, keep 'em from harm, and give 'em y'all's Holy Spirit without measure, as y'all do for me. In the name of y'all's Son, Jesus, we pray, amen."

"Amen," said Jayden.

It wasn't difficult to find Arabella. She had abandoned her night vision apparatus which now hung against her bosom like the world's largest medallion. She used a lighter she had found as a torch, which also made her visible from the doors.

Marshall, though lugging far more weight than Jayden, scrambled over rubble speed bumps so quickly that Jayden could barely keep up. The flame seemed as bright as the sun through the goggles. Marshall faced her. "What are y'all doin, Arabella?" he said, stripping off his goggles to make eye contact. "The flame y'all's holdin' up high can be seen for miles around."

"Marshall, earlier you had said, 'Use a flashlight or a butane lighter; and as soon as we find either one we split up, you go your way'—or did you forget?"

"Y'all left us back there wearin' goggles. A lighter near the windows ain't followin' directions, which y'all agreed to do back on the mountain, under the condition I would leave y'all for the Golgoths—big important promises often slip that steel-trap mind?"

"Sorrrr-eeeee. You should give clearer directions instead of contradicting yourself, big-bad leader."

Marshall glowered down at her. "I outta jerk y'all bald," he said.

"C'mon guys. Did you get what you came for?" Jayden asked her.

"Mm hmm, yes," she said.

"Marshall, we have a long walk back. What say we strap on our goggles and make short work of the TN-107?" Jayden said. He strapped his on and faced the door.

"Let's go," said Marshall, his tone and body language broadcasting maximum irritation. Jayden led the way. Marshall spotted something, a small box. Furtively he picked it up, reached over his shoulder and secreted it into his already stuffed knapsack.

Marshall followed Jayden through the jagged glass hold of the door they had smashed fifty-six minutes earlier. All three stood outside surveying. "Arabella, walk straight ahead fifty paces," said Jayden.

"What am I, the bait?"

"Just walk," said Jayden. "We need to field-test the goggles outside to see how close we need to get to others before we spot them. And please keep your voice down. Whisper only. Once we start walking, make no sounds at all. Go."

They watched her walk about one hundred yards, stop, and turn to face the two. She gave Marshall and Jayden a 'what's up' gesture with her arms and head tilt.

"I can see her clearly as if in daylight. At night, we would spot them long before we get in their sightlines," whispered Jayden. "During daylight, we and they have an equal opportunity to see each other simultaneously. At night, with these, we'll have the clear edge."

"Damn. Booker is one heck of a smart kid, turnin' us on to these goggles. If we wear these on the night trail while Golgoths are at rest, we can make fewer stops and better time; walk with impunity all night; and sleep hidden away on rock ledges by day when them damned, white-painted cannibal freaks are easiest to spot."

"Easier to spot, and easier to perforate with these, I think you meant to say," whispered Jayden, tapping the thick arrow bundle tied behind and below his waist. "I like it."

"Okay then," whispered Marshall. "Let's grab Arabella and be on our merry way."

Arabella's knapsack filled with tampons weighed little more than it did empty, yet as the miles wore on she continually fell behind the two.

Arabella Pendleman did not think much about her deeply ingrained racism. A direct descendant of slave plantation owners who grew cotton in Georgia, she still resented her father for rescuing Aliyah, along with Dodie and Tatum. Grady Pendleman had passed down the family disdain for Black people. She asked him why he thought to bring Aliyah into their home. He laughed and told young Arabella not to worry. *Blackies have their uses*, he had responded. Hate, especially racial hate was to her simply another part of the peripheral nervous system, no different from all other autonomic nervous system controls she took for granted, like breathing, digestion, sweating, and shivering.

Growing up with Aliyah had developed into a complex relationship. Arabella had tolerated Aliyah's presence, provided she knew her place in the Pendleman caste system. There would be no dining together and no friendship. Every interaction with the family had to be strictly business, relevant to maintaining the harmony of their own mini plantation resort. Aliyah knew the game well and had consented to play it. Dodie bonded with Aliyah through their mutual love of Christ, and Bible readings. Dodie had become more of a true sister to Aliyah than a best friend and close confidant; Dodie regularly reasoned Aliyah out of the most bitter and resentful episodes, bolstering her strength in the Lord, helping to foster her love and forgiveness— even for Arabella.

I hate you, Marshall, Arabella thought, struggling to keep up. She found it difficult to think and walk at the same time.

I hate negroes and hate your phony God for making them. I never should have left the resort. Comfort and security are all gone, my world is upside down; everything has changed. Booker that little Bama booger challenged me; he believes, actually believes that he's better than me, cleverer; speaking that French bullshit like he's some kind of intellectual. Con-man coon. And now Aliyah's taking orders from him. Little bitch-coon thought she was hiding her hate from me…hiding behind that religious mumbo-jumbo, Christ's love, blah-blah. I saw the hate in her beady little coon eyes. And Booker? Uppity little stain said he'd personally deliver me to the Golgoths if I ever make another racist comment. Aliyah and Booker, black devils.

Forced into a light jog to prevent Marshall and Jayden from widening the gap from her, she smirked while pondering the other objects she had found in the women's section and secretly slipped into pockets.

Cold Bodies

Marshall turned back to make sure Arabella had not fallen too far behind. Jayden suddenly stopped. "See somethin?"" Marshall whispered.

"Yeah, a deer. This area is lousy with 'em," Jayden whispered back.

"Mm mm mm, deer are tasty. You like rabbit?" Marshall asked.

"Never had it. At this point I'd eat a vulture's asshole. You hungry?" Jayden asked.

"Starvin' like Marvin. I could eat a bag 'a maggots," said Marshall "Bring anything?"

"Emptied my bag back at the ledge 'cept for a few waters," whispered Marshall. "While we wait for pokey Arabella to catch up with us, quick, eat this. I can't guarantee it's still edible, but I only found two," he said, and handed Jayden a plastic-wrapped piece of beef jerky. "Quick let's wolf 'em down before she catches up and asks why we didn't share." They tore open the plastic coverings and quickly chewed the two leathery strips.

"So this Walmart got swamped in the First Flood, making this jerky forty years old or more. Not bad for forty-year-old cow," Jayden whispered.

"Felt like I just ate Solomon's sandal, but it hit the spot," Marshall replied. "Pocket the plastic wrappers. Leave no trace for Golgoths to find. They also track us by scent. I swear them things ain't fully human."

"No, man. They aren't. Part devil for sure. Biggest part of 'em was created below."

They stood quietly until Arabella got within twenty feet of them, then started walking again. Over the next three hours they paused only twice more before they intersected with the Appalachian Trail. Marshall stopped and saw a speck three quarters of a mile back moving toward them. "We'd better wait up for her. She might walk right past the Trail."

Ten minutes later, Arabella caught up. Glancing back to be certain she had seen them do it, Marshall and Jayden stepped off the paved road onto the rougher earth. The packs on their backs felt like mountains. Every joint, muscle, tendon, and sinew ached and throbbed. Jayden whispered, "Quick, let's get this side trek over with."

Marshall needed no convincing. Mustering every remaining ounce of energy, his long legs set a faster new pace. To keep up, Jayden used reserves he never knew he had. As they rounded a bend, Marshall slowed to a plod. Then he stopped.

Marshall's whirling brain struggled to compute the scene of death splayed out before him, made spookier by the eerie green night vision light.

Fear prickled Jayden's scalp. The three animals were so mangled that only his intuition suggested they had once been deer. Gut piles and intestines were carelessly strewn about.

Arabella caught up. Loud enough to momentarily distract the others, she gulped in a shocked breath; she gagged in her mouth and swallowed it.

Carefully avoiding deer innards, Marshall advanced slowly. He bent down. Using both hands, he grasped ribs and flipped a deer over from its left side to its right, searching for clues that only an experienced hunter would spot. He did the same with the next deer, and the third. He motioned for the two to follow him. They did.

Around the next curve they saw seven more eviscerated deer. The next fifty yards presented even more death. *Spring Mountain never seemed farther away*, he thought. *Spear and knife marks on bone. Golgoths done discovered the Trail.*

Jayden maintained two steps behind. Arabella fell close behind him. Jayden had never watched Marshall unwilling to disturb a branch or risk crunching old fallen leaves step so lightly on the Trail. Jayden imitated him, stealthy footfall for footfall. To their surprise, Arabella did the same. They picked their way forward until eventually they came to the drainage culvert leading back up to the ledge and to their friends. Marshall stopped. The two flanked him.

"Spears. That's how Golgoths hunted the deer. Them devils may or may not think humans use this Trail; ain't possible to say, but we all been leavin' breadcrumbs: we done left footprints and broken branches for miles. Y'all, this is just like the bed-time story 'a Hansel and Gretel who left real breadcrumbs so they could find their way home in the forest."

"I have never heard of Hansel and Gretel and their trail of breadcrumbs," said Arabella.

"Now y'all can bet Golgoths know that people are usin' the Trail." Marshall looked up and pointed to the trees above them. "Golgoths hid in them trees. They staked out a section 'a Trail during daylight, then hurled spears at the deer. Knowin' deer primally fear the smell 'a blood or decayin' meat the Golgoths moved downwind. They slayed the next herd, then moved again. They slaughtered as many as they saw. After killin' the deer they gutted 'em and sliced 'em up for food. They also took brains, eyes, and tongues. Then they dragged the meat to their campfires for cookin.' Since we ain't smelled fires so far: I think these Golgoths must be a-ways off. Now we all know that when Golgoths run low on people caught out in the open, they'll hunt animals on the Appalachian Trail."

"Marshall. I counted forty-two dead deer. How big was their hunting party?" asked Jayden.

Marshall hesitated. "At least twenty or more. Prolly' more if we count them spears I saw stuck high up in trees where they missed the deer."

"Not good, hoss," said Jayden. "At least to my way of thinking: this Trail is a trap. "If we're stuck with this Trail, for sure we walk at night from now on. I will only walk at night."

Marshall nodded. "Huntin' party weren't there this mornin' or when we left which was middle afternoon, else we woulda' run into 'em," said

Marshall. All three fought against full-length spine shivers thinking about how close they had come to a cannibal hunting party which far outnumbered them.

"They came up the trail just after. I'm surprised we didn't cross 'em tonight walkin' on the road. Musta' just missed 'em," said Marshall. "Guess is, they passed by while we all were in the Walmart. So now we know: Golgoths hunt in the afternoon. Which means that we all need to do our huntin' and meal prep strictly in the mornins' then settle down and sleep during daylight. We wake near sunset; eat cold leftovers: pack up, and then walk in darkness."

Jayden gave two thumbs up. "Rest by day high up at inconvenient elevations, like we've done. Golgoths are not stupid."

"No," said Marshall, "they ain't: but I can tell you they are lazy hunters. They lie in wait for food to come to them. Not like me. I track my food or cast lines into streams and rivers 'til I catch a fish. Sometimes I noodle."

"Say what?" asked Jayden.

"Noodle. I'll reach 'round down just under water level along river and stream beds, feelin' 'round for big old channel cats—I mean catfish. I shove my hand down their throats and pull 'em out. Really good eatin,' catfish. Anyway, as we were sayin' if we make ourselves scarce like we been doin' high up them drainage culverts on ledges, Golgoths ain't gonna burn the energy to barefoot hike up them tough grades."

Jayden nodded. "That theory makes sense if we're sure not to break branches and leave clues on our hikes up culverts, because compared to you they might be lazy trackers, but they are excellent trackers, hoss. When do we tell the others?"

"Tomorrow, Jayden. Let's get up to the ledge. And Arabella: don't y'all say a damned word to 'em tonight. Me and Jayden'll do all the talkin' in the mornin.' If they all 'r asleep up there don't wake 'em up. Read it back to me."

"You and Jayden will do all the talking in the morning, Marshall."

The steep climb up the natural drainage depression depleted them completely. The three teetered over the ledge lip onto flat rock, Marshall first, then Jayden, and finally Arabella. Jayden and Marshall only made it three feet in then sat down hard, too exhausted to wriggle out from their knapsack straightjackets. Strapped into their backpacks, listening to the slow, quiet breathing of Aliyah and Tatum, Jayden and Marshall sat like that for ten minutes. Both Booker and Dodie were snoring. Amused despite his body's discomfort, Marshall thought, *Dodie, the tiniest little ferret 'a the bunch snores like an old man sawin' wood.*

Marshall worked himself out of the backpack, grabbed a water bottle from a pocket, and left it where he had dropped it. He took the day's final pull of water and swished it around his mouth. Still tasting the petrified beef jerky he wished dearly that he could brush his teeth. He found his bedroll, removed his boots and goggles, and zipped into his sleeping bag. Arabella and Jayden watched him groggily. They decided that if Marshall could muster the energy to find his bedroll, remove his boots and goggles, and zip himself into his sleeping bag, so could they. And they did.

As he did every day, Marshall awoke to dawn, the best time of day to hunt, facing an eastern sky painted a delicate rose color, hazy thoughts still colored by the most detailed dream yet of Spring Mountain. Birdsong served as his back-up alarm clock. He had fallen asleep on his right side. When he tried to turn over, pain, stiffness, and uncomfortable tingling jolted him fully awake. Slowly he managed to roll over.

His gaze fell upon Tatum. *God. She's even more beautiful asleep than awake*, he thought, seizing the chance to commit every contour of her face to memory. He could not help but compare her to his common-law-wife, Delilah, who rejected his God, murdered his baby, and pushed him out of the only home he had ever known, LeConte Lodge, his happy place. *No comparison. Completely different women. This one's spirit is kind, and her mind is open. Truth be told, lookin' at her arouses a longin' in me far more powerful than Delilah ever did.*

Scanning around, he saw no one else awake. Freed from his sleeping cocoon, he inhaled deeply of the chilly morning air. *Mid-fifties*, he guessed. Quietly he slipped on his pants; pulled on his sweatshirt; laced up his boots; and tip-toed to his knapsack. Reaching inside it, he grabbed his slingshot and emptied one translucent plastic box of steel ammo balls into his right pocket. *I won't need this many…not unless I'm wrong about Golgoths bein' far away sleepin' off last night's glut 'a venison.* With one final glance back at Tatum and the others, he disappeared silently over the lip of the ledge to go kill breakfast.

Down now, he stood on the Trail imagining the hunt. He reversed direction heading south, back to a grove they had passed yesterday. Walking left, he arrived at the white oak grove and clearing he had scoped out yesterday. Listening, he glided quietly into the grove. He saw acorns, old and decayed acorns from last fall or winter, and fresh ones. *How did the squirrels miss those? Edible but not very tasty to people. But a banquet for wild turkeys.*

Fresh droppings informed him that big, yummy birds had just spent the night in these trees. Wincing at the stiffness in his lumbar spine: he bent over, untied his boots, then tied the laces of both boots together into a makeshift pole-climber. Hugging the impossibly fat trunk of the tree next to where the birds gathered, he leaped up and slammed down the lace hard against the rough tree bark. Pulling with his arms, pushing down against the field-rigged bootlace pole-climber, he made it up nine feet to the lowest branch, thick enough to support his weight and disappear from view. Reaching into his right pocket he freed a steel ball. From his left hand dangled the slingshot. *Nothin' to do now but listen and wait*, he thought. He used the quiet time to untie and properly retie his boot laces for when it was time to pounce, a simple task he found exceedingly challenging while hugging a branch and grasping his weapon.

From a distance he heard a gobbler. *Could be a tom, could be a jake.* He had hunted them before and recognized sounds made by males of the species, different from females. *Sounds carry. They'll be hungry for breakfast. A rafter of gobblers. If nothin' happens here in the next fifteen minutes, I'll come find y'all.*

Then he heard the distinctive clucks, chirps, and whistles of a relaxed, happy hen. *Goll darned close. Fifty feet, maybe?* He steeled himself. In the past he had heard a hen's yelp, which she used to warn toms and jakes of a nearby predator. Yelps would mean the jig was up; that his quarry were now aware of his threatening presence and would escape. *If little miss turkey senses me, the entire rafter will escape and none of us gonna eat.* He tried pulling back on the slingshot. *Be lucky to sink one ball into one bird from this crazy position.*

The unwary whistling and turkey song grew louder. Then he saw her searching for the proper sized breakfast acorn with her big black ostrich-like eyes. He judged her weight to be fifteen pounds. *Fat, toothless, and ugly: which is just how I like my hens*, he thought jokingly. Silently he pulled back as far as he could on the leather slingshot pouch. *If the shot don't reach 'er, I'll jump down and finish 'r by hand.*

He had mastered the slingshot as a boy. Now that he was a man, aiming the lethal weapon felt like second nature. He rarely missed his target: he shot best when the bird or animal was moving, flying, or running. The hen walked slowly, so close now that her feet crunched old leaves. His hyper-sensitized hunting-mode brain picked up every nuanced sound of her. *Aim for center mass and thump 'er heart.* He released the shot: it found its target as a tuft of breast feathers detonated like a puff of smoke. He heard a distinct yelp of panic as he watched the bird flop about. He dropped his slingshot and slipped off the branch which had served him well as a hunter's stand.

He reached into his pocket for his lock-blade knife. In four long running strides he covered the distance to the wounded hen. He crushed his boot down onto the oscillating neck. Rather than suffocate the hen, he squatted down and humanely severed its head. He wiped the bloody blade clean on moss; pocketed the knife; and grabbed its legs. He walked back and picked up the slingshot. *Wish I had time to hang the bird and age it. So much tastier that way. But oh well. Thank y'all, Lord, for today's meal.*

He stopped before the culvert which led up to his fellow hikers. He plucked and gutted the turkey just off the Trail side, then kicked leaves and branches over the entrails and feathers. He ascended hundreds of feet until he crested the rock ledge. He flopped down the bird and looked around. *Still sleepin.' Oh well.*

As quietly as possible, he set up the new camp stove against the ledge's eastern rock wall. Using the lengths of paracord, he created a canvas tarp lean-to covering the stove by affixing rope ends to scrub plants growing out of the rock face. He weighted down more lengths with loose, heavy stones and tied the sides closed, hemming in the stove completely like a tent. He slipped over the ledge again and returned with long sticks he had trimmed with his camp saw to equal lengths. Back inside the lean-to, he used a bit of paracord to bind the sticks together at a point over the stove, a small teepee frame. From the teepee's apex, he lashed the feet so that the bird's mass now dangled a foot above the burner. He turned the gas knob until he heard the hissing of the propane, then used a Bic to ignite the burner. It went up in flames with a whoomph! He nodded at his morning's work. He sealed the bird inside his makeshift oven.

While waiting for breakfast to roast, which would take all morning, he decided to hike to North Indian Creek for fresh water and a wash-up. He pocketed his toothbrush, toothpaste, and soap bar. He grabbed an empty water bottle. When he came to the rotting deer, across his eyes flashed a mental image of Tatum and the others screaming in panic at the gruesome charnel, too frozen with fear of Golgoths to proceed. He set to work dragging one ripe carcass after another to the right-side drop, where he hurled them down out of sight. Using a sturdy stick as a shovel, he hockey-shotted the gut piles and fly-covered intestines over the same drop-off, one after another. He watched them slither down into the poison ivy and understory growth like absurd blue-red anacondas.

At the stream, he stripped and waded in. He yelped at the bracing cold. Finding a suitably flat submerged rock, he sat and soaped his body head to toe. He moved upstream a little to refill his water bottle and brush his teeth. *Ahh, much better*, he thought, licking his clean teeth. Using the soap bar, he then scrubbed his socks and underwear clean. Back on the bank, he put on his pants and boots. Bottle in his left hand, wet underclothes in his right, he walked back, appraising his former trail clearing work. *Blood and soil have become one. Jayden'll keep quiet 'bout us seein' all them butchered deer last night, and so Tatum and the others won't know what they're steppin' on 'less Arabella opens her big fat trap.*

On his ascent up the culvert, he looked around and saw more culverts leading up to other ledges. He thought about the decision at which he and Jayden had arrived last night, after carefully reasoning it through, to only walk at night from now on. *How's everyone gonna feel 'bout tryin' to sleep as a group durin' the day? They gonna wanna talk. Everyone's gettin' acquainted, pairin' up, discoverin' each other. Nobody'll be able to nap. The night hike gonna feel like the Bataan Death March. We' all gonna be sleep-walkin.' Dead tired. Walkin' tired ain't safe. That's how accidents happen.*

He reascended to the ledge and saw Booker sitting up. He stretched and yawned.

"What smells so good?" Booker asked.

"Fresh roasted turkey."

Booker's eyes flew open. "Serious? Hot-diggity! Every twenty-fourth of November my folks would open cans of turkey and gravy and cranberry sauce. Oh yeah, and they'd whip some hot water into boxed taters. So good! We gave thanks to God for our food, for our lives, and for each other. 'Thanksgiving,' they called it. This'll magically transport my icy cold heart back to happier times. Respectable job, killer!"

Marshall grinned. "Aw shucks."

"But hey," said Booker, "if I can smell it, can't the Golgoths?"

Now everyone was awake.

Infectious

Marshall stood with his back to the rock wall. He closed his eyes and prayed in silence. *Father in Heaven, please give me y'all's Spirit. Gimme the strength to complete y'all's mission. In the name of Jesus, I pray. Amen.* He opened his eyes and briefly made eye contact with all. Finally, he spoke.

"We all 'r headin' to a new permanent residence, to join up with God's Church. Last night in my dreams, I saw the Mountain of Springs. I saw purty new log cabins awaitin' us and felt love all around. But I felt somethin' else, too."

"Me too!" said Tatum. She leapt up. "I saw the cabins! And I saw crazy catapult thingies, like big wooden slingshots."

"Saw 'em too, hoss," said Jayden. "Catapults."

"Trebuchets, they're called, and yes. I saw them too," said Booker. "I also saw a room filled with cutting and stabbing weapons."

Marshall held out both palms. "I got no doubt that we all had a similar dream last night. Like the dreams that brought us together. God's Holy Spirit at work in us."

"I didn't," said Arabella. The others stared at her as they would a drowned rat floating dead in their swimming pool.

"We all got us a crazy long ways to go into an uncertain future," said Marshall. "A future requirin' some bigtime violence before it settles down. 'Course these visions might-could be showin' us that God's Church is buildin' up defenses against Golgoths that ain't never gonna see action." Marshall tried not to let feelings of doubt bleed through. "Though for certain I understand if any 'a y'all wanna turn back. Decide now. I'll pack y'all's bags with enough food and water to make it back to whatever safe havens got left behind, and I'll pray day and night for y'all's safety."

Tatum walked over to stand beside Marshall. She flicked her eyes at each person. She looped her arm inside his. "I'm with him."

"Me too," said Booker. "Whatever is happening up on that mountain is real. Each of us lived content in our bubbles of unreality, thinking we could live safe from Golgoths, prolonging the inevitable. Everybody dies, that's a fact. There's a giant boulder balanced over every head I see, including mine. It's not a question of if those boulders will fall on us and crush us, only a matter of when and where. If a Golgoth kills me then let it be in hot battle, if that's what God's Church is prepping for."

"Amen," said Jayden. "Better than waiting around for them to ambush me someplace."

"Cheery," muttered Arabella.

"Amen," said Marshall. "We all could stay in our wombs waitin' to die alone, livin,' and dyin' for nothin'. Or get born to where things are happenin,' where we can live and die surrounded by love for somethin' real.

And them defenses we saw in dreams are just to psyche out the Golgoths; peace through strength. They ain't never gonna be a battle. Maybe."

Aliyah and Dodie, never taking their eyes off Marshall, nodded. He looked then at Jayden, who gave him the thumbs-up. Finally, his gaze fell upon Arabella. She stared at him blankly.

"I had a different dream," she said, "so Marshall you're wrong about us all having the same dreams. This means you could be completely off track about everything: like walking during the day. You thought that was a clever idea. Then last night we had to step through a slaughter scene."

"What? Marshall, what is Miss Congeniality even talking about?" asked Booker.

"What's congeniality?" said Arabella.

Marshall shot her the death stare. She stood, defiantly. Marshall turned to Booker. "Last night we found slaughtered deer remains on a section of Trail slightly north of us. I went there this mornin' and cleaned it up."

"Okay. But what does it mean?" Booker pressed.

"It's a sign, Booker! The Holy Spirit has revealed to us the Golgoth pattern," said Marshall. "By day they hunt humans along roadways; we all seen 'em. And look what happened to y'all's parents before dark. We all knowed 'em to hunt people only at night, right? Now we know they also hunt trails for wild game. Which for us means, I need to hunt in the mornin,'" he said, pointing to his roasting tent. "This works out good because mornins' are when game critters take the biggest chances 'cause that's when they are hungriest. Same with fishies. So from now on we gonna eat breakfast, then sleep durin' daylight hours. After a quiet dinner and when the sun is down, and while the enemy are restin' far from the Trail, usin' night vision gadgets we will walk. Arabella, y'all seem happier than a dead pig in the sunshine, so you can go do whatever suits your fancy."

Arabella sniffed. "My dad used to say that. You just told me I'm blissfully ignorant."

Marshall gave her a cold-eyed stare. "Y'all ain't never could do nothin,'" he muttered.

Booker nodded. "Your plan makes sense."

"Last evenin' in Unicoi at that Walmart place, me 'n Jayden sourced everythin' needed. Everyone gets a pair 'a night vision goggles and a solar charger. I will hand those out shortly. Don't lose 'em or break em, or y'all gonna hafta' follow the person in front real close, like holdin' on to their shirttail. Won't be easy for either of y'all 'n it'll slow us all down. So keep them goggles charged. They really work. Thanks again Booker for turnin' us all onto night vision. Y'all just buttered our corn, good buddy."

Everyone looked at Booker. He blushed and nodded.

"We're all rested," said Marshall. "I sure as heck can't get myself back to sleep right now with y'all movin' 'round makin' noise, sunlight penetratin' my lids. No way." As the words left his mouth, stemming from the plan formed by his heart and in his mind, he experienced a massive internal gut-punch of guilt. *Ignore the Holy Spirit at y'all's own peril.* Glancing at Tatum, this thought he bulldozed aside.

"You're right, Marshall," said Booker. "Which is another reason I suggested you grab cloth tarps. I assume you got enough for everybody?"

"Man, it's like you can see the future. Are you a prophet too like our blond-headed friend up there on Spring Mountain?" said Jayden.

Booker grinned.

"He's only a parrot," said Arabella. "Spits back what others thought up, so of course it always sounds good."

Booker stood with fists balled. He took steps toward her. Aliyah leapt up and grabbed his arm. "No, Booker. Don't let her bait you. You're better than that."

"As I was sayin,'" said Marshall. "I think it best we all separate today, but not far apart, up here on this mountain. I found other places we can use as individual campsites. This'll eliminate chatter and bein' heard by Golgoths. Best we ain't all clustered together makin' us ripe for easy pickins.' I got six tarps with me. Which leaves us one short. Not enough for all seven 'a us to have one. We can pair up," he said, and glanced at Tatum. "Overhead, tie your tarp which makes a great sunblock. I also got a ton 'a bug repellent. Y'all need to use it. Mosquitoes and ticks are hungry for y'all's blood. Nights without bug repellent are a livin' Hell. Now, this mornin' I took a nice sudsy bath in the stream. Next time I get naked, I'll be slatherin' on repellent head to toe. Little suckers bite right through clothin' y'all: but only those who ain't wearin' repellent. So do it."

"Marshall and I will share if he permits: then we'll have plenty of tarps to go around," said Tatum. He whipped his head toward her. "I promise not to make a peep," she whispered, making a zipper move across her lips.

Marshall felt that if given the time, he would never tire of gazing into her eyes and explore her innermost recesses. Now, under time constraint the most he could manage was affirmation, punctuated with a single nod: *permission granted.*

"Tatum's comin' with me over yonder," Marshall pointed to a spot at the same elevation as the ledge upon which they stood, about one hundred yards north. "Booker's camp is that ledge to the south."

"Booker, if you're good with it, I'll share a tarp with you," said Aliyah. "Somebody has to protect you from the wild beasties."

Booker laughed and nodded. "Sure thing, Amazon warrior princess. You sit up swatting bugs while the king takes his rest, as it should be." Aliyah smirked.

"Jayden," said Marshall, "north of my campsite will be the most ideal spot. Flat rock surrounded by trees. It'll be short work tyin' up the drop cloth for shade. Best part is, y'all get a direct line of sight to the Trail. Like a huntin' stand."

Jayden nodded. "I'll keep all the arrows, for now," he answered. "One of these mornings, why not let me teach an archery class? Then each of you will carry your own bows and arrows after that."

"Teach me this morning!" said Dodie. "I'll come with you, if you want."

Jayden worked hard to stifle a grin. "So, Aliyah's not the only Amazon warrior princess in the village. I see how it is," he said, acknowledging her attraction to him with a knowing grin. "Sure, Dodie. Come with me."

Booker unknotted the archery bows fixed to Jayden's backpack, freed one, retied the bundle, then stuffed a dozen arrows into his knapsack, razor tips-up. He held the bow. "Not all the arrows, good buddy. Better to have it and not need it, than to need it and not have it."

"What about me?" cried Arabella.

Marshall appeared thoughtful. "This here ledge we're on is the biggest one 'a all. Y'all seem comfortable here. Take it. This whole thing is y'all's."

"Alone? I won't be safe here alone!"

"How d'ya figure? If Golgoths use the trail between now and darkness, Jayden will fill 'em full of arrows. His weapon has tremendous range and he's an ace archer: a proven sniper 'a Golgoths with a documented kill count. Nothin' to worry about, Arabella."

Arabella stared blankly at Marshall. Everyone fell silent as they studied her. All noticed her expression change; animated now, as though she were engaged in conversation with an invisible person. Then, recognition, as though the internal discussion had concluded: she returned to reality. Noticing everyone looking at her, she smiled. "Fine with me. I'll stay here. Get me when you're ready to walk."

Something about her eyes just then tugged at Marshall. Apart from the ember of distrust he had felt toward Arabella from the moment he first saw her: his suspicion of her now glowed a little brighter, burned hotter. He brushed past it—though something deep down urged him to trust his gut. He pondered this. *Is the Holy Spirit tryin' to warn me? Ignore its counsel at y'all's own peril,* he thought. *For sure, she carries a darkness in her. The spirit 'a hate, chaos, and mischief—it runs her. But what can I do? Tie her up? That'd go over well with the team.*

Hours later after everyone had explored their assigned campsites, they gathered again on the ledge. "Raise a hand if y'all ain't never eaten turkey before," said Marshall. Everyone's hand went up except for Booker's. Marshall smiled. "Oh my. Y'all's tummy-tums are in for a special treat then, mmm mm. Y'all got enough to drink?"

Everyone except Arabella smiled, but all nodded. "Okay then. Grab your mess kits," he said. All watched him enter the lean-to cooking chamber; all heard the steady hiss of bottled gas cease. He emerged with paracord looped around his hand, from which dangled the browned, steaming body of the turkey. He reached into his knapsack front pocket to grab a never-used folding knife. He lowered the bird onto a clean, flat section of rock where no foot had trodden, and proceeded to carve off drumsticks and juicy white breast meat. "Come on over," he said, wearing an excited, self-satisfied grin. "Breakfast is served! But before we bite into it, let us give thanks to God for his bounty today." Marshall said grace. Aliyah, Booker, Dodie, and Jayden said a collective "Amen." Tatum, unfamiliar with prayer, imitated them seconds later. Arabella sat in stonelike silence.

Everyone came back for seconds. Booker and Tatum both came for thirds. Tatum returned for a fourth time. As she stood over Marshall holding forth her plate, he gave her a long, head-to-toe appraisal. He wanted her to see him do it. He shook his head.

"What? What is it?" Tatum asked.

"Nothin' much. Just scratchin' my head, tryin' to figure how such a perfectly formed little lady can put away this many calories without plumpin' up like a moon holdin' water. That's all. Like y'all ain't eaten in weeks."

A sly smile. "Perfectly formed. I'll bet you say that to all the girls."

Marshall laughed. "Only say it to girl birds, lately, I'm afraid. Also y'all's only the third girl I ever met, the first bein' my mama. I meant to say, there ain't an ounce 'a fat on y'all's body yet you out-eat everyone, every time."

She flexed her right bicep. "Girl power. What I could do to you with my arms is nothing compared to the damage I could do with my legs."

Marshall grinned and said nothing. He doled another helping of white meat onto her plate, then enjoyed watching her luminous dark blue eyes sparkle. His facial muscles relaxed as he became momentarily swept underwater by a wave of feelings unlike anything he had ever felt before.

"I need to ask y'all somethin,'" he whispered. But then he felt eyes on him. "Pay no mind."

After the feast Booker yawned, reminding Marshall of their need to set up campsites and get rest. With a sense of urgency he emptied his knapsack. "Do y'all mind?" Marshall asked Jayden, who gave him a thumbs up. Marshall also removed the night goggles from Jayden's knapsack. To Booker and Jayden, he handed drop cloths. He paced off twenty feet, unspooled the paracord, cut off three equal lengths, and handed one to each. He took out the remaining unused folding knives and passed them out, along with night goggles and a charger. He dismantled the camp stove and placed it in his knapsack. He rolled up and attached his bedding to the backpack frame, and said, "Arabella, gonna leave the lean-to in place here for y'all to use."

"So very white of you," Arabella said, shooting a glare over at Booker and Aliyah. Booker's face reflected her hate. Aliyah took Booker's hand and pulled him toward his bedding and knapsack. She left him there while she squared away her own bedroll. Jayden, also stiff from the prior day's heavily burdened hike rolled his eyes, stood with a grimace, and packed up.

Marshall and Tatum shouldered their backpacks. "Okay. Let's move out: follow me and watch your footin' 'cause it's a long painful roll downhill to the Trail if y'all slip." He and Tatum disappeared quickly over the ledge. Jayden followed with Dodie close behind.

Booker gave one backward glance at Arabella. "Bless your heart. Have the day you deserve," he said, eyes on her. Arabella shot him her right middle finger.

Arabella moved her bedding into the cooking lean-to. It smelled of cooked food. *Pleasant enough. Shady enough.* She stretched out listening to wild bird sounds, watching the silhouette of sunlight and leaves dancing against the canvas top and sides.

Now, she carefully laid plans to give life to the idea that had implanted itself last evening, while seething with hate, separated from Marshall in Jayden in the dark Walmart. At first debating within herself that it would be going too far, crossing too cumbrous of a line: she had rejected this idea. Now she smiled wondering how she had ever doubted herself about it.

She thought of her dead father, handsome and strong in her memories; she ran the idea past him. In her vision, the ghost of Grady Pendleman nodded his approval. 'Proud of you, Bella. All the Pendlemans are here. We are all so proud of you. Be strong for us, until the day you join us.'

Marshall and Tatum said their temporary goodbyes to Jayden and Dodie, who walked past them on their way to the northernmost campsite, a two-hundred-yard hike away. Tatum looked up at the giant boulder marking their campsite, behind which was a flattened area. They hiked until, behind the boulder, Marshall set down his pack and fluffed out one of the new drop cloths.

"Tell me something. How did this rock get here?" Tatum asked. He watched as she looked up at higher elevations. "It's not made of the same stuff as this mountain, or foothill or ridge—whatever you want to call this boulder. It's like a giant had a pocketful of these hundred-ton stones and accidentally dropped one here."

"Gimme a hand with this tarp?" Marshall asked. "Hold that corner to the tree level with mine while I tie this corner," he said. He looked out over the vista and swept the air with his arm. "A long time ago all this— everythin' we all see—was entirely covered in a miles-thick sheet of glacial ice. But glaciers don't ever just sit in one place. They move real slow-like. Eventually and very slowly, they grow small again. When this one melted, its hard blue ice sheared off bits of mountainsides and carried them along its path to the sea. When things thawed and glaciers melted, millions 'a rocks, bigguns like this and littler ones ended up sinkin' and settlin' all along the glacier's path," he said. "It might a' started as a chunk 'a mountain miles away, like up in New York, so it ain't gonna be made of the same stuff as this here mountain."

As he walked over to tie her tarp corner to the opposite tree, he patted the boulder and said, "Like this little pebble right here. It'll block the view from the Trail just fine. I'll bet that flat area ten yards up is where the boulder originally landed. See the depression? Then over thousands 'a years, gravity and earth movements gradually shifted it downhill to where it sits today."

"Huh. I never knew," she said. "By the way, for a rough-and-tumble mountain man you seem like a well-read guy. Booker has nothing on you."

He smiled. "Thank you. Wasn't much else to do where I came from. Well…the last ice age ended 'round ten thousand years ago. Humans lived through it. We all 'r a resilient lot. We always find ways to win."

"You think humans will survive this period…this rise of the Golgoths?"

Finished tying their temporary shelter in place, he stood before her. He took both of her hands in hers and held them against his stomach. "God's will be done. Atheists believe that God and Satan are manufactured beins' designed to take the place 'a good and bad human drives and emotions. Like so people can blame 'em when their sins whip 'round to bite 'em. But it's all cattywampus; none 'a these i-dears' can explain Christ's supernatural works that happened two thousand years ago, and the perfection of his actions, his words, his timeline, and his story."

"Works?" asked Tatum.

Marshall nodded. "Restored life to dead folks; gave vision to the born-blind; made permanent cripples walk; healed many thousands of ailments; walked on water; turned water into wine; cast out demons who feared him. Jewish scribes at the time accepted these good works—how could they not? —but they spread word that the healins' and raisin' up dead Jews were 'cause of sorcery. Them Jews were tryin' to protect their power over the Jewish people who propped 'em up; let 'em live in luxury. But the entire world changed 'cause these things did happen, Tatum, believe it; and believe in the holy, righteous God. We all are sinners; much 'a what we think 'n do does offend him. He sacrificed his only begotten Son so that we who love the Son won't have to die twice to atone for it all: death of our bodies, then death of our souls."

"You mean Hell?" Tatum asked.

Marshall nodded. "Permanent separation from God. It ain't good enough to live a decent life. Y'all can't work your way outta prison. Bein' a 'good person' can't save us from God's Judgement, because why?"

"Because we're all sinners who fall far from the righteous behavior God demands?" said Tatum.

"Right! But if we love the Son, who gave his life for us, and repent, meaning change our ways, the Father forgets every evil thought or selfish, stupid, wrong thing we ever done: He just blots it out so we can kneel clean before 'im. God did it for love, Tatum, because our Father in heaven knows us completely; and he loves us completely. I for one love 'im back. My heart and soul belong to 'im; for this reason I'm hikin' to the Spring Mountain: I wanna serve 'im."

She glanced down at their hands which were still entwined, then she looked back up at him. "I'm beginning to understand, Marshall. Your faith in God is infectious. I always figured that if God exists, he must hate me; hate us, for sending Floods and making Golgoths. What you just told me is compelling. I need to learn more," she said, and released his hands.

"God loves a questionin' mind and so do I. Listen; I picked up on y'all's wirin' straight from the get-go. Can't see it, touch it, taste it, then y'all have doubts. I get it. But tweren't it them dreams that moved y'all outta safety and onto the Trail?"

Tatum nodded. "Evidence enough for me that magic exists."

Marshall flashed her a grin. "Magic. I like it. Indeed it is. Faith is like them tests they used to give in schools, with four clever wrong answers but only one right answer that earns the passin' grade. It took hundreds 'a years followin' the death of Siddhartha Gautama, the Indian prince known as Buddha, to spread through Asia. It took hundreds of years followin' the death of Muhammad for Islam to spread. But faith in Christ blazed through the Middle East, Europe, and Asia with an unparalleled exponential growth rate followin' the death and resurrection of Jesus of Nazareth, because tens of thousands 'a Jews either directly benefited from his supernatural healins' or they were close to someone who had. Also the twelve Apostles of Christ willin'ly allowed themselves to be tortured, imprisoned, and murdered under false charges rather than recant what they'd lived through with Jesus, and the world's first "Christians" for hunderts a years willin'ly accepted the same fate, 'cause Christ asks this 'a his followers, to go all the way to the Cross with 'im. It all happened over such a short period of time. Nothin' like this ain't never happened before Christ, or after Christ. His enemies in Judea, Greece, and Rome wrote 'a his supernatural works, because to deny they happened would 'a caused a revolt; too many witnesses to the works lived still, and them elite sinners viewed Jesus as a threat to their profitable hold on power. Instead they propagandized the miracle works as "sorcery" and labeled Jesus a tool 'a Satan. Yes, those writins' from Christ's enemies are submitted as evidence to his otherworldly powers that coulda only come from God. So yes, Tatum. Faith in Christ should come plum easy to the critical-thinkin,' science, 'n evidence-based truth-seekin' souls. And iffn' it don't, the most powerful parasitic propagandist, plaguin' us since humanity began, has successfully blinded them to the plain truth right there in their faces."

"Satan?" she asked.

Marshall nodded.

"Hmm, wow. I never thought about this; any of this. Feeling a bit panicked, like I need to catch up in a hurry. I mean, this is eternity we're talking about here: mine, yours, everyone's."

Marshall slowly blinked and nodded. "Y'all'r gettin' it."

Tatum grew quiet, lost in thought, but then she focused on Marshall's eyes and frowned. "Now, buster: what was it back there you wanted to ask me until you told me to 'pay no mind'?"

His face fell, grip loosened.

"Tell me!" she pleaded. "What was it?"

"Oh. Right. I forget."

"Liar! Tell me!"

Marshall toed the ground with his boot. "If you unintentionally got pregnant, is there any circumstance where you might consider abortin' the baby?"

She released his hands. "That's what you wanted to ask me? No, oh my God no! That's pure evil! Oh my God, never. Do you think I'm evil?"

A single tear spilled from his eye. "I've only just met y'all. Sorry. Question's been hauntin' me, is all."

She blinked and perceived something terribly painful lie behind the question. "Well, that's fine. I don't ever want to discourage you from asking me anything. I'm just a little shocked by the question. It's okay. Ask me more."

"Last question of the day, I promise: do y'all find me attractive?"

With her left hand, she reached around his neck and pulled him down to her level. She kissed his mouth, teasing his tongue with hers.

So warm, he thought. *So delicious*. He felt her quickened pulse through her chest pressed tightly against his. She gazed into his eyes.

"I have spent my life in the company of women; no men at all besides Grady, for whom I felt daughterly things, and my real dad who got taken by Golgoths when I was too small to remember much about him," whispered Tatum. "Marshall—I didn't even know myself. Never did I waste time thinking about men, or God, or the purpose of life, or having children. Those possibilities all seemed so…remote and unattainable. Then I met you. You make me feel things; believe things."

"Like believin' in God, maybe?"

She nodded. "Like that. With you I feel…like I'm becoming the woman God made me to be. I feel my womb, now. Because of you, your male strength, I'm not only thinking in new ways—I'm feeling things never felt before," she said. "Did I say too much too soon? Sorry. I'm so bad at peopling."

Again, Tatum pulled Marshall to her lips and tongue; greedily she explored, then paused. "I find myself very drawn to you, Marshall. I feel more for you than just a friend. Do you believe me? Please tell me that you believe me; that I would never try to deceive you. And that I'm not evil."

He inhaled the intoxicating animal chemistry uniquely her own, like a secret that had burst inside him. His hands found her hair and plunged into it.

He felt a switch click deep inside just as he had hoped it would when he decided the team should split up for the day; saw Delilah's face outside their lodge door on their last morning together, her eyes and mouth replaced by the baleful, defiant, hate-filled face of a stranger, or a demon. In Tatum's warm blue eyes, Delilah's cold darkness found no reflection; like a ghost made of steam above a hot coffee mug, Delilah's face melted away to where he no longer remembered it; abruptly he ceased worrying about her safety. The relief was physical, like an incalculably heavy weight suddenly lifted from his spirit as one door closed, and Tatum flung another wide open.

"I believe y'all, yes."

Blood Trail

At one point Arabella had lightly dozed. When she came to, she remembered standing naked before the approving gaze of Hostis Dei in a stone building where sunlight shone through colored glass. Fully awake, her mouth felt dry, slack, trembling. Her eyes throbbed, dazed from dreams and horror drugged.

The sun position suggested to Arabella that the window of opportunity was now. From her pack she withdrew the two small, garish objects that nobody else knew about that she had taken from Walmart. She stuffed them into her left and right pants pockets. She disappeared over the ledge and made her way down the culvert to the Trail. She walked north until she found a second culvert head. *This must be the Booger's. The next one would be Tatum's, then after that, Dodie's.*

She started the ascent toward Booker's camp, heart pounding not from exertion but from the thrill of the potential result. The culvert was clear of leaves and twigs which rendered her footfalls silent thanks to runoff from countless rainstorms. Sensing how long it had taken to descend from her ledge down to the Trail, climbing up, she knew that by now she had to be close.

Above she saw a ledge and a lean-to. *Aliyah and the other Booger.* Moving with more stealth than she believed possible she dared to hike further up to within five feet of the ledge. She freed the two-ounce bottle of patchouli perfume from her left pocket. She unscrewed the cap. The stink of it wrinkled her nose. *Women used to put this on themselves to feel more attractive. Seriously? Rancid! Absolutely disgusting,* she thought.

Being extra careful not to accidentally drip any onto herself, she made her way back down the narrow drainage path tapping drops of perfume every two feet or so onto the dirt. She paused after emptying one of the bottles and casually tossed it off to the side, careful to not let any of it touch her skin or clothing. She reached into her right pocket for the second bottle and continued dripping the reeking oily liquid until she reached the Trail below. She still had drops remaining. She distributed these equally where the culvert met the Trail. Having created a clear scent path for Golgoths to follow, she tossed the empty bottle nearby. "Mission accomplished," she whispered, and grinned. She walked south back along the trail until she arrived at her culvert. She thought of Golgoths, and what they do to people like her. Frightened, she sprinted up the drainage path leading back to the relative safety and obscurity of the ledge. She re-entered the lean-to, laid back down, and waited.

She did not need to wait long. When there remained only ninety-minutes or so of daylight, the stillness was pierced by Aliyah's distinctive scream from a distance. She smiled. "Got 'em! Aliyah can pray to her God when Golgoths breed her before they cut her alive and screaming to pieces and eat her dark meat. Booger Bailey will be someone's dinner tonight," she said aloud with a shiver of fear and delight.

The scream woke Marshall. He turned to Tatum, on her back naked beside him, eyes wide open in panic. He whispered, "If we can hear it, so can the Golgoths. Stay here." He rushed to pull on his pants, tripped over his feet and fell on the ground. He slipped on his shirt and stuffed his feet into his boots, the tying of the laces crude and rushed. He patted his pants right pocket. Satisfied with the quantity of ammo balls and the lock blade knife, he grabbed his slingshot and a machete and took off in a sprint south toward the sound.

He saw Booker's lean-to. His heart thudded out the primal beat of panicked terror; his thoughts raced. *It was your decision to split up, because stealin' sugar with Tatum meant more to you than group safety,* his inner man accused in an inculpating tone. He slowed as he approached Booker's campsite. Then he recognized both of his friends. Whatever had happened to them—clearly it had happened all at once.

Aliyah crouched behind Booker. Both still dressed the same as when he had last seen them hours before. Booker stood like a Roman statue, unmoving, unblinking as if in bas relief carved into dark soapstone. Marshall could see a pulse beating thickly at Booker's temples; arrow nocked, taut bowstring restrained by nerveless fingers, compound bow pulled all the way back. Marshall's eyes followed down in the direction of Booker's aimed arrow.

Two Golgoths, arrows protruding from ghostly white chests twenty feet away, lay dying. Marshall could see dark blood burbling up from entrance wounds like nauseating artesian wells. Booker suddenly turned, arrow aimed at Marshall, who threw up his hands.

"Shoot me, Booker, and y'all can forget about turkey leftovers tonight." Recognition dawned on Booker's face. He lowered the bow and relaxed his tension of the bowstring. Aliyah broke down and started sobbing.

"What happened?" Marshall asked as quickly he closed the gap between him and them. He put his arms around both, pulling them close. Booker's breathing remained erratic; he refused to peel his eyes from the dying Golgoths. He managed to speak through the pounding heart caught in his throat. "Aliyah caught a whiff of something strange. I stood up to investigate. That's when I saw those two Golgoths coming straight toward me. They saw me seconds after I saw them. They started running straight at me. I grabbed the bow. I got lucky with my shots. My first shot missed because I was so panicked. I'd never used one of these damned things before. The second arrow missed the mark, too. But the third hit, and when the first Golgoth dropped, the second one stood there stunned. It gave me enough time to load one more. By then I had the hang of shooting arrows.

I did not miss that demon."

"You're a natural," said Marshall.

Meanwhile, Tatum had dressed and had run over to warn Jayden and Dodie of the Golgoth attack. Marshall could now hear the alarmed, angry cacophony of male voices floating up from the Trail. Having left Booker and the hysterical Aliyah, Marshall walked down the culvert. He too caught whiffs of a pungent, unfamiliar oily-rank scent as he descended. When he reached the point where he could clearly see the Trail, he froze.

Silently Marshall watched an arrow from somewhere swish downhill and thwap into the neck of a large Golgoth. He watched hands fly up to grasp at the arrow shaft, feathered tail protruding from the side. He watched the white monster drop to his knees, then onto his face mashed flat against the Trail. One by one, he watched five more fatal piercings as Golgoths collapsed, and life departed. One shot made him wince as it ripped through a Golgoth's belly causing him to scream piteously, but quickly was followed by a kill shot to the heart. There was no further sound.

Marshall descended the rest of the way and stood on the Trail, machete arm cocked and ready to swing at the first flash of white. He looked in both directions. Satisfied there were no more hunting party Golgoths expected, he rubbed his face in thought. Finding no answers, he worked to calm his racing heart, and prayed silently. *Heavenly Father, through y'all's Holy Spirit, please guide me now. Please let me know what y'all need me to do next.*

As the others made their way down to join him, an idea formed. With only a vague notion of their hierarchy and structure, Marshall had no clue how well or how poorly Golgoths communicated with one another. *Hide the bodies well.* He did not know for sure if this commandment was his own intuition or had come from someplace else. Either way, it felt powerful. He selected the Golgoth closest to him, clearly dead and fully bled out. He grabbed the ankles. Just then Jayden and Booker appeared.

"What are you doing?" Jayden asked Marshall.

"Hiding evidence," said Booker. "Marshall doesn't want the entire home colony to send scouts looking after their missing hunting party and find them all shot up. Imagine if they did. This entire Trail would become a danger zone for us. They'd set traps up ahead. I mean to Golgoths the Trail is another road, of sorts. Golgoths may already suspect people use the Trail. If they find dead comrades they'll surely know."

Marshall nodded. "Not only a lethal archer, Booker, but y'all 'r a war chief: nailed it dead bang."

"I killed these animals, Marshall. What do you mean Booker is a lethal archer?" said Jayden.

"Walk up this culvert a ways, y'all 'll find two dyin' or dead Golgoths with holes in their hearts. Booker did that. Listen Jayden, I know how good y'all pluck that guitar, but when it comes to pluckin' a bowstring, by far y'all 'r the most accurate, lethal sniper alive today. Y'all just saved all our lives. After we relocate these here cadavers, gents, I'll be needin' y'all's help."

"With what?" asked Jayden.

Marshall answered. "We need to figure out how they tracked Booker and Aliyah. Smell anythin?'"

Both sniffed the air. "All I smell is perforated bowel," said Jayden.

"Let's get these corpses well-hidden off the Trail. Then I'll show y'all what I mean," said Marshall.

Working together, they dragged the two bodies down the culvert from up near Booker's ledge. Marshall had identified a drop point about twenty-five yards south, with dense understory scrub growth and leafy foliage with a steep drop seventy feet down from the Trail side. After the final bodies were rolled down into green-covered obscurity, Marshall looked up. "Red sky in mornin' means sailors take warnin.' My wise ole dad taught me that early. Biblical rain comin' tonight, which is a good thing."

"Great," said Jayden. "Not sure if night vision goggles will fare so well in a downpour. Don't know much about electronics but I did read that stuff does not do well in water."

"Great point," said Marshall. "We'll use my poly-whatever-you-said tarp I'd packed from home and cut ponchos out of it. My point is rain gonna wash away the scent, boot-prints, and blood evidence. By tomorrow, if Golgoths get wise to us 'n send another party along the Trail, rain'll wash away our footprints and other signs of travel."

"Tell us about the tracking," said Booker.

"Yessir, 'bout that," said Marshall. "I smelt somethin' strange too, all the way down, like it was followin' me; an awful stink. Ain't never smelt nothin' like it. Jayden, go stand by the culvert, sniff around."

Jayden did. "Yep. I smell it." He rubbed his nose. "God-awful reek, whatever it is. You're saying this stench leads all the way up?"

Booker and Marshall nodded. Jayden poked his boot through the poison ivy and weeds. He thought he saw something. Removing an arrow from his quiver, he used it to knock the small, empty glass bottle out of the weeds and onto the Trail. He sniffed it, made a face, and nodded back. "Somebody sprinkled this foul-smelling liquid like an arrow pointing straight up from the Trail to you and Aliyah."

"Who in the Hell would—" The same suspect's name hit all three at once. *Arabella.*

Booker's face changed. All charm, humor, intellect, politeness, and compassion had fled. The spirit of hate rose and filled all gaps large and small. "I am going to cut her throat." He started walking south on the trail toward the ledge they all knew well, Turkey Ledge, as Booker had already named it for his memoirs someday. *After today it'll be known as the Sacrificial*

Blood Stone, he thought.

All heard a female voice coming from twenty feet up the culvert. "Booker, stop." He did. He turned. Aliyah, Dodie, and Tatum closed the gap and stood on the Trail, facing Booker. They trotted up and stood in front of Jayden and Marshall. It had been Aliyah who called him.

Aliyah spoke: "Booker, this isn't the way of the Lord. Do you think Jesus couldn't have summoned legions of angels to save him from the Cross? He let them torture and murder him, out of pure love for his Father and for us, his Elect. Love your enemies, Booker; or let hate consume you. Choose wisely," she said.

"Aliyah this was attempted murder. Hello? That murdering bitch Arabella nearly got away with it! Golgoths would've found our bodies and none of you would know it was a cold-blooded murder planned by her. This isn't hatred; this is justice, and self-protection. Recidivism, know what that means? Do you, Aliyah?"

She shood her head. "No, Booker. Tell us what you think it means."

"It means that Arabella will only just do it again if we give her the chance. If I don't act now she'll keep trying until we are both dead. Or all of us. There's no love there. And Marshall, you see the way she looks at you? There's evil inside her; the same spirit as the one running the Golgoths. Hate owns that bitch: I'd be a fool to give Arabella another chance to hate me to death. My mama didn't raise a fool. So, all of you just back off and let me do what must be done."

"Booker. Aliyah's right, y'all need to know. About God, about Christ. This ain't what God wants," Marshall said as he lightly laid his hand on Booker's shoulder.

Booker narrowed his gaze. "Tell me, Marshall. You have a good relationship with the Holy Spirit. What does God want?"

Marshall closed his eyes, then opened them. "Mercy. Show mercy, and it will be shown to us."

Booker shifted his gaze between Aliyah and Marshall. "That's it, then. See y'all later. Maybe you people will make it, and maybe you won't." He took ten paces north up the trail until Aliyah's voice arrested him.

"Stop, Booker, please! Don't leave me."

"Then come with me, Aliyah. I have no plans to walk another mile with Arabella, that succubus from Hell."

"Marshall, do something!" cried Aliyah.

"Y'all gimme a moment, please," Marshall said. Booker walked, but something told him to stop and turn around. He watched Marshall drop to his knees and form a triangle with his palms pressed flat on the trail. He bent and pressed his forehead against the backs of his hands. Silently he prayed. Everyone remained quiet. None had ever seen such focused prayer. At no time did Marshall move at all. It was difficult for Jayden to confirm life, seeing no rise and fall of Marshall's chest. All watched a large wolf spider crawl over Marshall's neck and finally back to ground, which in his focus he ignored. Finally, Marshall raised his head. He stood with eyes still closed. He opened them. He looked in their direction, but none thought he was seeing them.

"'Therefore go out from their midst, and be separate from them,' says the Lord, 'and touch no unclean thing. Then I will welcome you."

Tatum stared at Marshall in wonder.

"I appeal to you, brothers, to watch out for those who cause divisions and create obstacles contrary to the doctrine that you have been taught; avoid them."

"I recognize that sentence from the Bible!" said Booker. Slowly he walked back to the group, incredulity animating his face.

"Marshall?" said Jayden. "Hoss?"

"As for a person who stirs up division, after warning him once and then twice, have nothing more to do with him. If anyone comes to you and does not bring this teaching, do not receive him into your house or give him any greeting, for whoever greets him takes part in his wicked works. Take no part in the unfruitful works of darkness, but instead expose them. Do not be deceived: bad company ruins good morals.

"Do not be unequally yoked with unbelievers. For what partnership has righteousness with lawlessness? Or what fellowship has light with darkness? What accord has Christ with Belial? Or what portion does a believer share with an unbeliever?"

Marshall ceased talking.

Booker took a deep breath and wiped angry tears from his eyes. "Working through Marshall, God is telling us the right thing to do. I've read these words he's speaking. They're from the New Testament. He's speaking the Word of God, people," said Booker. "Verses word for word, spot on. Not like I have them all memorized but I recognized them immediately. I doubt Marshall committed chapter and verse to memory. I think we all know that words are not his strength."

Marshall fell to his knees, face in his hands. Tatum ran to him. She cradled his head against her waist. She took his wrist and pulled. He uncovered his face; awkwardly like a man awakening from a dream he stood, again looking at everyone, but this time they all felt he was seeing them.

"You a big Bible reader, Marshall?" asked Booker.

"I try, Booker. Because my memory for written words sucks, mostly I use it for lookups. Why?"

"Incredible. You nailed every word—"

Marshall stood with his arms outstretched. "Arabella's out; she is shunned. Everyone, hear me: we go on without her," he announced. "This is God's mercy. If any of y'all got a problem with my decision, y'all can stay here with her."

Tatum held his hand in silent solidarity. Booker still appeared vexed, denied his retribution. Jayden was amazed, suspecting that he had just eye-witnessed a bona fide mini miracle. Aliyah and Dodie wore their puzzled shock like children. Tatum fell deeper into Marshall's orbit.

No one spoke.

Marshall released Tatum's hand. "I'm goin' back up to break camp and pack my stuff. It'll be dark in forty minutes. I'm givin' myself twenty minutes 'til I return here. I'll stand in this spot slicin' six rain ponchos from my waterproof tarp 'til the last of the western light turns black. Then I strap on goggles and start walkin' north. Any 'a y'all wanna walk with me had better be here when I start walkin' and hold to my decisions from here on out; or y'all can stay behind or go different ways. It's y'all's choice."

Without further delay, Marshall strode north to the bottom of his narrow drainage culvert leading up to his camp. Tatum studied the faces of Aliyah, Booker, Dodie, and Jayden a moment longer. Abruptly she broke eye contact and sprinted to catch up with Marshall.

Dodie pressed herself against Jayden. "Can anyone please tell me what just happened?"

Aliyah answered. "Marshall's prayer for guidance got answered."

Booker nodded. "Dreams-in-common. Marshall the rough-hewn mountain man falls into a fugue state, who admits he doesn't have an eidetic memory for written words, suddenly becomes a vessel of God: yes, these are signs and wonders given to us from a higher plane of existence. I believe, Lord. I believe."

"So you forgive Arabella?" Aliyah asked.

Booker grunted. "As long we put her behind us, Aliyah. Truth be told I won't lose a minute's sleep if Arabella ends up excreted from Golgoth bowels, but sure. Mercy for Medusa; whatever."

"We're losing time," said Jayden. "Marshall and Tatum walk without us in seventeen minutes."

Red Rain

"Not bad rain ponchos, Marshall! Maybe in Spring Mountain they'll make you the official tailor!"

"Hah," Marshall said. "Never crossed my mind to bring scissors; had to use a knife. Glad they more or less fit. The object ain't to keep our entire bodies dry. Not sure if that's even possible. Water hits the ground and splashes up. Prepare to get soaked. But we gotta keep this headgear dry. Did y'all slather on the bug repellent I gave out? With rain comes mosquitoes; clouds of 'em. If y'all wanna repel 'em, cover every inch 'a skin with repellent."

Everyone except Dodie nodded. "Dodie, do it now," said Marshall.

"I'm not getting naked here in front of all of you!"

"I didn't get nekkid," said Aliyah. "Neither did Booker. We just sorta reached up and down on ourselves. You can do it, Dodie."

Dodie shook her head. "Next time. It's dark. Let's go. Will Arabella be…okay?"

Booker glared at her. "That's an HP, not an MP or OP or YP."

"What?"

"Her problem. Not my problem, not our problem, and not your problem."

Dodie shook her head. "Leaving her behind feels so wrong."

"Me getting raped and cut up for bait, and Booker getting cooked and eaten up on the ledge by Golgoths she deliberately lured up there for that purpose—would that've felt right to you?" said Aliyah. "Come on, bestie. We live in the real world, a ridiculously hard world. Every little decision we make is a big decision. We place our trust in God to help with those decisions. Marshall has, so suck it up and let's walk."

Jayden took Dodie's hand, giving her a protective nod. Aliyah took Booker's hand. Tatum stood on her toes, threw her arms around Marshall's neck, and kissed him, long and wet. "Ooooooo"—said all, with smiles all around. Marshall smirked. He noticed how Tatum's eyes radiated life even now, in the gathering gloom of twilight.

"Stay close this time and stay quiet. Whispers only. Let's roll," Marshall said, setting off along the perfumed ways of the summer night.

"How did you leave it with Arabella when you left her up on the ledge?" Booker whispered to Marshall.

"Well, since y'all asked: first off, Arabella confessed to plannin' this attempted murder from the moment she found the smelly stuff at the Walmart. I told her that she is alive only through God's grace. That she gotta use her goggles and hike only at night, back to Georgia or wherever. Told 'r I know for certain she ain't welcome at the Mountain of Springs. I left her food and water, a knife, the tarp, and pieces of paracord. I told her not to follow us. And that if we all see 'er again it definitely ain't gonna end well for 'er. I ended it by tellin' 'r she looks like death eatin' on a cracker."

Jayden laughed hard and covered his mouth.

"What does that even mean?" Dodie whispered."

He bent and pressed his lips to her ear. "It's a Smoky Mountain redneck's way of saying she looks like pale poop. He got in one last dig." Dodie giggled.

They passed North Indian Creek and hiked east, mostly uphill miles. At a point Marshall felt was the summit of Iron Mountain, he called for a rest. "Let's break the fast."

"Breakfast?" whispered Aliyah. "It's like midnight."

"Good mornin!'" Marshall whispered with a grin. He reached into his bag and withdrew the plastic envelope filled with roasted turkey. "When the sun is fully up, I'll be wishin' y'all goodnight! This is our world now, for a long while."

After he and Tatum had eaten, he whispered, "Grab your water bottles and mess kits. I see a clear mountain stream." To the others he whispered, "Tatum and I 'r gonna go check it out, make sure it's safe. Y'all can fill up after we get back. Enjoy your breakfast, back in a jiffy-jif."

About twenty yards back down the trail, Marshall veered off and walked ten paces to an artesian spring percolating up, burbling gently into a thin, sullen stream of clear mountain water. He removed his goggles and Tatum followed suit. They filled their bottles, screwed on caps, then rinsed off their tin plates. Speaking in muted tones, he said, "Been thinkin' 'bout what we did before we fell asleep. How d'y'all feel about what I did to you back there?"

She smiled. "Oh Marshall, no words! I've dreamed of you throughout my entire life and now you're real. I would ask you the same, but I know it wasn't your first time."

"How in the heck would y'all know such a thing?"

"No virgin man in the history of virgin men was ever that good with his hands and mouth, I suspect. Those were practiced moves, buster."

He found it difficult to stifle a laugh. Then he grew serious. "I guess y'all could say, I was married. Back at LeConte. I'll tell y'all the whole truth of it if that borin' garbage is somethin' y'all really wanna hear."

"I do! Oh yes, please tell me."

Marshall described the day he found Delilah; how recently it blossomed into something more. About her disdain for babies and for any 'God talk' as she called it. Then he told her about the self-inflicted abortion, and about the poisoning of their baby with May Apple root and how she told him to leave, and how prayer revealed the epiphany that brought him to the Trail.

"God, Marshall. I am so sorry all of this happened to you." Recognition animated her face. "So that's why you asked me if I would ever kill a baby inside me. Listen," she said, and grabbed his cheeks. "I am not *that* woman. I will never hurt you. And as for that witch I have only one thing to say: her loss is my gain. Maybe God intended for us to meet. He knew you needed somebody to watch your back."

She wiped a tear from his cheek. She knew what it meant. Relief, joy, and rebirth. "I think I'm fallin' for y'all," he said.

She shook her head.

"No? Don't want me to?"

"Oh my God, yes! Yes, I do. It's just that I was about to tell you the same thing. You beat me to it. You can't be first in everything, you know. First one to the Trail, et cetera."

They embraced. He buried his bearded face down into her long, smooth neck. Marshall said, "We should be gettin' on back. They'll wonder what happened to us."

"Just five more minutes?" said Tatum.

He saw her grin and understood. "I wanna give y'all somethin.' A gift. But believe me, it's more a gift to me than for y'all." As Tatum hugged a sapling for support, while kneeling behind her Marshall's tongue danced, darted, flickered, and swirled, until thoughtfully she covered her mouth to stifle her own screams.

"Where've you two been?" asked Dodie, mischief in her tone.

"Washing up," answered Tatum. She darted a sideways glance at Marshall. "In point of fact, I'm quite certain that I have never felt this clean." Marshall snickered. Dodie covered her mouth. "C'mon guys," said Tatum, "follow me, I'll take you to the stream. I'm sure General Tojo over here—I mean Marshall—can hardly wait for the forced march to resume."

Theatrically he punched his left palm with his right fist. "Y'all make it quick," he said.

Tired, circadian rhythms in disarray, aside from bathroom stops, they pushed through the Iron Mountain range for uncounted hours until temperatures plummeted. The wind swept through endlessly, cold, and sharp as a blade. It howled through trees, inverted leaves so that their silvery underbellies now faced up and surrounded the hikers with forlorn hooting noises; spooky, grim omens. Dead limbs and branches liberated by blasting air currents crashed down around them like mortar fire.

Then the rain hit. At first it had announced its impending arrival with a fine mist, which increased to a steady drizzle. Bolts of lightning spanned the entire breadth of the black horizon followed by teeth-rattling thunder rushing in to fill electrified air vacuums. What soon followed were loud baseball-sized splats against Marshall's makeshift polyethylene head covers, sparse at first, but jarring. The skies then opened into a full-blown monsoon.

The Trail turned muddy fast. Despite the no-talking rule in effect,

Dodie scratched at her maddening mosquito bites while dropping profanity bombs every few minutes; the rain pelted their ponchos so loudly that nobody heard her. If not for night vision goggles they would be walking in a completely lightless environment.

Walking the downhill stretches proved the most challenging. Each slipped or stumbled going down on their butts. Marshall wondered when it would end. *If not before daylight, where 'r we all gonna camp? What safe, warm, dry place is a-waitin' out here in no-man's land? None*, he thought. *Any survivin' roofed structures are lowland, where Golgoths hunt. Dear Lord, they're all countin' on me. I'm countin' on y'all. Please deliver us all from this night 'a water.*

Seven hours into the soggy hike, Marshall felt the inexplicably strong urge to look up, which could destroy his night goggle lenses, but the urge only grew stronger. He stopped. So did Tatum and the four behind him. He leaned down and pressed his lips against Tatum's left ear. "Please lift y'all's poncho for me."

"Here, in front of everyone? How kinky!"

He smiled at the flirt. "Seriously. I need to look up without drenchin' my night goggles. I need y'all to make a kind 'a roof for me. Think y'all can do that?"

Immediately she held her poncho straight out in front of her. Rain collected quickly. He knelt. He found that her sweatshirt underneath was dry. He used it to rub the goggle lenses clear of water dots. He crouched and lowered his head to her mid-thighs. He chanced the tilting up of his head. He scanned trees running high up the small mountainside. "Nothin' but trees," he grumbled.

Then, he spotted a shape that did not belong. A perfect square. *What in Sam Hill is that?* He blinked. Up the hillside he saw what appeared to be a hunters cabin, high enough never to be touched by the two Floods.

He stood. Marshall turned to the group. He pointed up toward where he had spotted the cabin. He made the 'follow me' arm-hand gesture and commenced his slip-sliding ascent up the steep grade. Before, the group when walking had followed drainage culverts, which worked in dry weather, but this side trip proved far more dangerous in a monsoon. Dry culverts had become muddy torrents. Climbers were swept back down to the Trail from water pressure and slippery surfaces. Marshall used trees as walking sticks. Progress up the steep slope was arduous. The raggedy, makeshift tarp poncho and goggles made it impossible for him to keep turning around to do progress checks on the others. So, he climbed. *Got nothin' better to do tonight,* he thought.

He stopped, grabbed a sapling, and turned to look at his followers. Imitating him, they were keeping up.

He believed they were heading in a slightly diagonal line from the Trail to the cabin above. *In conditions like these what cannot be seen must be felt.* He climbed awkwardly, slowly, but steadily. The navigator in his brain suggested that he was close to the cabin. All he saw ahead of him were more trees. Then the sky flashed with lightning. *I saw it! Seventy yards up, thirty yards northwest. Darn, son. Your diagonal was just a tad bit aggressive*, he thought.

He continued up but now bore lightly left. Ten minutes later, they all stood on what was obviously a manufactured flat area that had no business up here on this mountain. In the greenish glow of the goggles they watched rain pelt off the corrugated metal roof, raising a roar equal in volume to the rhythmic thunderclaps. *This cabin is enormous,* Marshall thought. Single-story but at least sixty feet in length, forty in depth. Glass windows covered with wooden shutters with crucifixes carved in their middles. The door was one solid piece of wood. *Heluva big tree died to make this door.*

As the followers caught up, he saw that the cabin door handle was a black iron latch. He pushed down on the black spade-shaped latch button. Nothing happened. He pushed against the door with his shoulder. Above the clamor of rain-pelted steel and thunder, he heard creaking. Using his shoulder again as a battering ram, he hit the door with a three-foot running start. The old semi-rotted door casing splintered. He grabbed the latch and pulled hard. The door opened outward with creaking noises loud enough for him to hear above the din. Everyone heard the rusted old hinges screaming in agony. He stood outside with the others staring into the black maw. Tatum stepped past Marshall and went inside. He soon followed her, and the others joined them.

"Well, this sure is Jim Dandy," said Jayden, staring at a stone fireplace with dried firewood stacked near it inside a wrought iron ring. "This main living room area was an open floor plan with a woodburning oven, rustic and sturdy kitchen table, and hand-hewn wood chairs. Everything coated in decades of dust. Home sweet home!"

Rain assaulted the steel roof so violently that the group could barely hear one another talking in normal tones. Everyone became forced to dial up speaking volume. "Look, Marshall," yelled Tatum, pointing at open doors. She walked inside the first room. "Oh, will you look at that. Now there's something I haven't seen in oh, about two million years. A real bed!"

"Okay to make a fire, hoss?" asked Jayden.

"Absolutely, hot as y'all want. Tonight smoke only got one way to go and that's straight to ground."

While Jayden made a fire, Booker went in the next room. "Yes! Bed in here too."

"Yes!" said Dodie. "A bed in here too!" she said, as she tried not to be seen scratching welts covering her chest.

Marshall opened a door and found a bathroom. In it was a toilet with paper still on the roll, and a shower. He wondered about the water supply, most especially about hot water. In the closet inside the bathroom he found the answer: a water heater powered by liquid propane gas. He tried turning on the bathroom sink. He grimaced while trying the lever. After loud rusty burps, water ran into the sink. He located the liquid propane gas valve and turned it on. *If I can light the pilot, we all gonna have ourselves a nice hot shower.*

Marshall returned to the living room. A fire blazed in the hearth. He removed his still dripping poncho by the door, shook it off, and hung it on one of the hooks. He slipped off his goggles and hung them. He removed his knapsack and set it by the door. He closed the door to prevent light from escaping. He walked to the fireplace. "Tatum, can y'all pass me one of them pom-poms?"

"What?"

"Y'all know what. Them cotton wads y'all ladies like to…once a month. Sorry, I'm only acquainted with pads for the purpose."

Dawning recognition. "Ah, sure. Feeling a little crampy are we?" she joked.

Marshall laughed. "Now look I don't wanna get anyone's hopes up. But if I'm right, I'm thinkin' we all might just have us a nice quick warm shower tonight."

Tatum's mouth slackened. She closed it. "Quit playing. That's cruel."

"No-no, not playin.' Serious. Hand me one. I need somethin' to use as a torch to light the pilot."

Tatum shook off and hung her poncho; hung up her night goggles; and rested her knapsack next to Marshall's. She reached inside then handed Marshall a tampon. He went into the kitchen, found a long meat fork, and impaled the tampon onto its tines.

"Jayden, not sure how long we gonna be here, but for sure we need to let the fire die before midday. Rain is tampin' down smoke preventin' it from travelin' to distant Golgoth nostrils, but when it clears up, whew! That furnace 'a yours will announce our presence for twenty miles in all directions," said Marshall.

"Roger that, hoss."

Marshall held the cotton over Jayden's now roaring fire until the tampon torch ignited. He quickly ran into the bathroom cupping his hand around the cool blue flame. He pushed down on the little red pilot valve release and inserted the forked torch. The pilot lit. He shook the flaming wad into the toilet. He flushed. "Toilet works," he muttered. "Thank y'all, Lord!" Tatum stood outside the bathroom door watching, but she gave him space. He opened the hot water heater valve to ON. There was a woosh of ignited propane gas as flames underneath the water heater roared into hot life.

He held Tatum in front of him while waiting for the water tank to heat. They made out like desperate teenagers. He found the strength to break the seal of their lips and release her. She watched as he reached into the open tiled shower enclosure and tried turning the shower valve. It barely moved. He manhandled it left and right until it moved more freely. He pulled on it. Plumbing behind the tiles coughed and groaned. Water from above soaked his sleeve, ran cold, then hot.

He opened both sink faucets; the water flow was brown with rust, but then the brown gradually diminished; flecks became sparser; and the water flowed clearer. Same with the shower which he left running on cold setting. He turned to Tatum. "I had prayed on the Trail for God to deliver us from this night. See now, how he works? It ain't a one-way relationship 'tween us and God. It's two-way."

She pressed her left cheek against his warm, thick chest. She looked up at him. "Those words you spoke back there, when you knelt on the trail asking God to help with the Arabella and Booker situation. Those were not your words, were they?"

His mouth pressed against her scalp. "Not sure what I said."

"Now this," Tatum said. "Mini miracles, each. Supernatural. Beyond the explainable earthly realm. Marshall, I believe. I believe; I believe; I believe. God loves us. Let's spend the rest of our lives loving him back."

Marshall smiled. "If we live, then we will. Long in his service."

"Together?" Tatum said.

He kissed her head. "God willing."

The Hunted

At nightfall, following Marshall and Tatum's lead, the four paired up under showers to stretch out the limited hot water. Tatum found dusty but fluffy towels in the bathroom, enough for everyone. "This is how our great grandparents lived. Sure could get used to this in a hurry," said Booker.

"Yeah, Marshall. Why don't we just stay here?" said Aliyah.

Marshall laughed. "Propane gas runs out. This may have been y'all's first hot shower, but it sure weren't mine. Up on my mountain I had propane gas: a hassle foragin' for small tanks. Eventually I ran outta tanks. Then I took cold showers and hey, I survived the shivers and so will y'all. Just enjoy the blessin.' In y'all's prayers tonight, give God a special thanks for deliverin' us from the storm."

"Bet your lily-white butt I will," said Aliyah, smiling. "That shower was the best thing I've felt in my entire life!"

"Hey now," said Booker in a deadpan tone. "Good to know you set your feel-good standards so low. I can't lose now."

Jayden lost it. Sitting by the fire he soon collapsed to the dusty floor on his back, laughing uncontrollably. None had ever heard Jayden laugh like that. It was infectious. Soon everyone joined him.

Later, between clean white sheets, Jayden, and Dodie, also Booker and Aliyah, further explored one another's bodies. By morning not a single virgin remained in the house. Everyone except Marshall seemed content to remain in bed. "Where are you going?" asked Tatum.

He kissed her forehead. "If they ask where the boss went, say he's gone fishin.'"

"I've never eaten a fish. Are they better than turkey?"

"Different. Gotta go, lover," he said, kissing her mouth. He left her with a smile and headed back out into steady rainfall and winds markedly lighter than the night's monsoon.

In the time Marshall was gone, Aliyah, Dodie and Tatum gathered up everyone's second set of clothing from their knapsacks. In the shower, they took turns scrubbing tops and bottoms, socks, and underwear, using the powdered detergent and stiff bristle brush they found under the metal bathroom sink. After thorough rinsing, they used Booker's length of paracord to rig a clothesline by the hearth's still orange coals. Then they hung all the clothes by the source of dry heat.

"I'm starving," said Tatum.

"I'm starving too," said Aliyah, "but I think you have intestinal parasites, Tates. I've never seen anyone put it away like you."

"I'm hot. My body is a furnace. I just burn it up."

"Better check Marshall for burns," Dodie joked.

"Hah-hah. Listen itchy-bitchy," Tatum said, looking at Dodie. "Are you okay? I see welts."

Dodie scowled. "Those awful critters just *love* me. Remind me never again to blow off Marshall's wise advice to use bug repellent. Ever. Before I set foot outside this place again I'll be taking a bath in his bug juice. You have no idea how badly these things itch."

The door opened. Marshall walked in with six brook trout already gutted, hanging over his shoulder from a length of clear fishing tackle. "Did I hear y'all's hungry? Jayden, it's still rainin' so it's okay to fire up that woodburnin' kitchen oven. We all 'bout to have delicious baked fish for breakfast; light and flaky; high in protein; can't beat it." Jayden immediately set about the task. Marshall looked around. "What's with the clothes? Didn't think they were that wet."

"We hand-laundered everyone's socks, undies and spare outerwear," said Dodie.

Marshall smiled at her, and at Aliyah and Tatum. "The good Lord could not have paired me up with better travelin' companions. Y'all are such a blessin' to me." He removed his poncho and shook it out.

"You're drenched," said Tatum.

"Great fishin' weather," Marshall replied. "Rain washes worms into the streams. Mornin's are when fish feed. Dummies thought they were eatin' a plain-old worm, but mine came with a bonus: a needle-sharp hook. I will say that the southern sky is much lighter than the rest. Fairly sure this storm is gonna move out sometime today, which means we all get back on the Trail tonight. Meanwhile, along the way I spotted deer. Y'all like deer meat?"

"I don't even know if I like fish: I never ate a fish, never ate a deer," said Aliyah. "But if you like it, then I know I will too."

This made Marshall smile. "Jesus told the Apostle Peter three times to 'Feed my lambs.' Well I ain't good enough to kiss Peter's foot but I know enough to keep feedin' y'all. Okay then, I'm headin' back out for a bit. Once the oven's hot just pop in the fish. Lay 'em on a grill or on a piece 'a steel. Turn 'em once after twenty minutes. Be right back," he said. Donning his poncho, he grabbed Jayden's bow and seven arrows. "Well buddy, I can't work this thing good as you can, so I'm takin' extra ammo in case I miss."

Jayden smiled.

Forty minutes later Marshall returned with the bow and six arrows in hand. He shook out and hung up his poncho. "You're short one arrow," said Jayden.

"A keen eye y'all have. That's because it's stickin' outta the doe outside. I'll gut and cook it after breakfast. Then we let our fire die out, for good."

"First try at archery and it's a bullseye. Damn. You are one lucky sonofabitch, know that?"

"Wasn't luck. The Lord is feedin' us. I had help. And I never miss a movin' target. I've kilt animals fifty feet away throwin' rocks at 'em."

"Mmm, so good!" said Aliyah, as she tucked into her brook trout.

"Good chow, hoss," said Jayden.

"Right? We'll do fish again soon, I hope," said Marshall.

"Our next stop might be a reservoir on the Virginia border," said Booker.

Marshall nodded. "Apt to be loaded with large and small-mouth bass and walleye, and more of these trout."

"What's deer taste like?" asked Tatum.

"Deer meat or venison tastes really good if y'all prep it right," Marshall answered." Find any canned food in the kitchen cabinets?"

"Only salt and pepper shakers. That's it."

Marshall smiled. "I'm goin' outside to butcher the deer. Jayden, if y'all can keep the kitchen oven near as you can to a constant state 'a hot coals versus flames, I'll salt the venison to take off the gamey edge. It'll give us somethin' to munch for a coupla' days after proper cookin.'"

Marshall went out and dragged the deer part-way into the woods fifty feet to the cabin's north side. Using paracord around the animal's rear hooves to hang it from a lower limb, he gutted it; peeled off the hide; and sliced the raw meat into chunks small enough for the iron oven's compact interior.

But then in his peripheral vision he thought he saw a flash of red behind the cabin. *Trust your gut,* he told himself.

Holding the bloody knife used to dress the deer, he walked behind the cabin. He saw the big propane tank. *Prolly' could live here takin' hot showers 'n sleepin' in warm beds for a good long while, 'stead 'a hikin' the muddy Trail for weeks. So temptin,'* he thought. "Lord, lead me not into temptation," he said.

He examined the rear window and glimpsed his friends warm and dry inside. He thought of last night with Tatum.

Then he bent for a closer look at the ground beneath the window. He saw two muddy boot prints, their outlines visible against the dark gray gravel. *Them prints are fresh.* All at once he went cold. He studied the prints more closely. *Golgoths don't wear shoes. What—"* suddenly the world went dark as he collapsed face-down in the gravel.

"Marshall! Marshall!" Tatum called his name as she knelt beside him. "You didn't come back. I was worried. Oh my God, are you all right?"

As consciousness returned, squinting from rain in his eyes, he reached inside the head area of his poncho. His hand came out bloody.

"Oh my God—what the heck happened?" screamed Tatum. "Did you trip and hit your head?"

Marshall sat up, palms supporting his weight: the sharp gravel stones dug into his palms. The pain shooting up his arms from his wounded palms helped him to focus. "No, lover. This is flat ground. I thought I'd seen somethin' or someone movin' back here so I moseyed 'round to check it out. The next thing I see is y'all standin' over me."

Cool rain did not cause the atavistic shiver tingling his spine. It was the stealth of the attack that chilled him. *Why did I not see it comin'? Have I grown civilized…complacent? Prideful? Is that my sin, Lord, pride? Is this why y'all's Spirit didn't warn me of danger?*

"Look under the window, tell me what you see."

Tatum inspected the ground closely. "I see fairly small boot prints; small enough that they could even be mine."

"Were y'all ever back here?"

"Nope. None of us have left the cabin."

"Someone musta clubbed me good. You sure none of y'all left?"

"Until now I've been inside the entire time with these people, Marshall. I came out to see what was taking you so long to return and to tell you the kitchen oven is hot. Whoever attacked you wasn't any of us. They're too interested in stealing kisses every chance they get."

"Hah. Can you blame 'em?" "Take my hand," Marshall said. Tatum pulled him to standing. He then followed from under the window the small boot prints until they disappeared, swallowed by the flood muck. "I'll pray the Holy Spirit; maybe I'll get a clue or two 'bout what just happened. In the meantime, follow me. Could use y'all's help carryin' an oven's full 'a venison: and Tatum, please don't mention this to anyone. Okay?" She nodded, though he felt anxiety, fear, and hot anger radiating from her like a pyroclastic cloud. He led her back to the window and picked up the bloody knife.

While Jayden took control of the venison roast, the three women repeated their laundry scrub-down with all remaining dirty clothes. Everyone changed into dry clean clothes. The mood inside the cabin felt infused with romantic endorphins and high optimism, everyone putting distance between themselves and bad memories. An emotional rebirth was happening for all, except for Marshall and Tatum.

Boot prints. Small. Female.

"Tatum, may I have a quick word?" said Marshall. He stood outside their bedroom door. She entered. He closed the door behind her.

"What size boots does Arabella wear?"

She understood what he implied. Her hand covered her mouth, eyes wide. "But how could she follow us all those miles through that insane storm, hide outside in the woods all night, then sneak up and attack you all by herself?"

He shook his head. "Darned if I know. With all the rain, not even Golgoths coulda' tracked us up here. From the Trail, this culvert looks pinky-size, so unless she was followin' real close behind no way could she have seen us leave the Trail. Besides, we stayed inside 'cept for my two food trips and believe me I woulda' sensed her or anyone else lurkin' out there. I was on full alert for stalkin' deer."

Tatum looked down at her socks. "On the Trail, a person can only hike in one direction or the other. I had hoped Arabella headed south, by now a good chunk of the way back to the resort we left, where she was queen bee surrounded by creature comforts, but no. Think about it, Marshall. That stunt she pulled with the perfume was attempted murder. She's not intent on making it to Spring Mountain because you told her she's unwelcome there, and we kicked her out of our group. She hates black people; she hates the concept of a living and merciful God. And now that we kicked her out she hates all of us equally. She trailed us, hanging back just far enough so she wouldn't be discovered. She means us severe harm. I don't think she has any other goal, at this point. I think she hit you with a rock trying to kill you and would have kept on hitting; but either she thought her one heavy blow did you in, or something must've spooked her away. Maybe you should've let Booker end her. God forgive me; I can't believe I just said that."

He noticed Tatum's shivers. Marshall embraced her. "We did the right thing," he whispered. "The Christian thing. People can accept Jesus Christ, repent of their sins, and be saved at any time; hearts can change even in them minutes right before death. But once the body dies all chances 'r gone, and God's grace with it. The unsaved face Judgement. God wants us to be merciful so we all can receive his mercy. What I decided back there was mostly for Booker; so the kid can grow up with a lovin,' merciful heart. 'N my daddy raised me never to lift a hand against a woman, ever. Y'all's the weaker sex; it ain't right to put a hurtin' on women, and children. Not ever. That's what he taught me 'n I believe it's right."

Speaking against this chest, she replied, "I believe you. But if Arabella comes at you again, I swear I'll poke out her eyeballs with a stick. Do you believe *me*?"

He held her tighter. "I like our prospects for livin' long, peaceful lives on the green mountain. But I do believe I'm fallin' head over heels in love with y'all, Tatum Winters." He felt her smiling against his chest. "But for now, what's say we all join the hootenanny in the kitchen for some fresh chow?"

"Mm, sure smells good in here," Marshall said, then walked to the cabin door to crack it and keep an eye on the weather outside. The storm left the same way it had entered, tapering down to a drizzle. He knew that soon it would be a light mist, and by nightfall, clear. He figured they had three hours to prep before descending back to the Trail. He closed the door. He felt the laundered clothing by the fire. In an hour it would be bone dry. "How's the venison?"

"Take a look. I think it's done. Don't want to overcook it," said Jayden. Marshall walked to the wood stove. He grabbed one of the two smooth hot wooden door handles and opened it up. "Oh Jayden. Archer, astronomer, musician. Now we all can add chef to the resume. Nailed it! Let's slice it up and fill plastic bags so y'all get an equal share. Then we all can retire to our bedrooms for a two-hour nap."

Jayden smirked. "Nap, uh huh, so that's what they're calling sexual congress these days." Using the tampon fork, he removed the first enormous hunk of smoking roast and smacked it down on the wooden table.

Marshall grinned. "I do mean nap, Jayden, not sex; else we all gonna be zombies tonight on the Trail. We're supposed to be sleepin' right now and yet here we are."

Jayden nodded. "My sleep-wake rhythms are messed up bigtime. You're right." Working together they quickly sliced up pounds of perfectly roasted venison. "Yo hoss, we have a problem: there aren't enough plastic drop cloth bags for all this. Guess we're leaving most of it here to rot."

"Heck with that!" said Marshall. "Be right back." He returned holding a box of thirty-gallon trash bags.

"Where the heck did you find these?"

"Remember when I followed y'all outta the Walmart, and I paused to pick somethin' up?"

"Nope. Don't remember."

"Stealth, brother. Y'all didn't see me grab that petrified jerky neither. Anyhow, I stuffed these into my backpack figurin' we'd need 'em to keep somethin' dry at one point or another."

Jayden shook his head. "You are one prepared jake, let me tell you."

They did their best to equally distribute sixty pounds of roast among six bags. "Now that it's cooked, we can munch on this for days. Tastes a heluva lot better than that dinosaur leather we ate on TN-107, don't it?" said Marshall.

"Not sure. Let me take a bite of my share," said Jayden. He did. His eyes rolled back in his head. "Best thing I have ever tasted. Seriously. So good. I'll stop now. Time to shut my eyes."

Marshall announced a two-hour nap period and reminded everyone to slather completely with insect repellent. Tatum followed him inside the bedroom and closed the door. Immediately they stripped off all clothing and commenced fevered and greedy mutual consumption, to the point she had to bite the pillow to avoid disturbing others. After, they closed their eyes in ecstasy, and in the abject worship of love.

The absence of light woke Marshall. As gently as possible, he disengaged from her. She snapped awake. "What's wrong?"

He kissed her mouth. "I don't wanna leave."

"So don't."

"I must. We all must, lover. It's mornin' in our troubled world. Time to face the new day."

"Night."

He smiled. "Confusin' ain't it? Yes. Let's get dressed and make some noise."

He did, and Tatum followed. Together they packed the knapsacks with laundered clothes. "Wake up, Elect!" he yelled, the steel fork in his right hand banging the aluminum cook pot in his left. Rubbing their eyes, Booker and Aliyah came stumbling out of their bedroom; Jayden and Dodie lurched out next. "Grab your clothes," Marshall said. "Whose paracord?"

"Mine," Booker groaned.

"Me and Tatum 'r packed. Don't forget to pack your ponchos. See them bags 'a hot roast on the table? Y'all get one. Each of us gets ten pounds 'a food which should last us all more than a week."

"Except for Tates," yawned Dodie. "Hers will be gone by noon tomorrow." Everyone laughed, especially Tatum. Packed up, they donned their night goggles and stepped outside.

"Brrr. Got cold out here!" said Aliyah.

"Once we all 'r movin' trust me, y'all gonna be glad for the cold," said Marshall. "Lots 'a sweaty uphill hikin' in our future."

Everyone groaned. Marshall turned and faced the cabin. He took a knee. "Heavenly Father, we thank y'all so much for this port in the storm. Y'all 'r our salvation forever and ever. Amen."

"Amen," said the five.

Marshall walked down the steep decline and merged with the shadows gathering around him. He relied on grabbing trees to slow his descent, and hoped the others were imitating him. They did, and therefore none slipped and broke their bodies rolling down the steep grade.

A quarter hour later they reunited on the Trail. Both Marshall and Tatum did a three-sixty, not knowing with absolute certainty whom or what they were hoping to spot.

Boot prints. Small. Female. Marshall and Tatum shared the same thought as their eyes met; it was a silent exchange reminding them of their agreement not to reveal the incident to the group.

Satisfied the group was alone for the moment, Marshall led the night's first steps north along the muddy Trail, praying they learn how not to drown in the unfamiliar, unfriendly ocean of darkness separating them from the promise of God's peaceful community.

"Remember: whispers only," he reminded them. He glanced at Tatum. Fleetingly their eyes met. He thought back on how he had intended to confront lethal dangers alone, responsible only for himself; in Tatum's eyes, and looking back at the group, he felt the weight of leadership pressing down on his spirit. He wondered how many of them might die along the Trail from injuries, infections, or snatched by Golgoths before ever reaching the lush Mountain of Springs.

Funnel to Hell

The Trail rose and fell, but then seemed to rise for good. The White Rocks Mountain section felt like one ceaseless uphill grade. Marshall and Jayden were able to bear it slightly better than the others, conditioned to the crushing physicality of carrying far greater pounds for hours on end during their Walmart side trip. To the rest, the twenty or so pounds they carried uphill felt every bit as heavy as all that by now.

Marshall, sympathetic to their plight spotted a small stream off to the right. He stopped, held up his hand, turned, and whispered, "Let's take these packs off awhile and refill our water bottles."

Everyone groaned their relief and set the packs down onto rocks scattered along the trail side versus into the sucking mud of the Trail itself. Each grabbed a water bottle. All together they picked their way over to the stream. They bent and filled up their water bottles, removed their goggles, splashed cold water on their faces, then slogged their muddy way back to their knapsacks.

"What I wouldn't give for a nice lounge chair right now," whispered Dodie.

"I don't know what one of those is," whispered Jayden, gazing up at the stars. "You know, guys: the problem with stargazing in the old world before the Floods was light pollution."

"What's that?" Tatum asked quietly.

Jayden spoke in low muted tones. "In Pre-Flood days, nations were so lit up from so many electric lights blaring that astronauts saw them from orbit; they could identify major cities based on light concentrations. Light from the ground diffuses light coming down from stars, planets, and galaxies. Astronomers had to build observatories in remote places where light pollution wouldn't interfere. They built domed structures on top of island mountains in the middle of the ocean, or in dark deserts: remote places away from civilization. Government agencies were even launching telescopes into space. Now, ever since the First Flood knocked out all the electricity, when we gaze at the stars, we see everything clearly."

Dodie rested her head against his shoulder. "What do you see up there?"

Jayden shrugged. "Yo hoss: mind if I take a few minutes to set up my scope and star-gaze? Been weeks."

"Not at all," whispered Marshall. He figured if Arabella or some other lunatic was stalking them, this little break might force a reveal. As Jayden unlatched his knapsack and pulled out his portable telescope, Marshall and Tatum walked down the trail back to where they had passed two good-sized rocks. They sat on the rocks facing back down the Trail watching for Arabella, or whichever stealth operator had tried to kill Marshall.

Jayden steadied his collapsible tripod as best he could on rocks along the trailside. Dodie rested her hand on his back as he peered through a small viewing lens, fiddling with focus knobs. He tilted it, locked it into place with one knob, then fine-turned a dial. He stilled his breathing. "Wha—"

Dodie removed her hand from his back as he jerked away from the device optic. He appeared shocked as he stood erect, mouth open in an unlovely yawp.

"What is it, Jay? Tell me!" Dodie whispered.

He turned to her. "Jupiter—the planet Jupiter. I believe it has moved closer to earth. That it's twelve-year orbit around the sun has changed."

"What?"

Still looking, he whispered, "The sheer size of Jupiter—around three-hundred-eighteen times as massive as Earth—means it also has an outsized gravitational pull on our planet. At the peak of that warped orbit, Earth undergoes hotter summers, colder winters, as well as more intense periods of drought and wetness. No wonder we're getting super floods. Jupiter formed four times farther from the sun than its current orbit. Its migration inward through the solar system to its current orbit took only seven-hundred-thousand years. Nothing moves that fast in our solar system. And...holy crap! Stars appear brighter."

"You're only just noticing this now? Tonight? What about two weeks ago in Nashville?"

"Apsides, Dodie. I was certain I'd been looking at Jupiter's perigee weeks ago, but it's closer now to the sun and to earth than it ever was."

"You're saying this caused the Two Floods?"

Jayden nodded. "Absolutely Jupiter's movement could have caused flooding. And if it keeps changing, the next thing heading our way will be volcanic activity like this planet hasn't seen in about two billion years."

"Oh my God," she said aloud then covered her mouth.

"I mean look around you," he continued. "These mountains were formed by a major tectonic orogeny. Right where you're standing used to be volcanically active. If Jupiter grows any closer, drowning in water will be the least of our worries. Volcanoes will bring floods of molten rock."

"What are you two whispering about?" Tatum asked quietly.

"You don't wanna know," whispered Dodie. "End of world stuff."

"Creeping out my buddy here, Jayden?" Tatum asked.

"Myself, that's who I'm creeping out."

"How do you know all this stuff anyway? You could be off," said Tatum.

Jayden ignored the question. "Anyway, I need better equipment to prove my hypothesis. Hoping they have one where we're going. Thought I glimpsed a powerful Dobsonian telescope in a dream about Spring

Mountain. I promise not to speak about planets and stars 'til we get there. If we ever get there," whispered Jayden. "Hey hoss, thanks. Had my fill of the stars for a good long while. Can we get a move on?"

They walked without incident, high up through the White Rock Mountains until walls of rock and trees fell away into breathtaking ledges and pine-choked ravines. A sense of relief swept through all as they started walking downgrade into the Cherokee National Forest. Marshall stopped at a particularly soggy point, bent over, uncovered flat rocks, and pulled large pink earthworms from underneath. He slipped these into his knapsack.

"Marshall, my mama told me never to kiss a man with worm-breath," whispered Tatum. Dodie giggled. He grinned at her then pressed on. They came to a road. Jayden unstrapped his bow and nocked an arrow. Marshall, understanding the threat, stood behind Jayden with open hands. *Road crossin' ahead.* Jayden loosened his bundle and handed a bow to Marshall.

"Where y'all keepin' them strings?" asked Marshall.

"Side flap pocket. Just reach in."

Marshall strung his bow and nocked an arrow. Booker also loaded up. The three walked in a line across Highway 321, scanning the road with night vision. No movement spotted. Once across, Marshall stood with Booker and Jayden; all three motioned back across for the three women to follow. Into more woods they walked until, on the right, all six removed their goggles to take in the beautiful site of the gibbous moon reflecting off vast, serene fresh water. "What's that?" whispered Aliyah.

"Watauga Reservoir. Means we're still in Tennessee, but the Virginia border is close," answered Booker in a happy whisper.

"Booker," whispered Marshall. "These are lowlands. Does the map suggest any safe places we all can hole up in durin' daylight?"

Booker struggled to map-read in moon and star light. He saw a symbol that resembled a narrow footbridge somewhere up ahead just off the trail leading out into the reservoir. At the end of it, he saw a symbol of something large protruding up out of the water. "Marshall. On the map there's a dam, and what looks like a defensible position. It would be tough to spot us if we could get out into the reservoir and onto this big round obelisk, whatever it is; on the map it resembles a castle tower with battlements and arrow slits with a deep moat separating us from the Trail."

"Hmm. Sounds promisin.' Let's check out the reservoir, y'all," said Marshall."

"Yes, let's," Booker agreed. "Since there's only one ingress, the footbridge, we have enough arrows to wipe out an entire Golgoth colony. They'd have to cross the narrow bridge to get to us well out of spear-throw range. All we'd have to do was keep firing until the last fiend fell."

"Can't lose, really," said Marshall. "I seen Golgoths over my lifetime, never armed with anythin' 'cept cuttin' and stabbin' weapons. I ain't never seen a gun in my entire life, 'cept pit'chers in books. The Floods carried away or rusted out even simple metal machines, which guns are. Floods also soaked and destroyed all the bullets people 'd put in 'em. Even if Golgoths discovered bows and arrows like Jayden did, they'd be like sittin' ducks on that footbridge because we all'd be firin' from behind cover. But this place is so remote, I can't even imagine it ever comin' to that. I like the odds."

"Hmm. I like those odds of firing arrows behind cover. Okay, let's go check out this obelisk. It's on the way, right?" Jayden chimed in.

"According to the map the obelisk is only feet off the Trail," Booker answered.

Walking took them past Watauga Lake to their right, peaceful and serene, reflecting Heaven's light. Though each felt the eerie stillness. *Too good to be true* skipped across everyone's thoughts. Anxiety would follow them wherever they went; each recognized and accepted the danger and risks of traveling through Golgoth country. Still, they found that body of water calming somehow and strangely enticing.

"Marshall—look right!" Booker whispered. "The footbridge. And look, two cement obelisks. The one at the other end of this walkway is six-sided, not cylindrical. I see now: Iron Mountain Fault, Watauga Dam, Tennessee. We have arrived."

Marshall walked off-trail. For a minute, the group lost sight of him. He returned. "The bridge is solid steel on concrete pilins,' and I'd say it's 'bout a hun'dert yards to the big cement obelisk. The bridge dips down but then levels out. Very sturdy. There's a hardened steel gate blockin' the bridge to keep people out. No way can we pry open that steel lock without heavy iron tools," he said, rubbing his beard. "I got camp saws and paracord. We'll throw together two quick ladders. Climb up one ladder this side then down the other on that side." He reached into his back pockets, pulled out the coiled wire garrote-like saws, and handed one to Jayden. "Ready?"

"Let's do it."

Goggles on, in the woods they wire-sawed through the straightest low-hanging green limbs and hauled them to the Trail. While the others kept the limbs stable, Jayden and Marshall fast-sawed four six-foot poles and twelve sixteen-inch rungs. Marshall felt uncomfortable sacrificing the spare twenty feet of paracord, wishing he had not left the fifth length and a perfectly good drop cloth with Arabella. *Waste*, he thought. To squeeze twenty-four lashings out of a cord that was only twenty feet long, Marshall calculated each lashing could only measure ten inches. Lashings would need to support his weight of over two-hundred pounds. *Clove hitch knot or constrictor knot? We gonna need them ten-inch lengths again up the Trail, I just know it. Clove hitches gotta be easier to untie tomorrow night. Constrictor knots under my weight? They'd tighten down so hard under I'd need to slice 'em off. Okay, clove hitches it is. I pray this works.*

He tied the bottom rung looping the cord over the rung, around the pole, looped around the nub and outside of the pole, then tied a perfect clove hitch knot. He did the same with the top rung. "Okay gang, ya'll watched me knot down a few rungs: how 'bout taking a stab at makin' the other ladder while Tatum and I finish this one? Space the rungs twelve inches apart. My boots are twelve inches heel to toe, just eyeball 'em as a guide."

Tatum pulled his head down to her mouth. "You know what they say about men with big hands and feet."

Smiling, he bent down and whispered, "Well? Is the rumor true?"

She held up her right hand, forefinger and thumb separated by one inch. He poked her shoulder hard. She giggled.

After ten minutes of lashing work, they admired their two six-foot ladders. Marshall shouldered one; Jayden the other: heads down they trod carefully down the slippery grade to the gate. Marshall hoisted his ladder up and over the gate, pole tops clearing the fence tilting back toward him. Jayden dropped and carefully positioned his exterior ladder to integrate with Marshall's on the other side, making one 'A' shaped ladder.

Marshall ran back up to the Trail. "Who's goin' first?" he whispered. No one volunteered. "So y'all wanna be the last one standin' on this side after the rest of us are safely over?"

"I'll go first!" said Aliyah. With the grace of a cat, quickly she scaled the ladder, swung her right leg over at the top, and found firm footing on the top opposite rung, then scrambled down. She hit the metal footbridge with a resounding metallic thud.

Marshall smiled. "Excellent, Aliyah. Everyone see what she did?" All nodded. Dodie went next without issue, followed by Tatum, Booker, then Jayden. Marshall went last. The rungs felt firm. On the footbridge, he pulled over the opposing ladder. He and Jayden shouldered them again. Marshall walked first with Jayden seven feet behind him. The others followed. Booker holding Aliyah's hand, then Dodie, and finally Tatum. All imitated Marshall's deliberately cautious pace to minimize sounds from boots impacting steel. The stillness and quietude of the reservoir was acoustically different than any environment the group had experienced: where the smallest sounds carried clear and far.

The sun pushed up against the twilight, and with it, a nautical blue rind heralded the daybreak. The color reminded Marshall of Tatum's eyes. He knew she was somewhere in the back. Regretfully he knew that today, none of the couples would enjoy distance and privacy. Just then inside he felt as blackish and blue as the sky. *More than anythin,' I wanna be closer to y'all, Lord. I wanna believe y'all brought Tatum to me. If I'm wrong 'bout her, if I missed the Holy Spirit's signs somehow then please, this is me beggin'—send 'er away. I wanted Delilah but that union whuddn't ordained by y'all; I know that now, which is why it failed. And now here we go again, 'cept this time we know that I ain't never wanted the company of a human anywhere near like I want hers, but Lord, I refuse to sell myself another fiction ever again. In the name of y'all's Son, Jesus Christ, I ask please either ordain our union, or send me clear signs to leave her be. Otherwise outta caution I'm gonna hafta cut 'r loose. No one ain't never comin' between me and y'all again. Amen.*

Marshall had been careful not to accidentally bang the ladder against the steel walls or safety guardrails, also not to step on the occasional bird skeleton on the walkway, which now emptied onto the concrete obelisk that jutted up sixty or seventy feet out of the water. As the brooding blue eastern sky became speared with rays of yellow orange at the center, Marshall gently set down the ladder. He leaned it against the solid four-foot cement wall, atop which was more of the same steel pipe guardrails. He slipped off his goggles and held up his palm for the others to stop.

Yet again, Booker nailed it. This obelisk, whatever it is…perfect for our needs, Marshall thought. He wondered how they would relieve themselves. He walked three-quarters of the obelisk's perimeter. He could not make out the purpose for the 1940's menacing machinery occupying the entire middle, rusting and sinister, built for mysterious heavy-duty activity; a crane boom from which dangled a thick steel cable and massive hook designed to swing out over the water. *What in the Sam Hill did these men hoist outta the water with this thing, submarines?* The lightening sky revealed concrete and steel areas in the middle of the obelisk, purpose unknown, with holes that could permit a man to disappear down inside the concrete. He felt better. *There's our toilet. Plenty 'a privacy from the deck, and a hole down to nowhere with rainwater fillin' the bottom. Perfect.*

At the halfway point he marked his territory with his knapsack, then positioned the ladder on the railing to jut out over the greenish-blue water. He completed the final third of the circular deck walk back to the footbridge, and to the group. All had removed their night goggles. He motioned with his hand to follow him. He stopped at the quarter mark and pointed inside the morass of metal and concrete, and at the hole. "Toilet," he whispered. They followed him to his knapsack. "I'm tyin' my drop cloth to the railin' right here, so Booker and Jayden, if y'all wanna stake claims at the other two quarter marks, we'll each have a bit 'a privacy," he whispered. "I'll drop a line and baited hook from the ladder. If y'all wanna eat venison that's fine, I will too, for now. Later though, thinkin' fresh crappie could be on the menu," Marshall whispered.

"Marshall, my mama told me never to kiss a man with crappie breath," whispered Tatum. He laughed and noticed that indeed her eyes were the color of the sky just before dawn.

"Crappies are a kinda fish y'all find in still water like this, Tater-Tots, ya giddy slip of a girl. My mama told me that if a woman ever gets uppity, just drop a few earthworms down 'er shirt when she's sleepin' and that'll tune 'er right up."

Tatum punched his stomach. He let out a hiss, teeth clenched, smiling. "I wish you wouldn't call me that," she said. "It's not at all dignified. Fartface."

"You two are a trip," laughed Aliyah. Booker, Dodie, and Jayden joined in the sorely needed levity. "C'mon, Booker, said Aliyah. "Let's take the south quadrant. Okay with you Dodie?"

"Sure! Perfect view of the beautiful, stepped dam! How cool is that?" whispered Dodie, scratching at scabby welts on her arm.

"Really cool," whispered Booker. "Marshall and Tatum have the scariest view of all. See that gigantic concrete funnel over there? Seriously, I am not even joking, that thing ranks as one of the most terrifying things I have ever laid eyes on. What the heck is it? A portal to Hades?"

"Circular emergency spillway," whispered Jayden. "I've read about them. Though that's the craziest one I've seen and the first I've seen in-person. Would not want to go anywhere near that big sucker during a flood. Can't see the outfall downstream so it must be a long way down the valley."

"What's it for?" asked Booker.

"When there's a flood, the overflow swirls down into that yawning concrete finned funnel like a giant flush toilet, except water rushes around it with the force and velocity of a maelstrom," Jayden said, drawing a circle in the air with his finger. "A huge high-volume pipe made of concrete or steel buried deep in the earth carries the water downhill to a lower elevation outflow, probably to a river somewhere in the valley."

"What would happen to us in a heavy storm if we kayaked over to the spillway?" asked Aliyah.

Jayden shook his head. "You'd get caught up in its event horizon, circling around it no matter how hard you paddled until it sucked you all the way down inside. Imagine tons of water crashing down on you, pushing you into an airless pipe for a mile or more. Your life would end in a high-velocity drowning death, for sure. Only a powerful boat could escape the vortex once the boat got too close to the edge. Maybe not even."

"Like a black hole in space, but on earth," said Booker.

Jayden nodded. "At least a black hole would be a quick death. Tatum, you said each lady packed a blow-up kayak, right? Let's all paddle over to the spillway before we rest, take a closer look," he whispered, trying not to smile.

"Yeah, ah, that's a big no," whispered Tatum. "C'mon, let's pitch camp and take a nap. Anybody else beat?"

Everyone nodded. Drop cloths flew up and bedrolls unfurled in under sixty seconds. Marshall cut four three-foot lengths of clear nylon fishing line, tied hooks to each end, and tied their opposite ends to the main length. He impaled the squirming worms onto the four hooks and lowered them all the way down below the water line. He tied the spool to the ladder rung. *Twenty-percent chance that I even get one fish,* he thought.

Everyone ate cold venison. There were no biting insects, only flies attracted by the venison. The sun came fully up and burned away the night's chill. They laid on top of their sleeping bags, cool enough under the shade of their cloth roofs. Sleep came quickly and deeply. Each dreamed of the yellow-haired man in white linen robes, smiling down at them on Spring Mountain. Tatum had vaguely dreamed of the green hill on the mountain, but this was the first time that the prophet Gabriel's face had appeared within Tatum's unconscious mind.

Clang! Clunk. Bonnngg. Bing! Thunk. Splash.

Sounds—alarming, alien, and very loud rudely pulled them back to unwelcome consciousness. "What the—" Booker said.

"Shhh!" cautioned Marshall. He launched into motion leaving Tatum sitting up wide-eyed and terrified. He maneuvered up onto the concrete-steel center ironworks to avoid walking straight through Jayden and Dodie's campsite. He arrived at the mouth of the footbridge, right hand shielding his eyes from the sun. Rocks and stones that had not been there last night lay near the halfway point of the footbridge. He panned the area and saw no sign of life. Birds near the opposite end of the bridge had stopped tweeting but had now restarted. *Not a group 'a humans, otherwise them birds woulda scrammed for a good long while. No telltale flashes 'a bald white painted enemy stalkin' them woods.* His haggard brain flashed only one name.

Arabella.

Wedge

As far-away pilgrims off the Appalachian Trail puzzled over the lobbed rock assault waged upon them: at Spring Mountain, the prophet Gabriel held his first meeting with Gunny Powell, outdoors on his tower deck. "Ah, so, you're the brass hat around here?" asked Gunnery Sergeant Patrick Powell. Gabriel's face registered no recognition of the title. "Head honcho. Pointy-head. Guy in charge." Still shaking hands, Gunny Powell found the grip dry, warm, and respectfully firm. The blinding sun beamed hot as a torch directly above them outside on Gabriel's wooden deck. Gunny found himself wishing for just a little shade.

"I am indeed the brass hat, Gunny. I trust that my friends have made you feel at home." Gabriel did not release his grip or cease staring deeper into Powell's corneas and optic nerves. Gunny felt it. On some level he sensed an intellect, vast and cool, like nothing he had ever experienced before. "Please call me Gabriel."

Gunny nodded vigorously. "Everyone always used to call me Gunny. After a time, even my dad did. Yessir, I feel at home. I was a little bit scairt' of leavin' my home for half a century, but the second I got here I knew God had steered me right."

Gabriel smiled and released his grip. "He always does, Gunny. What did my friends say to you in the first sixty seconds of your meeting them, do you recall?"

After stroking his beard, Gunny nodded. "Sorry to disturb you, sir. The Lord of Hosts has need of you. We serve the Lord Jesus Christ, sent here by his prophet who lives among us. That's what they said pretty much word for word. Are you he?"

Gabriel nodded. "Do you know what a prophet is, Gunny?"

"Well sir, I do love reading my Bible. Prophets are ordinary men with God's finger on 'em. He uses 'em, and they consent to being used. Mostly for communicating God's thoughts to other people. Like John the Baptist. Now he is my favorite prophet. I like his fire. The man had balls of steel. He didn't care who he offended. The way he took on King Herod, laying that guilt trip about his illegal wife, oh yes. But tyrants in command couldn't face their sins and would do nothing that might chip away at their power; and so like every prophet who came before him, John ended up executed."

"All bodies end up dead, Gunny. But some souls will live on. Will yours? Are you one of God's Elect?"

Gunny's eyes widened. "A'course I am, don't you doubt it! I am all-in with the Man Upstairs," he said, jabbing his index finger at the sun. Sweat beaded on his forehead. "He let them Jew tyrants kill his only begotten Son just to save my worthless ass. I owe him more than my life." Now the sweat dripped onto the decking material. Gunny swabbed his face on the sleeve of his summer wool khaki Marine shirt. Then he noticed thousands of people gathered to stare at them on the deck. "Sir, why are all of these people gaping at us?"

Gabriel smiled. "I'm something of an introvert, Gunny. My public appearances are measured, and purposeful. They know no one else like me, or like you. We are mysterious to them. They want to know more about us."

Gunny laughed. "I could be grandfather or even great grandfather to all of 'em. You are so right. They bury me in questions all day and all night about the world before The Floods. I'm the most popular guy on campus. 'Cept for you, a'course."

Gabriel's face turned stony. "You appear overheated. Shall we move inside where it's cooler?" Gunny gave a high-energy nod. They moved inside.

Gabriel motioned to a thick green vinyl reclining chair. Powell sank into it. He found it incredibly comfortable, firm, and cool. Gabriel sat on the floor, legs folded under him, white linen robe billowing about him. *Like he's growing up out of the floor, hovering like a ghost,* Gunny thought.

"Let us speak plainly, Gunny. Yes, I am a prophet of God. He touched me in the third grade. Changed me. Gave me more…capacity, let's say, than given to others born of the flesh. He revealed knowledge, imparted wisdom, and speaks to me."

Powell sat actively listening and pondering. "May I ask, sir: does the Lord speak to you in words? Like a voice? Like my voice right now 'cept only you can hear him?"

Gabriel nodded. "Yes, sometimes. Heaven's voice sounds like my own voice; the voice of the Lord's Holy Spirit comes from inside me: I hear it as plainly as I hear you now. He speaks to me in dreams. He shows me movie scenes. Only you and I, and also the other eleven founders of the community who are all my age are old enough to remember television and moving pictures, so imagine if I tried describing this to any of the younger Elect: not one could relate to the simile. Sometimes, the Lord plays movies of future events, like previews, never long, only snips. Enough to know what to expect, then supplies knowledge and wisdom to act upon the information."

"Are you able to ask him on what day I'll die, and how?"

Gabriel shook his head. "It does not work like that, Gunny. I spend most of my waking hours in prayer. Sometimes the Lord responds immediately, sometimes days or weeks, months, or even years later, with the precise answer to my question. The answer might be through a sign, and then I see plainly how it connects to a former prayer." Gabriel inhaled deeply and let it out slowly, his eyes locked on Gunny's eyes. "What I've told you just now about my two-way communications with God is more than I have divulged to anyone. Please know this."

"Sir. I feel honored. Thank you. Let me know how I can help the cause."

If you please, let me ask you some questions."

"Yes, sir. Fire at will."

"You don't believe that I am what I say I am, is that not true?"

Gunny shifted in the chair, making it squeak. "I believe that you believe it, sir."

Gabriel smiled. "Hannah was the first girl that you kissed, underneath the willow tree. You had spent the afternoon catching Monarch and Tiger Swallowtail butterflies in a net, long enough for Hannah to look closely at them. One thing you may or may not have known: she loved those butterflies more than any of God's other creatures. But she loved you even more than butterflies."

Powell's mouth flew open. Tears pooled in his eyes. One ran down his left cheek. "But how did you…"

"When Hannah got smashed to death by a snowplow skidding down the icy mountain road, at her viewing, you stood by her casket holding her hand. What you may not have known is, Jesus—Jesus—was holding your other hand. Her parents, Herb, and Terri, and you, were the only ones she allowed to call her Banana. They buried her in a white Holy Communion dress with lace and puffy sleeves, and black patent leather shoes buffed to a perfect sheen. You put your fingerprint on one, deliberately, so that she would go to her eternal rest with something of you to keep close. She was the one true love of your life, Gunny. She was the purest soul you had ever known. The gentlest of all."

Gunny broke down and cried hard. He covered his face, as his entire lean body hitched and jagged. Gabriel allowed him his privacy. "Is she… will I…"

"Yes, Gunny. You will embrace Hannah again. For you have faithfully loved and served the Lord. You have done his work that none of these young people can conceive of doing. Yet."

Gunny prayed: "My God, my dear sweet Lord, forgive me for ever doubting this man, your living prophet. Please have mercy on me, Lord, for I am just a stupid, stupid man."

Gabriel rose and placed his right hand on top of Gunny's head. "You are a deliberate man, stubborn to the core. Once you decide on an outcome, you judge not your effort, only your result. Many people who claim to love Jesus fall away during grim times, such as losing the people they loved most in this world. They grow to hate God for failing to intervene: to stop the truck, the bullet, the disease, or the evildoer. Not you, Gunny. You decided to love God and you never wavered, not even for a moment. That is why the Holy Spirit gives you such strength, so much so that the Lord requires your service, here, now. Will you take orders from me, God's servant, and from me alone?"

Gunny raised his eyes to meet Gabriel's. He felt the magnetic pull. "Yessir. God, yes. But I have little to offer. Only my unflinching loyalty. Obedience without question. I'm not particularly good at anything. Got no unique skills or talent, apart from telling a bunch of kids what it was like back in the day, maybe. What can I do for someone like you, sir, with all your power?"

Gabriel stroked Powell's head. "I have nothing that was not given to me from above. And as for you, please permit me to correct you. Indeed you have great skills. War is a skill."

Gunny blinked. "Are you expecting a war, sir?"

Gabriel closed his eyes. He sat back down on the floor as before, hands steepled under his chin. "Salvation belongs to our God, who sits on the throne, and to the Lamb. Our Lord said, 'Behold, I stand at the door and knock. If anyone hears my voice and opens the door, I will come to him and eat with him, and he with me.' Tell me, Gunny. What does the New Testament tell us about the end times?"

"Depends on which translation you read. I left two other versions at the armory. The New International translation reads 'Then they gathered the kings together to the place that in Hebrew is called Armageddon.' Though lately I've been favoring the Aramaic direct translation, how Christ formed his sentences in the popular language of the time and region, sir. 'And he shall gather them to the place called, in Hebrew, Megiddo.' Did my feeble old brain remember right? I'm sure you know."

Gabriel nodded. "And of the whole world, to gather them to the battle of that great day of God Almighty. Behold, I come like a thief. Blessed is he who watches and keeps his garments, lest he walk naked, and they see his shame."

Gunny nodded. "Golgoths are naked even in winter. I've shot 'em in winter. But sir. Armageddon is the Greek name for Tel Megiddo, an old mound about thirty klicks southeast of Haifa; a trading hub for millenniums. I was there once with my outfit for Krav Maga and sniper training from the Mossad. Megiddo is no bigger than a football field. If that's where God's decisive battle will be fought, first we'll need a few large ships to cross the Atlantic to go fight it; and that tiny town of Megiddo won't hold the half of us."

Gabriel stood. "Permit me to show you something," he said. He walked to an old wooden roll-top desk and raised the cover. He rifled through cardstock folders until he extracted a yellowed paper. He walked to the green vinyl chair and held it out. Gunny took it. "Please read it aloud."

"Lenape Indian deed, March 3, 1691. He is called Mehgheetow 'chief of the Perkiomen savages.'"

"Did you just say Megiddo?" Gabriel asked.

Gunny examined the remainder of the document. "This was a land grant from William Penn, the Quaker. He founded the Province of Pennsylvania, a North American colony of England. I learned in school that he was an Indian lover, but I had no idea he loved 'em enough to give 'em this mountain, this entire valley, and all the land around here for miles."

"Gunny, who authored the Book of Revelation?"

"Saint John, The Apostle. Exiled to the Island of Patmos. I love the entire New Testament. Everything is crystal, especially Paul's Letters to his Churches. But I never quite connected with Revelation. Seals opening, plagues, earthquakes, and stuff I can't quite get clear in my head."

"God revealed a name to Saint John. John only knew what he knew; could only relate the name he heard to lands with which he was familiar. He didn't even know America existed at that time. 'Meh-geet-tow' is the name he heard from God, so naturally his rational mind believed it to mean the tiny village he knew which when you say it aloud sounds exactly the same: Megiddo."

"Hmm. Makes sense."

"Gunny: you and I are sitting in the land grant known as Mehgheetow, the ancient Native American name for all of Spring Mountain."

As dots connected, Gunny buried his face in his hands. "Oh, my dear Lord. I had no idea. Do others know about this? And what about other signs John's prophesy revealed about the end times final battle?"

Gabriel nodded. "I have been preparing the community of Elect for the coming violence; and yes, Gunny: Christ himself as well as John prophesized that there will be signs in the sun, moon, and stars. On the earth, nations will be in anguish and perplexity at the roaring and tossing of the sea. Men will faint from terror, apprehensive of what is coming on the world, for the heavenly bodies will be shaken."

Gunny shrugged. "Floods, sure. But the sun moon and stars seem pretty normal to me."

"They are not. This was revealed to me. A young man with strong earthly knowledge of the heavens, a self-taught student of astronomy is on his way here. My friends recovered a powerful Dobsonian telescope from a flood-damaged store, perfectly preserved. They erected a cabin on the highest point here on Mount Mehgheetow, with a roof cut-out to block the elements but the hatch opens for celestial observation. This astronomer man, God willing, shall observe the heavens and provide us with details."

Gunny nodded. "We are here, then. End of line. I don't suppose you know which side will win. Was this revealed to you?"

Gabriel shook his head. "Only that the Lord knows the beginning and end. He reveals to me, his lowly and unworthy servant, what he wills. I am a killer of God's enemies, as you are. I shot dead thirteen first generation Golgoths when I was eight years old. It requires great faith and strength of spirit for an adult to kill a man, to take from him everything he has or will ever have. But I was only a third grader. How can you help, you asked? Train the young men. Take your strategy from me but teach them gritty tactics and field discipline. Your role is to make soft men hard, because the enemy holds a numerical advantage which, in war, typically means their victory is assured."

"But we have God on our side. Don't we?" asked Gunny, sounding a bit panicked.

Gabriel stared at him with unblinking, hypnotic eyes. "If you were a student of the Bible and have studied God as a character throughout the millenniums, then you would know that his policies toward humans never change. He helps those who help themselves, and who glorify him. He is nothing if not for consistent; all promises kept. We must prepare the men. Drill them for war. Help us to help ourselves, and to glorify God."

"Do they know this? The men?"

"You have seen our armory. The catapults. Earthworks. Napalm bombs. Your mortars. So have they all. I doubt they believe that their leader's war preparations are based upon unfounded paranoia," Gabriel said, lips flattened into a self-deprecating grin.

"How many Golgoths?"

"Approximately seventy thousand."

"Christ almighty," muttered Gunny. "Golgoth weapons?"

"Swords, spears. But they also found one M2A1 tripod-mounted Browning .50 caliber machine gun with over forty-thousand rounds, mounted to the flatbed of a working vehicle."

Gunny sprung up out of his chair. "That thing will cut us down easier than a chainsaw! And what do we have to go against that beast? I have three mortars and one M1 Garand with a thousand rounds. The armory where I lived has no firearms. When it was operational they manufactured rounds for mortars, mostly."

"You see the archaic weapons we have. We can win a fair fight, but their machine gun unbalances everything. You must destroy it with your mortars. Please understand that once you destroy their one modern weapon with your mortars, your mission is over. We will fight the Golgoths using traditional Roman methods and tactics. Close up fighting, intimate, and brutal. Your assistance in drilling the young fighters is why I asked you here today. They lack your instincts and mindset. You must reveal your inner killer and let it flow into them."

"Roman style?"

Gabriel nodded. "You are familiar with the testudo formation? The triple line? The wedge?"

Gunny beamed. "The wedge! —the Roman phalanx. They'd put the least seasoned men up front. Behind them were the guys who could afford good armor and weapons to act as spearmen and swordsmen. They put the veterans of combat in the back, so that when the first two lines got tired or wounded, knowing by that point the enemy was also battle-weary, the hardcases would move up front and enjoy the mop-up. Those unfortunate new recruits, poorly trained, who would launch javelins at approaching enemies before melting back behind the rich guys—they died first. Sort of canaries in coal mines."

Gabriel slowly closed his eyes and lowered his head. "Go on."

"The wedge was great when the enemy was hurling shit—I mean, throwing javelins, stones, throwing axes. They'd form a tortoise shell with their shields that nothing could penetrate," said Gunny, visibly growing excited.

"But the wedge formation was unbeatable. The Legionnaires became a saw, basically—a human saw. Simple physics. A sharp point drives deep into the body of enemy soldiers, while a thickening mass behind expands to further divide their forces. Same as a wooden wedge can split a log, a human wedge can smash an opposition force. Behind the wedge point, deep lines of the best troops concentrated their killing power against a weaker enemy. It would force a gap widened by the rest of the formation against an enemy that got compressed into a smaller space," Gunny said. "I thought I noticed fresh earthworks piling up around the perimeter. Is that what you're going for—building a kill box?"

Gabriel nodded. "Kill bowl. Earthworks will slow them down but not stop them. Our catapults are capable of hurling napalm bombs overtop the earthworks to incinerate Golgoths assembled on the other side; even still, many fighters will escape the flames and make it over. They will concentrate inside this steeply graded battlefield with Elect and Golgoths trapped together inside the earthworks. The steep grade will give the wedge formation of Elect an insurmountable advantage, forcing the enemy to fight a true uphill battle. Imagine trying to climb a child's sliding board with a large whirring chainsaw pushing you back down."

Gabriel watched Gunny's eyes moving rapidly side to side as the order of battle events played out in his mind. "You're right. You know, you are so right. Yessir, taking out the M2A1 gun with my mortars followed by firebombs to reduce Golgoth numbers, which then leaves the rest of their spearchuckers to face a wedge formation: this plan can work, even if we're outnumbered."

"Our catapults will thin their numbers. We have all the spears, swords, throwing axes, knives, and shields that we need," said Gabriel. "More than enough. We have secure shelter for the women and children. Now all that we need are to drill these men in close knife fighting, spear and axe throwing, swordsmanship, effective shield use, and maintaining formation lines while under Golgoth ground attack. From you, they must learn how to hold the line. How to fight through grief, loss, pain, and the shock of watching your friends die. To protect the helpless. To be brave and upright that God may love them. I cannot teach this. The powers of Heaven believe that you can. Learning of your existence and finding you was not something I earned. It was given."

"Gunny Powell, reporting for duty, sir!" he said with a salute. "This is right up my alley."

Gabriel smiled. "Knew it would be, Gunny."

"When do I start?"

Gabriel inhaled deeply. "Now."

Gunny's eyes sparkled. "Sir, who will lead at the point of the wedge in battle?"

Gabriel hit him with a look so powerful that it caused the battle-hardened soldier a spine tingle.

"I will."

Bye-Bye Dixie

Fast walking around the perimeter deck of the obelisk, Marshall stopped first at Booker and Aliyah's camp. "Nothin' to worry about. Go back to sleep." He crept back around to Jayden and Dodie's site, tiptoed around it again, then whispered, "No threats. Rest if y'all can." He returned to Tatum. He stretched out on his left side; she showed him her face, worry etched into every crease. He knew Tatum would not fall back to sleep today. "I suspect it was her. Arabella. She tossed rocks onto the bridge to send a clear message that she is shadowin' our every move. That she has power over us."

"Marshall, she knocked you over the head! Put you out cold! God only knows what she might've done if I hadn't missed you and come outside looking for you," she whispered. "You showed her God's mercy. I would never doubt you, or doubt God. You said he reaches out to sinners. What about Golgoths? Are we to forgive them?"

"We are to pray for them. Pray that if it pleases him, to save them as he has saved us. Kill them only in self-defense or defense of others," said Marshall.

"What if they capture me? Will you let them take me?"

Marshall frowned. "Thou Shalt Not Kill. This Commandment has tripped people up for over five millenniums, Tatum. It means don't commit murder. Kill equals murder. Doesn't say don't defend the weak and innocent against murderous evildoers. Or self-defense. It means don't murder people."

"She tried to kill Booker and Aliyah," whispered Tatum.

He nodded. "Yes she did. And she'll be judged by God for that."

"Shouldn't you neutralize the threat she poses to us?"

"Like I said: I spared Arabella mostly for Booker's sake. I want the kid to grow up with a lovin' heart. He watched his parents get cooked in front of 'im. Kid carries a boatload 'a anger and hate none of us can figure."

"You're angry: about Arabella; about that witch who murdered your baby," she countered.

He nodded. "Yessum, sure enough, I am angry. But anger's different from hate. God gets angry, too. Jesus Christ bunched up cords and whipped the moneychangers from the temple, flippin' their tables. God punishes; but God don't hate. I mean that slaughter just happened to Booker weeks ago. His hate burns bright; and I'm sure God don't hold it against 'im for killin' that Golgoth. That was self-defense, mostly. If I kill outta' defendin' myself or y'all, I'm prepared to stand before my Lord and answer for it. But Tatum: God ain't askin' me to cold-blooded execute that woman."

Tatum blinked. "But Arabella will lead the Golgoths straight to us, and we will all die because you let her live. See my point?"

He nodded. "I know where y'all 'r comin' from. But Tatum, we all 'r goin' to a place of pure love. I just," he whispered, rubbing his face, "I wanna plant seeds of love, water 'em, shine sunlight on 'em, and watch 'em grow. Every time we hate or hurt someone, or kill 'em, I think we all experience, dunno how to say it…stunted growth. Am I makin' sense?"

Tatum reached out her right hand. Gently she stroked Marshall's bearded cheek. "Yes. When she attacks next, you'll face a hard decision. I mean if you catch her in the act."

He nodded. "I'll do whatever it takes to protect the group. God knows I will, even if y'all doubt me."

She took his hand. "I would never doubt you. Before the rocks woke me up, I dreamed of the man surrounded by light on the green mountain. And all the people. So many! Nursing babies, little kids playing, wild animals acting tame, begging for food. Is this the same dream everyone's been talking about?"

Marshall nodded. "Y'all dreamed of the prophet Gabriel! First time?"

"Yes! Well, it's the first time I saw his face. He looked straight at me with his arms wide open and smiled!" she whispered. "What does it mean?"

"Y'all really wanna know? The answer may flip yer' insides out," he whispered.

"Tell me!"

His eyes never left hers. He did not blink. "God's been knockin' for y'all to open up to him since childhood, Tatum. Somewheres along the way, deep down y'all believed in 'im for the first time; maybe y'all thanked 'im in earnest for somethin,' I dunno, but somehow at some point y'all opened a locked door inside; so God moved in to fill that void; made a home inside, active all the time even while asleep. We all were created to be in fellowship with God, and we feel empty 'n lonely 'cause we live apart from 'im due to sin. But now that y'all wanna please 'im, God is givin' y'all dreams; signs; answerin' important questions; helpin' y'all to decide things. He's helpin' y'all to love yourself, love others, and show mercy."

Tatum nodded. "You're saying love is a decision, not a feeling?"

"Sometimes it's both," said Marshall. "Like when you decide to love him, and to love his Son who voluntarily died, takin' our sins and the Father's disappointment all into himself—and rose again for our sake," he whispered. "Like when you decide to pray even for your enemies."

Tatum blinked rapidly. "Marshall: did I choose God, or did God choose me?"

Marshall smiled. "Jesus told us that 'No man can come to me, unless The Father who has sent me will draw 'im, and I shall raise 'im up in the last day.' So God drew y'all to Christ, his Son. Like I said: he knocked again like he's been knockin,' but finally y'all opened the door a crack." Marshall's gaze penetrated deep into her eyes. He shrugged. "What it means is: God feels y'all are worth savin.'

"Oh wow. So God really knows me? Knows me completely and even after knowing me, he still wants me?"

Marshall beamed. "Yes! Now y'all are gettin' it! Y'all were that lost sheep that God loved so completely that he left behind the rest 'a his flock to go rescue. This is why Christ calls us his Elect: 'cause God elected us to follow Christ. I mean everyone is free to follow, and God wants 'em to— oh boy does he ever. But y'all felt the pull of the livin' God, Tatum, as did I. We coulda' rejected 'im and served ourselves instead, like Arabella and Delilah; like them Golgoths followin' their wicked god, whatever that damned thing is; but we choose to obey the one true livin' God. And now y'all 'r dreamin' right along with the rest of us. That's a sign from God! Welcome to the Elect. Y'all's one of the Elect, now, Tatum Winters! God knows us completely and loves us completely."

Never breaking eye contact, she kissed his hand. "I do believe you would sacrifice yourself for us and kill our enemies. I want to believe everything you said just now. I want to know everything there is to know about God, his Son, and this Holy Spirit that moved inside me.

"Know too, Marshall, that if your heart were colder, harder, more selfish, less merciful—I don't know if I could trust you like I do. Or want you this much." She kissed him again and did not stop. She broke their kiss with an unrestrainable smile. He found himself kissing her teeth, until he realized. He smiled back.

The soporific sound of reservoir water as it lapped against the concrete below soon sedated them back down into full sleep.

The sound of a jumping fish woke Marshall first. By the height of the sun, he figured they had about three more hours of usable daylight. He pulled on his pants, peered down, grabbed the line, and tugged. *Weight.* He felt the familiar heart-pound. With his right hand he spooled up line around his left elbow and hand, in loops. He saw large fish hanging from three of the four hooks, very much alive, and he smiled. As gently as possible so that none would wriggle off the hook and drop to freedom, he looped and looped until he was able to hoist them to the concrete surface with a wet splat loud enough to wake Tatum.

Tatum had never seen a living fish before, fascinated as they flip-flopped. She grimaced when Marshall removed the hooks. He noticed her watching. "Those things are gills. Think of 'em as fish lungs. Fish use 'em to filter oxygen from the water into their blood, the way we use lungs to pull air into our own bloodstreams. We drown under water because we run out of oxygen and die slow, painful deaths. That's what y'all 'r seein' in reverse. They're drowning in the open air."

He gutted them alive and scaled them quickly. Tatum appeared horrified. "It was a mercy," he whispered. "Hop up for me?" Tatum stood. "Drag our beddin' over there?" he pointed. "I'll set-up the camp stove under the canvas, let the flaps down, and we'll fast-cook these crappies."

"They're big! Way bigger than those trout you caught."

He nodded. "We'll all eat well in about thirty minutes."

Everyone sat on the railings eating fresh fish. "Mmm. So good," said Booker and Aliyah."

"You've really outdone yourself, hoss," said Jayden. "I didn't smell smoke, so breezes must be blowing east out over the water."

Dodie's eyes rolled up to whites. "Can we eat fish every day, Marshall?"

He laughed. "We'll see what bodies 'a water the Lord provides for us along the way. All I can say is, I'll try. By tomorrow we all should be well into the State 'a Virginia. There'll be rivers and streams to cross, and maybe also fish. One day at a time."

Tatum finished her apportionment, then reached into her knapsack. She pulled out a quarter pound of roast venison. Marshall grinned. "What!" she said.

He shook his head. "Nothin.' Remind me to keep my extremities away from y'all's mouth. Y'all might eat them, too."

Tatum's eyes gleamed. "There's a thought. I wonder if your extremities taste like venison, or stringy old shoe leather."

Marshall smacked her knee. Their eyes met, and locked. The others noticed the wordless depth of their bond. It made Aliyah, Booker, Dodie, and Jayden feel happy to see it, and curiously secure. The other two couples felt the same romantic inertia budding within themselves, but with Marshall and Tatum, to them it felt a little like they were getting new, ageless parents to model.

The sun had again hidden itself beneath the western horizon. Indigo turned to denim blue, which minutes later slipped down into lifeless black. After taking turns at the toilet and packing, each donned night goggles. Marshall and Jayden grabbed the ladders and led the way back across the footbridge.

"I don't remember these rocks, hoss," whispered Jayden.

"Shhh. Don't wanna alarm the others. We got us an Arabella problem."

"You have *got* to be shitting me."

"It sure ain't Golgoth behavior. What other crazy persons do we know?" Marshall whispered.

"Could be anyone who isn't a Golgoth. We picked up a tail somewhere along the way, maybe? A wannabe?"

"Who clobbered me over the head behind the cabin and threw rocks at us last night? If y'all were a lone hiker, wouldn't y'all hang back and keep watch; spy us out for a bit to make sure we all's decent folk; then make an inner'duction in the most non-threatenin' way? Ask if y'all could tag along; plead a case for safety in numbers and offer to share the load?"

Jayden thought about it. "Yeah. Totally. Must be Arabella. She hates us. She really knocked you out?"

"I was inspectin' small muddy boot prints behind the cabin which now I know were hers. Then lights-out. Never passed out before. It sucked. Try never to do it. Tatum thinks she was tryin' to kill me; that she woulda' finished me off with that rock if somethin' hadn't 'a spooked 'er off."

Through clenched teeth, Jayden said, "I will end that bitch."

"No. Y'all won't," said Marshall. "She'll end herself. That's how it works. We all 'r products of our own decisions. Y'all don't want executin' a woman on y'all's conscience, good buddy, believe me. I was angry; I coulda' done her days ago, but the Bible said no. Arabella can still repent."

Jayden seethed in silence. After positioning the ladders, everyone made it over the fence just off the Trail. "Untie all them paracord lashins' from the ladders. If we need new ladders we'll just make more," Marshall whispered. Aliyah, Dodie, and Tatum dug into the task. Aliyah stored all twenty-four lengths in her knapsack pocket. "Good job," said Marshall. "So, what's our next destination, navigator?"

Booker examined his atlas. "If we push hard we can make Damascus, Virginia, before sunrise. The Trail leads into Southwest Virginia from the Cherokee National Forest here in Tennessee; it crosses the state line about four miles south of the town of Damascus, Virginia. We'll need to find a place to camp either before we leave the woods, or after, because the Trail takes us onto roadways, but only for a few miles, including Highways 58 and 91. So, if we make it to Damascus while it's still dark, we should keep trucking straight on through that town while Golgoths are dead asleep. Otherwise we need to hang back in Tennessee and find another high elevation forest camp for the day. If we walk through Damascus in daylight…"

"Damascus," whispered Marshall. "Damascus. What a lovely name! We all's goin' to Damascus!" Energized and upbeat, he grabbed Tatum's hand and took the lead.

Fifty-fifty chance she'll come up from behind us like she did to Marshall at the cabin. I want to be the one to sink an arrow into that lunatic animal, thought Jayden. He took the rear with Dodie beside him, ears pricked looking backwards more than usual.

"Worried about something?" whispered Dodie.

Jayden abruptly dived off-trail to grab a large dry brittle branch with smaller branches sticking out. He snapped off the small ones and left them behind in the middle of the clear trail. He did the same with lengths of the larger branch. "Just earning my keep like a good soldier. If you should hear anything weird like a snapping branch or so, grab me."

"What if I just grab you for no reason?"

Jayden smiled. Dodie held his hand, and it made her feel safe. "So what do you make of Marshall and Tatum?" she asked.

"Huh?"

"What I mean is, I grew up with Tatum. She wanted no part of the Bible readings that Aliyah and I did every day. Never once. She claimed to be an atheist, and bisexual. Cut her hair short like a boy since forever. When she got breasts, either she bound them, or wore loose clothing and boy jeans. Then one day she meets Marshall and all of that, her entire childhood persona flipped—snap! —just like that. Don't you find it a little weird?"

Jayden smiled. "I'll hold onto my answer until you finish making your case."

"My case," said Dodie, squinting. "Okay: she claimed to like girls more than boys, and she was besties with Arabella forever. Now suddenly she's first to abandon Bella to the Golgoths, and she's head over heels for Marshall, who happens to personify the stereotypical big bearded muscular Viking. I just don't know what to make of it."

Jayden remained quiet. "I have the Bible memorized for the most part. It's how I got through the days after Golgoths took my folks. This bit might help you make sense of it. 'For the unbelieving husband has been sanctified through his wife, and the unbelieving wife has been sanctified through her believing husband. Otherwise, your children would be unclean, but as it is, they are holy.'"

Dodie walked in silence. Then she whispered, "You're saying Tatum really does believe in God now? That through Marshall's strength in the Lord, she is changing? Her core is changing…her heart is new?"

Jayden nodded. "Looks that way. I believe we're made by God to love him; and those who don't feel incomplete because they're missing out on that essential relationship. I believe people are born to sin; and some learn to hate and embrace hate, like your friend, Arabella; but I don't believe that most people are born evil or start out hateful. Some are, maybe; like that Hostis Dei guy."

"Who?" Dodie asked.

"Leader of the Golgoths. My parents told me he lives in a stone castle in the Valley of the Forge, an apostate of the devil himself; possessed by pure evil. Worships the moon god, or some such garbage. But most other people I think are like empty rooms. God wants to fill us, but then so does that other ancient spirit, Satan; the devil. So they both move in and start a tug-o-war. Fairly sure we know which spirit won over Arabella, versus Tatum. Do you think us meeting here was by accident? God joined Tatum to Marshall. Obviously, Marshall is bursting with the Lord. You saw what happened back there. He may talk like a redneck rube but trust me, the man is literate; only not on my level, or Booker's, where we read and retain Bible chapters and verses. The fact that whole verses came to him in prayer the afternoon of Arabella's attack tells you everything you need to know about the man. The Spirit runs him."

"You think the passages were given to him by the Holy Spirit?"

Jayden nodded. "God is strong in him. Call me unsurprised that Tatum is caught up in his aura. She invited the Spirit in," he said, and shrugged. "Conceivably she initially bought in only to get closer to Marshall. We can only speculate how it happened, but now she is a believer; I see it; and that beautiful bright light is pushing out all the old darkness. So, no. I absolutely don't think it's weird. I think it's an amazing thing to witness."

Dodie smiled. "I think you're amazing, Jayden Bonner. You see people. I mean really see them. There is so much more to you than just amateur astronomy, guitars, and shooting arrows into Golgoths."

He smiled, then stopped. He held up his hand. Dodie stopped, eyes wide, ears straining. He conducted a greenish night vision three-hundred-sixty-degree search of the woods. He controlled his breathing. Dodie did the same. Sound had carried from somewhere far back in the distance.

Both had heard the unmistakable sound of breaking sticks.

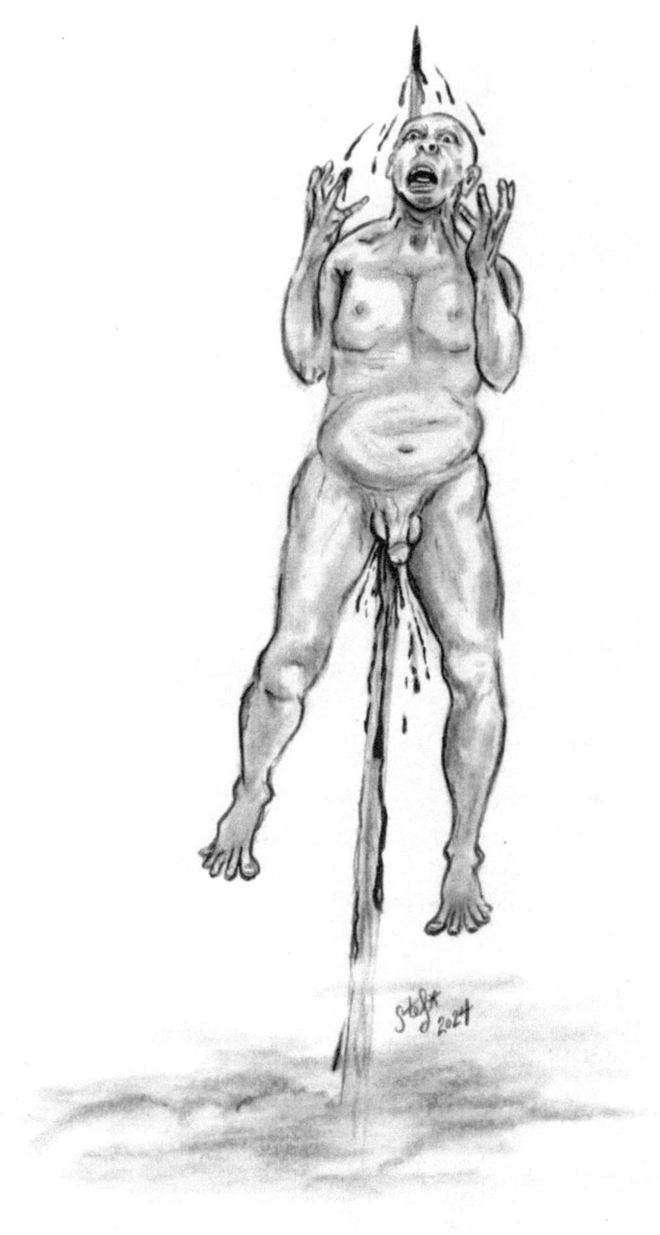

Moon God

"Spoggs, according to our law, what becomes of Golgoths found guilty of falsely accusing other Golgoths?" asked Hostis Dei.

Spoggs felt his bowels turn to water. He knew that somehow he was implicated in this latest palace intrigue which would lead to a decidedly horrifying death, for someone. Like now. He attempted to clear his constricted throat. "We execute them for bearing false witness."

"Not we, Spoggs. I execute them."

"Forgive me, m' Lord. They die by your own hand."

"Repeat the unsubstantiated rumor."

Spoggs cleared his throat. "A tribe member named Drogo was alone in his cabin. Five Golgoths reported overhearing him praying to a false idol."

Hostis Dei stood in the doorway. Normally by this point, sixty seconds into their exchange, Spoggs would be noticing an impatience vibe, the lord-master anxious to get back to his cathedral of Breeders. This afternoon, he seemed truly engaged.

"These Golgoths are under your command, Spoggs?"

"Yes, m' Lord."

"The Golgoth they accused, this Drogo: have you sensed any friction between any of the five Golgoths and him?"

Spoggs thought carefully. "Yes, m' Lord. I believe these five envy him, for he follows orders better than they do. Brighter, more intelligent, thinks critically. Always praises you, and prays to our Most Merciful Moon God, Hubal."

"Did you interrogate the accused?"

"M' Lord, yes."

"He denied the charge?"

Spoggs nodded. "Yes. Even when I placed his balls between two planks and stood on them, m' Lord. I said that if he did not confess to the charge I would slice his balls off. Drogo said to do whatever I must, and that he prays to Hubal that we see the truth of it."

Hostis Dei nodded. "Go now. Bring me his five accusers." Spoggs turned and ran. Hostis Dei stood in the doorway, watching Spoggs do his bidding. Three minutes later, Spoggs returned with the five. They stood fifteen feet away at attention, in a line, facing the door with their heads down.

Hostis Dei commanded, "Look at me. I will see your eyes." One by one visibly nervous Golgoths looked into the unsettling eyes of their prophet. "You will step forward when I point to you. I am going to ask each of you one question. You must answer truthfully. The others will not hear the question or your answer. You," he pointed. The man furthest left slowly shuffled toward Hostis Dei, visibly trembling.

"Did you hear Drogo praying to a false god? Do not blink. Look into my eyes."

"Yes, m' Lord." Hostis Dei continued to stare. The member's bladder released; urine trickled down his white-painted calves and pooled at his feet on the concrete.

"Step back," said Hostis Dei. The man did. Dei pointed to the second. The man slowly approached, shivering in the heat.

"To which false idol did Drogo pray?"

The man tried to swallow but failed. There seemed to be a thick, hot obstruction in his throat. His desiccated lips appeared blue. "Drogo prayed to the false idol, Jesus Christ."

"Step back. You," he pointed to the third in line. The man shivered like in winter. "To which false idol did you hear Drogo pray?"

Terror jumped nimbly down the man's throat. "Drogo prayed to Allah, m' Lord." The man felt the sinister vacuum of Hostis Dei; as though Dei's eyes attempted to pull the man's soul out through his eye sockets. The man believed that if he sustained eye contact further, surely he would go mad.

"Get back in line. "You," Hostis Dei pointed to the fourth. The man swaggered up proudly. He was broader and fitter than the other four. "To which false idol did Drogo pray?"

"M' Lord, to the Hebrew God, Yahweh." Forced to meet Hostis Dei's magnetic gaze, and to observe up close the lightless grin frozen on Dei's face, the man felt his grip on sanity slipping away. He broke down and wept.

"Back in line." He pointed to the last man who needed no prodding. He slithered more than walked up to his leader. "To which god did Drogo pray?"

His entire naked flesh marbled into goosebumps in the warm night air. "To the Buddha, m' Lord. I once saw him carving a figure on a foraging mission. It's hidden somewhere. Give the order: I will find it."

"The rest of you, approach," the leader commanded. They did. Spoggs urgently needed to relieve the hot wetness cramping in his lower intestine. "I have a job for you to do immediately. Each of you get an axe and a knife. You will walk to the uncut woods. Each will fell a strong sapling twice as tall as a man. You will strip off all branches. You will sharpen the narrow end to a dull point. Bring them to the Breeder Pen. Be back in one hour, at nightfall. I will meet you there." The men turned and ran.

"Spoggs. Bring the bicycle generator and the spotlights over to the Pen. Use the post hole auger. Five holes, three feet deep, three feet apart. Numbers divisible by three are best, are they not? Spread the word: mandatory full assembly in one hour at the Pen."

"Yes, m' Lord." Nerves no longer permitted restraint of Spoggs's bowels. He walked to the nearest latrine and lost the battle.

As twilight descended over Valley Forge Park, campfires broke out along the rolling miles of blackness, like orange-yellow cracks in the earth near an active volcano. A Golgoth pedaled a stationary bicycle power generator. A bank of moveable LED stadium lights flickered on, which bathed the Breeder Pen in something close to daylight. Females within the fenced area shielded their eyes. "Spoggs," said Hostis Dei. "Bring me the five."

"Yes, m' Lord."

As Hostis Dei moved into the light, a ripple of conversation carried through the crowd. The prophet surveyed the beautiful sight. It calmed him to know more would soon arrive and swell his ranks. He gazed downhill upon seventy-thousand silent Golgoths who stood together over the flats and hills of the national park, a ghostly white army under a thin cuticle of a moon: the sight of it sent blood to his privates.

Hostis Dei grabbed his electronic bullhorn and directed his gaze skyward. "Hubal, moon god, lord of the Ka'aba, we praise you and worship you." The silent crowd exploded in loud cheering. Hostis Dei held up his hand then continued praying. "We thank you for the strength in our bodies. We thank you for our daily food. We thank you for the power you have given me to lead your people to freedom from tyrannical false gods. We thank you for the wisdom to recognize your strength. As you work by night, rest by day, so it is that we gather here to enforce your commandments tonight. In your strength, there is truth. The pagan gods have no part in truth. Theirs are weak kingdoms of lies. We know that in your kingdom of strength, oh Most Merciful Moon God, Hubal—lies are intolerable. Your immutable law prevails."

He glanced at Spoggs, who advanced from the front of the crowd with the five accusers of Drogo, roped together. Spoggs raised his hand. From behind the Breeder Pen, five of his fellow generals materialized from the shadows to stand by his side. Each carried an extraordinarily long wooden spear upright like a flag.

Spoggs knew these generals conspired to replace him as Hostis Dei's first-in-command. Outmaneuvering and outsmarting them occupied much of his time. To him, this night's spectacle could only help reinforce his standing. He would stand, and point, and make the other generals do the wet work. *Fear and respect.*

"These Golgoths falsely accused one of our own. This is blasphemy!" Hostis Dei shouted into his bullhorn, startling tens of thousands of Golgoths. "What separates us from animals but for the rule of law? Thou Shalt Not Bear False Witness is a law so keenly important that even their lesser God stole it from the one true lord of the moon. Therefore, under the laws of Hubal, blasphemy is punishable by death. But not a proud, easy death, no.

Hostis Dei lowered his bullhorn, wishing to speak to the accused at normal volume. "Disgraced Golgoths," he said, panning the five. "I have interrogated you myself and hereby certify your guilt. I sentence you to death by impalement. The breeders will fall asleep to your piteous music as you give vent to the nightmarish agonies consuming your bodies. Your insanity should last for one or two nights. Hubal can forgive the member who screams least and lasts longest. Yours shall be a sour death. There is no honor in it," he said. Two collapsed to the ground sobbing, and screaming, which pulled the other three down with them. One tried to run but bonds held him tightly.

Hostis Dei turned to face his Golgoth army. "Hear me, followers!" he shouted into the megaphone. "Let this be a lesson to you all. Do not lie. Do not steal. Do not covet. Obey the law of Hubal. Look up at him now, each of you. Say this: Hubal, please give me strength and never let me fall."

All Golgoths chanted the words in unison.

"Spoggs," Hostis Dei called as he lowered the bullhorn. Now he spoke in his normal terrifying tone. "Proceed, one at a time. Two generals hold, one aims, two impale, all five lift him up. Spoggs, you cut the wrist ties. Drop the first into your left post hole. Three face the crowd, two face the Breeders."

Spoggs walked eight paces to the other generals. In hushed tones word for word he repeated the supreme directive. He pointed to the first of the whimpering condemned Golgoths still collapsed on the ground. A general sliced the rope connecting one accused to the others and pulled the freed Golgoth to standing. The man refused to walk. The general and another dragged him to the bright side of the stadium lights facing the Breeder Pen.

One general stood behind and kicked the back of the freed Golgoth's knees, while another general forced his face-down neck to the ground, pinning it with his foot. A third general took a wide stance between the ankles. The fourth and fifth generals grabbed one of the long poles; one held the base, the other grasped it tightly four feet from tip. Both braced the pole firmly against their right sides.

The general at the top of the pole struggled with the task of placing the point against the panicked Golgoth's rectum.

"What's the hold up?" said Spoggs.

"It's a shitty mess down there. Shadows. Can't find the target."

Spoggs adjusted the stadium light deck left one inch. "Better?"

"Yep that'll do it." The general positioned the point of the pole against the man's rectum and, with the cooperation of the general behind him, twisted and worked in five inches. It would advance no further. Spoggs picked up his knife, positioned the tip carefully and pushed it in, giving the man a surprise rectal episiotomy.

High reedy screams of mortal fear and agonizing pain were heard all the way in the back rows of the assembly. The horrid sounds did nothing but increase in frequency and volume, chilling all who heard them. Spoggs, along with the other generals stood watching the pinned Golgoth's muscles tensing, his screaming face turned to the side. The general closest to the writhing condemned chuckled, as did the generals standing on his neck and ankles.

Spoggs gave the order. The two holding the pole further tightened their grip. With all their strength they shoved forward as if operating a battering ram against a locked enemy door.

Keening screams pierced the night. Seventy-thousand onlookers remained silent. Everyone present had heard the typical sounds made by dying humans, but none had ever heard anything quite as horrifying as the agonies vented by the first of five Golgoths condemned to death by impalement.

Females in the Breeder Pen yelped; others who were sobbing continuously did so louder. Spoggs spoke to the other generals over the high-volume wailing. "The point must travel up behind vital organs and follow the spine. Don't screw this up." He cut the wrist bonds from the condemned. The man's arms flailed in a sickening attempt to reach behind himself.

Spoggs said, "All together now, I want every hand on the pole here," and he demonstrated. The general standing on the condemned man's neck remained in place to prevent escape. He tolerated desperate hands cloying and scratching at his calves. Spoggs grabbed the pole.

"On three, we lift. One…two…three." The smoothness of the motion surprised even Spoggs, as the impaled member slowly rose six feet, another foot, then another, until he reached a height of twelve feet above the ground. "Impaling consists of one step at a time," said Spoggs, in the authoritative, confident tone of an experienced leader. In a coordinated shuffle, the generals positioned the bottom of the pole over the furthest left post hole. The impaled Golgoth's thrashing hands higher up caused the generals to lose their aiming of the pole base. Spoggs took a knee, grabbed the base, and guided it directly over the hole.

"Lower the pole down a hand's length until I see it go down." They did. "Good. Now on my count of three, everyone let go…one…two…three." As they released, the weight of the condemned and gravity dropped the pole base down fast and hit bottom hard. Spoggs looked up in time to see the man's buttocks when it connected. He watched the body sink a full twelve inches further down. "Ouch," he said, and the others laughed. "The point is now somewhere up behind the ribcage. Twist the pole so that he faces the breeders," Spoggs barked, mindful of his leader's specific command. He wondered about this. *Is his goal to instill fear in the Breeders? Or to magnify the condemned Golgoth's humiliation, with pretty young females watching him die so ignominiously?*

The five generals obeyed. Feces and blood trickled down the pole onto their hands. After achieving final position they wiped their hands in the grass. One grabbed soil from the post hole excavation and rubbed it on his hands like crude soap and water. The others then followed suit. They faced four more impalements and a leader highly intolerant to slip-ups. They looked up at the condemned member high in the air, fascinated. All five and Spoggs shared one common thought with every onlooker:

Better him than me.

All watched in gruesome fascination as the condemned pressed his feet against the blood-slicked pole in a fruitless attempt to push himself up, and off. The generals watched with cruel fascination as the impaled Golgoth's hands clawed his own face in agony. They delighted in the symphony of howls and laments, unnatural even in their sadistic experience, which was vast. The condemned tried to grasp the pointed pole top and to lift his nearly two-hundred pounds up and off, to no avail. *Simple physics,* Spoggs mused.

Each Golgoth witnessed the horror as ordered and took in every sickening nuance. Captives behind the Breeder Pen fence were mere feet away from the carnage; they cried or screamed, witnessing the stages of grief and terror settle upon faces of the condemned. Each knew her own life would soon end in a similarly cruel and inhuman fashion.

The party of five generals led by Hostis Dei's top trustee, Spoggs Reichert, repeated the steps to impale the four remaining Golgoths. "How do you get to Carnegie Hall?" Spoggs asked the four condemned. "Practice." By the third impalement, the five generals seemed to have the procedure down. Each new impalement took less time than the preceding impalement. "I predict numbers one, two, and five will last four days or more," he said. "Anyone care to wager against it? Five pounds of fresh prime sweet human meat. Who'll take that bet?"

"I will," said one. "I bet not one of these make it past three days."

Hostis Dei, silent throughout the impalement procedure, stood taking it all in. He faced his generals and spoke. "Three is the best number in all the universe. I will sweeten the bet with one of my Breeders. I will allow the winner to select one. Also, Spoggs: this Drogo who stands falsely accused and innocent of the charges, whom you tortured, also gets a Breeder. I want every follower to know that the lord god Hubal is hard, but fair." More aroused and energized than he had felt all year, his enormous penis standing straight out from his loins, Hostis Dei turned to the crowd. He raised the megaphone to his mouth.

"I must pray to lord Hubal. As his earthly prophet, I pray for strength and enlightenment which lord Hubal gives to me according to his will, not when I demand it. Therefore I cannot promise you a date when we will defeat the Elect army; take their lives and resources, which Hubal has promised us. Not yet. Not until he reveals it to me. But hear me, Golgoths: Hubal has revealed one great truth to me that I have not shared with you until this night.

"Before the close of the lunar year, each of you will receive his own Breeder or young boy of your own choice. Women of breeding age, children so young and tender. You may each convert Breeders to our faith and start your own tribes, or feast on their flesh. Whatever pleases you also pleases our lord above," he said, and made a grand show of looking up at the moon. "Be fruitful and multiply, repopulate the world, spread Hubal's seed everywhere. This belongs to you, though only if you are willing to fight for it, in Hubal's name, and for his eternal glory.

"Goodnight."

Four days later, the final unfortunate last man died in agony from dehydration, septic shock, blood loss and exposure. The women and girls in the Breeder Pen wept non-stop for their own fates, and for each other's fates. They prayed the Father in the name of his Son, Jesus Christ, day and night for absolution and deliverance.

Spoggs Reichert collected on his winning bet.

Black Water Demon

On the third day after crossing the Tennessee state line into Virginia, over his morning bird hunt Marshall had discovered a large patch of blueberry bushes growing wild. Lacking any form of bag, he removed his hooded sweatshirt and undershirt. He used the undershirt to create a vessel. This he filled with ten pounds of the bluest, ripest berries he could pick. During the fourth night, the team walked southeast, as the Trail ran parallel with the James River visible on their left. A rich and fecund tidal smell cloistered about them.

"Mmm, these are so good!" Aliyah whispered through her final mouthful of blueberries.

Tatum was making her share of the sweet treat last as long as she could. Everyone else had gorged themselves on their shares of berries in the first night of walking. "I see you looking, Booker, but no. You rushed through your supply. Let this be a lesson in conservation. Mmm, so sweet! So, tart! Absolutely amazing…"

"Your cruelty is exceeded only by your loveliness, Tatum," growled Booker. At this, she giggled.

"Booker, we all's gotta be gettin' close to the footbridge. How wide is this river?" Marshall whispered.

Booker pulled out his atlas. "Close to the bridge. We arrive any second now. Width, let me calculate…zero-point-one-two miles."

"Maybe we all passed it?"

"No Marshall, we definitely didn't pass it," whispered Booker. "The Trail crosses the river at the footbridge. Impossible to walk past it. We'll make a left turn straight to the river. The Trail picks up again on the opposite bank."

What they could see of the river through trees suggested that it was running fast and high. *Three straight nights of rain,* Jayden thought. *Outta be running like rapids.*

The Trail did indeed turn left and did bring them to the southern bank of the James River. Marshall and Tatum stopped. They stared. They turned back as the others caught up. "Booker how long is the bridge?" whispered Marshall.

"Six hundred twenty-three feet."

"What's it made of?"

"Steel and wood. Footnote says it is an obsolete train bridge that Pre-Flood builders converted into a footbridge. They kept the existing foundation blocks, cutwater pieces, pile caps, and piers that stick up out the water. So yes, Marshall: if it's sturdy enough to hold trains and stand after two Floods, you can be sure it can hold people walking."

Marshall removed his night goggles. The others followed. "Hate to state the obvious, y'all," he whispered. "Floods took the bridge, carried it away somewhere downstream. God only knows where all that steel and wood is now. All that's left are the stone and concrete foundations."

"Aw hell," whispered Jayden. "Six hundred feet across? We can't swim that."

"Marshall. What about the kayaks?" Dodie said.

"Right!" said Tatum. "We prepped. Knew there'd have to be water crossings. Even brought foot pumps to inflate them."

Marshall reached out and tousled Tatum's hair. "Don't know if Eve was a blessin' or a curse to Adam: a mix 'a both, maybe. But y'all three ladies are purely a gift to the world." Tatum beamed. Aliyah and Dodie giggled. "How heavy are they?"

"Thirty pounds apiece," said Aliyah.

"Hot dang! Y'all carried 'em this far wonderin' if the juice was worth the squeeze. Tonight, thanks to y'all's hard labor, we all are wealthier than King Midas. Okay then. Can one 'a y'all find me a big straight stick?"

Jayden restored his goggles and blasted into the woods in a fast trot. Forty seconds later he returned holding a hard, heavy branch about four feet long. He handed the branch to Marshall who put on his goggles before he grabbed it. The others strapped on their goggles. "I'm gonna chuck this into the river. Imagine ten feet in your mind. Y'all know what ten feet looks like. Watch the stick: the second it hits water start countin.' Count the seconds it takes for the stick to travel ten feet. Keep y'all's counts private, then come whisper in my ear."

Tatum looked at him curiously. Marshall took a wide stance, feet planted; he leaned back as far as possible, lifted his left leg, and violently launched forward like an Olympic javelin thrower. The stick flew straight and true. Jayden guessed the distance from Marshall's arm to the plop at one-hundred-sixty feet. *Ain't the channel but close enough*, Marshall thought. Everyone watched the splash and mentally counted as currents carried the stick the length of two people. Marshall removed his goggles and bent his head.

Tatum removed hers and pressed warm lips against his ear. "Two seconds," she whispered, then licked his ear. He laughed. He licked his right index finger and pressed it into her ear in response. She giggled.

I'd walk a thousand miles just to hear that happy sound, he thought.

In turn, the other four whispered into his ear. Marshall did the math and said, "Channel currents are movin' at seven miles an hour. Which means that if we all 'spect to paddle across and launch right here, fightin' that wicked flow we'd end up a long ways yonder downstream, nowhere near the Trail, no matter how hard we worked them dinky little paddles. It also means we all'd need to pick through them dense woods on the other side to find the Trail again…" he said. He paused to make more mental calculations.

"Twelve-hundred feet to be safe, Marshall," said Booker. "Beat y'all to it. I don't know exactly how fast we can paddle but let's say it's only two miles per hour on a flat mill pond. That gives us three and a half, four minutes to cross if we're really pushing it. Now, the currents are weakest closer to the banks. If we can cross the channel above the Trail mouth in three or four minutes, then we can coast to the other bank and to the Trail."

Marshall grinned. "Said it before and I'll say it again. You are one smart guy, Booker Bailey." Aliyah backhanded Booker in the stomach. Booker feigned agonizing pain. Marshall looked around, and up at the florid, slightly sanguine moon. "It's nice and flat here, and bright. Let's prep the kayaks right where we all are standin.'"

The double-action foot pumps allowed for quick inflation. The four-piece aluminum-nylon paddles flew together into straight sturdy pieces. Marshall insisted each team carry their kayaks exactly as he and Tatum carried theirs, both standing left of the kayak, grasping the black nylon rope spanning its length.

"Maximum control of the crafts, carryin' 'em this way," Marshall whispered. "If y'all snag and rip your raft, guess who's swimmin' tonight? Not I, folks. Not I." Marshall mentally paced off twelve hundred feet, then stopped. "Hang on a hot minute," he whispered, and disappeared through thick brush leading down to the riverbank holding his machetes.

They heard chopping sounds gradually growing louder. He emerged four minutes later. "It's only twenty feet from here to the water. The river is way over its banks due to days 'a thunderstorms we all just slogged through. I chopped us a clean path to the riverbank so no snaggin' these balloons on any sharp stuff. Just carry 'em like we did, and closely watch me and Tatum. Aliyah, can y'all please hand each of us eight of them short paracords we recovered from the ladders?" She did.

Maintaining cautious footing, Marshall and Tatum made their way down the cut-out path. Marshall removed his backpack. Tatum followed suit. Marshall tied his heavier pack to the cross-front nylon rope and webbing, then tied Tatum's lighter back to the cross-back rope. "Load balancin,'" he whispered. They stood in pungent, murky river water up to the tops of their boots. He lowered his kayak's flat bottom to the water. Marshall held it steady as Tatum climbed into the front seat. He handed her the paddle. He stepped in as gently as possible. He turned back. "I'm the heaviest of us. Between me and fatso up here and our knapsacks, this sucker is at capacity. So be careful."

Tatum whipped the paddle backwards, clonking him on the head. "Leaner than you are, tubby," she said. Everyone laughed. Having sensed group anxiety, Marshall was willing to take a little pain to lighten tension.

She reads me like a book, he thought. Gently he grabbed the paddle from Tatum's grip. "What'd they used to say in old-timey days? Bon voy-idge?"

"That pronunciation sounded just exactly like a Smoky Mountain backwoods redneck sadly attempting to speak French," said Booker. Everyone laughed again.

Marshall paddled left then right, trying to establish a rhythm that was both powerful and fluid. His first sixty seconds felt awkward. Spray from the actions sprinkled Tatum. "Hey! Knock it off, dorky!" she said.

He found his rhythm, and powered the kayak in as straight a beeline as he could toward the scrubby northern bank. Two minutes in, he guessed they were in or close to the channel current. He knew too that, while in all appearances he crossed over by rowing in a straight line, the other bank with its endless trees and scrub all looked the same in the greenish light of the goggles. *Likely we drifted hunnerts' 'a feet downstream from where we all started.*

"Getting tired yet old man? Need your young strong girlfriend to do some of the arduous work?"

He laughed. "Not yet, smarty pants. Besides, y'all are my figurehead."

"What the heck is a figurehead?"

"Hunnerts' 'a years ago," he huffed, "shipbuilders would carve a beautiful woman's bust on the prow of wooden sailin' ships. They all believed it brought sailors good luck." He wished he could stop and wipe itchy sweat from his forehead. Goggle lenses started to fog inside.

"When we get settled into our next camp, you might just get lucky, sailor," Tatum said.

Her words flushed him with renewed vigor. The clock in his head announced the four-minute mark. The northern bank appeared less than a hundred feet away. To their right, Marshall and Tatum saw one of the concrete supports looming up from churning murky depths. He paddled furiously with every ounce of energy in his reserve. He slaked, allowing the currents to position them directly parallel with the eerie concrete obelisk. *Damn bank all looks the same. Moorin' this balloon is guesswork,* he thought.

He knew that above the bank, where the original footbridge had terminated there would be a flat gravel area identical to the spot where they had inflated the kayaks. "Six-hunnert'-twenty-three-feet south of this exact point," he muttered. He barreled the kayak straight until woody growth arrested progress. "Hop out here," he said. Tatum did. He stepped forward to the front seat and onto mushy ground. He pulled the kayak out of the water a little, taking care not to rip or snag it. He unstrapped his machetes and hacked his way up the bank. Minutes later he returned. "Bingo."

Tatum smiled. "My hero!" To prove it, she pulled his face to hers and tongued his mouth.

"Mmm. Wow. Okay, now that my head is spinnin' let's unstrap our gear and carry it up to the Trail, then we stand up the kayak makin' it easy for the others to see, kinda like a lighthouse. We'll wait for 'em down here." Grinning, they untied and carried their gear to the flat landing, then descended back down to the mucky river bank. Booker and Aliyah, still seventy feet west, spotted Marshall and Tatum's flailing arms and the kayak standing tall. Booker paddled while Aliyah waved back. Finding his own powerful rowing cadence, Booker steamed his kayak straight at Marshall and Tatum from about twenty feet out.

"Whew! Man, that was a workout. I'll need a massage this morning," said Booker.

Aliyah snorted. "Use your left hand, Booker: give yourself a massage. It'll feel like someone else is doing it," she said. All four laughed. The two new arrivals carried gear and kayaks up to the landing and returned down to welcome Jayden and Dodie, cruising in quickly.

"Booker, you freakin' nailed it again, pal," said Jayden, huffing air. "Twelve-hundred feet was a great guesstimate. If you had figured it any shorter then we would've been forced to paddle upstream against currents to get here: and these crazy currents might've ended us."

"He's my smarty-pants," said Aliyah, grinning.

Jayden and Dodie stepped out of the kayak into the reeking river muck, and carried their gear uphill, followed by the others. Marshall removed his goggles and wiped stinging sweat from his eyes. He took a knee, praying for clarity in planning the next steps.

Everybody froze.

Directly across on the southern bank where they had stood not half an hour earlier, the woods were engulfed in flames, a forest fire spreading quickly. Jayden was first to break the stunned silence. "Hoss. Golgoth tribes will see the fire and smell it for miles around. We can't stay here. They'll be crawling all over the Trail. We need to put plenty of distance between us and the river before we make camp."

Just then they all heard a sound: a female in distress judging from the pitch, timbre, and loudness. "Sounds like it came from the river," whispered Tatum. "I am so creeped out right now."

Booker and Jayden pulled their bows and nocked arrows. Marshall grabbed his slingshot and tapped his right front pocket to confirm the ammo. He led the charge back down the cut-out to the water's edge.

"Golgoths are onto you," screeched Arabella, voice now unmistakable. She was two hundred feet southwest of the hikers, still well within the channel currents, paddling toward them. "I dragged dead Golgoths up out of the ditch and set them on the Trail. I even arranged them into a nice big arrow pointing north. I'm sure the next hunting party made a great report to their leader. Now I bring you the gift of fire! Now they consider the Trail a road like any other; now that people have fought back and beat them, the Trail is going to light up with Golgoths! They'll have it covered up ahead of you," she screeched. "You're walking straight into your deaths!"

Rage came to boil in all, except for Marshall. *Keep your head, son.*

"You are all going to die!" She threw back her head, body racked with maniacal laughter. Aliyah and Dodie shivered. They knew Arabella could be most unpleasant and difficult to live with, but they had no idea until now that some unclean spirit had fully moved inside her.

"Die, you bitch!" Tatum screamed.

Booker and Jayden exchanged glances. They both took aim and pulled back their bowstrings.

"No!" said Marshall. He stepped in front of them. "Y'all wanna kill 'r then y'all gotta shoot through me first."

Jayden lowered his arrow. "Marshall, she keeps trying to kill us. This isn't murder. It's self-defense. Be reasonable!"

"I'll handle it," said Marshall. "As long as I'm leadin' then the decision and consequences are mine. Booker, please. Stand down."

Shooting Marshall a death stare, Booker lowered his arrow point. Marshall reached into his right pocket. "Can she swim? Arabella. Can she swim?"

Dodie looked at Aliyah. Both looked at Tatum. "Yes," she said. "We've seen her swim before. She's a fine swimmer."

Marshall took aim. He pulled back the pouch, stretched the surgical rubber bands to maximum length; he timed the rise and fall of Arabella's paddles like anticipating a bird's next move or flight trajectory. *Clank!* The ammo ball hit the paddle head he had aimed for dead on. The noise and shock tremors along with the kinetic energy of the shot made her drop the paddle. It flew into the current, and it was gone.

"*Dead!* You are all *dead!*" she screamed. They watched as currents carried the kayak east, passing between two of the ominous concrete-stone bridge supports spanning the channel. Her screams, hysterical, lunatic, continued unabated, but the volume faded gradually as the mean current carried her toward the ocean faster than Marshall knew he could run in a full sprint. They stood watching through goggles as the tiny greenish point on the water's surface grew smaller and smaller until it winked out of view.

"Currents'll keep 'r in the channel," said Marshall. "Miles east 'a here she'll get caught up in an eddy current that's gonna move her outta the channel, closer to a bank. From there she can doggie paddle to land. If so, she'll be so far from us that it ain't possible for her to catch up with us again, ever. Ain't gonna be no more Trail for that demon: only highways and roads. Then again she might get carried all the way to the Atlantic, east to land's end. Friends, she is in God's hands now. Whether she lives or dies ain't ours to decide. It's the Lord's."

"Golgoths will get her for sure," said Dodie.

"In the wise words of Booker: that is an HP—her problem—not my problem, our problem, or y'all's problem," said Marshall. "Whatever happens to her next is between Arabella and God's will: our consciences are clean. I put her away from us for good. Y'all can just put it all on me. Thank you for not fillin' 'r with arrows," he said, looking at Booker and Jayden. "Swallow your bile. 'Vengeance is mine, sayeth the Lord.' Which means it ain't y'all's and it ain't mine, gents. Y'all gonna get your chance to kill the real enemy, and so will I. So how 'bout we just save the anger for real battle? We are God's arrows. Trust him to aim us.

"And Jayden, y'all's right. We need to get far away fast from Arabella's signal fire. Let Golgoths think it started from a lightnin' strike or natural causes, but we all can be sure they'll come—now that Arabella pointed them corpses straight at us. Booker, what's the highest point we can reach by mornin'?"

Booker pulled out the atlas and traced the Trail with his finger. "Twenty-eight-hundred-feet. Big Rocky Row. Bound to be nice rock ledges."

"Or Golgoths," muttered Jayden.

Kill Box

"How much longer, Marshall?" whispered Dodie. "My feet are killing me. My back feels like someone took a big hammer to it."

"You can say that again," whispered Aliyah. "I feel like a little piece of nasty smelling something stuck up in the treads of some monster's shoe."

It had been nine days since they had kayaked across Virginia's James River. Marshall felt the strain in his friends, and in his own body. What they needed most at that moment was a ray of light beaming ahead at the end of an impossibly long, dark, and exceedingly dangerous tunnel. "Booker, please tell me that we all have finally arrived in Carlisle, Pennsylvania. Multiple river crossins.' Rain, rain, and more rain. Bring us good news."

Booker cleared his throat. "Good news and unwelcome news. Which do you want first?"

"Good news," said Tatum. "I am now answering for Marshall, in case nobody noticed." Marshall crept behind her, reached under her arms, and tickled. She squirmed and giggled.

"The good news is this: we are indeed near Carlisle. Now what this means is it's the end of the Trail for us. Spring Mountain is only two more nights away," Booker announced.

Each of the other five quietly applauded. Dodie jumped up and down.

"Now," Booker continued, "we can't take roads because for sure they'll be crawling with Golgoths. We're close to Gabriel's turf, but about to be even closer to Satan's apostate, the prophet of the Golgoths: Hostis Dei."

There was a dead moment of silence as they exchanged glances. "And we've run out of Trail. So…" Booker whispered. He traced a line left to right across the paper, "It means that if we go the way I want to go, we should be safe and snug as bugs in rugs."

"Which way might that be, mister navigator?" Marshall asked Booker.

"We'll be walking the old Norfolk Southern Railway Company track from here to Phoenixville, to Route 29 which becomes Gravel Pike. From there to East Park Avenue, cross a deep creek, and from there we hike a different trail up to Spring Mountain. Two nights and half a day, and it's over."

Despite the volume risk, everyone cheered, including Marshall. "So, what's the bad news, Booker?" asked Tatum.

"Bad news is, I have the nastiest itch in the middle of my back, and if Ali doesn't use those long pointy claws of hers to scratch it I will surely go berserk. You won't like me."

"Gladly!" said Aliyah, and she did. Everyone laughed.

"Au contraire," said Jayden. "We love you."

"Good memory! I taught you that French term way-way back."

"You've taught all of us," said Jayden. "Now that we know what we're looking for, does anybody see this old rail track? I see nothing but scrubby-ass woods."

The others fell silent and still as Booker again studied the map. "Weird. Because we should be right on top of the old Norfolk Southern rail track, according to this map. Do you know what they look like? Railroad tracks, I mean."

Everyone nodded yes. "To get to the Trail we had to cross over parallel steel rails, at times," said Aliyah.

"Yes exactly," said Booker. "Keep looking for parallel steel rails stretching to infinity. Floods may have changed the landscape, but the right-of-way should be easy to spot even in the dark with night vision goggles. Even though without any maintenance done to it in half a century, knowing the earth always reclaims what man has developed, a railroad right-of-way will still look like a big wide break running east-west. Don't look at the ground. Look right and left for what seems like a road, a trail, a big wide carve-out. Look through the trees. Look past them."

They spread out, hoping to find rail tracks as Booker had described them. Dodie was the first to call out something. "Stop!" she whispered. Look right, between all the scrub growth. Do you see what I see?"

Jayden stood beside her. He followed her finger east. "Well butter my butt and call me biscuit!" Jayden said. "Two parallel lines close together like they stretch off into infinity. Guys, I think the Dodester found the rails. I'll go check it out." He launched himself through low growth and winterberry bushes, then slogged through squishy earth. As the soil firmed, gravity pulled him downhill faster than he would have liked, down seventy feet until his boots crunched onto weedy gravel. He looked west and saw a tunnel. Train tracks disappeared into its arched-shaped, gaping black stone maw.

Jayden lacked the patience to climb back up the incline to tell the others of his discovery. He whistled loudly to get their attention. He jumped up and down, waved his arms making the 'come hither' gesture. "Are they blind and deaf?" he muttered. With a heavy heart he started the difficult climb back up, but then he heard the squish and crackle of descending footfalls; he saw Booker first, then saw the others behind him. He stood back on a wooden railroad tie and waited for them to come to him.

"This is it," said Booker in normal speaking volume. East-west. Norfolk Southern line for sure. Notice we're in a valley. Means whatever sounds we make won't travel far. We can quit with the whispering."

"I'd rather we all don't quit just yet," whispered Marshall. "When conditions are right, I can hear sounds bouncin' 'round from miles away. It's how I hunt. Golgoths are hunters."

"Of people," added Aliyah with a shiver."

"But sure as Grandma goes to bed with the chickens, them Golgoths can't see us down here," said Marshall. "Our own hidden, private road. We can pitch camp anywhere. No need to seek higher elevations. Look, the eastern sky gonna start to blue up in a half hour or so. Booker, two mornins' from now we all gonna be standin' on the actual mountain of our dreams. Y'all found this road, God bless us."

Marshall turned and started walking along the gravelly right side a foot's distance from the wooden railroad tie ends. He thought he smelled creosote. "Smell that? Tar. Don't know why but I've always loved that smell," he whispered. "Hard to believe it still stinks after so many decades."

Tatum took his hand. "All those young couples making babies. You think we'll fit in with them?" she whispered.

Marshall remained silent as they walked another hundred feet. "Tatum, I don't want to scare y'all off or risk pushin' y'all away from me. I feel like I'm the most blessed man alive because it feels like y'all 'r returnin' my affection just the same; with the same intensity. Delilah was my common-law wife. When she murdered my baby and kicked me off my own mountain, for what reasons only God knows, I reckon pre-Flood people would call that a divorce. I am free to marry. So, if the Good Lord decides to send me a woman for keeps someday, one who loves as fiercely, whose spirit belongs to Jesus, well, sure. You can bet y'all's perfect little ass I'll want to start a family with her. Why, whatcha y'all thinkin?'"

It was her turn to remain silent. Then, "If you asked me to marry you, bear your children, and love no other for rest of my life, I don't know if I would say yes."

Marshall walked a little slower. The sun pushed away the twilight and birthed the new day with eleemosynary rays, letting him know there would be no rain anytime soon. Yet he felt a twinge of dashed hopes like what drove him from LeConte. He looked down at her and released her hand. "Y'all don't know?"

Her eyes bored deeply into his. "Because my answer would not be yes. It would be hell yes, ya big fat dope! It feels to you like I'm returning your affections with the same intensity: to me it feels like I love you more than you could ever love me."

He grabbed his chest and breathed heavily.

"Please don't scare me like that! My old man's heart can't take the strain. Seriously. Don't play with my feelins' even in jest."

"I won't, and now I see. What you are really saying is…that your heart no longer belongs to you. It belongs to me now. You need me to nurture and protect it?"

Marshall nodded and jabbed at the now turquoise sky. "The Lord has my heart and soul. Always has always will. It belongs to him. But the rest 'a me belongs to y'all, little brat."

With her left hand, she reached over and grabbed his crotch firmly. "These belong to me now, too."

Marshall whipped down his right hand, struck her butt firmly, then grabbed one entire cheek in his big hand. He squeezed firmly. "And this here's my property," he said. "Ain't nobody touches it but me. If they do, multiply that spank by the number 'a stones 'tween these steel rails to reckon whatcha got comin."

Tatum reached out her right hand. "Deal," she said. Marshall shook it.

They walked in silence for a quarter mile. "How did they do weddins' back in Pre-Flood days?" he asked. "Gold rings, unity candles, Churches, receptions, ever'one dressed up like penguins. A priest or pastor read from the Holy Bible. She said, 'I do' he said, 'I do.' I think we all 'r past all that now, ain't we?"

She nodded. "We shook hands on our union. That's a good enough contract for me. Wait," she said. She spat into her right hand and extended it. "Do it!" she said. He smiled, spit in his hand, and shook hers. "Okay now it's official. We're married. When can we get working on the baby part? I feel my old womb drying up like a slug in the sun."

"Well, as soon as we make camp, 'less y'all wanna scramble up that bank and hug one 'a them saplings right now…" he said, jabbing his finger toward the steep wooded track side.

She laughed. "Too much pressure with the others close behind, otherwise heck yes I'd meet you in the woods right now."

Marshall never felt more optimistic for the future than he did at that moment. So exuberant that he playfully hopped up on the rusting steel rail and attempted to walk along it without falling off.

Then he stopped.

Tatum read his face and stopped. He looked at her with a pounding heart though not in a happy way. He dropped to his knees and pressed his ear to the steel. He motioned with his hand for the others to stand quietly. He felt vibration.

"Booker, Jayden—them bastards musta been right behind us. A huntin' party. They followed us on the Trail then down to the tracks. Hopefully, it's only one small group like before."

Jayden looked at Marshall. "Don't know about anybody else but I am sick of running," he announced. "I would rather stand and perforate these demons."

Aliyah, Dodie, and Tatum stood wide-eyed with fear.

Marshall took a knee, closed his eyes, and tilted his head to face Heaven. After three minutes, he nodded and stood. "Son, y'all get to perforate. We gonna set up a kill box. Split up. Y'all 'n Booker 'r both good archers but Jayden, y'all can shoot the eye outta a flyin' bird from fifty yards. God's assassin. Booker, Aliyah, and Dodie: come up the bank with me and Tatum. I ain't gonna risk Jayden getting' distracted in any way. I don't trust myself with a bow so I'll use my slingshot. A steel shot to the temple can kill or at least knock down a Golgoth. Go! And be quieter than corpses! Mornin' ain't broken; it's still dark to them. Use our supreme advantage to ambush 'em: night vision."

That sense of creepiness came over Tatum again. She realized with something like despair how dramatically she herself had changed. *Will we ever have a day without fear? Without death?* Marshall glanced at her. He thought she looked pale and dismayed, but there was no time to comfort her.

They divided as Marshall had said. Jayden scrambled up the opposite bank alone, where he explored his options until he settled into his sniper hide. Marshall and Booker knelt together behind a big fern plant, giving them optimal visibility down to the tracks but also camouflaged them from below.

Marshall stilled his breathing and strapped on his goggles. The others perceived his calm and forced themselves to attempt the same. The hunting party appeared around the west bend a quarter of a mile back, white naked males holding long spears straight up. They marched in no formation along the tracks. Aliyah, Dodie, and Tatum had taken cover behind thick scrub. Marshall glanced back: he saw faces of fear and panic like three frightened rabbits.

Marshall whispered to Booker, "Let Jayden shoot first. They'll all be searchin' for him, backs to us. Aim for center 'a their backs: go fer' heart 'n lungs. I'll do head shots. Steel y'all's selves. Keep them heart rates low 'n minds clear."

"Heads are small targets. You could miss," Booker whispered.

"I ain't never missed a movin' target. When any 'a my headshot Golgoths drops or stumbles, fire your arrow at center mass when he's down. When some turn to look at y'all I will put out their eyes. Maybe kill 'em outright. If they come at us I will cut 'em to pieces. Tatum," he whispered sharply. "Hand me the two machetes strapped to the back of my pack. Also reach inside and pull out a box of ammo." She did. She handed him the weapons handles first.

He made a mental note of her concern for his safety. *Dear Lord, thank y'all. I love this woman.*

As Golgoths drew closer, they afforded Aliyah, Dodie, and Tatum their first-ever clear look at this species in motion. Hair plucked clean. Entire bodies painted white. The pendulous swing of genitals as they walked. Body language radiating hate and hunger. The complete absence of fear, pity, or remorse. Evil in the form of a singularity, a hive mentality. Tatum imagined that wordless chemical or spiritual commands got transmitted into them from a powerful, dark, purely evil entity.

All three shivered. Booker counted twelve. *Goths outnumber us two to one,* he thought. *Always in numbers divisible by three.*

The rearmost Golgoth closest to Jayden silently dropped from an arrow that sailed easily through one side of his neck and out the other. The man in front of him heard the scuffling of rocks. As he turned to investigate, an arrow broke through his teeth, severed his spinal cord, and protruded from the back of his neck.

Brilliant! thought Marshall. He made a hand motion toward the back of the assembly. Booker nodded and unleashed his arrow through the heart and lung of the Golgoth closest to his embankment.

Jayden fired an arrow into the fourth rearmost Golgoth closest to him, another neck shot. *He's aimin' for necks. So Jayden has a favorite kill shot. Likes to watch 'em drown in their own blood,* Marshall thought.

Now the eight remaining Golgoths stopped directly below Jayden and Marshall. They scanned the scrub on both sides. Jayden nocked an arrow and shot a man through the skull, then watched him collapse dead. *Missed his neck. But still fun. Like I poked out his battery,* Jayden thought.

Booker aimed for another man's center mass: the arrow went low and pierced his kidney along with other vital organs. The man dropped to his back, howling. *Shock or pain: I don't care which; scream on, devil,* Booker's thoughts raced.

That was when all Hell broke loose.

Two large spear wielding Golgoths rushed up toward Marshall and Booker just as two others scrambled up the opposite bank to get Jayden. Marshall saw Booker had nocked and taken aim. "No need to even say it," Booker muttered. He let the arrow fly. It hit one of the two on Jayden's embankment squarely in the middle of the shoulder blade. The man's howl sounded wet, and burbly. *I pierced a lung,* Booker thought, as he watched fascinated at the fruitless reach-behind attempt to pluck out the source of his undoing.

The Golgoth he had shot through the back on the opposite bank turned. Booker saw the bloody razor-tipped arrowhead poking out of the chest. Even wearing goggles Booker recognized blood leaking down in stark contrast to the white body paint. Jayden shot the second attacker's chest only feet before the Golgoth's long spear could reach him. The Golgoth dropped from the heart wound, dead before his brain had time to question it.

Two Golgoths continued the uphill charge to kill Marshall and Booker. Marshall released an ammo ball directly into the left eye of the forward Golgoth charging up at him. The eye popped like a tiny water balloon filled with gel. The man howled and grabbed at his face; though covering the mangled eye with his left hand he continued to lurch toward Marshall. Booker fired an arrow at the second charging Golgoth's center mass. The man moved erratically; the shot missed entirely. Two Golgoth spear tips were now only feet away below them.

Marshall grabbed the machetes and stood, making himself the obvious target. As both Golgoths charged at Marshall, Booker aimed for the heart of the one closest to Marshall, nocked his arrow, pulled—released. His arrow caught the Golgoth in the left lung. The shot only slowed him. Both enraged Golgoths continued to charge uphill at full speed. Preposterous animal noises bellowed from their white flared noses like enraged elephants. Both bore down on Marshall, spear tips now three feet away from piercing him.

Marshall closed the long machetes together. He held them out in front. *Lord be with me.* As spear tips entered his swing range, he burst the big knives outward and apart, hoping the knives would sever the spear shifts. They did not. However, they did deflect the spear shafts far enough apart where they could not pierce him without the attackers finding new footing and taking new aim.

Machetes extended, Marshall rained down on the two Golgoths with speed and body weight behind the knives, and with a downhill gravity assist. Each blade hacked through collarbones and deeply pierced abdomens. The men still stood. Mortal shock animated their grotesque faces.

Marshall pulled, and his machetes came free from the bodies with wet sounds. He dropped one blade, held the other high over his head, and brought it down upon the left man's head, splitting it open like a ripe melon. He tried to pull it out but could not. The wounded comrade charged at Marshall, who deftly sidestepped. The man's weight combined with his wound caused him to fall. He got back up. This time when he charged, Marshall was ready. He picked up the other machete and swung it sideways like a baseball bat. It connected with the neck and sunk halfway through. When Marshall pulled, the machete came free. In a graceful move he got behind the man and repeated the swing. The head came off cleanly. The body dropped, the heart still furiously pumped blood out through the neck.

Booker had nocked another arrow. Now he relaxed his pull on the bow.

"Marshall!" yelled Jayden as he scrambled up the hill. "I saw that, hoss. You were a man possessed! That was incredible!"

Tatum's terrified face had relaxed a measure though her breathing remained just this side of hyperventilation. "Wicked," was all she could say.

"That was some serious swordsmanship!" said Booker. "Man, what you just did wasn't human, not even close, like a dexterous bird of prey closing on two rodents at the same time! I stand humbled. We all skip lightly through the garden of your thinly restrained violence."

Marshall took a deep breath then shook his head. "Y'all sure do have the words, Booker." Tatum ran to Marshall and threw herself against his chest. He opened his hand. The bloodied machete slipped to the ground.

She sobbed into his chest. "For a second, I thought they were going to…"

Marshall cut her off. "Have faith in the Lord. It was all his doin.' His Holy Spirit works through me. I'm merely the knife. His is the hand that wields it."

She nodded against him. "I love you, husband." She said it loud so that everyone could hear. "I love God and his Son and his Holy Spirit. God and you saved me in every way a tragic woman can be saved. Thank you-thank you, thank you…"

Marshall consented to hold Tatum until her crying ceased, but his mind was elsewhere. He removed his goggles and the others followed. When Tatum released him, he looked at Jayden who was holding Dodie in a comforting hug. "We need to hide bodies like before. I think we'll mosey a ways. Make camp somewhere up along the banks. I'll string fishin' line 'cross the tracks at ankle level. At best, if Golgoths see it they'll think it's a cobweb and try to walk through it. Worse case they'll try to step over it. At least one gonna accidentally hit it. The other end 'a the line will hang over a shrub with discarded old glass or metal danglin' so that if we all hear clinkin' it'll wake us up, and we'll unload more projectiles into them white walkin' abominations. Sound like a plan?"

Booker and Jayden nodded. "Kinda brilliant, hoss," said Jayden.

Marshall nodded. "All credit goes to God. Besides: Booker's the brilliant one."

Booker grinned. "So Marshall, for the record: how do you feel after your first sublimely gory Golgoth kills?"

Marshall looked at him. He considered the simplicity of the question, and the source. It deserved a frank response. "Same as when I kill animals, Booker: nothin.' I feel nothin' at all. We do what we gotta do to protect each other. Now, help me drag these bodies uphill and outta sight. We gotta assume that these here won't be the last of 'em on the rail tracks huntin' us."

Booker and Jayden snapped-to and followed him down to the blood-stained kill zone.

Raw

Marshall disappeared downhill with his slingshot and spool of fishing line. Half an hour later, he deliberately kicked the line although he had assessed it well before the hunt. Bottles tied next to iron rail spikes clinked and jangled. Booker and Jayden emerged from the scrub and scree at the top of the embankment, arrows nocked and pointed at him. In his left hand, Marshall held forth two pheasants.

"You were testing us," said Booker, accusingly. "Didn't think we'd hop to it fast enough."

Marshall grinned. Under a bright morning sun, he shielded his face with his left hand. "Not testin' y'all, Booker: I was testin' the alarm. And it works! Let's eat."

After breakfast, each couple crawled to their drop-cloth lean-to and collapsed, exhausted from the adrenaline rush of battle followed by massive let-down, bellies full of wild game, and weeks of walking with an end finally in sight. Marshall's alarm never clinked a warning: all was peaceful.

Marshall awoke from dreamless sleep. He studied Tatum, memorized every contour of her petite, triangle shaped face.

He thought of Delilah, which raised questions within him about blindly trusting another woman: something he had sworn never to do again, to never feel pain like he had felt back home. *How'd I ever allow myself to be taken in by 'r? We were kids, both of us. Just dumb kids. Lord, forgive me, and forgive 'r diseased soul.* He tried to imagine being with Tatum in five years, ten years. *Is my grief over the baby and Delilah mixin' with these new feelins'—the most intense ardor and passion I have ever felt—to beguile me, Lord? Did y'all deliver Tatum to me as my wife? Please gimme a sign. I need to be certain. Ain't never gonna let me be deceived again. Help me, dear Lord. Give me y'all's Spirit without measure.*

Tatum's eyes opened. Seeing him, she smiled, yawned, and stretched. Fully awake now she lay watchful, a slight grin spread across her face. "I know you have doubts about me," she whispered, her words confirmed by his guilty expression. "You said it yourself: I'm an empath, remember? At least that's what Aliyah and Dodie have called me. So be warned, buster: whatever you feel, I feel, too."

Slowly he closed his eyes. "I worry, is all. I let myself get burned bad up there at LeConte. It hurt, Tatum. Hurt so bad that I decided only to love God. To never feel anythin' for another woman. I refused to go through it again. Then I saw y'all's face. Somethin' behind them eyes...the way y'all moved, the way y'all looked at me—Click! Click! Click! —it just happened. I had no control. Womanly charms pulled me in, but then I got to know y'all's core. It felt like y'all was scrapin' the residue of a dead existence from my eyes. Y'all changed everythin' and even thawed my icy blue heart, a little.

"But still, even now, a part of me stays locked up in a secure vault deep down. What if y'all were to pick that lock and get at it, then crush it? I don't know. All warmth in me would turn to permanent ice. I wouldn't like myself. The spirit 'a hate could just glide right in, find the place swept clean, empty, ready for habitation. Then what? Would God still even want me?"

Tatum placed her soft left hand against his cheek. "I know. All I can tell you is what you've taught me: that love is more than a feeling. It's a decision. I decided to make this journey. I decided that my feelings for you and that my feelings for God are real. My love is out now, growing by the hour. I feel healthy, whole, and so incredibly good for the first time in my life. If I should decide to stop loving you, yours wouldn't be the only insides to break—turning to permanent ice. I see God working through you. And who is greater than God? None. To reject you is to reject him. Then what are my options?" she whispered. At no time did she blink or break contact with his cheek.

"Try to see it from my place," she said. "I've thrown in my fortunes with you: good or bad; no matter what happens. I don't want to miss out on the chance of living an authentic life. I dream of the green place; see all the couples having babies. I want to bear your children. Stand with you or fall with you in battle. I love you, Marshall. I'll share you only with God because he comes first, and yes, he brought us together: I feel it. I want to be your second, and you want me to be yours. Neither of us has the strength to separate. It would disappoint him. So please, let me pick your locks. Don't hold anything back. Let me love you. Please?"

A male cardinal flittered down, sleek red wings, black face, tall head tuft. The bird perched on Tatum's extended forearm. The tiny head tilted left and right as though somehow it were examining them, questioning. It remained for half a minute before it flew off. A tiny red feather floated down and landed on her forearm.

A sign 'a trust. Thank y'all, Lord, Marshall thought, as he pinched the feather. "If we both make the same wish on this feather, the wish is gonna come true," he whispered.

Tatum smiled. "Well, then I wish for a long and happy life raising a family as Mrs. Marshall Langar. Your turn."

"I wish for God's Spirit to make a home in Tatum and me, without limit, and in our children and in their posterity. And in our friends. Now, we both blow on the feather."

Together they blew. The feather floated up, and out of sight. "Wish granted," said Tatum.

Marshall nodded. "Wish granted." He covered her mouth with his, then replaced his mouth with his right hand as he kissed her neck and kissed all the way down. Muffled trills escaped through his fingers. All her muscles went limp. A satisfied smile animated her face. She turned over, forehead against the bedding, and raised her hips toward him.

"Plant your seed, husband," she demanded.

Jayden guessed they had fewer than thirty minutes of usable light. "Marshall, I'm going to spool up the fishing line."

Marshall awoke to the disembodied voice of his friend, which had floated uphill from a distance. He had fallen asleep atop Tatum. She too had dozed. Now both snapped fully awake.

"Thanks Jayden," Marshall yelled down just loud enough to be heard.

"I truly hate to leave this spot, lover. Don't get y'all's knickers in a knot but wife: we need to dress in a hurry and break camp," he said, gently withdrawing from her. She groaned, but then rolled onto her back and pulled up her bottoms. She reached into her knapsack and pulled down her second dirty top.

"What I wouldn't give for another one of those warm showers and clean clothes," she said.

"I'm sure the Spring Mountain Church got that covered. Let's get there, shall we? We're close. Feel it?" Marshall said.

"Mm hmm. The shower is calling us," she whispered.

"I'll be honest, lover. I like y'all better raw. Mmm mm mm, deee-licious!" Marshall licked his lips.

She frowned. "Quit teasing."

"Serious! I love y'all's crust. Don't think I'm gonna let y'all scrub away all them tasty bacteria and sexy pheromones, oh *hell* no."

"Try and stop me. Animal."

The six assembled on the tracks and faced east, the sky behind them a cloudless orchid. Steel rails stretched off to infinity, or so it felt. Unlike the Trail with its ever-changing elevations, vistas, water crossings, and mix of terrain under their boots, the flat railway was the epitome of monotony.

"I preferred the Trail," Dodie said. "And my feet still hurt. Can we please get there already? Sorry to whine."

"Next time we stop, I'll give you a foot massage so good it'll make your ears tingle and toes curl," promised Jayden with a sideways smirk. "You'll feel finer than a frogs tail split four ways."

"Yeah, right. Whatever that means."

"Hold me to it, woman!" he whispered. She smiled.

Marshall donned his goggles as did Tatum. "C'mon y'all, let's move," he said, setting their pace at three-and-a-half miles per hour which those with short legs found a challenge to maintain. The distance between Marshall and Tatum from the four others gradually widened. Tatum would tug his sleeve and cast glances back. To give the other four chances to catch up, he would stop and press his ear to the metal rails, listening for vibrations. As they caught up he would resume his pace.

"Dodie's right, you know," said Booker. About the dreariness of this rail hike. Back on the Trail the hours passed quicker. Here, they draw out like molasses."

"What's molasses?" said Aliyah.

"You serious? You're seriously asking?"

She nodded.

"I'll pour some on your stomach, rub it all over then lick it off. You can taste my finger and tell me what you think."

Aliyah giggled.

Twelve hours of walking had started to feel more like twenty-four when the hint of navy-blue light appeared above the eastern black tree line. Marshall scanned the endless trees and scrub covering both embankments. He spotted big leafy ferns and a flat area atop the bank. He stopped allowing the others to catch up. The sky brightened more every minute. He removed his goggles. They all followed suit.

Marshall pointed. "Make camp up there. I'm gonna go kill our breakfast."

"Marshall," said Dodie, "You do realize that it's been like a month since any of us have had any vegetables. You probably consider fish a vegetable." Everyone laughed including Marshall. "I mean, don't get me wrong: I adore your food. It's just that I feel the need for vitamins and minerals. If it's all the same to you, I and Aliyah would like to forage for greens."

Marshall turned to Jayden. Jayden nodded.

"Soon as we set up camp, Jayden, y'all and Booker grab bows and quivers and stand guard while they rustle us up a nice salad," said Marshall.

"What protein are you going for today? Birds?" asked Jayden.

"First thing I see, whatever critter I scare up. Maybe a nice ripe skunk. Pairs well with mashed taters if y'all can find some. Seriously though, if y'all spot any bird's nests, grab the eggs."

Marshall walked to the left bank, removed his backpack, grabbed his slingshot, and ran across the tracks and up the right bank until they lost sight of him. Tatum lugged his backpack uphill, looked around until she found a nice, secluded spot, set everything down, and set up camp for both. By the time she started downhill, she ran into Aliyah and Dodie who moseyed about, bent over, and pulled at leaves. Booker and Jayden each kept one foot on the railroad tracks to sense vibrations, bows at the ready.

"What'd ya find?" Tatum asked.

"Dandelion leaves so far. Lots," said Aliyah.

"I found these sticky purple seed pods," said Dodie. "They smell a little skunky.

"How do you know the pods aren't poisonous?" asked Tatum.

"Saw birds eating them. Good enough for tweets means good enough to eat," Dodie said.

"Good point," said Tatum. "I'll see what I can find." After forty minutes Tatum identified wood sorrel, orange-yellow mushrooms growing on dead wood, oyster mushrooms on trees, and morels poking up from the soil. She harvested so much that her hands could barely hold it all. She picked her way back to camp and dropped everything into a pile at the foot of her sleeping bag. Tired, she laid down fully dressed atop her sleeping bag and dozed.

She dreamed of Spring Mountain.

Everyone here seems so busy! Women and children milling about. No animals this time, though. Those earthen walls are new, like cliffs hemming in the bowl of green mountain. That's exactly what it looks like—a giant brown bowl with a giant grass-green ladle filled with wonderful people inside. Happy people soup! Men standing in lines holding shields and blades longer than Marshall's...

The sound of Marshall's whispering from a distance slowly lifted her from this most pleasant dream. She opened her eyes.

"What are those?" she heard Dodie ask.

"Rabbits, Dodie," she heard Marshall answer. "Really tasty, y'all 'r gonna love 'em. First ones I've seen outside of LeConte. Somehow their ancestors survived the Floods. How'd your foragin' go?"

"Come on up to camp and we'll show you!" said Aliyah, in the tone of a schoolgirl itching to show daddy her latest art project. Aliyah and Dodie led the men up the bank. Tatum watched, then appeared holding out the hem of her shirt like a shelf covered with mushrooms.

"Wow, Tates! You found so much more than we did!" Dodie said.

"I read a magazine article once about foraging," Tatum said. "Pre-Flood people used to do it for fun. Even though they paid currency at stores for the same stuff, it gave them a thrill to just go get it themselves, not paying anything. I remembered what to look for, although this is the first time I've looked for it. And there it was, just like the article showed. Mushrooms are good for you. Boost your immunities a whole bunch."

Marshall walked fifty feet away to behead, gut, and skin the two rabbits, not wanting flies to gather on the gut pile near the team later while they rested. He returned; set up the cooking tent; and set the rabbits to roast. After they began to brown, he placed the light aluminum mess pot onto the flame, emptied three of his water bottles, and sliced bite-sized chunks of roasted rabbit into it. The remainder of the meat he stored in two of the rinsed-dried venison plastic bags. "Okay, ladies. Add y'all's greens. We'll have a delicious nutritious rabbit stew in no time," he said.

Tatum tossed in mushrooms, morels, and sprinkled in wood sorel for color. Aliyah and Dodie added dandelion leaves, wild garlic, and onion bulbs, and the purple sticky seed pods. Marshall brought the stew to a boil then turned down the flame to let it simmer. "Y'all," he said, "and Booker, correct me if I'm wrong: if we all sleep 'til three o'clock, givin' us maybe six hours' rest, but then we start walkin' right away 'fore it gets dark, we all can make it to the Mountain tomorrow mornin.'"

Booker checked his atlas, estimating their current location based on their walking speed multiplied by hours walked. He traced the line using the same speed estimate to Spring Mountain. He nodded. "We could do it. It'll be a hard day, though. That's more walking without a break than we've done. Dodie's feet might fall off. Plus, what about Golgoths during those last hours of daylight? I still can't clear my mind of how you julienned those two big demons."

"Who is Julie Ann?" Marshall asked.

"Never mind," Booker said. "I'm not sure this juice is worth the squeeze."

Marshall nodded. "I understand the risks and discomforts."

"Yeah, sure," Dodie whined.

"Given this railroad cut-out, I doubt very much Golgoths gonna crash down these high sides and set up a kill box like we all did to them," said Marshall. "If anythin' they'll come off the Trail back there followin' up on their huntin' party that never returned."

"Because we slayed every damned one of them," said Booker, a note of barely suppressed joy simmering in his tone.

Marshall continued. "If more Golgoths walk these rails lookin' for their own and somehow find the bodies, they gonna call an army down on us. And they ain't never gonna catch up to us. But y'all: what if they communicated to a tribe ahead? We encountered that huntin' party at night, right? That's a deviation. What if them demons 'r comin' at us right now from up ahead?"

Booker nodded. "We are on the most direct route to Spring Mountain, so no way did any tribe south or west of us pass information to tribes east and north of us. It'll be three o'clock before we can blink. You need to decide."

Marshall closed his eyes, hands pressed together over his lips, fingers extended in prayer. "I ain't feelin' an attack in the next few hours. I think it's worth spendin' one less day exposed and another night walkin.'"

"A warm shower would be worth a hard final push," said Aliyah.

Jayden appeared thoughtful. "My dad used to say, 'Son, when you see light at the end of the tunnel don't crawl, don't walk, don't run—sprint your ass off.' After weeks of walking if we really are that close, I vote we go for it. Let's get this done, bros and sisses."

"I'm with you, Marshall. Whatever you think is best," said Tatum.

Did the Spirit show him danger? Can't ask him now, in front of everyone, she thought.

"Then it's settled. Let's eat." Using his spoon, he equitably attempted to ladle equal portions of greens, meat, mushrooms, and seed pods into everyone's aluminum mess pans, serving himself last.

Aliyah dug in first. "Mmm! Good! Tastes like chicken!"

"That's the mushroom, the big yellow one. It does taste like canned chicken," said Tatum.

"Eww!" cried Dodie. "Don't eat the seed pods! Yuck. Tastes skunky."

Jayden examined the pods. As he ate his portion, his mind traveled back through all his readings trying to place where he might've seen them. "Tatum, the morels and mushrooms really make this something special," he said. "And Marshall, I've never eaten rabbit before. This is the best meat I've had on this journey. Good shootin' there, hoss. But these marijuana pods boiled up with animal fat are going to make the next six or eight hours feel very strange."

Marshall clapped his hands to his face. "Marijuana!"

Side Trip

"Huh? What?" asked Dodie.

"You picked these pods?" asked Jayden.

She nodded; eyes rheumy.

"Dagnabbit!" said Jayden. "And we just cooked them with the meat. Chemicals in the pods bond to fats in the meat. Each of us can now expect to feel…off our game. Unable to focus."

Dodie choked back tears. "Are they poison?"

Jayden laughed and shook his head. "No, Dodie, not poison. They mess with your head. Pre-flood people used these pods to alter their reality…mentally escape present anxieties. To relax and feel artificially happy. Many people consumed daily doses of 'self-medication.' All I know is, we need our wits about us. We're at war with Golgoths everywhere we turn."

Jayden patted Dodie's hand. "What I'm saying is that we're all about to go on a little head trip. Read about it when I was a kid. People did it for fun. I went exploring offices in my building; one day, I found a rolled-up cigarette of the stuff in a bottom drawer, and a lighter.'

"Tell me you didn't," said Dodie.

He smirked. "I did. Coughed 'til I thought I'd die. Didn't take much, though. Spent the next hour or so staring at a wall reminding myself to breathe, following my thoughts wherever they led me. Made me emotional, too. I felt like I loved the world, like I was one with it. Gave me a raging thirst and bottomless appetite. Anyway, guess I'll feel it again soon. I'm done. No more for me. C'mon, Dolores, let's lie down and I'll make your achy feet sing. Marshall, see you at three o'clock packed and ready to rock. Can't wait to get to Spring Mountain and play my guitar. Beginning to lose my fingertip callouses," he said. Dodie was so upset she didn't object to Jayden's use of her birth name. Aliyah refused to look at her.

Tatum's eyes were wide saucers. She continually glanced toward Marshall for comfort. Booker took Aliyah's hand and led her away. "See you at three," he whispered.

Tatum rushed over and hugged Marshall, lips pressed tightly against his chest. "I'm scared."

Marshall held her for half a minute. Then he whispered, "Come with me to bed." She pulled back to meet his eyes. He smirked mischievously.

They stood together. Marshall bent and unlaced his boots. He stepped out of them, toeing off the socks. He removed his two shirts, pants, and underwear. He stood naked before her. He pulled off her two shirts. With his left hand supporting her naked back, he gently lowered her to the sleeping bag. His left hand supported her ankles while his right removed her boots. Her socks he pulled off with his teeth. She giggled.

"You truly are a beast, Marshall Langar." She looped her ankles behind his thighs and pulled him inside.

"That was intense," he whispered.

"It took us both forever! Slow-slow build, then wham! Together! Never-ending waves so sharp and deep. Unreal. The best ever."

He frowned at her. "So y'all 'r sayin' all them times before weren't so great?"

"Marshall, I didn't mean—"

He broke out laughing. It infected her. "Y'all's face…priceless." The two guffawed and could not stop. He collapsed onto his back to her left, covered his mouth with his left hand, hers with his right to muffle the merriment. The snorting hilarity refused to pass. Their stomachs ached and still they laughed, tears streaming down faces. He managed to whisper, "I used up my water in the rabbit stew. Can we split one 'a yours?"

Through laughter, she nodded. He crawled to her backpack, reached down and reverse-crawled with a bottle. He handed it to her. "Ladies first," he said. She managed to calm herself long enough to take a drink. She swallowed the entire bottle. "Pig!" he said, which started her chortling harder than before. He crawled back, grabbed a bottle, and drained it. "Dopie Dodie and her damned marijuana pods," Marshall said.

Tatum had to turn over and bury her face in the cloth, body wracked with peals of laughter. The sight of her lithe form, muscles contracting, rib bones heaving, immediately forced him back to where he was. It took them both thirty minutes to climax together. Again, he laid to her left, head propped in his right hand. He lightly traced lines over her skin as far down and up as his left hand could reach.

"What do you suppose Heaven is like?" Tatum asked.

Marshall considered it. At first he weighed a myriad of possible pithy responses about their torrid romance. His mind wandered. He wasn't sure if he was in a state of trance as when praying or feeling the effects of the marijuana. He closed his eyes and just went with it. He followed his thoughts wherever they led him.

"Soft gold light, incredibly bright, with blues and reds like sunlight, yet the light's source gives no heat. Patches of flowers thirty feet tall, sunny faces framed in colorful petals. Everythin' glimmers! The basic elemental buildin' blocks 'a life sorta resemble precious jewels and metals on earth, only better; brighter. Streams, dazzlin' rivulets so clear and sparklin,' murmurin' over beds of diamonds, emeralds, rubies, and sapphires. In the distance a structure 'a such monolithic size and grandeur, nothin' on our planet could compare to it, like stackin' our Mount Everest next to the thirteen-mile-high Olympus Mons volcano on the planet Mars. I might call it a cathedral, or a castle. A temple grand enough to hold three billion people, each with their own mansions inside. Like you could fit a million Saint Peter's Basilicas inside it. Still, even that inadequate description falls pretty limp against the splendor, the vastness, the majesty of what Heaven is like."

"Oh Marshall. I want to live there! What are the people like?"

"A sound—as though every atom hums together to form music more deeply satisfyin' than any human-generated notes. People in Heaven ain't like nothin' relatable in our carbon-based frame of reference, 'cept in basic shape. Everyone's made 'a the same element as the cathedral, the room, the grass, the flowers. People in Heaven move like us, but their skins 'r sparklin' gold; everyone's the exact same height, size, and color. Each wears a similar long, flowing raiment, principally white, though some have blue trim, others trimmed in purple. Gender? I'm seein' one who definitely has feminine facial features and bearin.' I see her holdin' a silver cat. I can *hear* feelins!' Even the cat's! I feel the animal's utter contentment restin' in them golden arms. No energy in all the universe coulda' pried it away.

"In Heaven, language is moot. People there see themselves through the eyes of people, and creatures that were once pets here on earth: feel one another's thoughts; feel the equanimity, the lovin' warmth of their welcomin' spirits. When we arrive, we all are new friends for others to play with, to love. We all feel special; wanted. In this place, joy feels like spirit-liftin' ecstasy! No anger or grief, no sadness: not a trace. And time loses all meanin.' The past, present, and future coexist. An hour, a year, ten thousand times a million years: time elapses without any sense of it passin.' People 'a Heaven look backward and forward like lookin' out a window. In Heaven, people can ride a dinosaur or float through a black hole that ain't even been formed yet. There, people feel completely present all the time."

He opened his eyes to find Tatum staring at him in wide-eyed fascination. "I'm back," he whispered. "Sad to leave, but happy to be back with y'all, lover. Where I just went, I did not wanna leave. I ached to stay. Mountains 'a green reachin' to the sparklin' blue-green-yellow skies, impossibly high. A peaceful deep green lake the size and depth of an earthly ocean. I think maybe the Holy Spirit just gave me a little preview of what's to come.

"Or maybe it was just marijuana," she said.

He shook his head. "Seemed pretty clear; that magnificent expansiveness and that pervasive sense 'a joy, love, and perfectly harmonious peace. Again, 'joy' ain't nothin' but a noun here, misused to describe a fleetin' chemical reaction in the human brain. In Heaven, joy is a force, sovereign and transcendent."

She rolled over and straddled him. "Wanna hear something spooky? What you just said didn't really sound like you. I mean it was you, of course. But the words seemed...not your own. Anyway, we'll go there together, husband. But not yet. Not yet," she said, and kissed him, until again she felt heat, hard and urgent, pressing up against her. She looked down upon his face, and at thick neck muscles straining.

She smiled. "I have tamed a stallion, and he is mine all mine. God, he is beautiful. Thank you, Lord God. I don't deserve him, and I don't deserve you, and I don't deserve your Son, Jesus Christ."

Pale blue and white lights exploded like mini supernovas behind her closed eyelids. He groaned and covered his mouth. She collapsed and buried her face against his neck until her breathing normalized. She rolled off onto her back. He looked over.

"Get under the covers, wife. Don't wanna wake up with a big hairy spider on your tummy."

"Eww-uh! Okay," she whispered. Together they slipped inside his bag. He zipped it from the inside, spooning behind her. Sleep came quickly.

"Marshall. Yo Marshall. Wakey-wakey. It's quarter to three," Jayden whispered, with Dodie by his side.

They jolted awake. "I was dreamin' of the green mountain," said Marshall.

Tatum nodded. "Me too. I was in dirt cave there. But it was weird. There was a narrow crawlspace up in the dirt roof. I climbed up inside it, just barely able to fit, then it arched, pitch black in there, then the arch curved downward for what seemed like forever," she said with a full-body shiver. "I was hiding from Golgoths. They were trying to get inside the dirt cave. Like, thousands of them."

Jayden frowned. Marshall watched his face. He appeared thoughtful. Then, "Hoss, what if we get all the way there and it's just another deserted mountain? I mean, isn't it possible the dream about the prophet Gabriel and his Church could be getting beamed inside our heads by a force other than God? Like, a trap set by God's opposite number?"

Marshall nodded. "Sure. After everythin' we all seen I guess anythin's possible."

"What then?" asked Dodie.

"Then we walk up through Canada to Alaska. I'm cravin' ice water."

Jayden, Dodie, and Tatum stared at him, hangdog. "Your faces," he said, as laughter billowed up from someplace deep and made the rounds. Aliyah and Booker heard none of it. But then they joined the group and laughter consumed them, too.

Regaining a measure of control, in hushed tones Marshall said, "Jayden: People lie. They promise dreams one day then deliver nightmares the next." He looked at Tatum. She felt Delilah's betrayal shot from fierce eyes like lightning.

"Our lovin', merciful God ain't never broken a promise or shattered a dream since the dawn 'a time. God has never changed. This dream, like a radio signal from someplace else, joined us all together in God's love. We walk under his protection. The Church of the Elect is waitin' while we all stand here jawin.'"

Marshall kissed Tatum's forehead. "We were all lonelier than ticks in an attic before we obeyed the dreams and met up on the Trail. Sad sacks, every goll-darned one of us. We grew up in the ruins of a society that had separated itself so far from God that he gave Creation a little jiggle and washed it all away, just to bring it all down to this time. God knows all truth, but he waited; waited; then did this great reset. He has seeded a new, fresh Church, free from corruption. He delivered to us friends for life, ones who will keep our secrets and ease our pain. No," he looked at Jayden. "What y'all r' suggestin' ain't possible. A Church awaits us. Let's pack up and be there by mornin.'"

Jayden nodded. "You're right, hoss. Just a random thought," he said. "Ever since I ate your rabbit stew, been having lots of them." That started everyone laughing again.

"Booker spoke to me in French and Latin. He wouldn't tell me what any of it meant. But it sure sounded good," Aliyah whispered. She nibbled his left ear.

"Yeah, we're revokin' Dodie's foragin' card permanent-like," said Marshall.

Dodie blushed. "Guys, I am *so* sorry."

Marshall said, "I'm kinda nekkid, otherwise I'd stand up and give y'all a hug, Dodie. I'm kinda glad for our screwy stew. How 'bout you, Tatum? You glad?" She gave him a coy grin and vigorous nod.

"But yeah, no more giggle-weed. We need our minds workin' tip top. This last leg could be the most dangerous. Where there are Elect y'all can bet Golgoths are there like wolves, eyeballin' 'em hungrily. We all r' walkin' through some risky mileage once we all get to…"

"Gravel Pike," whispered Booker.

"Right. Gravel Pike. We gonna be on roads for a while. Y'all remembered to solar-charge your goggles before you ate the silly stew?" Everyone nodded. Jayden laughed. "Okay then git, so we all can put on clothes. Y'all pack your stuff. Meet on the tracks in five."

The Last Mile

"How much farther to Gravel Pike, Booker? I realize y'all can't really pinpoint where we all are," whispered Marshall.

Booker walked while finger-tracing his map. "Best guess, we have about an hour; ninety minutes maybe."

Marshall stopped. The others fell in behind him. He pressed his left ear to the steel rail and held up his hand for total quiet. He stayed like that for over three minutes. He stood up, removed his goggles, and so did the others. Eyes adjusted slowly to the darkness, with an eerie assist from billions of stars and a small highly polished silver coin of a moon riding just above the rails ghostly, high, and free.

After he re-established eye contact with each, he said, "We got enemy on our tail. I'm guessin' Arabella's little arrow a' corpses lit up the Golgoth coconut telegraph. Every Golgoth south and west knows 'bout us by now."

"Coconut telegraph?" Jayden asked.

Marshall did not speak. He perceived something like fear in faces and body language. "Like that last huntin' party we ended, they tracked us from the Trail. They walked while we slept yesterday. Instead of restin' tonight, they decided to lose sleep and press on. They wanna kill us more than they wanna kill anybody, 'cause we beat 'em good."

Marshall rubbed his face and hair. "Vibrations are there, but faint. I'm gonna guess they are a good three miles behind us. So, either we set up a kill box here and deal with 'em in the dark using the advantage of night goggles and surprise—"

"Or we push on, stay out in front of them, deal with the road, and get to the safety of the Mountain with no more delays," whispered Jayden. "Hoss, you know damned well how dearly I love ghosting these abominations; and I know you're not against it; neither is Booker. But the ladies might want to get up to where we're going as soon as possible. And last round included several life-ending close calls for you and me. We nearly bought it, friend. What say you, Dodie?"

"Me? You're making me decide for the group? I don't want the pressure, Jayden. Not fair," she said.

"I say we walk on," said Aliyah. "Just feels right. We've come this close and nobody's wounded. Let's go all the way. Finish the trip. I had a dream like Tatum's today, kind of. I was in a cave, but above ground was a war, maybe? If that's our future, Marshall, then ending a dozen Golgoths here won't make a dent. What if it's not twelve this time but thirty, fifty?"

"More time on the Gravel Pike Road in daylight means more exposure," said Tatum. "While we lose another day sleeping on the ground. Aliyah's right. We need to push on."

Marshall nodded. He wore his goggles like a necklace, grabbed Tatum's hand and recommenced walking. This time, somehow everyone managed to keep up with him.

"What's that down there?" Aliyah asked. They walked across an incredibly old and sturdy steel railroad bridge undamaged by the Floods.

"That's the Schuylkill River," Booker answered. "An old Native American name. Saw it on the map. Know what it means?"

"What does it mean, Booker?" asked Marshall.

"Means we're about to leave the tracks and start walking to the mountain!" Everyone high-fived each other.

"Goggles on," said Marshall. "As soon as we step onto pavement we need to be bug-eyed alert. You see anythin' move, even a little, call it out. Me and Tates'll look straight ahead. Aliyah and Booker, each take a side and cover our left and right. Jayden and Dodie, y'all got our backs; look behind y'all. Three-sixty visual coverage always. Got it?"

"Got it," whispered the five. On the north side of the river, corpses of commercial buildings and homes crouched eerily in rotting piles. The rail tracks disappeared into a thick grove of trees.

"Hey Marshall, better stop," said Booker. "Up ahead is a steel bridge high above the road. We'd have an ugly time climbing down the stone supports. Best we cut through these trees at a forty-five-degree-angle, straight to Gravel Pike."

"How long from there to the Mountain?" asked Marshall.

"Four hours."

"How long 'til dawn?"

Booker hesitated, then, "We've walked twelve hours since three o'clock yesterday. We have two hours or a little more before we lose the goggles. Three hours on Gravel Pike brings us to a big stream crossing and an uphill hike through the woods. So technically we'll be on a road for an hour after the sun comes up before we hit the smaller mountain trail."

Marshall nodded. "Remember y'all's jobs, people. Anythin' moves: y'all run up and tell me real quick-like. With any luck, the Golgoth huntin' party behind us 'll keep to the tracks all the way east. Damned devils are good trackers. They followed us in Carlisle down the hill to the tracks. Broken leaves and branches; boot prints; squashed plants; little rocks turned upside down; hairs from our heads: these are how they figured out where we went off Trail. Let's make it harder for 'em this time. Follow me through the woods single file. Don't drag y'all's toes; lift knees high and take flat steps only. Don't let any low branch rub on y'all's heads. The goal is to leave no trace. No rain in days. We can do this."

Marshall flat-stepped off the overgrown gravel onto terra firma covered in brown pine needles. He threaded his way through a crossword puzzle of small dry pine branches without snapping any. It was slow-going. He ducked under low branches without touching them, careful to leave no hair or clothing fibers for Golgoths to find. The others did their best to imitate Marshall's every move. Only Dodie stepped on one small twig and snapped it. She bent; picked it up; and pocketed the pieces.

Marshall set foot on cracked asphalt. Weeds grew up through the cracks. The road stretched steeply uphill in a northeast direction. He stepped to the middle and waited for all to join him. "Booker, are we all standin' on Gravel Pike?"

"We are."

"Wee doggie! Finally. Now ya'll remember, me and Tates look straight ahead. You two cover the sides. Jayden and Dodie, look behind and *keep* lookin' behind. Walk backwards if y'all gotta. Okay let's move."

"I can hardly believe it," whispered Tatum. She held Marshall's hand. "The Church at Spring Mountain; the prophet Gabriel; the community we've always longed for; the promised land of our dreams! So close. Do you think they'll make us feel welcome?"

"Oh for sure, lover," said Marshall. "These are our people, God's people. The only man there who gonna eat you, is me."

She grinned. "I'm overdue for another of your thorough cleanings."

He released her hand and reached behind to his backpack to free his machetes from their Velcro stays, one in each hand.

"Worried?"

Marshall nodded. "The last stretch gonna be the most dangerous. I had a dream, a nightmare really, about a Golgoth stronghold where their leader lives. It gave me the feelin' of a hive, or hornet's nest, venomous Golgoths everywhere. I think we're near it."

"What makes you think that?" she asked.

"From where we all started, which way were all Golgoths headin?'"

"North. Same as us. Though it could be a coincidence."

"I don't believe in coincidences, Tates."

She remained quiet. "There's something you're not telling me. Don't you trust me?"

The force behind his whisper increased. "Not thinkin' 'bout Golgoths right now; and I don't like talkin' 'bout LeConte, you know that. About her; about Delilah."

"I understand completely, husband. I only just wanna know what you know about them."

He looked at her. "I'm sorry, but I just told you a lie. I swore I would never do that."

"Then please. Tell me."

"The nightmare I described weren't mine: it was *Delilah's*. On our last mornin' together, she told me that she had dreamed 'a the top Golgoth,

Hostis Dei. Told me that he called her to himself. Like we have dreams 'a God's prophet, the yellow-haired man, Gabriel, callin' us to him? She dreamed 'a his opposite number, Hostis Dei, the sublime potentate 'a all murderers. She told me that his mountain 'a power is at a place named Forge Valley, or Valley Forge. I looked on my map when we laid over at the cabin. Valley Forge National Park is only 'bout a two-hour walk east 'a here."

"Dear God. That's so close!"

"Tatum, sorry I lied. Won't happen again, I promise. I wanna build a wall as high as the stars between her and y'all. To me, y'all 'r a gift from God, an angel made flesh. She is corruption, decay, infection, rot, and all things unclean. An abomination, like a gassy-ripe, sickenin' odor in my memories. I refuse to think about 'r let alone talk about 'r. Please don't make me think back on all that."

"Marshall," she said, reaching up to grab his neck. "I told you early on I will never press you for anything more than you want to give. I completely forgive your harmless lie if you'll forgive my pressing you about enemy intel. I know you only meant to keep me from worrying, and also you hate thinking about her. I only want to be mentally prepared for anything. If those freaks try to hurt you, hear me now believe me later: I will kill them."

She reached into his knapsack, pulled out his already-strung bow, held it in her left hand, and an arrow in her right. "I'm serious. Anyone who tries to hurt you gets dead. I don't care who it is."

Marshall smiled. "You sure are a fierce little thing. Thank you, Lord. You know what fer.'"

The biggest smile came upon her face.

Marshall slowed his pace. "Did you see something?" she asked.

A shape in the middle of the road ahead appeared human to her now as well. She nocked an arrow and pulled back the bowstring.

"Marshall, what is it?" said Booker, who ran up with his bow at the ready, followed by Jayden. Aliyah and Dodie caught up. Marshall let them see for themselves.

"Sitting and laying on top of each other waiting for us? That doesn't quite seem right, hoss," said Jayden. "They aren't moving.'"

Walking at a cautious pace, the three men stood in a line with the three women close behind them, as they cautiously advanced toward the anomaly in the middle of Gravel Pike. Thirty feet away now they recognized what it was. "Lord have mercy," whispered Jayden.

Booker stiffened. In a low growl, "I watched my parents go out like this."

Old kills thought Marshall. Adult skeletons arranged in obscene sexually explicit poses into a deliberately appalling diorama. *They wanted survivors to find this. A warnin' to go no further up this road. They don't want people addin' themselves to Gabriel's Church.*

"Bones picked clean by birds, insects and bacteria a long time ago," whispered Booker. "Decades of exposure. Whited bones."

"Ossuary from Hell," whispered Jayden. "What do you suppose it means, hoss?"

"We got Golgoths on our tail. Let's keep walkin,'" Marshall said, and they did, but did not immediately resume formation. Jayden and Booker flanked Marshall to speak with him while the women trailed behind. "Meanin' is clear, Jayden. Golgoths know about the Church, have known about it for decades. They formed their own about a two-hour walk east 'a here at a place called Valley Forge, their epicenter of power. I'm sure every road leadin' to the Church is one long necropolis designed to slow travelers long enough for Golgoth patrols to slaughter 'em."

"They're afraid of Gabriel adding to his numbers," Booker muttered. "Can't let anyone slip through. Can only mean one thing."

"War," Jayden leaned closer to Marshall. He whispered. "They mean to destroy the Church."

Marshall nodded. Trouble crossed over his face like a cloud shadow lazily carving a dark path through a serene reservoir. "Tatum already knows we're close to Hostis Dei: I told her. If y'all wanna tell Aliyah and Dodie that's on y'all. Me, I'm gonna stay focused and quieter than dust in a tomb for these last miles. How many more, Booker?"

"Twelve miles to go. About this war—"

"I think it's preordained, Booker. Y'all done memorized the Bible," Marshall whispered.

Booker fake laughed. "Lemme get this straight: we all just left our high elevation places of safety to walk just shy of a thousand miles for a damned month—into a war zone? C'mon, man. You're talkin Armageddon? Guess what, Marshall. That war takes place in Israel. That's not our problem."

"Ain't an OP— got it. I hope y'all 'r right, Booker. For all our sakes I dearly hope y'all are. We all need to get back in formation: Jayden, y'all and Dodie in the rear; Booker, please take the middle so y'all and Aliyah can be scannin' our flanks. Any sounds or movement please stop me. 'Cept for the huntin' party behind us, let's hope all them other Golgoth patrols 'round here are still asleep."

Jayden fell back, grabbed Dodie's hand; immediately the two resumed looking behind them. Dodie unlatched a bow from his backpack. She felt around inside a pocket until she found a string. She looped a string end into the bow tip notch. She paused to flex the bow, tip against the asphalt, to complete the stringing. Jayden stopped to allow her time. She grabbed an arrow from his quiver and nocked it. The two sprinted to catch up to Aliyah and Booker.

Jayden bent over and kissed her cheek. "Tiny but lethal," he whispered, smiling. "Dolores the viper. And sexy as they come. I do believe I am in love, little miss."

"I should hope so, moron. You've certainly taken enough liberties with my body. I would never give my love to someone who isn't my husband."

He grinned. "Mrs. Dodie Bonner. You have my whole heart. Now please: keep looking behind. One day I'll teach you how to aim and shoot that arrow."

"If I see one Golgoth you can bet I'll figure it out right quick."

The group had spotted what remained of child skeletons moldering along the roadside, long ago picked clean by animals and bugs. Marshall saw those tiny skeletons and prayed for the soul of his own dead child. "What's that river on the right, Booker?" Marshall whispered. Without incident they had walked up the steep grade which had flattened through Collegeville, now in Rahns. Marshall and his followers hiked Gravel Pike where thirty-three years prior, the young prophet Gabriel walked through the First Flood with eleven of his eight-year-old followers. They had just passed the tall Norway Spruce tree which, during the First Flood, after third-grader Gabriel reacted to an image flashed into his mind by the Holy Spirit of God, sheltered him and his eleven followers from first-version Golgoths.

"Perkiomen Creek. Gravel Pike follows it. We're close to the trail that leads to Spring Mountain," Booker answered in a whisper.

"Good. 'Cause look east," whispered Marshall. Dawn rapidly broke through the gloom like an unwelcome guest. They stripped off their goggles.

"Golgoth wake-up time," whispered Jayden.

"Only about an hour until we get off this road," whispered Booker. "Park Avenue, then an uphill hike on a trail through the woods—and we're there. The next sixty minutes bring the highest likelihood of encountering Golgoths."

"No Golgoths here!" whispered Jayden, an hour later.

Marshall grinned. "Don't sound so disappointed."

They walked across the decrepit, but sturdy remains of the same arched steel footbridge that Gabriel, leading his eleven school mates crossed on the slippery arches during the First Flood that were then a mere two feet above the turgid rapids. The trail mouth that led up to Spring Mountain was unmistakable. Several steps in, Jayden spotted an artesian well. They paused to fill their water bottles with clear, delicious mountain spring water.

Pulsing with hope and optimism, with kisses all around, the six marched up the Trail, feeling lighter than air.

Reborn Hard

After an hour of steeply inclined hiking, their boots finally stood on the aged asphalt of Spring Mount Road. The team briefly paused to drink. Their bodies had become so conditioned from many weeks of ceaseless hiking that none breathed heavily. "This is it," Booker whispered. "On the right. We're parallel with the summit of Spring Mountain on our right."

Marshall nodded and smiled. "Beautiful," he whispered. "The green slope. I can barely see it, though. Looks like the Church 's been busy buildin' up some high dirt redoubts 'round the perimeter. Not sure how we all get inside."

"A fortress!" whispered Tatum. "Every castle has a drawbridge somewhere."

"Oh my God! I can hardly believe it! We really are here!" whispered Dodie.

"Amen and Hallelujah!" whispered Aliyah.

Marshall nodded. "Y'all are so right, Tatum. Let's walk downhill and keep our eyes right. Must be a way for folks like us to get in."

"But not Golgoths," she whispered.

"Not them, lover. They ain't welcome here. Only God's Elect are welcome here."

"Marshall," Tatum whispered, "are you sure God elected me? Chose me?"

Marshall nodded. "Yessum he did. God chose y'all and loves y'all completely. If not, God woulda' abandoned y'all back there to selfish passions like he did Arabella." Downhill they walked. Tatum held his hand and energetically swung it forward and backward. At times she skipped like a little girl.

Whenever she glanced at Marshall she found him deep in thought. "A covered bridge," he whispered. "Did y'all see one of 'em in your dreams?"

It was Tatum's turn to grow quiet. "A footbridge with a roof made of wood shakes, Y-shaped beams holding it up, painted red, crossing over a small stream."

"Y'all seen it!" he whispered too forcefully. "I believe that right there is our way in. We gotta find it."

The downhill grade made it an effortless walk. Marshall observed that the earthen berms were taller than he was by two at least, with a gradual slope up. Across the green grassy hill he saw that inside of the dirt moat was a sheer vertical drop. He puzzled out the reasoning. *It's like they wanna invite Golgoths inside the bowl, then they made it nigh on impossible for 'em to climb back out. Ain't no kill box: it's a kill bowl.*

The grade flattened. Tatum was first to spot a darkness interrupting the solid brown dirt wall. She stopped. She pointed. Marshall stared. They walked closer. They looked at each other. "That's it!" they cried together at full volume.

A gravel path led from the road to a large, thick wooden door in the side of the dirt wall, taller than a man and as wide, with no visible hinges. The others caught up to them. Nobody spoke. Marshall used the knife edge of his right hand to pound on the door. His effort met with a hollow booming echo. He pressed his ear to it, listening. He heard the creaking of footfalls on wood. "Who goes there?" came a male voice.

"Marshall Langar, Jayden Bonner, Burl 'Booker' Bailey, Dolores Sealy, Aliyah Freedman, and I am Mrs. Tatum Langar."

"Tatum—you are married? And you just told everyone my secret name! Oh my God, Tatum!" Dodie screeched.

"Yes, I am married; and Dolores is the name your parents gave you. It's a pretty name. Be proud of it."

Jayden grinned. "Cat's out of the bag, Dolores."

"What is your business here?" said the voice.

"Gabriel called us here," Tatum said.

With a loud metal-to-metal grinding against a background of creaking wood, the heavy door opened inward. The group saw a footbridge leading to daylight at the other open end. Sixteen young men stood at attention facing each other across the six feet of wooden floor planking. Each wore identical uncolored linen pants and shirts, covered in kusari—samurai chain mail armor worn by Japanese elite warriors in past centuries. Jackets, hoods, gloves, vests, shins, shoulders, thigh guards; Marshall saw that even their forehead guards and tabi socks were of the tiny interlocking steel rings. Each wore a sword about his midsection inside a hemp scabbard hung from a rope belt. He also spotted one smaller blade, attached by a hemp loop. Each stood holding up a spear twice as long as a man.

The man who greeted him was older by twice their years. A beautiful, petite woman stood by his side. He wore linen but not armor. Dark hair, as tall and broad as Marshall with a thick black beard and mustache salted with silver hair. "Welcome, travelers. My name is Drake Childers. This is my wife, Nicole."

"Welcome!" she said, with a voice so high it sounded childlike. Her eyes sparkled. Her middle-aged beauty stunned all six. She smiled.

Now that right there must be the warmest smile I ever seen, thought Jayden.

"Won't you please follow me?" said Drake. "The prophet Gabriel has been expecting you."

Tatum's eyes filled with water. "Oh my God. He really is real. I've dreamed of him!"

Marshall nodded. He reached out his hand to Drake. "Marshall Langar, it's an honor, sir. We all dreamed 'a Gabriel, and this place. We all believe the Holy Spirit pulled us here."

Drake grinned and shook Marshall's hand. "Marshall, we are all so thrilled to meet you and your friends. You are not the first to sojourn here from afar, following your dreams," said Drake, "but Gabriel believes you are the last. He has mentioned all of you by name to me, every week, for months," Drake said, eyes locked with Marshall's until he made eye contact with the others. "Come, all of you. Meet the Prophet, Gabriel, whom I have served for three and thirty years."

Drake walked beside Marshall on his left as the others followed. "Gabriel knew you were close. He sent me down here to greet you personally." Drake turned and led them along an asphalt path past a unique chalet building. Uphill stood the only two-story structure with a wooden deck on the second floor.

"From our dreams!" said Aliyah.

"Oh. My. *God!*—squealed Dodie.

"Holy moly," said Jayden.

"The man of light," muttered Booker. "With the finger of God upon him."

Tatum closed the gap and held Marshall's right hand. "I'm nervous! Suddenly this all got real!"

Marshall smiled. "Don't be anxious, wife. God is good. God is great. We all have obeyed his will. Nothin' to get worked up about. The opposite." He released her hand and placed his right hand against her chest. "Y'all's heart feels like it's gonna explode out this skinny little ribcage, wife. Relax."

"He can see inside us, Marshall! I…I spent my life apart from God until you came along and opened my eyes—"

"Until God put me in y'all's path, like a finger pointin' the way. God opens eyes: 'twasn't my doin; and not Gabriel's. It was all the Father's doin.' God chose and saved y'all. He knows every inch a' y'all's heart: the good, the bad, and he loves y'all absolutely. So nothin' to fear 'cause now y'all believe. All y'all's sins, every single one of 'em are forgiven; wiped clean. God don't see 'em. He sees only y'all's love for his Son, and that's all he sees. Now, through his prophet we all 'r gonna learn what the Father expects from us. Be strong, 'cause whatever it might be, easy or hard, this we all must do. Understand?"

She looked at him, eyes brimming with tears. "Mm hm. Yes," she said, nodding. She looked up at the tall man on the deck, his yellow hair moving in a warm summer morning breeze, his linen robe bleached white from the sun billowed at the sleeve and hem folds.

Gabriel watched them, hands steepled at his chest. He smiled. He lifted his right hand to them. All six lifted theirs in response.

"Nervous, Booker?"

"Crapping my pants, Jay. You?"

"Copy that, Booker. My diaper overfloweth."

Dodie overheard. Though she tried to hide it, tears rolled down both cheeks.

Drake led them inside the dark wooden building and up the stairs. He bid them pause on the landing. He ran downstairs and returned in a hot minute holding a stack of seven white molded plastic chairs. He stepped through the wide opening leading outside to the deck. They watched Drake on the deck as he hurriedly unstacked and hastily arranged chairs. He stood in the doorway and motioned with his hand for the six exhausted but exhilarated pilgrims to join him.

Six dry throats swallowed hard. They stepped out onto the deck into the brightening morning sunlight filtered through clouds in strange shapes scudding slowly overhead. Each sweated, though the air felt deliciously cool.

Gabriel gazed out over the expansive property. When he heard many footsteps and heavy knapsacks flopping down upon the deck, he turned to face the group, arms at his sides, face expressionless. "Welcome to Spring Mountain, home of the Elect, and to your new home as well, should you wish it," he said, voice low and compelling. "I feel like I already know each of you."

"We feel like we know you, too! From our dreams!" Aliyah said.

The six stared in awe. Gabriel smiled. "Please sit. Let us talk about what God has in mind of each of us, shall we?" Following Marshall's lead, each took a seat. Gabriel folded his legs underneath him and sat on the deck before them. He made long eye contact with each in turn. "Raise your hand if you are ready to be Baptized in Christ, our Lord."

Tatum searched Marshall's face. "It means the symbolic washin' away 'a sins from our former lives. Purification or renewal, and admission into the Christian Church. Baptism is a symbol of our commitment to God," Marshall whispered.

Gabriel smiled. "Excellent. And you must be Marshall." He nodded. "The Spirit is strong in you, Marshall; a knight who defends the helpless and yet carries no hate. Yes, you are so correct, and so eloquent. The greatest prophet, John the Baptist, made the first immersions in the river Jordan. After he Baptized Yeshua—"

"Yeshua?" Booker said.

Gabriel looked at him. "You must be my scribe, Booker."

Booker smiled, nodded, and pantomimed writing in the air.

"Yeshua is the name given by God to Mary, mother of the Christ," said Gabriel. The Greek spelling Iesous became the Latin IESVS, from which comes the English spelling Jesus. The Hebrew spelling Yesua appears in later books of the Hebrew Bible. Sadly, over millenniums, men changed the name to Jesus. John The Baptist was his cousin, conceived in a womb too old to conceive, the second miraculous birth. For your convenience I shall use the name Jesus. It was John who baptized Jesus. It was Jesus's Apostles who baptized thousands. If any of you wish to be born-again to the Lord Jesus, and to the Father and to the Holy Spirit, I am offering to baptize you."

"I do!" said Tatum. Her hand launched up like a catapult.

"You are Tatum," Gabriel said. She nodded, nervously. "Recently, the Spirit has made its home in you, Tatum. You are the stormiest woman I have ever met. Your love is ferocious, fiery, pure, and true. The Spirit has increased and magnified your strength and your resolve." She blushed crimson.

"Here, take this," he said. He removed a chain hanging from his neck threaded through a hole in a door key and handed it to her. "God willing, you will never need this."

"Thank you! But what is it?"

"Plan B, should it ever come to that. You may remove it from your neck only when the moon turns from blood back to bone. Anyone else?"

Every hand went up. Gabriel's grin widened. "Splendid!" And you are Aliyah, and Dodie." They nodded, nervously. "The Spirit has resided in you throughout your lives. Your loyalty to the Lord is noticed in Heaven." The two glanced at each other and nodded with their mouths wide open.

"Jayden, last but by no means least. My astronomer and my archer, and the community rock star. You are the Lord's zealous warrior and diviner of the heavens.

"Thank you for inviting us," said Jayden.

Gabriel nodded. "If you are familiar with past agricultural methods, you would know that wolves would raid herds of sheep, and sheepdogs would bravely attack and drive off these vicious, powerful predators. Often it would cost the dogs their lives. They laid down their lives to protect the sheep and were loyal only to the shepherd. You are the Lord's brave attack dog, Jayden. Loyal to the death." Jayden, unsmiling, nodded his acceptance.

"God has smiled upon each one of you. He has conjoined you together as friends, but also as mates. Two bodies have become one flesh."

"You know about us?" said Dodie and shot a brief glance at Jayden.

Gabriel nodded. He panned the group. "All of you have enjoyed carnal knowledge of your mates. If you wish it, after your baptisms; I will use the power God has given me to consecrate your unions in Holy Matrimony. Do you want this?"

Faces of the women flushed like three little pomegranates.

"You mean, as in, marriage? For real?" said Aliyah, who stared at Booker, her head back.

"Would that be so bad, being Aliyah Bailey?" he asked.

"Well, I… well. Just that I haven't thought much about it. Marriage is a big deal."

"Fine. If you don't want to…"

"Booker, I didn't say no or yes because you never asked me."

Theatrically he knelt on one knee before her. "Aliyah Freedman, I do find myself quite taken with you despite the massive age gap, you being sort of an old wrinkly spinster and all." She smacked the top of his head and feigned disgust. "Though I am hopelessly in love with you and fully devoted to serving and protecting you for as long as I breathe air. Will you? Please? Marry me?"

Aliyah blinked away tears. She smiled, nodded. "Yes," she squeaked, as Aliyah's tears flowed freely now. She knelt and hugged him.

"Whuddya say there, Dolores? Wanna get hitched?"

She shook her head. "Such a romantic Neanderthal. Call me Dolores again and I'll eat your face off. Marry? Only because I have nothing better to do."

Jayden laughed. "Normally takes me about an afternoon to pick through a new melody and lyrics, trying different chords, combos, poetry, and riffs. But the entire time we were walking, our fearless leader banned me from singing and playing my guitar. It took me just south of a month to write you a love song you inspired, and right now it only exists here," he said, poking his head. "If you marry me, I'll play and sing it for you, and dedicate it to you in front of all those people out there. I think it's pretty good. As in Elvis Presley good. But if you say no, forget it. No song for thee. So is that a yes?"

Dodie openly wept. She smiled. "Yes, Jayden. I love you so much."

Tatum looked at Marshall. He smiled. "We all's 'r already married, Gabriel. But it sure would be a blessin' if y'all would make it official in the eyes of God."

"Magnificent!" said Gabriel. He rose to his full six-foot-four height. "I would be delighted. Today is a day of days, one the Elect will never forget."

As Gunny Powell drilled Gabriel's legions of soldiers, women and children gravitated down to the clear-running stream which flowed underneath the covered bridge. Though the stream was shallow, Gabriel knew where to stand in a darker pool about four feet deep. He motioned to Tatum. She waded in. "I baptize you with the Holy Spirit and with fire," he said. When she came up out of the water, her eyes rolled back showing only the whites. She said, *"Pater Noster, qui es in caelis, sanctificetur nomen tuum. Adveniat regnum tuum. Fiat voluntas tua, sicut in caelo et in terra. Panem nostrum quotidianum da nobis hodie, et dimitte nobis debita nostra sicut et nos dimittimus debitoribus nostris. Et ne nos inducas in tentationem, sed libera nos a malo. Amen."* Gabriel completed the third immersion. No sooner had Tatum blown water from her nostrils than Booker pounced.

"Oh my God!" he shrieked, wide eyed, pointing. "She just said the Our Father prayer in perfect Latin! Tatum! You've been seriously holding out on us! Why didn't you say you speak Latin? All this time we could've been practicing our skills, girl!"

Tatum shook her head. "What? I didn't say anything."

Gabriel smiled at her. "You spoke in tongues, Tatum. Latin, to be exact. Booker is correct. You were given the prayer Jesus gave to the people over two-thousand years ago. My dear Father in Heaven, how generously and without limit you have poured more of your Spirit into Tatum. Thank you, Lord."

"I'm…I don't know what to say," said Tatum.

Gabriel held out his long arms. She hugged him. He closed his hands around her. "Our Father in Heaven filled all voids in you because you invited him in which is nothing short of a miracle. I know because something like it happened to me when I was a little boy. It changes everything, doesn't it? How you see the world. How you think."

"Teach me to pray, as you pray. I have so much I want to say to our God…so many thanks to give."

"Your husband will teach you better than I. The Spirit owns him, Tatum, as it owns me. Now Marshall, come back in the water with us, won't you?" He did. "Take her hands where I can see them. That's it. Look at each other. I—state your full names—" which they did, "take you—say them again—" and they did, "to be my husband or wife," both grinned while saying it, "to have and to hold from this day forward, for better, for worse, for richer, for poorer, in sickness and in health, to love and to cherish, for as long as we both shall live. This is my solemn vow. Say I do." They both said it. "I now pronounce you husband and wife. You may kiss the bride."

Marshall and Tatum fell together. They touched noses, eye to eye, then kissed with the boiling passions of a lost world, of generations reaching backward through time, urging them on to an uncertain future, now and forever cleansed of all past mistakes, ready to regenerate new, holy, better than ever.

Gabriel smiled, but the smile faded quickly. He pointed at Aliyah, and she joined him in the water. His left hand held her right shoulder, his right hand her waist. "I baptize you with water to cleanse you," he said, then immersed her head briefly under the cold mountain water before he pulled her back standing. "I baptize you with light and with fire," he said, then dunked her again. "I baptize you to be born anew, awake, and ready for the day to come," he said, and gave her one final immersion. She came up smiling, and spontaneously hugged Gabriel.

Booker and Aliyah, then Jayden and Dodie followed. The three couples climbed out of the stream and stood on the asphalt before Gabriel. He spread his arms wide. "I say this to you all with the full authority of God: What God hath joined together let no man put asunder. In other words, divorce is not an option. Only bodily death can absolve you of this blessed union. You are no longer two hearts, two bodies; you are now one heart, one body."

The entire Church applauded, including soldiers in training, when the newly blessed couples followed Gabriel back up the asphalt path. "Drake," said Gabriel, "Please have someone bring their backpacks to the cabins, and would you please escort our new wives and show them how to use the propane gas hot water?"

"Oh my God! Hot showers? Really?" said Tatum.

Gabriel smiled. "Almost like I can read your minds, isn't it?"

"Kinda spooky, yes," said Aliyah. She appeared nervous.

"Please know that we have communal shower stations, as propane gas is difficult to source, however, I had these cabins built special for you three couples, each having your own private showers. Eventually we will convert all water heaters to bioethanol fuel, which we plan to make and store in abundance. Then every family will have their own shower."

"Why us?" Jayden asked. "We just arrived; we have no seniority. What's so special about us?"

Gabriel nodded. "Return to my tower, men. Let's discuss the future. My hour groweth near."

A Time to Kill

"War is coming," said the prophet Gabriel. "Holy war. Not every Elect knows this. Of course some suspect given our unique focus on military preparations this year, however many have not fully faced it…internalized it. Though all are acutely aware of the Golgoth threat in general."

Marshall nodded. "Are y'all sayin' we all 'r in the end times? I mean, I've suspected as much. Glimpses in dreams."

Gabriel nodded. "For we do not wrestle against flesh and blood, but against the rulers, against the authorities, against the cosmic powers over this present darkness, against the spiritual forces of evil in Hellish places."

Booker looked up, and added, "Permit me to quote the Lord, Jesus Christ: 'But concerning that day and hour no one knows, not even the angels of Heaven, nor the Son, but the Father only. For as were the days of Noah, so will be the coming of the Son of Man. For as in those days before the Flood they were eating and drinking, marrying, and giving in marriage, until the day when Noah entered the ark, and they were unaware until the Flood came and swept them all away, so will be the coming of the Son of Man. Then two men will be in the field; one will be taken and one left.'"

Jayden lowered his head and raised his hand.

"Yes, Jayden?" said Gabriel.

"Sir, the end of the New Testament describes an ultimate battle between people devoted to Christ against those who worship the Antichrist. Armageddon. On a hill named Megiddo. Goes something like this, 'Then they gathered the kings together to the place that in Hebrew is called Tal Megiddo.' But Gabriel, I thought the name of this mountain is Spring, not Megiddo."

Gabriel grinned. "More about that later."

Jayden shook his head. "I'll take your word for it, as I'll take your word for all things. I simply needed—"

"Accuracy, yes, Jayden. You are meticulous and scientific by nature. You question everything. Which is why tonight, I would like for you to assess the heavens. Report all anomalies."

Jayden nodded. "I will. If I may be so bold as to ask, what does it sound like?"

Gabriel frowned. "What does what sound like?"

"God's voice."

"I would not know, Jayden. The voice is my own voice, internal, not external, just as clear as you hear me now. Thoughts that are clearly not my own, formed into words also not my own, but delivered to me in my own voice if that makes sense. Sometimes graphic images and scenes, like still pictures sometimes, like moving pictures other times. For example, I saw all of you coming. I watched multiple conversations you had along the Trail. Consequently I knew all of you, intimately, before you ever arrived. This is more than I have ever told anyone about my relationship with God."

Jayden's eyes sparkled in wonder. "Wow." Marshall and Booker sat with their mouths hanging open.

Gabriel blinked slowly. "When I was eight, I watched the only world I knew become submerged in a deluge. One morning, I received a massive bolus of knowledge: of Holy Scripture; scientific; biological; agricultural; languages; even medical knowledge. It wasn't there before—couldn't have been there—yet there it was, as though advanced knowledge became compressed into a hypodermic needle and injected directly into my mind. I cannot explain this, other than to say that with my third-grade education, at eight years old, suddenly I was able to solve advanced calculus and discrete mathematical problems in my head. When I led a group of eleven children here, I found myself applying this gift to solve real-world problems, such as how to fit object A around two tight bends inside of building B. This was given to me. I did not learn it. With knowledge, and the Holy Spirit of God came the confidence to lead. Moreover, to develop what is very much a two-way relationship with the Creator of the universe. But Jayden, I received no knowledge of the cosmos, so I need you. We need you."

Jayden appeared stunned and fell silent.

"And Booker. What does the New Testament tell us of the signs for Jesus's return?"

Booker cleared his throat. "Immediately after the distress of those days the sun will be darkened, and the moon will not give its light; the stars will fall from the sky, and the heavenly bodies will be shaken."

"Do you see, Jayden, why tonight I need you in the high cabin, surveying the sky through a powerful Dobsonian telescope?"

Jayden snapped to. "You really have a Dobsonian?"

Gabriel smiled. "An exceptionally fine and powerful one, yes. Thought that might pique your interest. Back to you, Booker. After the great battle, what happens?"

Booker said, "I'll quote Jesus Christ from Holy Scripture: 'And then the sign of The Son of Man in Heaven will appear and then all the families of the earth will mourn, and they will see The Son of Man who comes on the clouds of Heaven with miracles and many praises. And he will send his Angels with great trumpets, and they will gather his own Elect from the four winds, from all the ends of the heavens.'"

Gabriel tented his hands. "Yes, Booker. But then in Revelations we learn, 'Then I saw an angel coming down from heaven, holding in his hand the key to the bottomless pit and a great chain. And he seized the dragon, that ancient serpent, who is the devil and Satan, and bound him for a thousand years, and threw him into the pit, and shut it and sealed it over him, so that he might not deceive the nations any longer, until the thousand years were ended. After that he must be released for a little while.'

Booker nodded. "Many Bible scholars believe that after the Holy War Jesus will return with angels to separate the Elect, meaning we whom he loves and who love him from those who do not. He will judge both the living and the dead. The Elect shall return to Heaven to live forever with Jesus, and with the Father. The condemned get to spend eternity with Satan in a hot room with no doors."

Gabriel nodded. "Go on. Some interpret Scripture far differently."

Booker shrugged. "Yes sir, you said it; I have always struggled to reconcile that another school of thought leans more on the Book of Revelation, which tells us 'they came to life and reigned with Christ for a thousand years.' That every Christian whose body ended, going all the way back thousands of years, returns to bodily human life when the Son comes, and before his thousand-year kingdom here on earth begins. Those who do not love him do not return to life until after the universe is destroyed. And when they do, a great gulf separates them from the Elect, who live with Jesus."

"Heavy stuff," said Jayden. "What do both scenarios have in common?"

"War," said Booker. "War is inevitable. I think I'm of the Rapture school of thought. That's when Jesus—I mean Yeshua, The Son of Man—returns. When it happens, living bodies get caught up in the clouds along with the resurrected dead who loved him while alive. Yeshua the shepherd brings his entire flock home to Heaven as one, to the New Jerusalem, where we get new forever bodies that don't wear out.

"Think about it, guys," Booker went on, eyes open wider than Jayden and Marshall had ever seen. "We are all just spirits living inside meat shells. Spirits, I believe, are not unlike the old computer programs they had going in Pre-Flood. God is the Great Programmer. He designed every one of us far away in Heaven, then, like with boy Gabriel's sudden knowledge injection, our programs get implanted inside fetuses, no two programs were alike. He knew us before the womb; the Bible is clear about that. So, when the meat shell expires as all meat does eventually, our programs enter sleep mode. Spirits don't feel time passing. Two thousand years feels identical to a night's sleep. The program wakes up someplace else, in a new, permanent body. I've often thought the new bodies are made of dark matter, which we know exists but cannot be measured."

Gabriel threw open his arms. "Booker, my scribe! This understanding did not come from your astute mind, but rather it was given to you by the Holy Spirit. Oh, blessed are you! I do hope you know this. Tonight, when Jayden explores the heavens, I ask you to please tarry here with me. I would like you to help me document certain truths for the perfect sanity of the written record, should anything happen to me in battle."

"Y'all 'r gonna fight, Gabriel?" asked Marshall.

He nodded. "It is my duty. It is every man's duty to fight evil. I am no exception."

"But y'all 'r God's prophet! Y'all need to lead the people! God depends on y'all! The Church too!" said Marshall.

"Which is precisely why God called you here, Marshall. Jesus will come, if not right away then soon. If it is his will to lead an earthly Church, then so be it. But until he does, someone must make decisions and lead should my body die in battle. That someone, Marshall, is you."

"No! *God*, no! I ain't qualified!"

Gabriel smiled. "You might not believe in yourself, but God believes in you. It shall be you; God wills it. Would you like to hear my opinion as to why God chose you?"

Marshall nodded, his face a reddened mask of confusion.

Gabriel held his arms wide apart. "Precisely because of the grace and mercy you showed to Arabella, the one lost sheep of your flock. Every other Elect in your position would have been quick to cast the first stone at her. Never once did you succumb to Satan's temptation to hate; or seek vengeance; or to mete out justice without compassion; nor did you permit those under you to fall into temptation and wound their souls. You are as lethal a warrior as there ever was, but without the hardness of heart that may sometimes lead such men from God's narrow path. These are the qualities God seeks in the one who would shepherd his Elect."

Marshall hung his head. He covered his face with his hands. He remained like that, and the room fell into grave silence. Finally, he looked up. "In battle, promise me that y'all ain't leavin' my side, Gabriel, not even for a hot second. I ain't no prophet and can't lead the Church community, so I'll make darn sure y'all survive."

Gabriel smiled. Booker thought that smile was the saddest thing he had ever seen. "I understand. Marshall," said Gabriel. "Now, we haven't much time. At first light tomorrow, Drake, my number one and my rock since the First Flood, along with Gunny Powell have been arming and drilling our forces. They will show you around the field and the armory."

Marshall nodded. Gabriel continued, "We foraged many bows and arrows. Jayden: tomorrow I'd like you and Booker to see Drake and Gunny about recruiting an archery core. Once you have your men, I'd like you both to train them on firing accurately under pressure, since you both have this experience. Your trained archery core will be strategically placed inside along the earth works."

"Got it, Gabriel," said Booker. Jayden nodded.

"But on the eve of battle, however, I want you both up here on this deck firing arrows into every Golgoth who makes it over the Spring Mount

Road earthwork you walked down to get there," Gabriel said, pointing, "until you run out of arrows. We will napalm bomb concentrated groups of them, but we need snipers to pick away at individual infiltrators. There are many more Golgoths than Elect: winning this war for us means massive attrition in the first thirty minutes. Immediately we must disable their advanced weapons and reduce their ranks until Golgoth troop numbers roughly match Elect troop numbers. It all comes down to math. Inside the entire perimeter, I need a ring of archers doing the same, as I know the enemy will pour over the earthen berms from all directions, though nowhere as concentrated as here facing Spring Mount Road. Here is where you and a few good men will get no breaks whatsoever. You will fire and keep firing until your fingertips are bloody nubs."

"Can y'all see the future, Gabriel? Do we win?" asked Marshall.

Gabriel shook his head. "Sometimes I receive glimpses of future events, as the Father and his Holy Spirit deem me worthy to receive; but not of this, Marshall, no. Our bodies might all die here under the blood moon; but take heart, for we are all saved. We will all meet again in the Kingdom of God. Jayden, you asked why I am giving Marshall, Booker, and you this special treatment. Now I hope you understand why. Assuming that we prevail, you and your wives will help lead the community to life after war. I command an army of people your age who have never killed an animal, let alone a fellow human. You three are cool-headed experienced killers of Golgoths. Drake, and Gunny Powell, are proven hunters of Golgoths. At this moment of epic change in the world, this makes you five God's most valuable assets at this time.

Marshall glanced at Booker and Jayden. Confident that he was speaking for all three, Marshall said, "We all came here to live or die for Christ."

Gabriel nodded. "Praise God for sending you here, to defend your new home. I too am a killer. I shot dead a Golgoth precursor group of men who hunted some of my initial followers when I was eight years old years before the rise of the Golgoths."

Dots connected in Booker's brain. "We saw decades old child skeletons a few hundred feet before the Norway Spruce off of Gravel Pike on our way here. You mean these skeletons were kids who followed you?" he asked.

Gabriel nodded. "They followed me and the eleven Elect out of the perishing elementary school, but then they rebelled against my leadership; which is the same as choosing not to follow the living God who possesses me. I slayed their slayers that very same night. Later, as I sought to secure fallow grounds for growing our crops, while recovering information from area libraries, I killed one-hundred-forty-seven Golgoths over the years in close hand-to-hand combat."

"My God! That's an army!" said Booker. "Sorry. Forgive me."

Gabriel spent over one minute studying their eyes. "Gunny Powell has slain even more. Men: together, we five are God's vanguard of elite warriors. Any questions?"

Jayden raised his hand. "What do you mean the Elect here haven't killed animals?"

"I have forbidden it. God is restarting something here. Animals are his creation, too. The Floods devastated their populations. Here, they mingle safely and gently with humans. Nature's dangerous animal predators lick human babies until they giggle. Here the animals act more like pets because they feel no threat. This is a sanctuary of life. All life."

Jayden raised his hand again. "So what do we eat?"

"Plants, Jayden. Plant protein. God made us omnivores in order to survive, allowing us to eat almost every living thing. But not a sparrow falls without his knowledge. Here, we respect God's complex creatures not destroyed by the Floods, like Noah and his ark. We believe God wants animals to repopulate the lands."

"Man cannot live on bread alone. Or salads. Frankly, I'm starvin,'" said Marshall.

Gabriel smiled. "Soon it will be brunch time. I will send my chefs over to your cabins. I promise, when we reconvene again, you will tell me it was the most satisfying meal you have ever eaten."

"I don't know…" said Jayden.

"You will. Also, humans who eat only plants live longer and healthier than those who eat flesh. Besides, Golgoths prefer to eat plant-fed Elect. Our flesh is purer, less gamey, far more tender, and succulent."

Booker, Jayden, and Marshall stared at him, mouths agape. Gabriel suddenly burst out laughing. People down below had lived their entire lives having never heard Gabriel laugh, not once. Now he was roaring. Everyone stared.

"The expressions on your faces right now!" he managed to choke out through laughter. "And who says God's prophet can't have a dark sense of humor. Joking, gentlemen…" He laughed so hard he could barely finish the sentence. The others quickly became sucked inside his laughter. All four cut loose, and it felt particularly good to vent fear, frustration, dreams, and nightmares, and to unload extraordinary stresses few humans faced in Pre-Flood eras. Gradually, all quieted. The nervous certainty of an impending war with armed, demonic, intelligent, and organized cannibals returned to their minds, along with the memory of the Golgoths each had slain: the reality of the impending conflict threatened their very sanity.

Booker, Jayden, and Marshall decided with iron certainty that they could and would obey this man, selected by God before they were born. Follow him into battle without reservation. An inevitable conflict, foreseen billions of years before God had formed the earth, all according to his plan.

War was unavoidable. Each accepted the steely truth of it.

Jayden raised his hand. Gabriel looked at him. "If the Elect prevail, do you know what happens after the battle?"

Gabriel shook his head. "No. All that is certain is: Golgoths are a pox, an unclean scourge upon the earth. Our Father finds their very existence offensive. Knowing the Church of the Elect is open to all, any of these men could have scrubbed off his white paint, defected from their hive, knowing we would take them in. They know we keep to ourselves and live peacefully. But not one has chosen to defect from cannibalism and pure evil. Therefore it is God's will that his people, the Elect, find and exterminate every last one of them, clearing the way for the Son of Man's return. Not one Golgoth can be permitted to live. They are unsalvageable 'programs,' to use Booker's visualization."

Jayden asked a follow-up question. "Force strength, them and us?"

Gabriel steepled his hands under his chin and closed his eyes. "I have been shown migrations of Golgoth colonies down from the north and up from the south. They will number close to seventy-eight thousand warriors. Our Church is sixty-thousand fighting-age males, and as many females. Nor have I counted the now twenty-four thousand children among the Elect's total number."

"Golgoth warriors outnumber Elect warriors by eighteen thousand. Not good," muttered Jayden

"All them Golgoths down south been walkin' north on roads, which is why we walked the Applachian Trail. So they all been migratin' to Valley Forge National Park, assemblin' for battle with the Elect?" asked Marshall.

With eyes still closed, Gabriel nodded. "Did you see mass migration, or did the Holy Spirit give you this knowledge?"

"Neither. My common-law wife...a woman I knew in Tennessee saw this in a dream. One time, she told me about it." Marshall sensed Booker and Jayden's surprise at learning this closely guarded dimension of Marshall's life before the Trail, and he felt their eyes boring into him.

"Is she still alive, Marshall?" Gabriel asked. He opened his eyes and explored Marshall's face.

"Dunno, maybe," he shrugged. "I reckoned she'd stay there on the mountain in Tennessee, 'cause she kicked me out."

Gabriel shook his head. "If she dreamed of Valley Forge, it means she was called to the apostate, Hostis Dei, whose spirit is owned by his infernal father, Satan, the prince of this world who reigns in Hell. Golgoths believe they worship Hubal, the moon god, which is merely one of the many faces of Satan."

Marshall remained quiet. Then, "I would never doubt y'all, Gabriel. I just never reckoned she would ever leave the security 'a the mountain lodge. Golgoths killed and ate her parents; she was too 'scairt to venture back down into their territory. But she was just fine sendin' me out to face danger." He jetted air out of both nostrils in disgust.

Gabriel nodded. "For the sake of your peace, I hope you are right about Delilah."

"I never told you her name."

Gabriel looked at Marshall. "Golgoths have captured women and girls along their journey, delivered to Valley Forge as slaves of Hostis Dei. After the battle, you are to free these Elect, and assimilate them into the Church of the Elect.

"Others there are brides of Satan," said Gabriel. "Listen closely: inside Hostis Dei's lodging originally built as a chapel of God, you will find women. Those who do not bear the mark of the crescent moon on their bodies must never be allowed near the Church of the Elect. If any have conceived, the children are also unclean. It will be a mercy to decapitate these cursed young lives and stop their hearts with minimal pain. Or you could wait for them to starve, or somehow survive and mature. They are a virus that would eventually multiply and threaten the Elect decades from now, if left alive."

"God told you to kill women and children?"

"No. This was not given to me from above. Experience and logic, Marshall. When the time comes, pray the Father in Jesus's name for guidance in the moment. Under no circumstances are you to bring any of these here."

Marshall closed his eyes to escape Gabriel's stare. He shook his head. "Wow," he muttered. "So many lost souls."

"Wide is the path to destruction, Marshall. Each of us are the summary consequence of stacked decisions every day. I know that you know this. Take heart, son. All things serve the Lord. God is love. Act accordingly, with love."

"I never told you her name was Delilah," said Marshall.

He smiled. "No, you never did."

Marshall shook his head. "Y'all 'r a true miracle of God. He runs y'all completely, don't he, Gabriel?"

He nodded. "Since the age of eight. For more than three decades, and for an eternity still to come. God choses and uses whom he wills. He has chosen you and your five pilgrims and clothed each of you in immense power. Live up to his trust, Marshall. Submit to him alone. Give all glory to him. Be grateful and humble. Love every member of the Elect church, even those who vex you. Be slow to anger. Love intensely, with unselfishness all around."

"Amen," said Marshall.

Gabriel stood. "Mankind once had a dream that they were inherently good. People lived for themselves and not for God; they turned to idols and materialism and pleasure; for millenniums they loved this dream. But now the day of God's final Judgement is at hand: the Elect, we who love Christ shall have all of our sins cast into the deepest ocean trench. God has forgiven us and does not see our sins. For the Golgoths: each faces Judgement. When their bodies die, their spirits will be judged for every sin against the Holy God. The human spirit never dies; haters of the living God will spend eternity separated from him. But beware: all dreams are over, and evil is fully awake, and it has never been hungrier. We have so much work to do. The book of Ecclesiastes tells us that there is 'A time to love and a time to hate, a time for war and a time for peace.'

"Killin' time is here," said Marshall.

"Amen, hoss," said Jayden.

"About time," Booker muttered.

"God wills it," said Gabriel.

Starry-Starry Night

"Please come with me, Jayden," said Gabriel as he stood in the doorway of Jayden and Dodie's cabin. Jayden followed Gabriel as they hiked up the grassy grade. "I know you must be very tired," said the prophet.

Jayden gave him a wan grin. "Especially after eating that amazing veggie pizza. I feel like I could crawl into bed and sleep for a week. But I do understand the importance of this task you're putting on me. Thanks for the Matcha tea: you were so right about it; I can feel my road-weary brain beginning to sharpen up a little. I thought green tea only grows in Japan?"

"We have a large bioethanol-fired heated greenhouse, and many smaller ones," said Gabriel. "They produce zero emissions detectable by eye or nose. You passed them on your hike. We set them back from the road, making them difficult to spot without Golgoth's risking being spotted and killed by our sentries. As you know, Golgoths hunt along all Pre-Flood roads."

"Where is the Dobsonian telescope?" asked Jayden.

"See that lonely cabin up there?" Gabriel said, pointing. "It's the highest elevation, about five-hundred-twenty-eight feet. And of course we've not suffered light pollution since the First Flood; thus your view shall be wholly unencumbered. The Dobsonian telescope has never been used, until now. As a boy I received much knowledge from God about Holy Scripture and practical skills, but little of the heavenly bodies. We do not know how to properly use the telescope and would not know what we're looking at if we did know. You are the first and only stargazer among the Elect. I have anxiously awaited your arrival, and your clear observation of heavenly movements. I sense changes foretold in Scripture are happening above us as per Christ's prophesy, but the certainty of it has not been given to me."

At the cabin, Gabriel opened the door. A blast of musty-hot, pine-flavored air blew back at them. He lit a candle with a wooden match. He used the candle to light twelve more candles. He opened three casement windows.

"How were you able to install real working residential glass windows to fit all of these cabins?" Jayden asked.

"Foraging. Floods wiped out much, but we salvaged everything usable, including door and window glass, screens, and hardware. Everything you see in our community—your cabins too, now—represents twenty years of incessant labor. Local pin oak and maple trees supplied the wood."

Gabriel unfolded a stepladder and climbed to the cabin ceiling. He turned a small crank handle clockwise. A lid opened to the sky. Directly underneath the lid sat a large cylindrical object covered with a drop cloth. Gabriel carefully removed the cloth to minimize the release of dust into the cabin's stale interior air.

Underneath reposed the most beautiful gleaming white telescope Jayden had ever seen. The Dobsonian scope had been affixed to a blue seventy-two-inch vertical double-scissor lift table. Jayden's eyes sparkled in the candlelight. "Love at first sight," he said.

"Better not let your wife hear you say that. Go ahead, climb on. I'll crank you up as high as you need to clear the roof: tell me when to stop cranking," said Gabriel.

Jayden positioned himself on the steel lift. He inspected the small finderscope and focuser on the side of the telescope. "Anchors away!" he said. Gabriel cranked. The flat table supporting Jayden and the heavy telescope lifted slowly and smoothly until the light-gathering tube end of the scope protruded through the cabin roof. "A little more…another three inches…okay stop. Gabriel, do me a favor please? Blow out all the candles."

Gabriel did. Darkness swallowed the cabin interior like a coal mine.

As Jayden tilted and focused the telescope, Gabriel sat on the floor and prayed, attuned to Jayden's breathing. He sensed Jayden's pulse quicken over sounds of movements as Jayden took the big telescope on a tour of deep space, moving it on its azimuth turntable.

Jayden studied the stars and called out their names, more to himself than to Gabriel, breaking the silence. "Aldebaran, Capella, Pollux…Procyon, Rigel, Sirius. Dear God. Oh, my dear sweet Jesus."

More movement. Gabriel made no sound.

At the sixteenth positioning, Jayden said, "Please light the candles and crank me down. I can't look anymore." The moment the candlelight returned, Jayden leapt down and sat on the floor with his back to the log wall. He gulped air.

"You look like you've just seen a ghost," said Gabriel.

Jayden attempted to find his center. Breathily he responded, "I have."

"Please, the suspense is killing me. What exactly did you see?"

Jayden cleared his throat. "Every star making up the twelve constellations of the zodiac, is what I saw. Aries, Taurus, Gemini, Cancer, Leo, Virgo, Libra, Scorpius, Sagittarius, Capricornus, Aquarius, and Pisces. Please understand that I know these like the back of my hand. Gabriel: every solitary star forming the zodiac has become a supernova! All at the same time! An astronomical impossibility."

Gabriel nodded. "My knowledge of these matters is limited. What would you say are the odds of this happening?"

"How many stars are there, two hundred billion trillion, I believe? Take that and multiply it by itself and still you would never find one chance of this happening. It is impossible. Not possible."

"All things are possible with God, Jayden."

"Well then there's your answer! God has exploded every star forming the twelve constellations at precisely the same time. I've lived through a Flood, grew up in a world dominated by cannibals: this is by far the most illogical, disturbing thing I have ever seen," said Jayden.

"You know, recently I thought nights seemed brighter," Jayden continued, "and blamed it on Jupiter's changing orbit. Weeks ago back in Tennessee on the Trail, we stopped to refill our water, which is when I looked through my little portable telescope. I'd noticed Jupiter's orbit appeared strange, but there was nothing weird then with the constellations. So the supernovas all just happened, Gabriel. The light from these supernovas is drowning out all other starlight. It takes lightyears for their glow to reach earth. Which means…"

"This was planned an unfathomably long time ago by the God. Is that all? What about planets: you mentioned Jupiter?"

Jayden tried to stand but slumped back down. "Jupiter has moved closer to earth during its long orbit around the sun, and I just confirmed the orbit has extended. Jupiter's orbit has always been twelve years; I would guess that now it's taking twenty years to go full circle. With my low-power scope I'd thought I'd spotted this weeks ago, and now using your scope, I am certain of it," said Jayden.

"Floods every sixteen years," added Gabriel. "Jupiter's orbit is causing them?"

"Absolutely! There's your second answer. Jupiter's new proximity to earth when its orbit brings it around is causing floods. And if it moves closer still…"

"What? If it does, then what?" asked Gabriel.

"We are cooked, prophet. Game over. All of this, everything you know gone, just gone. Buried first under feet of magma and volcanic ash, and then in a few years covered in miles of ice. The great freeze."

Gabriel smiled.

"Seriously, what's so funny? This isn't funny. I am terrified here!"

"Don't be. You have no reason to be. This is merely our Heavenly Father showing us that he is in charge, not us; and that the Son of God, the Christ, the Messiah, will revisit us soon," said Gabriel. "Jayden: Rejoice! This is a time for joy, not for fear! God is sending his Son back to us! Do you not see what this means? Wars, signs in the heavens. The Second Coming of Christ! You just confirmed it!"

Jayden nodded. "I'm not scared of Golgoths. Not scared of much, truth be told. But what I just saw? Let's just say that I am more freaked out right now than I have ever been in my life. Everything really is about to change. I've heard your words, the Bible's words, God's Word, everyone's words. Guess I never let it in, until tonight. I am beyond freaked out. Can I go back now? Be with my wife?"

Gabriel nodded. "Go, son. Please ask Booker to visit my tower tonight at his earliest convenience. I will close up here, then head down. And Jayden," he called to him. Gabriel studied the candlelight reflected in the young man's eyes. He laid his hands on Jayden's shoulders. He squeezed, and gently shook them. "Thank you. Your observation did not just make all my dreams come true. You made my life complete. When I die tonight, I will depart a happy man, knowing God's Church will soon be in hands I am unworthy to hold."

"When you die tonight?"

Gabriel smiled patiently. "If."

"Booker Bailey! Thank you for coming. Here," said Gabriel. He handed him a blank notebook and a choice of pens. "Please have a seat."

Booker sat in the green Nineteen-Sixties vinyl recliner. "Gabriel you have referred to me as your scribe. And more recently, your archer," said Booker. He grinned. "I can multitask with the best of them. What did you want me to write about?"

Gabriel assumed his lotus position on the floor in front of the recliner. "Interview me. For the record. Younger generation Elect find me unapproachable, a mysterious otherworldly figure, and thus they fear to ask any probing questions. If I do not survive battle, my scribe can circulate my words."

Booker opened the blank notebook. He tapped his cheek with the pen and appeared deep in thought. "What was it like when you were eight years old, when God first touched you?"

Gabriel grinned, eyes closed, nostrils flared. "Before electronics replaced imagination, and before the Floods, the world was endless possibilities. When waking up in bed on the first Saturday morning of summer break from school; secure in our parents' cocoons; watching dust motes float lazily on whisper currents of sunbeams streaming in; wondering which friends we'd hang out with; feeling no pain; feeling immortal. Truly the objective of life is to live it backwards. To use our acquired wisdom to free ourselves to grow younger. Spiritually speaking, to become that eight-year-old again, to better understand God and his works as such.

"I lived separated from my parents for weeks, forced by government decree to shelter-in-place in school. Water from the Perkiomen, the creek you walked over on your trek here had become a river lapping at the school's outer walls. Out in front, a new river had formed, equally as deep, as wide, and as violent. I was sitting at my desk looking out at the Perkiomen. I missed my mom and dad; scratched at head lice; and followed my little boy thoughts whimsically to wherever they led me. Letting our minds wander: back then we called it 'zoning out.' I imagined that I was Noah, and my elementary school was God's ark."

Booker's right hand moved as fast as a polygraph needle over the paper. "At first, receiving the Holy Spirit of God felt physical. Respiration was the first change, like my nose had opened wider allowing in more oxygen. I saw lights, purple starbursts, not physical, and yet they appeared as real as heatless fireworks exploding in my face. The lice either died or jumped off. I never saw evidence of them after this. Felt my muscles harden, stiffen. Every corner of my being felt warm. Blood raged through my temples no less intense than the currents outside."

"Wow. I mean, this is amazing," Booker stopped him. "So glad I asked the question. Apart from these physical changes how did the sudden intrusion of God's Spirit make you feel? Were you scared? I'd be terrified!"

"Ah. The best part, Booker. Infusion of pure, indomitable confidence! Like no person or thing could best me. All fear was suddenly gone. Fear of blood, needles, pain; fear of adults, bullies, spiders, claustrophobia, ghosts, monsters in the dark and under my bed: Snap! I feared nothing. Empathy had always been there. I would protect smaller kids from bullies the best I could within my size limitations, but then suddenly, I knew that I could take human life without hesitation. Toward enemies no longer did I ever feel hot rage: I felt ice cold toward them. Yes, that noun is the most fitting. Warmth for all of God's creatures except for his adversaries who would eventually coalesce into the Golgoth tribe. And though I felt ambivalence I did not seek to destroy them. When they sought to destroy me or my friends, I did what I had to do and felt only the satisfaction that results from doing God's work."

"How did you kill?"

"Using my bare hands, mostly. One of the gifts I received that day was an ability to summon at will deeply repressed memories and images I didn't even know I had. I grew up watching martial arts movies involving hours of advanced physical combat. When I needed combat skills, mental reels from those movies came to me physically, like implanted muscle-memory. Golgoths attacked me with knives. I quickly moved out of harm's way. Everything slows down for me."

"What do you mean, slows down?" Booker asked, frowning.

"Real-world example: I see a knife aimed at my throat before it happens. The enemy thrusts weapons or fists or kicks at me; I see these happening in slow-motion while my body—at least it seems to me—moves in hyper-speed motion. Also I see the next movements before they happen. So with the knife example the blade misses my neck by less than a half inch, as I knew it would, because I had already foreseen the miss. The enemy is now off balance. My arm swings up into a high-speed, perfectly aimed, full-torque chop to the Golgoth's throat. When he falls, I stomp on his neck and finish him by crushing his larynx. He asphyxiates. The entire encounter lasts fewer than ninety sections.

"Sometimes I would run straight at a Golgoth and leap forward onto his shoulders before he had time to react and raise his blade. My hands met under his chin. I somersaulted over him but never released his chin. By the time my feet hit the ground behind him, kinetic energy had carried my full weight at speed with the Golgoth's neck in the vice of my hands. In an instant his spinal column where it inserts into the brain snapped clean apart."

"Whew, dear Jesus. Remind me never to bring your anger down upon my head," said Booker, eyes wide. He held the pen in his left hand and shook out cramps from his right. "You are the most lethal killing machine on earth! I could sit here all-night listening to stories like this! But I need to keep moving with the Q and A. How is it that you convinced eleven of your fellow students to follow you here and establish the Church of the Elect?"

"Immediate confidence, gravitas, maturity: God gave me these on that fateful day, and there was no hiding it," said Gabriel. "I did and said some things back in that homeroom class that confounded the teacher and astounded my eight-year-old peers. My new appetite for the knowledge of God and for everything he created: how all the dots connect, and cogs move together was on full display, especially to children who are highly perceptive. Advanced anatomy and mathematics, and skills were just— there, given. Love, the pinnacle of all emotions: I felt one with the world and every person in it, except for pure evildoers, predators, enemies of God seeking to wipe out his children. I did not feel hate for anyone or anything. Emotional students followed cool-headed, unemotional strength; they followed me because I demonstrated that my intellectual and moral spheres govern my emotions. God gave so much to me that day, in a measure not given since young David slung a stone at Goliath and defeated the Philistine giant and demoralized his army."

Booker tapped the pen to his lips. "Why do many follow Hostis Dei?"

Gabriel steepled his hands and touched them to his chin. "People follow Hostis Dei because they believe strength resides in wielding power over other people. Lust for power is how Dei manipulates them, and claims that Hubal, the moon god who we know is really Satan is the one true god."

Booker nodded as he wrote. "Back to your given knowledge of anatomy; let's explore that. This world lost all its physicians in the Floods. You are the prophet; the Church leader: do you also serve as the community doctor for the Elect?"

Gabriel sighed. "The closest thing to it. Medic might be the proper label."

"Please give me some examples of your doctoring. This is fascinating.

I've been super-cautious all my life because I can't just go to the hospital if I break a bone or get a deep cut."

"Delivering babies, stitching wounds, setting bones and dislocations, insect and snake bites, poison ivy rashes, mostly. I treat infections homeopathically; again, using knowledge given. Honey and garlic oil, and witch hazel, for topical anti-infectives. Whole garlic, beta glucans from mushrooms, arabinogalactan from larch tree sap, astragalus, echinacea, elderberry, oregano oil—too many to name tonight. I have it all written down in case a member of the Elect needs to take over for me; it is all there, in the desk, Booker. People sometimes get sick, but under my care they heal quickly."

"What about more serious stuff?"

"Ah, yes. My foragers recovered surgical tools and supplies, limb casting material, inflatable boots, great quantities of local anesthetic some of it expired and ineffective yet some still useful. I use a type of mushroom as a dissociative that makes patients not focus on the pain."

"A what?"

"Elect still feel pain as I make cuts, stitch wounds, and such, but their conscious minds are elsewhere. You asked for examples: I have performed countless tooth extractions, appendectomies, cesarean section births, melanoma excisions—"

"Oh my God, Gabriel. I understand you were given knowledge, but you were also given skills in surgery and diagnosis?"

"My hands simply know what to do. I never once made a regrettable movement."

Booker wrote down every astounding word, then stopped. He needed time to process this latest information. He shook his head rapidly to clear it. More questions were now coming to mind quickly.

"Food. Tell me about the food. Twelve kids arrive here; there's nothing to eat. Please do tell."

"Foraging, at first. Apples and pears; wild blackberries and blueberries; rude-growing corn; cranberries; dandelion flowers and leaves; groundnuts; hackberries; larch tree leaves and bark; morels; mulberries; mushrooms; onion grass; paw paws; peanuts; pokeberries; potatoes; rhubarb stalks; wild grapes; and strawberries."

"What about protein?" Booker asked. His stomach growled.

"At first we found beans; black walnuts; chestnuts; hazelnuts; mockernut hickory kernels; wild potatoes; pumpkin and sunflower seeds; burdock; and cattail roots. We have since cultivated soy and other beans, corn, potatoes, sweet potatoes, and grains. Our foods include an extensive list of complete plant proteins, sustainable supplies in abundance. We do fruit and vegetable canning to get us through the non-growing seasons."

"Don't you ever crave meat? Doesn't your body just…ache for it?"

"No, Booker. Nobody here does, not even a little. The body adjusts. It is a far healthier way to live. Our bodies lack no nutrients."

"If you say so. I will try. Why do you suppose God chose you to build and defend the Church?"

"Excellent question, one that I have pondered for decades. God revealed to us his loving merciful heart through his Son. Heart is one thing. No man can begin to understand the mind of God. Best we can do is guess at it based on our own limited points of reference which, in my case—why me? —meant analyzing myself. I believed in God as a kid. I had watched a TV movie about Jesus and the crucifixion when I was seven, the year before the First Flood. When the movie showed me Mary, mother of Christ, and his Apostle John, and Mary Magdalene who was Apostle to the Apostles, weeping at the feet of the crucified Christ, I kneeled before the television and wept also."

"None of us can relate to television," Booker interrupted.

"Electronic moving pictures projected onto tiny screens into homes. An imitation of life. Crying over the imitated murder of his Son is when God's Holy Spirit first entered me—shall we say stuck his toe in the door?—right at that moment. Later, the Spirit would be poured into me fully on that fateful day during the First Flood.

"My parents told me that I was the most stubborn, willful human they had ever met. As was Saul of Tarsus, whom God chose to become the last Apostle, and who ended up being the most effective Apostle. Paul was incredibly intelligent and resilient; he could never be bent by any force on earth, not even by Satan. I believe, in answer to your question, Booker that God chose me because I am stubborn to the death, and I am resilient. I see challenges and overcome them, instead of getting mired in analysis paralysis or tied up in knots of fear. I get things done when I know those things please God. As the impending battle does please him. We are nearing our final preparations for battle, and I am confident that no army has ever been more ready than we are."

Booker finished his notes. He thought momentarily of Aliyah waiting for him. "David had seven hundred wives who were princesses, and three hundred concubines. From what I've seen of the Church, marriage and children are strongly encouraged. Why not yourself, Gabriel? I'm sure you could have your pick of princesses among the Elect. Everyone here knows you are magic. Also, you are handsome for a white man. Are you gay? A eunuch? Sneaking around with a secret woman?"

Gabriel smiled. "Thank you, Booker. My strength was enhanced by God, as I have described, otherwise I am a physically normal heterosexual male with all the same drives as you. My celibacy, like my plant-based diet, is a decision. I live the life of a monk by choice. I only engage with Elect when necessary and communicate mostly through the public address system when I give my Sunday sermons, and limit face meetings to my right-hand-man, Drake. Otherwise, I choose to be alone with God, in prayer, without distraction. My one true love is God. I strive to be his most dedicated disciple by imitating Christ, and Paul of Tarsus.

"Booker, your body, my body: these are temples for the Holy Spirit to dwell within us. I chose to keep my temple as pure as possible. I would do nothing that might distract from or hinder my two-way relationship with our everlasting Lord. I strive to be like Yeshua—Jesus—aside from his omnivorous diet. He lived a sexually pure life as a man, as did Saint Paul. Am I special? No. I am a servant of the Father, as was John the Baptist who took no wife. Why should I receive special indulgences? God touched me for a reason; he chose me for a specific purpose. Marriage and procreation are not it. I am a vessel for God, an instrument. That is all I ever want to be, both in this world and the world after."

Booker wrote quickly, pausing to shake out his hand, but also to consider what questions Elect members might ask Gabriel if only they could summon the courage. "Earlier you said God communicates to you in words from within, and with pictures, and moving pictures. Has he ever shown you Heaven and Hell?"

"No. But I once received a vision of Marshall describing for Tatum his vision of Heaven. I suspect that it may have been given to him by the Spirit. The imagery and impressions Marshall described could be close to accurate. I like to think so. You should ask him."

"I surely will ask him. What do you think Hell is like? Sulfur and lakes of fire, people roasting?"

Gabriel lifted his hands. "Maybe so, Booker. We only have the Lord Yeshua's brief words given to his Apostles. We know that a great gulf has been fixed between Heaven and Hell, which no spirit may cross. He also described lakes of everlasting fire. But think about it. If you were sent to a prison filled with Golgoth spirits; in a place where the sun gives no light; and every soul preys on others as they do here in the flesh; would that be better or worse than lakes of everlasting fire?"

"Shh," Booker hissed. "Neither. None of that is good. I want no part of it."

"You are one of God's Elect, as are your parents. You will hold them again, Booker, I promise you, if you keep your faith and your love, son. The true riches shall be yours. I know that you hated Arabella Pendleman—"

"Wait. You know about that?"

Gabriel nodded, unsmiling. "Do not hate, Booker. Just don't. It seeps into your days and your nights until it consumes everything you once were."

"She tried to kill us, Gabriel!"

"So do Golgoths. They follow Hostis Dei, the earthly apostate of the moon god, Hubal who as we know is really Satan. They think the man in the moon is the one true god," Gabriel smiled ruefully. He pointed his finger toward the eastern sky. "Hubal was a pre-Islam pagan god in Makkah, just a red carnelian statue placed high inside the Ka'aba. Some say he was Nabatean, brought by travelers to the Quraysh tribe. Worshippers would pray to Hubal to divine the future and would even sacrifice their own children to him. Hubal is Satan: one of God's creations who turned against him. Satan is a murderer since his time in Heaven and the father of lies. Golgoths worship Satan. They do his infernal work. But I do not hate them, Booker. I kill them because it is God's will. They appear to be irredeemable and unclean to their cores: yet still, I do nothing out of hate. I do it for the love of God and his Elect. If it is God's will to redeem some of his lost sheep, to save some, then equally will I share in God's joy! A world is coming where hate shall be banished.

"Forgive those who despise you, Booker. This is your only weakness. Christ died for people that hated him. On the cross, Yeshua asked the Father to forgive his own murderers! If one act separates the Elect from those who follow Satan, it is that the Elect do not hate. We pray even for our enemies."

Booker shook his head rapidly, as someone coming up out of the water. "That's hard, Gabriel."

Gabriel nodded. "Yes, Booker, it is the hardest thing God asks of us. To follow Christ means following him to the cross and to love your enemies. Not everyone will like you; such is not possible. You will always have enemies, even here in the Church. Envy, jealousy, petty dark emotions: these are all of Satan. You must rise above them, Booker. Bless those who snipe at you. Forgive your enemies. But never let them harm you physically. Self-defense, and defense of others is of God. Yet you must forgive enemies when they show contrition and be gracious even when they don't; and you must pray that if it be God's will to save them, as he saved you, then please do save them."

Booker hung his head. "I'm sorry."

Gabriel smiled. "God forgives your sins, Booker. Try to please him. Give thanks by loving even the most insufferable of his people."

Booker nodded. "I will. Thank you for that. My last question for the night, before my hand falls off: Jayden seemed pretty shook up when he knocked at my door. What did he see up there?"

"From the book of Mark, I'm sure you have it memorized: 'But in those days, after that tribulation: The sun will be darkened, and the moon will not give its light; the stars will fall from the sky, and the powers of the heavens will be shaken.' At that time they will see the Son of Man coming in the clouds with great power and glory."

Booker's face turned ashen. "The stars are weird, aren't they?" Gabriel nodded. "In the Book of Acts it is written, 'The sun will be turned into darkness, and the moon into blood, before the great and glorious day of the Lord coming.' I see a bright yellow-white moon up there."

"When there comes a total lunar eclipse tonight, the moon will become blood red."

"For as the lightning flashes and lights up the sky from one end to the other, so it will be on the day when the Son of Man comes. That's from Luke," said Booker.

"Yes! And the trumpet! When these things happen, know that you are mere moments away from meeting Yeshua. From seeing the very face of God. Oh, Booker! What I and countless others who came before ached and suffered to see; you will see!"

"You. You didn't say *we* will see."

Booker watched as Gabriel's eyes came down from the ceiling, elation and wonder draining from his face. "Marshall, Jayden, and you must increase. I must decrease."

"I'm sorry. What are you saying?"

"The Lord is coming. There is a cup I must drink. A very bitter cup. Nevertheless, not my will, rather his will be done."

Booker shook his head. "Gabriel, please don't say that. It comes close to what Jesus said on the night of his arrest. He foresaw God's enemies killing him long before they killed him. You are special! A prophet of God he needs to keep alive for the good of his people."

"Everybody dies, Booker; most especially God's prophets, each of whom ended violently. But if it makes you feel any better, all prophets go to Heaven. Remember what I said. The greatest of God's Commandments is to love him above any human, and to love other humans as yourself. Do this, and you will live forever in the light of the Lord. Your name is written in Heaven, Booker."

Booker nodded, stood, and handed the pen and paper back to Gabriel. "It has been the honor of my life to scribe for you, sir," Booker said. He did not give any indication of wanting the conversation to end.

"Go now to your wife," said Gabriel. "Perhaps we will talk more tomorrow evening."

Rise of the Golgoths

"Gabriel. I need to speak with you. It's urgent," Drake shouted through the knocks.

The door opened inward. "Drake. I know."

"You do?"

Gabriel nodded. "Tell me what you came to tell me." Marshall sat quietly and listened.

"Luke pulled spy duty tonight. He used the fast row boat hidden on the bank of the Schuylkill to get back here. Luke needed ninety minutes to row from there to here via the river to the Perkiomen Creek, where he ditched the boat and night-hiked the rest. He said Hostis Dei assembled the Golgoth forces. They are armed with swords and shorter cutting weapons carried in their hands, otherwise they are naked. They march behind their truck-mounted machine gun which requires them to use highways or roads. Luke said he spotted no shields among them."

Drake expected some sort of reaction from Gabriel, if not to his words, to the wild notes of fear in his tone. Instead, Drake stared into an inscrutable countenance, eyes like starlight reflected off two blue-white glaciers.

"Did Luke hear Hostis Dei speak?" Gabriel asked.

"Yes. Hostis Dei welcomed Golgoths from the north and south. All traveling Golgoths have arrived. Hostis Dei gathered his army of approximately eighty thousand Golgoths and addressed them using his voice amplifier. Luke was able to catch and report parts of it—the key bits, anyway. Hostis Dei promised his army that if they slay all male Elect, that their deity, Hubal, will reward each Golgoth member with his own 'breeder' from among our women and girls to procreate and expand his tribe. Elect males are considered a primary food source. Golgoths know about our spring water, cabins, and agriculture. They intend to relocate to Spring Mountain after they defeat us in battle. Also, they suspect that we have cutting weapons, which they believe to be the extent of our defense preparations. Our earthwork perimeter walls were not mentioned. Nothing about the caves and tunnels."

Gabriel nodded. "Start the generators. Switch on the stadium lights and public address system. I will assemble the Church. The enemy will arrive three-and-a-half hours from now. And Drake," he said. He reached out and cupped his most trusted friend's bearded cheeks. "Be without fear in the face of your enemies. Be brave and upright, that God may love you. Safeguard God's people even if it leads to your body's death. Do this, and you will inherit life eternal."

Drake nodded, turned, and walked toward the generator barn. He stopped. He called over his shoulder. "The moon," he pointed. "Looks weird. Like it's beginning to bleed." Gabriel nodded once, hands steepled under his chin. Drake walked on.

Five minutes later, bright LED lights lit up the grassy bowl of Spring Mountain from night into day. The Elect, shocked into motion by the highly unusual beacon of light, fled their cabins in the woods; cabins on mountainsides; and their cabins along old roadways. They poured across the footbridge past Drake's sixteen elite guards like a fast-moving liquid current of men, women, and children. The guards kept the doors open. It took one full hour for all to arrive.

The murmuring din reminded Drake of a distant thunderstorm. Gabriel stood upon the deck of his tower. He held the microphone and thumbed it on. Speakers high on poles along the mountain's former ski trails crackled.

"God's Elect: hear me. The unblinking eyes of the Lord are upon us this night, with compassion, and incomprehensible love."

Murmuring and whispers immediately quieted.

"Undoubtedly you have deduced from our preparations this summer that war with Golgoths is imminent. For over five thousand years, God has afforded his prophets small glimpses into the future, that all generations may stand vigilant. There would be signs in the heavens to herald the decisive battle, known as Armageddon, and soon after, the Second Coming of The Son of Man, Yeshua, our Lord, the Christ, whom we love above all."

His eyes swept the mass gathering. Each member felt a personal connection. "Tonight is the night of Holy War, Armageddon."

Gabriel held up his arms to quiet a wave of anxious babble. "We have made our preparations as well as they can be made. Follow my instructions carefully for the Holy Spirit works through me. You are aware of the underground shelter network with air vents disguised as felled hollow tree trunks. Sixty thousand adult females and twenty-four thousand children will enter the miles of caves within the next ninety minutes. The crew will roll a boulder over the main entrance. Inside you will find sufficient food and water to sustain you for three days, and latrines have been excavated. There are well-disguised escape hatches deep in the woods, accessible by tunnels. If the main entrance is not reopened within three days, stealthily emerge through the hatches. The Spirit will guide you to a safe place two full days' walk from here, where the Elect will reestablish the Church. Newcomer Mrs. Tatum Langar carries the key that unlocks the Scranton armory, which is a secure fortress fortified with military ordnance.

Gabriel paused to gaze out at the reactions. "Men of God: tonight, each of you is a warrior for our Lord, and blessed protector of our Church of Elect. Some say childhood ends when you first realize you are going to die. I disagree. Childhood ends with your first kill, at that moment when you take away the only thing a man has or will ever have. Tonight, you Elect warriors will set aside fripperies and become men; you will do God's will; each of you will send unclean spirits that still haunt this world back to Hades. Together we will purify the earth for the Lord's Second Coming; as it was written, so mote it be.

"God helps those who help themselves; so we have, and so we will. Elect warriors, go now to the armory. Suit up in your chain mail. Gather your shields, your throwing axes, swords, javelins, and your daggers. I have mine here and will lead you to victory, flanked by newcomer Marshall Langar, my top battle general, brought here by God to help me lead. Together, Marshall and I will form the tip of the phalanx wedge. Those of you whom Gunny Powell has identified as hastati will form the outside of the wedge; you will take two javelins. Those named triarii will form the middle and carry only one javelin. Hastati: when you have broken or lost your javelins and thrown your axes, or you are exhausted, fade back so that the triarii will move outward and relieve you.

"There is one machine gun weapon the enemy possesses that would destroy us. The only means of bringing this gun to bear against us is by road, as the weapon is mounted to a vehicle. Spring Mountain Road is protected by earthworks. The vehicle will be driven up the dirt slope to the crest, as we have flattened a ramp leading from the road to the crest so that we might lure it into position. Directly across from the crest, Gunny has placed his mortars. He will use his explosive mortar weapons to disable that threat, and then he will join the archers here on this deck, to use his rifle on enemy fighters who drop over the wall. Some enemy will break bones at the bottom of the long plunge and impale themselves on a wide band of sharpened birch stakes.

"Archers assume your positions around the inner perimeter. Catapult teams: Golgoths are projected to fight with one javelin and one sword, but with no shields to protect them. Their naked bodies are painted white which makes them easy to spot. The gate into our community we will leave open and invite them in. Their main army will use this egress.

"Catapults will incinerate Golgoths climbing over perimeter earthworks and should significantly reduce their fighting force. Catapults will continue to pound the earthwork summit and the road. Golgoths who survive this, and the twelve-foot drop, archers will impale, or we the army will sift them like wheat. The wedge formation will drive them back toward the earthworks. After bringing to bear our mortars, our catapults, and our snipers, we will equal if not outnumber them for the battle.

"Remember, my compassionate children: these spirits are possessed by Satan and his demons; no longer are they men like yourselves. Cut them down with impunity. God wills it.

"Let us pray," said Gabriel. He held up his hands, closed his eyes, lowered his head. "Our father who art in Heaven: hallowed by thy name. thy Kingdom come; thy will be done, on earth as it is in Heaven. Give us this day our daily bread, and forgive us our debts, as we forgive our debtors. Lead us not into temptation, but deliver us from evil, for thine is the Kingdom, and the power, and the glory forever. Amen."

"Amen," came the response from every man, woman, child—even toddlers, like parrots.

"Also, please know that the time of Christ's second visitation is near. After the battle it might happen at any time, as was promised so long ago. Lord Yeshua is coming to embrace you! The Creator of all things! Men have lived and their bodies died praying to see what you will see, and so they will! — but not until Judgement Day, and the mass Resurrection of the Elect who died across the millenniums in Christ. For now, our brothers and sisters in Christ sleep. Your eyes of flesh may soon behold God made flesh, something that has not happened in over two thousand years, because your faith and your love have endured. Blessed be the Elect."

"Blessed be the Prophet Gabriel," all shouted.

"We will leave the lights on for one hour while you execute your assignments, then switch them off. Everyone will remain silent. We will offer Golgoths the dark, silent night in which to assemble outside our walls. We will lead them to believe that we are unprepared and at rest. At my signal, we will shock their eyes with blinding lights aimed at the road. Sergeant Powell and the catapult teams will unleash fiery Hell upon them. Go now. And may God grant each of you his indomitable courage and strength. Amen."

"And to you. Amen," responded every Elect.

Gabriel switched off his microphone. He walked back inside, where only a single beeswax candle illuminated his dark chamber. He sunk to his knees, pressed his forehead and hands flat against the wood floor, and for twenty minutes in tears he prayed for the strength to die well.

At the end, Gabriel straightened. "Lord, I am so scared. But thy will be done, Heavenly Father." He rose. He donned his full chain mail armor. He kissed his favorite Bible. He descended the stairs, walked outside, and took one last look at the structure he had called home for more than three decades. He turned his back to the tower and headed for the armory.

"I don't care what he said, Marshall," said Tatum. He read panic in her eyes. "I'm fighting by your side!"

He opened his arms. She fell into them. She broke down, her entire body heaved, wracked with fear and grief for a finality she felt deep inside. Her warm salty tears rained onto his armor of tiny steel rings sending microdroplets pell-mell.

"Thinkin' 'bout you is the only thing that can get me killed, Tatum," he said. Gently he pushed her away. He reached out; placed his hand over her heart; he felt the metal lump there pressed against her skin underneath her shirt. "Gabriel gave y'all this key. But he is only a prophet. Don't y'all see, wife? *God* gave it. He trusts y'all! If his Elect should lose the battle, through y'all's strength, God's people go on."

Head lowered, she snarked back nasal congestion. A pregnant pause, until finally, she nodded. "You're right," she croaked. She raised her eyes to him and forced a smile. "He saved me. His will be done, not mine. I mustn't think of myself. But you, buster," she poked his chest, "you need to survive, husband. God wills it. And I command it. Hear me: multiply two-hundred-trillion-trillion times infinity and still you will barely comprehend how proud I am that you chose me for your wife, because of the man you are, because of how you've played the bad hands dealt you since you were a little kid, because of the choices you've made, and this incredible relationship you have with God and all that you've done because of it, and all that you will do."

He smiled. "Hear me now believe me later: Y'all 'r the most allurin,' beautiful, captivatin' woman on earth. Ain't never told anyone this, but I believe that all through my life I have dreamed y'all were out there somewhere, custom-fitted to me. Warm heart, savage spirit, with the kindest eyes I ever seen. Y'all 'r my incentive to leave nothin' on the battlefield." He took both of her hands. "My love and abject adoration for y'all is like…like a well runnin' all the way through the earth and out the other side; there ain't no bottom to it; and now that I done fell in it feels like y'all's gravity only increases."

She pulled him down and kissed him. "Remember when you told me I smell like a raindrop?" He did remember and nodded. "You smell like home. Come home to me. See that you do. But for now, focus only on God."

He walked to his knapsack and unsnapped both machetes. One he looped around his belt so that it hung down against this right leg. He grabbed his long but light shield. *What a well-designed shield,* he thought. He looked at Tatum. "Go up yonder to the cave mouth. I'm goin' downhill. See y'all after," he said. She did not move. "I trust y'all: so trust me. Bye for now," and he walked outside, unwilling to extend the already long goodbye.

His head was now fully in the battle.

One man stood alone at bottom of the ski hill fifty feet from the covered bridge. Tall, long blonde hair, dressed all in white, covered by chainmail. Marshall trotted up beside him. Gabriel stared at the footbridge. After a time, he acknowledged the presence beside him.

"You forgot your throwing axe, sword, javelin, and dagger," muttered Gabriel.

"Nope. Didn't forget. Don't need 'em don't want 'em. Got everythin' I need right here."

"Marshall, we have drilled in the use of these. My battle plan depends on them."

Marshall smiled. "Good! Please use 'em. I done decapitated Golgoths with these," he said. He held out one machete for Gabriel to see. "Tonight—I will collect many more heads. To get to y'all, first they gotta get past me and my twirly-whirly blades."

"The Spirit is strong in you, son. Trust it. And I will trust your judgement. And your blades."

"Amen, prophet. God bless us all."

"Pray with me," said Gabriel. Marshall nodded and closed his eyes. Gabriel reached out his right hand to grasp Marshall's left. They bowed their heads. "Non nobis, Domine, non nobis, sed nomini Tuo da declension gloriam. Amen."

"Amen," said Marshall. What's it mean?"

"Not to us, Lord, not to us, but give glory to your name."

Marshall nodded. "Perfect. All glory goes to God. May I say a prayer?" Gabriel nodded.

"Heavenly Father. Y'all's will be done tonight. Whatever happens here is because y'all desired it. If my body dies, please keep my spirit; 'cause I'd rather live as a mouse behind the walls in Heaven eatin' crumbs dropped from the table of righteous men than to reign in Hell, separated from y'all. This is all I ask, Father, in the name of y'all's Son, Jesus—amen."

Gabriel squeezed his hand. "You will prevail tonight, Marshall. Of that I have no doubts."

Marshall recognized that this was his watershed moment, the apotheosis of his life. "*We* will prevail, Gabriel. For we are God's instruments on earth. His hands. His threshing scythe. Evil will not defeat us. For what can stand against the greater force that made all things?"

Gabriel hefted his sword. "We will unleash Hell on these demons."

Marshall smiled.

Behind them brave young men, silent and stealthy, assembled into lines by the tens and twenties. The only sounds Gabriel and Marshall heard were the muted rustle of chainmail as warriors fell into the wedge battle formation. Within the hour, the entirety of the green ski hill became covered with armed soldiers, tens of thousands, flanked by thick woods and a new dirt wall to the south, and enormous earthwork wall to the north.

Gabriel turned to watch Gunny Powell hustling between his three mortars sure and swift as a fox, triple-checking the aiming apparatus with the cool, confident bearing of a well-practiced instrumentalist. Above him, Booker and Jayden sat on plastic chairs, each flanked with his own plastic trash can overflowing with thousands of razor-broadhead hunting arrows. Dozens more full cans covered the deck surface, save for a clear area where

Gunny would lie prone with his ancient M1 Garand rifle and burlap sack of a thousand rounds.

"What do we do now?" whispered Marshall.

Gabriel looked at him. "Listen for the Golgoth vehicle."

Marshall shook his head. "Sorry but I ain't never heard a vehicle in my entire life."

Gabriel gave him a wan grin. "Don't worry you'll know it when you hear it. Also we should see it easily under the light of Jayden's supernova constellations. When I raise my javelin, Drake turns on the lights. Gunny fires his mortars. Teams unleash napalm bombs. Archers and snipers thin the herd."

Gabriel gazed backward at sixty thousand Elect soldiers in a wedge formation. Under red moonlight he saw his army fully assembled for the first time. It stretched up the hill to its summit.

"Thousands of Golgoth warriors will push across the bridge, Marshall. Thousands more will drop over the walls. We will fertilize the grass with their iron-rich blood."

"Ah," whispered Marshall. "Everythin' comes down to agriculture with y'all, don't it?"

Gabriel smiled. "God causes the sun to shine and plants to grow. But he needs we farmers to bring about his bountiful harvest. To raise his glorious order up from Satan's chaos. Let the blood of the Golgoths manure Christ's land."

Inferno

"Yes," Marshall whispered. "Gotta be the Golgoth vehicle I'm hearin' 'cause for sure that sound ain't natural. Ain't never heard such a thing in my life."

"When I was a boy," said Gabriel, "that sound was background noise day and night. Big cities were the loudest, though even people who dwelt in rural areas could not escape the mechanized sounds. Airplanes flew over day and night. It didn't matter where you lived: vehicles beeped, hissed, honked, and roared. The world I knew was noisy."

Marshall shook his head. "An ugly sound. I don't like it."

"Then Marshall, please see to it that after this night, no Elect ever hears it again. The Elect should always live simply and strive to please God. Humans proved our ability to organize into nations and societies which protect intellectuals. Peace, prosperity, and security allowed humans to share information, advance technologies, explore medicine, even the heavens. I believe it pleased God to see us reaching; see us advance and build upon shared knowledge to achieve great technological breakthroughs and scientific understanding. But haven't we proved all there was to prove? Except for the most important thing: that we love God back, with only a mere fraction of the intensity with which God loves us. Also that we can live together in perpetual peace. Humanity utterly failed at this. But the Elect have not failed God, and neither will you."

"It's why the old world ended, isn't it," said Marshall.

Gabriel nodded. "Tonight is our last chance to level the foundation and build a world without hate. The one God intended from the beginning: Heaven on earth."

Marshall shook his head. "It's still a horrifyin' world no matter how much love we all give it. Maybe God wanted to see us rise above his cruel, violent predator-prey ecosystem: to love peace as he does. Maybe he wanted to test how we'd handle a world that's violent by design, a world we enter violently and leave violently. I don't believe God is like a kid with an ant farm; I think maybe our time here is more like a test run before admittin' us into his Kingdom, to condition us, give us perspective that them angels 'a his can never feel. Y'all think?"

"Just so. Though none can know the unknowable mind of the Creator. Not even I," said Gabriel.

Marshall stared up at the blood moon. It looked back at him like the exit wound of a razor-tipped arrow. "Can we win this battle, prophet?"

Gabriel smiled. "With those whirring blades of yours, we just might."

As Marshall puzzled over the bizarre response, noise from the vehicle engine suggested the enemy had advanced as far as Schwenksville Road, possibly to its intersection with Sprint Mount Road. Elect whispers abruptly ceased. A pall descended upon the Elect army in battle formation on the green. *For these here gentle folk life just got real,* Marshall thought.

Marshall felt the familiar flood of Spirit and invincibility as before his battle on the railroad tracks, his face rubicund, body language placid calm. He glanced at Gabriel. *Need to hold a mirror under his nose to prove he still has a pulse,* Marshall thought.

Marshall heard human grunts and spitting: recognized the sound of bare feet slapping asphalt and sensed the quality of the engine noise change; he noticed Gabriel's grip tightening on his javelin. He heard twigs breaking fewer than one-hundred feet away on the outside of the upslope earthworks. The repulsive engine noise stopped. Most sounds ceased.

"In spiritu in veritate!" yelled Gabriel.

"In spirit in truth!" answered sixty-thousand soldiers. Gabriel raised his javelin. Stadium lights aimed at Spring Mount Road flicked on like dozens of supernovae, lumens from cold mini suns beamed harshly onto the ghostly lunar army of Hostis Dei. Naked and armed, thousands of white hands shot up to shield their eyes.

In his youth, Gunnery Sergeant Patrick Powell launched 120 mm shells through M74 light mortars at enemy positions in hot combat with almost perfect accuracy. After his tours of duty, the Corps rewarded Gunny with a cherry position at the Scranton armory as quality consultant and chief of testing. Tonight, this minute, his life's work would be tested along with his ability to train others. His four-man crew, named by him as Charlie crew, immediately assumed their positions. His five-man crews he named Alpha and Bravo manned the other two M74 stations. He smiled. "Oorah!" he yelled the Marine Corps battle cry. "Oorah!" answered all of his crewmen.

Gunny signaled to his own Charlie crewmen standing furthest from where he stood. His rangefinder crewman knelt and called out coordinates for aiming their mortar at the Golgoth truck. Powell pointed to the Alpha crew; he heard the team's rangefinder crewman call out numbers. "Alpha Team: FIRE!" Gunny yelled. The first team dropped their explosive shell into the mortar. A loud whoof sound; a sharp bright light; a large, pungent smoke ring hovered over the black gaping maw of Alpha Team's mortar. The truck exploded: all saw the truck rock. The shell had hit the engine compartment and exploded. Flames climbed from the now hoodless vehicle.

The M2A1 Browning machine gun remained intact, mounted to the rear of the truck facing them, threatening to mow down the Elect army like a buzzsaw. It's three-Golgoth crew got thrown from the truck bed when the 120mm round hit the front. Temporarily shocked and permanently deafened, but otherwise functional, they resumed firing positions in the truck bed. Gunny signaled to the Bravo Team crew. They fired and missed the machine gun. The shot went wild: high, wide, and handsome, into the indifferent earthwork where its shockwave horribly mangled seven Golgoths. Dismembered hands still clutched swords. Heads, legs, entrails, and bloody body parts erupted in a red and white volcano. The macabre sight temporarily disoriented the M2A1 Golgoth machine gun crew.

Powell was quite familiar with the Golgoth's terrible weapon; he knew it could fire six hundred rounds a minute. A grimness seized him. He had one chance to save thousands of lives. He peered through the scope of his mortar and grew still. "Lord, I've never asked you for much. The coordinates I call out to my crew: please correct me if I'm wrong. This is my last chance to save thousands of innocent lives." He studied the scope; and the coordinates in his mind infused him with a confidence and certainty never before felt. He called them out to his four crew members with a command to dial them into the mortar's aiming apparatus. "Charlie Team: FIRE!"

There was a flash of light and sound. Just then, Gunny heard the click of the M2A1 machine gun as Golgoths chambered the first belt-fed round, so that when they pressed the trigger their weapon would blast out six-hundred large caliber rounds per minute and slice apart the Elect army like blood-filled bags inside gelatin dolls. Then he heard the explosion.

Direct hit! thought Gunny. He smiled at the crippled, warped gun barrel, also at the spectacular shower of Golgoth gore still slopping down onto fellow demons.

"Red rain," Gunny muttered. "Oorah! Mission One accomplished," he yelled out to his three mortar crews. "Great work, men! Now, quickly, fire all remaining 120 shells into the white demons up along the ridge, then join the archers on the south wall," he commanded. He then sprinted toward Gabriel's tower, incredulity on the faces of his three mortar crews at the agility, speed, and strength of the lithe old man.

More explosions pierced the night behind Gunny as he ascended to the tower deck in time to watch Golgoth long-spears, thrown like javelins down from the earthwork, which pierced each of his fourteen crewmen's ribcages. He watched all fourteen of his men fall. In that split second his mind photographed white-faced enemies above. "I never forget a face you spear chucking demons," he mumbled.

Gunny brushed past Booker and Jayden. He lay in the prone firing position and picked up his loaded M1 Garand rifle where he had left it, next to his thousand-round sack of .30-06 Springfield ammunition. He took conscious control of his breathing. *These bright lights are a gift,* he thought, centering the scope crosshairs on the first face he remembered. He sent a bullet traveling at thirty-four-hundred-feet per second into the enemy's head. He watched the skull briefly expand, followed by a puff of gray, red and pink mist as the head vaporized. "Mm hm," he muttered, repeating the process with one reload in between until the fourteen Golgoths who killed his mortar crewmen fell, headless.

Briefly he glanced at Booker and Jayden, whose mouths hung open. "Oorah! That's how we do it, boys," he muttered. "When they drop over the wall aim for center mass. These headshots were highly unprofessional, but oh so satisfying, mmm mm. Now they know who they're messing with. Semper Fi, boys. Let 'em have it."

Unnatural shrieking pierced the silence. Cannibalistic Golgoths along the earthwork shook their heavy iron-tipped spears in primitive anger and discordant howling. *Hell's dogs*, Jayden thought.

Gabriel raised his javelin in signal. Thirty catapult teams released their simple tension machines. Fused explosive napalm pots whistled through the warm night air toward the Golgoth army thickly arrayed on top of the earth works. Large clay spheres hit earth and cracked open. Over a thousand Golgoths were ignited into screaming human torches as gallons of sticky, burning gel adhered to and blackened white skins.

There were screams of surprise, physical shock, and inconceivable pain. No amount of rolling in the dirt could free the Golgoths from death by intense roasting. The ground itself was covered in burning napalm. Catapult teams knew their mission and executed it swiftly, the result of Gunny's weeks of relentless drilling. Crews of four Elect cranked back the catapult tensioners; two of these Elect then loaded fresh clay pots of napalm and lit their fuses. In numbers equal to their smoldering dead, more Golgoths swarmed to the summit of the earth berms. Thirty Elect catapult teams unleashed their payloads. A thousand more Golgoths were incinerated in Hell's chorus of the damned, tormented in lakes of jellied gasoline. Elect who formed the long wedge up the ski trail vomited from the olfactory-scorching putrescence of petrol-seared human meat. Eight more volleys reduced the Golgoth army of Hostis Dei to numbers equal with those in Gabriel's wedge.

Golgoths leapt down into the bowl by the hundreds. Inhuman, agonized howls trumpeted from Golgoths dropping over the earthworks and getting impaled on the sharpened birchwood knives sticking up from the ground. Gunny continued his steady rifle firing as Booker and Jayden smoothly released arrows one after another. Killing soon became whimsical to the three Elect tower snipers: the killing was random, with no rhyme or reason, nor strategy or system. They were enjoying themselves.

Underneath bright stadium lights and a bloodshot moon, the first wave of hairless, thickly muscled, white-painted enemy to cross the footbridge hurled spears into the Elect's Roman testudo formation—shields held in front and overtop the Elect. Golgoth spears glanced harmlessly off the impenetrable tortoise shell of overlayed shields. Gabriel and Marshall heard footfalls slapping hard against the wooden plank floor of the covered bridge. Every Elect inhaled, bracing for bloodshed.

An image flickered across Marshall's mind of a paper wasp's nest with hundreds of barbed predators angrily attacking a creature considered a threat to the colony. Golgoths of unidentifiable age, spears in one hand, swords in the other, trundled across the narrow footbridge toward him and Gabriel, savage white faces—and something else—a pure, sifted form of hate. *Demons. The possessed,* he thought.

Low animal growls from Golgoth predators increased in pitch, timbre, and volume, as war cries filled the mountain.

Spears lowered, the enemy charged at Gabriel and Marshall at full speed, as hundreds more smashed up behind them became channeled up both sides of the wedge formation stretching far uphill. *Exactly as the Father showed me,* thought Gabriel.

Iron spear tips firmly caught Elect shields, inertia shoving the front line hastati backward against the ring of hastati positioned behind them. Gabriel and Marshall's shields met at the edges; several Golgoth spear tips thrust in between them. Marshall slammed his machete against the wood shafts severing the sharp ends. As Gabriel and Marshall helped to hold the front line with their shields, from the row of Elect behind them long javelins plunged down against Golgoths, each piercing a white body before it was quickly withdrawn like thousands of big bloody sewing needles.

Gabriel's well-planned meat-tenderizing cycle repeated all the way up the wedge of Elect. Using height to their advantage, Gabriel's sword with Marshall's machetes stabbed over, down, and between shields out into Golgoth bodies. Gabriel's heavier steel weapon bulldozed flesh and cleaved bone. Golgoths were now forced to stand atop growing piles of dead and dying fellow Golgoths to move close to Gabriel's wedge.

Marshall relied on brute strength and speed. Several of his blows cleaved Golgoth heads in two, like splitting coconuts. His misses lopped off ears, glanced off heads and traveled down with such force that his blade split collarbones and traveled into chest cavities deeply enough to sever arteries and vital organs.

Both Gabriel and Marshall chopped until their arms cramped, and the action itself became prosy. They hung back and rested while the line of Elect behind them stepped forward and commenced thrusting spears into Golgoth eye sockets, open mouths, necks, and delivered fatal blows to center mass organs. When hastati deltoids, forearms, and shoulders had become so fatigued that they started to miss targets, the best, biggest, and strongest fighters among the Elect known as the triarii moved up from the middle, fresh and strong, to give their front-line brethren a well-earned rest.

An endless column of diffidence and hate crossed the bridge, climbing over massive piles of their own dead to leap against the wedge. Elect held their lines with few injuries. As enemy numbers swelled inside the bowl, the

Elect wedge merely moved backwards further up the hill like a giant arrow in slow-motion reverse. The screams of the damned seemed endless, the iron-rich stench of blood, the fetid bouquet of unwashed man-sweat, and the unmistakable stink of offal from pierced bowels saturated the still night air. There was no escaping the heavy, malodorous atmosphere of death wafting throughout the whole of Spring Mountain.

Golgoths atop earthworks jumped down onto the impaled bodies of their fellows, but then their souls quickly joined them in the hellish afterlife, because Booker and Jayden rarely missed with their arrows, nor did Gunny with his bullets, from their firing positions up on Gabriel's tower deck. When Booker and Jayden did miss their targets, arrows entered limbs instead of center mass. Not once did either waste a single precious arrow with a completely missed shot.

Gunny exhausted his thousand rounds of ammunition within the first forty minutes. He saw something sticking out of Booker's bag. "Is that a slingshot?"

"Yes, Gunny, a very accurate and powerful slingshot," shouter Booker over the screams from below.

"Got any ammo?"

"In the bag. Three boxes of steel shot. Check Jayden's bag, he has some boxes, too."

Gunny Powell grabbed the slingshot and a box of steel shot. He resumed his favorite prone position but found it unsuitable for this type of firing. From the kneeling position he took aim and fired his first steel ball at a Golgoth who stood atop the berm. "Missed by five inches, dammit." Gunny opened both eyes wide, took aim on the same target, and released the shot. "Missed; overcompensated by one damned red pussy hair from his neck." He took aim again. This time Gunny felt that he had a bead on the Golgoth. Just as the Golgoth bent his knees in preparation to leap, Gunny let the shot fly. The steel ball directly hit the mouth of the Golgoth: tore through his closed lips and shattered front teeth in a spray of blood. Hands clutched the throat. The enemy stood there like that for two absurd minutes, until he fell face forward down the sheer drop from the earthwork onto a pile of white corpses, where he twitched, then lay still.

"Hot-damn!" shouted Powell.

"I saw it, Gunny. That was one hell of an amazing shot, Sergeant. I have a can of beer in my bag I've been saving for a special occasion. Bet you that single celebratory beer you can't do it ten times in a row," said Jayden.

"If I lose?" said Gunny.

"When this is over, you and I take a ride to wherever you came from, and you get me one of those Garands and a few cans of ammo. Hey

Gunny—this might just be the last beer left on earth."

"I was no superstar on the thousand-yard range but give me a moving target and I can hit anything. Watch." Powell repeated his slingshot success nine more times, smiled at Jayden, and commenced shooting out both eyes of ten more, which did not kill them outright but rendered them useless in battle. Arrows from Booker and Jayden finished them.

Gabriel's triarii drew back strong arms and laterally hurled their throwing axes down under their own shields hard against the ground, using the same stroke as someone skimming flat stones on a millpond. The sharp axes ricocheted up and severed Golgoth ankles by the hundreds and thousands, which took them out of the fight. Each slowly bled out and died within minutes.

Golgoths overflowed the covered bridge and the walls. Gabriel and Marshall saw the world only in the primary color red. The moon rose red, like a bloody bucket of guts. Red was the field of battle. Neither Gabriel nor Marshall would dare speculate how many Golgoths died versus how many were still in the fight. The reduction in Golgoth numbers happened gradually. The arrow-shaped wedge formation edged up the hill more slowly now than it did in the first few hours. Mincing and perforating continued until the great white push of Golgoths ebbed to a trickle.

For the first time since Gunny's mortar explosions and battle din, Gabriel felt that if he spoke, Marshall would hear. "It feels like it's nearly over," he yelled. "Though now I feel the presence of the demon, Hostis Dei, enemy of God, and the six generals who command his legions. For every Golgoth there can be no escape, no quarter. God wills it. Dei and his inner circle are more cunning than these," he said, waving his hand at the gruesome field of dead Golgoths piling ever higher.

"I believe y'all, prophet. How do we find 'em?"

"Through their hate, you shall know them. You shall feel their hate flowing into you, Marshall. Follow where the Spirit leads you, and you tell me: are they far?"

Marshall rested his arms and stared at the night sky. *Where are they, Lord?* Billions of cool white, dispassionate pinpoints stared back Marshall as if through a black sheet; the moon bled down like a giant red puncture wound in the stygian sky. Marshall's mind disassociated from the battlefield. He saw himself naked and shivering back in North Indian Creek. *Is this some sorta sign, Lord?*

He felt Gabriel staring at him, smiling.

"Moving and still pictures, Marshall. These are signs from the Spirit. Now, interpret the sign you received and tell me where to find the Golgoth leaders."

Marshall responded: "The worst of 'em are gathered yonder behind piles 'a their dead, hidin' out in the stream runnin' under the covered bridge where y'all baptized us."

Gabriel nodded. "The worst of them being Hostis Dei and his six generals. Let us bring five triarii. You," said Gabriel, pointing to the triarii behind him, "choose four of your best. Find me a second sword: I shall need two."

Marshall freed the second machete from his right side.

"We bring the battle to them. Are you ready to end this?" asked Gabriel.

Marshall nodded once. "Is a frog's ass watertight?"

Gabriel smiled. "Marshall, I feel like I've known you for years. I regret never having had the chance. So it shall be in the next world, my brother."

Marshall frowned.

Return to Zero

Gabriel and Marshall carried two weapons apiece and no shields. The five triarii each brought his shield, javelin, and sword. They found it hard to balance as they made their way over and through pestilential piles of death. Each slipped multiple times as the group scaled up and over slick intestines and disembodied organs, slippery mashed brains, and torsos coated in congealing blood.

"Do you sense our proximity to pure evil, Marshall?"

"Yessir I do," he answered Gabriel. They pushed forward through the mephitic gore. Fewer white warriors slapped across the covered footbridge. The point of the Elect's wedge formation, far too dense with their dead, forced fresh Golgoth fighters uphill along both long sides of the formation. Gabriel, Marshall, and five Elect watched the uphill flow of fresh Golgoth fighters slow from the earlier river to what was now a trickle.

It took Gabriel, Marshall and the four best Elect fighters twelve minutes to pick their way over the butchery and through the gore, until they stood upon a thin band of blood-soaked but otherwise clear asphalt twenty feet from the stream.

They stood for five minutes watching the footbridge to their left. "Pretty much they all stopped comin' across," said Marshall. "I can hardly believe what just happened. We were outnumbered by nearly twenty thousand and now most of 'em are dead. We really did this, and that right quick."

Gabriel shook his head. "Never make the grave mistake of sinful pride, Marshall. We are nothing, absolutely nothing. God prepared us. We are merely his instruments. All glory is his. Your battle will not end tonight."

Marshall considered the words. "Gabriel, y'all 'r so right."

"It's not over for you," said Gabriel.

Marshall nodded. "First things first. Let's cut the head off 'a this here demon, Hostis Dei."

"Your lunar deity is bleeding," Gabriel shouted. "Hostis Dei, enemy of God: you are an abomination in the eyes of the Lord. Come forth, unclean spirits. Show yourselves to the sainted Elect."

Spoggs Reichert, the highest ranking Golgoth general slowly rose from the stream bank like a basilisk, dripping wet, hands clutching a spear and a sword. To Marshall, the legendary cannibal seemed like a charcoal cut-out that was silhouetted against a black background splashed with stadium light. He wore a ghostly white mask of animal fury, cadaver eyes, not unlike a two-day-old dead fish. *Like a livin' skull*, Marshall thought.

Marshall sheathed both of his long machetes. He motioned to the triarii; the Elect warrior beside him handed Marshall his javelin and shield. Spoggs charged at Marshall like an enraged bull. Marshall held the shield horizontally with his left hand, out to his side. He charged toward Spoggs with the javelin in his right hand, twisted himself into exaggerated feints right-left-right, and jabbed at the kidney of Spoggs with the javelin. Spoggs arched his body to the right. The javelin missed, as Marshall knew it would. Marshall whipped his shield across. The edge caught Spoggs in the face. The blow did not damage Spoggs, only stunned him for a moment. Spoggs whipped the wooden shaft of his iron-tipped spear at Marshall's head. Marshall parried with his all-wood javelin, knocking the spear off course, then jabbed his javelin at the white legs of Spoggs. Spoggs side-stepped and swung his sword down at Marshall's collarbone. Marshall had just enough time to raise his left arm; his shield absorbed and deflected the energy of the sword's arc.

Spoggs plunged at Marshall with his spear. Marshall brought his javelin down onto the traveling spear hard enough to redirect the iron tip against the asphalt. Sparks flew. Marshall stomped onto the immobilized spear shaft and snapped it cleanly in half.

Marshall dropped his javelin and unsheathed the machete on his right hip. Spoggs swung his sword. Marshall ducked and jabbed with his machete. He missed center mass but opened a cut on the right shoulder of Spoggs. Enraged, unused to the sight of his own blood, Spoggs held his sword in the eagle position high above his head. With all his considerable strength Spoggs brought the heavy blade down in a chop. Marshall deflected this with his shield, but his shield got cleaved in two from the kinetic energy and extreme weight of the sword. If the sword had connected with Marshall it would have hacked him in half.

Marshall unsheathed his second machete. He knew that his lighter, sharper blades were no physical match against the Golgoth's heavy iron cutlass. *That heavy thing makes him slower,* he thought. Spoggs plunged the weapon at him. Marshall crossed his machetes into an 'X' and blocked it down to his right then quickly backed away.

It was then that a breviloquent moving picture spooled inside Marshall's mind. He felt himself watching the movements of his battle with Spoggs from a short distance away before all of the movements happened. He saw himself defeating Spoggs. *What the——,* he thought. *If I imitate these moves I see in my head I can beat this guy.* He held his machetes like daggers, tips down, cutting edges toward him. Spoggs raised his sword high to his right. Marshall windmilled the machetes up over his head and down, like a raptor tearing down at a large animal. Arcs of steel whirred too fast for the mind of Spoggs to process. Marshall spun in a fast counterclockwise three-sixty move that further confounded Spoggs.

In less than a second, Marshall's windmill blades came within kissing distance of Spoggs. Panicked, Spoggs chopped down with his heavy sword but too late. Marshall's right machete pierced the chest of Spoggs between his clavicle and left deltoid, as the left machete cleanly severed his right hand. In his peripheral vision Marshall saw the hand still grasping the sword handle as it clattered against the asphalt.

The eyes of Spoggs registered deep shock and surprise before his pierced lung could scream. Marshall sheathed his machetes, bent, and pried the severed hand from the heavy sword. With the sword gripped tightly in both hands, he charged forward with all his speed and strength.

Marshall buried the iron blade inside the chest, dissevering the dark heart of Spoggs Reichert. Marshall watched sixteen inches of blade disappear. He had a feeling the man he just bested was a demon of high rank, a man of unspeakable atrocities committed in the name of their god, Hubal. As if in answer, a feeling of peace swept through Marshall like a warm breeze.

The last thought crossing the mind of Spoggs was of him handing Isabella Albo's heart in a cloth sack to Hostis Dei. He was dead when his face smashed the asphalt.

There was a diabolical howl and a flash of white. Hostis Dei grasped a spear and a sword as he leaped over the stream bank and hit the asphalt running with ferocious speed. Gabriel rushed in front of Marshall. "This one is mine, sayeth the Lord," said Gabriel, sword in his right hand. He used his empty left arm to push Marshall further back.

Marshall stepped back. *Do not hinder the prophet,* spoke his inner voice. He could not be certain that this thought was his own. *Behold, Hostis Dei, the white goblin. The devil incarnate. Apostate of Hell.*

A peripheral glimpse of enormous sex organs slapping wildly against thick white legs appalled Marshall. *What is wrong with them eyes?* Marshall got a good close look now in the light. *Eyes 'a the evil dead.* A diaphanous glaze, something maleficent and wrathful smoldering behind them like post-mortem parasitic fireflies, or pernicious glow worms. *Abomination in the sight 'a the Lord. Gabriel was so right about that. About everythin.'*

The enemy of God came at Gabriel the same way Marshall had run at Spoggs, to his right then feinted left, sword and forearm parallel and cocked, liked an arrow nocked against a tensed bowstring. Moving like a tiger boxing in its prey, Hostis Dei used his overdeveloped left leg to launch into the air, waist now even with Gabriel's left shoulder, right leg up and folded for balance. As gravity pulled him back down Hostis Dei unleashed his right arm at Gabriel while twisting his torso, his awful head only six inches from Gabriel's.

Dei's sword plunged straight down through Gabriel's trapezius like a scorpion's tail. It penetrated down between the clavicle and scapula, puncturing the left lung before it retracted, quicker than a paper wasp sting.

In a state of panic, Hostis Dei failed to notice the short dagger Gabriel held in his left hand.

Hostis Dei's sword pierced Gabriel as Gabriel had known it would, for he saw it happen long before it did. Gabriel extended his left arm holding the dagger. Dei's inertia and weight did the rest. Through his pain, Gabriel managed to hold his arm and the knife rigid. The edge of his dagger shaved white paint from Dei's thighs as gravity brought the enemy's genitals down onto the sharp blade. Just as Hostis Dei's bare soles hit the asphalt, so too did his sex organs. Over the din of an amped battlefield, Marshall heard the squishy splat.

Castrated and nullified, Dei collapsed onto the asphalt clutching his denuded groin, face screwed into a grimace of unfathomable shock and pain, mouth open in a soundless scream. Dark blood gushed through his closed fingers.

The triarii witnessed the demon king succumb to his ultimate destiny. They could not look away. "Behold the boogeyman behind it all," said one.

"Doesn't look so tough now," another responded.

Several laughed. "Look at him. Hey Hostis Dei, give Hubal our warmest regards."

"No more breeders for this bad boy."

"Go straight back to Hell, demon."

It took precisely three minutes for the strong heart muscle of the demon Hostis Dei to push all eight quarts of blood out through the severed left and right superficial external pudendal arteries, a straight tap from the femoral artery.

Three minutes after piercing Gabriel, Hostis Dei was no more.

Gabriel Thomas collapsed to his knees, smiling. His right hand held up three fingers. "Dead in three minutes. The demon believed three to be his lucky number."

The five triarii froze. Marshall only knew Gabriel a short while; to these men, he was their everything. Marshall could see that each one of Gabriel's elite soldiers was broken inside. Each took a knee in respect, mouths frozen open in rictuses of pain and shock.

"Gabriel, oh my God, he's really dying!" cried one through tears. All wept.

Marshall watched five Golgoth generals quietly slink over the stream's bank, fully armed. They had just witnessed Hostis Dei, their immortal and undefeatable leader whom they feared more than death, bleed out dead in three quick minutes.

Marshall stood between five elite Golgoth warriors and the five Elect triarii. He recognized something in the faces of the Golgoth generals. "Greed," he muttered. It dawned on him. *After they kill me, they'll fight over which demon leads the comeback.*

The five Golgoth generals advanced on Marshall. He glanced up at Gabriel's tower. Booker, Jayden, and Gunny Powell stood watching everything. Marshall pointed at the generals.

Three were dropped; one from an arrow through the neck; another pierced through the heart; the third choked by a steel ball shot down through his esophagus. The other two Golgoths stopped. They hurled their spears up at the deck. One spear arced into the wooden deck and stuck, upright, two feet from Booker. The other pierced Gunny Powell straight through the liver. Marshall watched in horror as Gunny's face registered shock, watched Gunny hit the deck on his back, the Golgoth spear now vertical. It quivered. Booker and Jayden nocked and cocked two razor broadhead arrows. Marshall held up his hand for them to stop firing.

Unsheathing his machetes, Marshall charged the two Golgoth generals. In an inspired pirouette, he spun and whirled between them faster than a falling samara, until he stopped and turned. Later, Booker and Jayden would tell him his speed was unnatural, like nothing they had ever seen, a tornado of death. He watched their intestines spill to the asphalt as their knees gave out. Marshall knew that this scene before him more than any other horrifying experience would haunt him the worst. He just knew. *The most disgustin' deaths of all.*

"Eyes on the bridge and creek!" Marshall shouted to the triarii. Shaking off the imagery of the two Golgoths he had just eviscerated; he went over and laid the kneeling Gabriel onto his back.

"Still not over," said Gabriel. He coughed. Blood sprayed from his mouth onto Marshall's face.

"Can't you heal y'all's self, somehow?"

Gabriel smiled. Blood burbled onto his teeth from his stomach. Marshall felt ill seeing it. "I knew this was a one-way trip, Marshall." He reached up and cupped Marshall's bearded cheek. "God showed me my end before it happened. Perhaps his final test: would I act, knowing it would lead to my death. I passed the test, Marshall. I'm going home now."

"No! You led these people into war; you're the only one who can lead them out of it!"

Gabriel coughed. He tried to speak. At first it was a gargle.

"God showed me more. Tonight, you and our brave warriors clean yourselves, feed, take your rest. On the morrow, release the women and children through the escape hatches into the woods. Make them wait until the Elect have filled the caves with enemy dead. Your wives have experienced bloody battle firsthand. They will become leaders among our women. But those born and raised here must live their entire lives without ever seeing violence. Promise me."

Marshall nodded. "I promise, Gabriel."

Gabriel coughed up blood. Marshall sensed life force draining away. It wouldn't be long now. "Seal evil inside the tunnels with excavated dirt until they can hold no more. Cover every entrance with boulders. The worms below will grow fat, and the grass above will grow greener."

Gabriel descended into a coughing fit. Marshall found a new position behind to prop him up and give him something to lean against.

"You do love the green," said Marshall. Gabriel tried to smile. "Fifteen casualties against seventy-eight-thousand dead Golgoths. Gabriel, that is a miracle."

Gabriel nodded. "Yes, son. It is. But a bigger miracle is coming now. Hear me: Take your Trail hikers to Valley Forge. There you will find the last remaining Golgoth guarding a pen of women and girls. Destroy the guard and leave him where he lies, for the birds of the air to pick clean.

"You will see a cathedral nearby. Inside you will find more innocent captives, identified by the dead leader's mark on their bodies. They are victims. But any unmarked woman you find there is a willing bride of Satan. I can understand if you cannot bring yourself to kill a woman. Just know that if you leave them alive, at some point they will bring harm to the Church."

"Dear God, Gabriel."

Gabriel's words became a whisper. Marshall bent to hear what no one else could. "The Church of the Elect is God's restart. All evil must be eradicated and the face of the earth purified before the Son of Man returns, as it is written. You and your brave team will be that final mikvah," he said. A coughing fit, the worst yet.

"Rescue all innocent captives held at Valley Forge and bring them back here to become Elect. Baptize them as I baptized you and welcome them into the Church. Give our fifteen fallen heroes an honorable burial and see that their loved ones want for nothing. Read whatever passages you like from the Bible to the Church every Sunday until the Lord comes. Conduct marriages. Disassemble the catapults and repurpose the wood. The farms are well cared for and run themselves. Do this not because I, Gabriel Thomas, ask this of you. It is not I asking, but the Spirit working through me."

Gabriel coughed weakly. Marshall grabbed his hand. "I ain't much into public speakin,' prophet. In case y'all can't tell, the Elect think I talk funny. Please stay."

Gabriel patted Marshall's cheek and smiled weakly. "You will do fine. I suppose it's time to go. Though I would rather stay."

Marshall had known Gabriel for months, bonded to the magic man of goodness, light, purity, and warmth, through dreams. The man who owned his nights, infused there by forces outside the known universe. *Would I have walked away from Tatum if the Spirit 'a God livin' inside me required my full devotion? Would I have given up all when asked, as Gabriel has? Honest answer—I don't know if I'm that strong.*

"You are," said Gabriel.

"Oh dear Lord! Forgot sometimes y'all can hear other people's thoughts. Any regrets?" Marshall asked.

Gabriel smiled. Marshall found it simultaneously horrible, and beautiful. "Only one. That I never got to kiss Yeshua's warm hand. But you will, Marshall. I believe that you will. See you on the other side."

Marshall felt the hand go slack. He watched the chest collapse and rise, nevermore. Sixteen Elect casualties. Marshall closed his eyes and prayed.

Thumbnail Moons

The cabins prepared for Marshall and the hikers were clustered together in the southernmost woods. With the help of the five triarii, Marshall carried Gabriel Thomas's body to the cabin he shared with Tatum. Booker and Jayden carried Gunny Powell's body to Jayden and Dodie's cabin. Other triarii who watched in silence from the battlefield, including Drake, carried the slain mortar teams. Gently they laid bodies in front of Booker and Aliyah's cabin.

Marshall stood on his stone steps to address the assembled triarii. "Gabriel put me in charge 'til the Lord comes," he said, shaking his head. "I didn't ask for the job, y'all can believe that. He gave me an immediate mission for tomorrow. For tonight," he said, looking down at the dead, "I say, we all can't take our rest 'til these brave men take theirs. Find shovels. I will bury Gabriel. Booker and Jayden will bury Gunny Powell. Each of y'all will bury a member of Gunny's crew. Carve each Elect's name into the handle 'a y'all's sword usin' a dagger point. Use the swords to mark the graves. Go now, get the shovels." The men ran off in a double-time trot and returned from the barn holding shovels. By one-thirty a.m., the burials were accomplished.

Marshall spoke in a low tone, his eyes fixed upon the sword sticking up from Gabriel's grave. "Tomorrow we all release the innocent Elect from the caves into the woods and keep 'em there 'til we fill the caves with enemy remains and seal the corruption inside. Some of us gonna leave on a mission given to us by God, through Gabriel, to finally end this.

"I know y'all are grievin.' Tonight we lost an authentic miracle 'a God. A true prophet—and the purest, most righteous, sainted Elect anybody alive ever knew. He gave his life for us 'cause God asked 'im to. He knew he'd die violently in battle long before the fight; he knew he had no chance 'a survivin.' Imagine livin' with that knowledge ev'ry day 'n still runnin' the Church. Gabriel was the bravest man any 'a we all ever knew. I shouldn't say he *was* the bravest like in the past tense: Gabriel *is* alive, and his spirit gonna dwell forever with God in Heaven. We will hold a proper ceremony for 'im, and for these other brave Elect who gave their everythin' on the battlefield. The entire Church will attend and pray. Eventually we gonna carve proper headstones outta granite. For now, we all will follow Gabriel's order to clean up, eat, and rest before the hard work we all gotta face in the mornin.' Go now, and may God bless us all."

Marshall awoke to sunbeams and bird chatter from a lucid dream about thunder and bright lights, heralding the Second Coming of Christ on earth. He felt groggy. Every muscle, sinew, and tendon ached. He craved meat; his body demanded protein. He got up, dressed in clean clothes, gulped water, and walked down to the A-shaped Tudor building where he found bowls of shelled nuts. He chased away a squirrel and three chipmunks then helped himself. Refreshed, he walked to Gabriel's tower and found the microphone. He turned it on and blew into it. This met with audio feedback squeals. *Yep, it works.*

"Elect: Mornin' y'all: this is Marshall Langar. Our prophet tasked us all with a duty. Rise, quickly drink and eat somethin.' Meet me on the battlefield in fifteen minutes. That is all."

Every hastati and triarii awoke and obeyed. *Such discipline*, Marshall thought. He did not ask them to form lines; they fell into formation naturally, just as Gunny Powell had trained them.

When all were gathered, "This task goes to y'all who sealed the cave: unseal it, then open wide every emergency exit. Drake alone is gonna enter the cave. He's gonna move the innocents out into them woods through emergency exits. Once freed, Drake's gonna make sure everyone stays in the woods 'til summoned down here. Not before we completely pack them caves with dead demons and earth before final sealin.' Scoop up any organs or intestines. We ain't gonna leave a single trace 'a their cursed existence now that blood and soil have become one. Finish in ninety minutes. That's it, y'all. Let's get to it."

Was it a sense of awe that he felt? Something remarkably close to it as he watched the orderly, almost insectile organization of Gabriel's Elect army. Nobody slacked, which would have forced others to work harder toward their odious goal. He watched them stack charred bodies from atop and behind the earthen walls. On the battlefield, pureed human flesh was already beginning to bloat and attract flies. The vile sweet-sour stench of decomposing flesh hung over the Elect like a sulfur cloud, yet they labored on in silence, though he did witness his fair share of vomiting. Others used pitchforks to scoop blood-caked guts and other grisly leavings into wheelbarrows. They worked in teams, filling these same wheelbarrows with soil from the earthworks into the main cave entrance and into the woods, to fill emergency exits.

By the sixty-minute mark the earthen berms had been reduced by half. Marshall watched Drake pointing to teams, directing their actions. At last, when the berms were all but gone, Drake and his crew rolled the large boulder over the cave entrance for the last time. He and they then disappeared together into the woods to seal the hidden exits in the woods with heavy stones.

At the ninety-minute mark, behind Drake emerging from the woods high up the mountain, Marshall heard the crunch of many feet. He saw her. At the head of the procession Tatum walked beside Drake. Marshall dropped the mic and fled the deck. He ran down to the now cleared field.

She saw him and broke away from Drake. They crashed together. He lifted her and spun her around three times as she giggled. "Oh, Marshall. Put me down. I'm sure I reek. I just spent the night in a nasty place. Ladies were going number two everywhere and there was no real ventilation."

He sniffed her neck and hair. "Mmm. Cave-aged deliciousness."

She punched his chest, laughing. "You truly are an animal, Mister Langar."

He smiled. "And y'all wouldn't have it any other way, Missus Langar. Hey, we all need to move. Follow me," he said, and she did, up to the tower deck. He grabbed the mic. "Booker, Jayden: meet us at the tower with y'all's weapons and goggles. Aliyah and Dodie grab two wheelbarrows, plenty 'a food, small robes, and jugs 'a water. We all 'r leavin' here in ten minutes."

Aliyah and Dodie arrived first. "The wheelbarrows were gross, Marshall. We took them down to the stream to give them a good wash," said Dodie, "and still we beat the guys. How long does it take to fill a quiver with arrows, grab weapons and goggles, and get their butts down here?"

Marshall smiled. "In all fairness they all still got one minute left in the ten I gave."

Then Booker and Jayden appeared. "Well good morning, hoss," said Jayden. "Notice anything missing?"

"Your guitar and bedding."

Jayden smiled. "Yup. Otherwise, we look just like we have for the past month. You know it's kind of ironic when you think about it. We all left placid places, safe, sane, and stable—to walk for a solid month guided by dreams of a joyful, peaceful Church fellowship. We end up killing along the way. No sooner do we arrive and we're waging war, Roman style. And now we're all married to a buncha batshit-crazy women—"

"Hey!" Aliyah, Dodie, and Tatum called out. He blinked at them innocently and flashed a brief but charming little grin.

"Ain't peace something?" asked Jayden. "And I haven't played my guitar since Nashville. I say to Dodie, 'Baby, I need a haircut and a shave.' Dodie says, 'don't you dare.' Does feeling like I'm the last civilized man on earth make me the crazy one?"

"I gotta agree with Dodie," said Marshall. "If y'all 'r gonna be the rock star of the Church then please look the part, at least. Okay hikers, off we go. Booker: what's the shortest path to Valley Forge Park?"

Booker, atlas at the ready, traced his finger. He grinned. "Hah. Well guys—you'll love this—we're going back exactly the way we came on the mountain trail, to Gravel Pike, then pick up the Perkiomen Trail straight to the park. Nostalgia party! Round trip about ten hours."

"Which means we all likely gonna be walkin' back here in the dark," said Marshall. Now guys, it ain't gonna be just us on the hike back. This is a rescue mission. Gabriel said God wants us all to bring back Hostis Dei's prisoner girls and baptize 'em into the Church. Let's get movin,' 'cause time is crucial."

They walked back up Spring Mount Road and back down the mountain trail. Each took turns pushing the two wheelbarrows filled with stoppered earthenware jugs of spring water, berries, nuts, apples, sweetened cakes, and forty small, linen robes. "Is it okay to talk this time? I see you guys are all armed like before. Are all the Golgoths gone?" asked Dodie.

Marshall nodded. "It's okay to talk," he replied without further comment. Back on Gravel Pike, on the right Marshall caught glimpses of greenhouses through tree cover. *Exactly as Gabriel had described.* Further south on the right he spotted the tall Norway Spruce and remembered. *Kids. They were all only just little kids. Gabriel, I love y'all. But I ain't ready to lead the world's last survivin' Church, 'specially one this big. Heavenly Father, if possible, take this cup from me. Nevertheless, y'all's will be done, not mine. Amen.*

"Penny for your thoughts, husband," said Tatum.

"Trumpets."

"Trumpets?"

Marshall nodded. "'For the Lord will descend from Heaven with a shout, with the archangel's voice, and with the trumpet of God, and the dead in Christ will rise first.'"

Tatum appeared thoughtful. "Will all the dead believers claw out of the ground like zombies? That sounds, like, beyond creepy."

"Sorry for overhearing," said Booker. "Here's a thought, Tatum. What about the ones we just cremated on the walls? Ashes and bone bits. You think it's like when you drop a finished jigsaw puzzle, but then God makes all the pieces come back together?"

"What it sounds like," she said.

"Booker, please if y'all don't mind explain to everyone 'bout computer programs and sleep mode," said Marshall.

Booker gave his opinion that spirits are like computer programs in screensaver mode after bodies expire. Although no one present had ever used a computer, all understood how they worked. "Does the resurrection of the dead make more sense?"

Tatum nodded. "Sort of, yes. Yes it does, Booker. Thank you."

"Nothing to it, Lady Langar," he said.

"It amazes me how your mind works," she said. "When Christ returns, does that mean our 'programs' inside new eternal bodies will join the other programs in Heaven?" Tatum asked.

Marshall shook his head. "No, babe, it don't. Not right away, at least. The Bible says there's gonna be a thousand-year reign 'a Christ on earth. If we all go straight up to Heaven, which is called the Rapture, then there ain't gonna be Church on earth left for Christ to lead. The Elect are God's fresh start. I believe this. A second chance for humanity to live the way God originally intended. Some people gonna stay here and stay human; all the faithful dead gonna rise together to Heaven."

"Given free will, many rejected him," said Dodie. "Like Arabella, most chose to seek the approval of other people instead of God. They fell for the gods of this world, like Hostis Dei and others under the spell of the prince of darkness running this world."

"Satan?" asked Tatum.

"Yep. Most failed to realize it was the devil they worshipped, ev'ry time they cheated; lied; preyed on people; stole; and murdered their own babies," Marshall said, thinking of Delilah. "The greatest lie Satan ever sold is that he don't exist. Satan influences people and makes his home inside 'em, same way as God's Holy Spirit lives in us. They all don't see it for what it is, but we see it."

"Isn't it funny," said Tatum. "Like Arabella, whenever she felt bad, like when Grady died, she blamed God. The rest of her days she denied God's existence. She only trotted him out when she needed a scapegoat to blame. I never saw God and Satan working through people; I never once thought about it. Never knew I had a decision to make. I choose God. I feel him working inside me now. My whole life, he knocked on my door and I was too stupid to realize it."

Marshall put his arm around Tatum. "With God, nothin' ain't never too late while we live. Once our bodies die, all choice is gone and his Judgement rests upon us."

"Scary. Billions across millenniums have chosen unwisely," said Tatum, "just as I had. Seems so harsh."

"The judgments of the Lord are true and righteous altogether," said Aliyah. "Read that in a Psalm."

"No do-overs," said Booker. "Everything we say and do is recorded in Heaven's computer. I believe angels will make us sit and watch every moral decision we made in our lives, every careless word uttered, reliving them in moving pictures with sound. Sentenced to outer darkness many will cry and gnash their teeth as they learn precisely why they're getting separated from the light of God. All who loved Jesus—Yeshua—are automatically judged worthy to dwell forever in the Kingdom of light with God, sins forgiven. We get to skip the tribunal and the sins playback."

"Imagine! Every question will get answered," said Dodie. "The Bible tells us Heaven is a place of perfect happiness, where we who love Christ will be reunited with the Elect we loved whose bodies died before ours, not just blending into some faceless mob. I call it a fair deal, Tatum. Better than I deserve. Call me crazy, but I don't want to spend eternity in the dark surrounded by cannibal spirits."

Tatum appeared thoughtful. She nodded. "God is just and merciful."

"Amen, said everyone."

Marshall stopped. "Booker, y'all called the timin' 'a our hike to Valley Forge just right. Exactly three o'clock and here we all are."

"If we walk along Route 23, it'll take us past the Washington Memorial Chapel. If there is anything worth seeing then we'll see it from Route 23," said Booker.

"Okay, everyone back in stealth mode. Zipped lips," said Marshall.

Expressions on the faces of Aliyah and Dodie intensified. Tatum narrowed her eyes at Marshall. Booker and Jayden unslung their knapsacks and freed their bows. Each nocked an arrow. "Guys, seriously, what is going on?" asked Aliyah.

"Gabriel warned me about one last Golgoth hangin' 'round, the last 'a his kind, and some hostile females. Don't y'all worry. A coupla' demons ain't no match against the three of us."

"You mean six of us," said Tatum.

Marshall grinned. "Says my little murderer 'a mushrooms." She punched his chest. Aliyah and Dodie seemed to relax a little. "I don't know about y'all but me?" said Marshall "After last night's war, feelin' like I could sleep for a week straight. Let's get 'r done."

They made the final push eastward to Valley Forge, across the intact Sullivan's Bridge over the Schuylkill River, then a quarter-mile uphill climb to the severely Flood-damaged Visitor Center on the Joseph Plumb Martin Trail. Booker pointed east and so they walked east on Route 23.

"I liked it better in the woods. Cooler by ten or fifteen degrees. The sun blaring down on us kinda sucks," whispered Jayden. "Even now, hours past its peak it's still a damned furnace. Remember back on the Trail when Marshall joked about hiking to Alaska for some ice water? Maybe it's not so funny. I hate heat."

"Maybe we should just walk the Trail forever," said Dodie, quietly.

"I prefer the heat," whispered Aliyah. "What say you, Tates?"

"I loved the Trail," Tatum answered softly, and shot Marshall a conspiratorial glance. "If we ever get bored on Spring Mountain, maybe we could shake things up and walk North. See where it leads."

In a mile on the right, the majestic gray stones and bell tower of Washington Memorial Chapel came into view. "Marshall, look," whispered Tatum. She pointed at the expansive field directly across from the building, acres of tall grass recently trampled, dozens of small crude log cabins and thousands of makeshift tents, a rotting corpse crucified, the cross roped to a tall, pointed stone obelisk. Just east, five corpses hung impaled on tall medieval pikes, not yet entirely picked clean by vultures and crows.

Behind these was a rusting repurposed steel cyclone fence that enclosed simple huts without walls. Only thatched roofs shielded the girls and women underneath from the elements: naked, lying in piles of their own offal, urine, and vomit; some languid, others listless. From this distance it appeared they were either sleeping, or dead. "Dear God," whispered Dodie. Jayden pulled her close and forced her to look only at him.

The last remaining Golgoth, a hulking giant of a man, materialized from somewhere behind the enclosure. His face a smirk of enraged confidence, the man charged straight at them.

Moons and Scars

The Golgoth hurled his spear. Jayden reacted quickly falling into his assassin stance. But not quick enough. The fast-moving iron tip grazed his left shoulder. It bled. Dodie screamed. Jayden nocked and cocked: took aim; and released his arrow. His shoulder wound affected his aim. Instead of hitting the intended chest area of his enemy the arrow sunk low, slicing away a portion of the white inner thigh. The Golgoth yelped but continued to run, now only forty paces away. Booker then let his next arrow fly. It hit the lower abdomen at close range and traveled cleanly through. As the Golgoth ran, Booker caught a glimpse of the arrowhead protruding from the lower back. This slowed the enemy down but did not stop him. The Golgoth held his sword straight in front with both hands like a battering ram.

"Enough 'a this," said Marshall. He grabbed his machetes and charged. He formed an 'X' with his blades, trapping the Golgoth sword forcing it downwards. He leaped up to head-butt the huge white face. Nose cartilage fractured. Momentarily stunned, the Golgoth stood holding his face, eyes watering and wide open in surprise. Marshall extended his arms completely as though preparing to bear-hug him—then swiftly he brought his arms together with all his strength. The machete in his left hand severed the Golgoth's right hand at the wrist and sliced through half of his neck. Inside the neck, it kissed the sharp edge of the right machete somewhere in the middle. The aberrant head came off cleanly and hit the asphalt with a sickening sound. The body fell forward and sprayed Marshall's boots with gouts of dark blood.

Behind him, Marshall heard Aliyah and Dodie retching. He stared at the severed head for a few seconds, then he turned. "Sorry. Y'all weren't meant to see that."

"Oh, Marshall! That was the coolest thing I ever saw!" said Tatum. She ran to him and hugged him. Still holding the blood-slicked blades he opened his arms to her, rested his chin on her head, and regarded his friends with an expression of finality, and relief.

"The world is now free from evil men," Marshall said. "Satan rose and had his time. Now it is really, truly over, I think. Aliyah, Dodie, after y'all've pulled it together, please take the food and robes to the fenced area. See how many 'a these Elect girls can be saved. We can use the two wheelbarrows if one or two can't walk. Booker, Jayden: come with me and Tatum. We all need to get inside the chapel. Gabriel told me there are women inside; some are Elect bein' held captive; but some in there mean to kill us. I really ain't gotta clue what to expect in there; Gabriel was real cryptic 'bout this bit. Women could attack us. Booker, y'all up for anythin' and everythin?'"

"Heck yes," he said.

"How y'all feelin,' Jayden? Up fer it?"

Jayden examined his shoulder and found that the bleeding had stopped. "Right as rain. Mostly just surprised me, is all. You know me: I'll do whatever needs doing, hoss."

Marshall nodded, turned, and walked toward the Chapel. Booker, Jayden, and Tatum followed. "So, this is what a real house of God looks like," said Booker. "First one I've seen up close. I mean, I've seen photos of St. Peter's Basilica in Rome, and Gaudi's Cathedral in Barcelona. This one sure isn't those, but still it's the finest building I have ever seen."

Marshall tried the door latch. Locked. He tried shoulder-ramming and kicking. "Gimme a hand or a foot, guys," he said. They did. The door did not budge. "Nope; ain't happenin.' Come on, there's gotta be another way in here. Let's find it."

Marshall led them south to a two-story structure with the lower level below grade that appeared to connect with the basement floor of the chapel. He counted eight window openings, four on the east wall, three to the west, one to the north. He found the wooden door in the rear courtyard north facing wall. He tried the knob. "Locked," he said. "But did y'all hear that? This door ain't nothin' like that unbreachable submarine hatch out front." Marshall knocked on it three times. "Hollow and weak. Let's give it some serious what-fer, y'all." Marshall, Booker, and Jayden took a few steps back, tensed, aimed, then lunged forward to kick the door on its hinged side.

The hinges and wood were no match for a combined five-hundred-plus-pounds rammed against it. It exploded inward. A wave of cloying, hot, stenchful air blasted their faces.

"Help me." A close very weak female voice spoke.

Marshall could tell Tatum was about to say something, but he raised his hand for silence. Late afternoon sunlight struggled through filthy glass. Marshall listened. Hearing nothing, he said, "Booker, please tell me that y'all brought—"

"My solar-charged flashlight?" He clicked it on. Their eyes had not yet adjusted to the dark. The flashlight seemed as bright as the sun in this reeking tomb.

"Help…me…said the woman's voice." Booker shined the whitewash around the cavernous darkness, seeking a source behind the voice. He found a wooden table with a woman lying on it.

Tatum grabbed the flashlight and ran to the woman. Marshall and the others followed. The light beam went helter-skelter as Tatum's hands shot up to cover her terrified mouth. Marshall caught up to her. "Tatum? What is it?"

Tatum's eyes were saucers brimming with tears. Reluctantly, she directed the beam down. The woman looked like a human skeleton covered with skin. Her entire body was bald but for a few days' stubble on the recently depilated head, underarms, and pudenda. Her wrists were tied above her head: her impossibly thin thighs were spread apart, tied to eyehooks screwed into the thick table sides. Her sunken eyes appeared open and bright. Marshall's gaze met the glassine eyes of the victim.

"Don't…look at me," she croaked at him. Immediately he felt her shame and turned away, unwilling to add to her humiliation and misery. He glanced at Tatum; she read his expression.

"We couldn't possibly have gotten here any sooner, Marshall. You just fought a battle all night. You obeyed the prophet and his timing, which came from God. I can see it in your face: 'If only, if only,' no, Marshall. None of this is your failure." Ferocity of conviction animated Tatum's face. She would not break eye contact until Marshall nodded.

Tatum splashed light back onto the woman, reached down, and stroked her face. "My God. You're only a teenager. What's your name, hon?"

"M-M…Mary. Mary Wills."

Tatum bent down and, smiling, kissed and caressed the captive's forehead. Horrified, Tatum urgently wanted to run away screaming. Recently someone had red-hot branded a searing crescent moon symbol, a cuticle shaped scar two inches from point to point, into every tender inch of skin below the captive's neck. The torturer had omitted no part of her—not even the soles of her feet. Tatum had an unstoppable vision of red-hot steel being pressed into her own flesh, and she shivered. *Was he marking his cattle, is that what this was? No. He never thought another man would dare go near his stable of concubines. This was the last of Hostis Dei's entertainment before battle; pure cruelty for his own pleasure and amusement.*

Despite the redolent stale stink of burnt flesh, urine, feces, and low-oxygen hot air, Tatum's shivering only grew worse. She battled against billowing waves of nausea and horror. This was malevolent sadism, an evil so pure that it existed far down underneath any known limits. Violence rose in Tatum's throat like a storm. Hostis Dei had wanted his captive to suffer the agonies of the damned, as if sexual slavery was insufficiently sadistic.

Satan's nature, at work in man, hit Tatum all at once as she stared down at burned tissue. Wounds still oozed bodily fluids as epidermis fought to regenerate. Tatum rubbed her own face as she grappled with the deepest disgust ever felt. She inspected over one hundred wounds for signs of infection. Jayden stood frozen in the shattered doorway.

"Marshall. Machete these ropes." She held the girl's legs to gently straighten them when the bonds suddenly fell away. "Jayden, carry her to Dodie. She can't even weigh seventy pounds. She needs water immediately, but only small sips or she'll barf it up." Jayden shuffled over. Careful not to look too closely at the girl's ravaged body, his eyes glued to hers, he reached under the girl's shoulders and knees and lifted.

Cradled in his arms, he said, "Hi, Mary. My name's Jayden. I sing songs and gaze at the sky. I'm going to take you to my wife. She's going to take such good care of you. You'll be right as rain in no time, and safe from evil men forever."

As he walked, he looked over his shoulder and whispered, "Sixty pounds, maybe?" He glanced at her face. "I wrote a song. I think I'm going to give it to you. What do ya think? Would you like my song?" Weakly, she nodded, and tried to smile. Marshall and Tatum heard him singing:

You saved me
In every way
You saved me
Giving one more day
You saved me
We both know what's true
Maybe in some small way
I hope I saved you, too

"Wow. Never knew he is such an amazingly good singer," said Tatum. Desperately Tatum wanted to distract her own mind from the diabolism attacking her kind heart and gentle soul, like a virus. She refused to allow the spirit of anger, chaos, hate, and vengeance to seep in and control her like it had with the Golgoths.

"Now that we all know what to expect," said Marshall, "maybe whatever we find in here is better than Mary. I reckon there ain't nothin' inside that gets any worse than this."

Booker nodded. "Just want to say how glad I am that Gabriel sliced off that demon's junk. Fitting that Hostis Dei—may he burn in Hell for all time—departed this world minus his favorite organs that defined him; organs that drove him to rape girls and torture people. Satan has a whole red theme park awaiting that arch demon."

"Really, Booker? Do you think he'll roast for all time? Cool!" Tatum said. Booker and Marshall briefly made eye contact. Marshall grinned and slowly nodded. *That's my girl,* he thought.

Slowly they made their way through rooms and labyrinthine walkways, air cooler and mildew flavored. The tang of mold gave way to something awful, a cadaverine, putrescine smell, like rotting flesh.

"Skatole, giving off strong fecal odor," said Booker, sniffing the air. "Indole: mustier, with its distinctive mothball-like smell. Hydrogen sulfide, exactly like rotten eggs. Methanethiol, like rotting cabbage. Dimethyl disulfide and trisulfide, like garlic. I read about rot. Don't ask me why;

sometimes I regret being a walking encyclopedia. This is bad," Booker said. "You might've been wrong, Marshall."

"'Bout what?" Marshall asked.

"That it can't get any worse in here than poor Mary Wills. It surely can, and it will," said Booker. "The devil is real, and we're walking straight into its lair."

The eye-watering stench grew stronger as they neared a closed wood door. Marshall turned the knob. It opened. He grabbed the flashlight from Booker and shined the beam inside. He choked back nausea triggered by clouds of extreme redolence enveloping him; a sick stench; a ghastly rich sick-dead smell. 'Pffew. Oh my dear sweet Jesus."

When a woman dies, she sure does want us all to know about it, he thought. He closed his eyes and lowered his head.

"Marshall, what is it?"

He shut the door, swallowed hard, and faced them. "Torture chamber. What he did to Mary was a birthday party compared to what he did in there. No survivors," he said.

"How many?" Booker asked.

"Twelve. Some were skinned, vivisected, taxidermized. Others, hate to say it, got it even worse. I can tell you this: these girls were alive under Hostis Dei's knife. They felt every cut until they could feel no more. He kep' 'em conscious with ammonia; got rags soakin' in it beside every girl."

"Man, I can't see that," said Booker, "not even in my mind."

Marshall nodded. "I don't wanna talk about it. I can't ever unsee what I just saw." He glanced upward. *I done seen some awful things, but God Almighty, Lord, I ain't never seen nothin' so evil as this. Gabriel, if y'all can hear me: y'all sure didn't prepare me right enough for this mission.* Another terrible thought crept across his consciousness. *If we keep knockin' on the doors 'a tombs, knockin' to wake the dead, eventually, the dead gonna answer.*

Marshall walked on, haunted by images and memories of odors. No happy thoughts he conjured would shake these ghosts away. He felt the skin of arms, scalp, and spine attempting to crawl away from his flesh. Slowly, he collapsed to the dusty wood plank floor onto his back.

"Marshall! Oh my God, what happened?" Tatum yelled.

"Just gimme a minute, wife," he said. His face was covered in perspiration, lips blue, pallor white. "My blood pressure just bottomed out." He rolled onto his side and vomited. Tatum knelt behind him and stroked his sweaty face. She bent and blew air onto his face. After a minute, his color started to return. "Help me up," he said. Tatum pulled until he stood.

She cupped his cheek. "What just happened, lover?"

Marshall rubbed his face. "Just that I ain't never seen nothin' like what I saw in that room. I thought I understood the nature 'a evil. I knew nothing, until just now. I guess it was too much for my old man's heart.

Let's walk on."

Booker stood like a statue through Marshall's entire ordeal. Finally he said, "Don't ever scare me like that again, Marshall."

Marshall attempted to grin. "Will try not to my friend."

Concrete stairs led up to a door. Marshall ascended first. He tried the knob. It opened. He shined the light around the cavernous room. They were inside the chapel. He saw rows of old wooden pews polished glassine smooth by many faithful Elect sitting to pay their respects to God. He had never seen such grandeur.

"Wow!" Booker muttered. "Look at the colored glass! This is God's house."

"It sure wasn't God's basement back there, I know that much," said Tatum.

"Even the basement was holy before evil moved in," said Marshall. "Works the same way with people. Ideals are peaceful and pretty. Humanity is ugly, and very violent."

"Amen," said Booker. "Scripture is quite clear on this: 'You can enter God's Kingdom only through the narrow gate. The highway to Hell is broad, and its gate is wide for the many who choose that way.'"

"Tatum," said Marshall, "Booker just quoted God himself, from when he visited us in human form. Our bodies are like this chapel. Evil is a force like the Flood flowin' 'round us…like a river 'round a rock, forever pushin' to get inside. Our one job is to be strong in the Lord and seal that filth out," he said. "Nobody's immune to evil. Ain't only ever been one human who never sinned not even once; who was completely incorruptible."

"Yeshua? Jesus Christ?" she said.

Marshall nodded. In Tatum's eyes, he recognized the understanding.

"God sent his son and proved once and for all time that his Commandments, his peaceful ideals, are attainable. All's we gotta do as individuals is decide to attain 'em."

Tatum nodded. "Like everyone in the Church of the Elect on Spring Mountain."

Marshall nodded. "I love the people on the mountain but this here is how a church should look! I mean, look at the carvin' on those pews. The stonework, how it stretches up so high. The gorgeous stained glass," Marshall said. "The floorin,' the sanctuary. Can y'all feel the love? Whoever built this place truly adored God. In here, I feel God's presence. This truly is God's house. Now I understand what I'd read in the Bible: 'Passion for God's house will consume me.'"

"I feel another presence," said Booker. His keen ears had picked up a sound.

Booker stood at Marshall's left, Tatum at his right, the three in front of the altar. They stared down the main aisle at the wooden door in tomblike silence. The acoustics in the chapel allowed a whisper in the front to be heard in the back.

All three heard a sound like the rustle of cloth ahead to the right. They heard the same sound coming from the left pew directly opposite, also from left-right pews several rows behind closer to the front door. Now rising from the left: a bald pate, eyes, and a nose, the whole painted white like a female Kilroy. The hateful eyes stared at them. Rows behind also on the left, another bald female head rose up. Two on the right soon followed.

At a distance, Marshall stood transfixed by the two on the right. *The eyes. Haint' I seen 'em before?*

The two on the left stood erect. They walked into the main aisle. Both were naked, stomachs and breasts swollen from pregnancy.

"My God," whispered Tatum. *So, this is what it looks like to have a baby growing inside,* she thought. The two on the right stood. As they did, Marshall's knees felt rubbery. He felt lightheaded.

Before she had a chance to study the two new faces, Tatum sensed trouble. She whipped her arm around his waist. "Husband, what is it?"

"Husband?" said the taller of the two women on the right. "I thought I was your wife, Marshall," said Delilah.

"Well, if it isn't Booger Bailey and his traitor picininny, Aliyah," said Arabella, standing beside Delilah.

Booker loaded an arrow, drew, and pointed it at Arabella's naked chest.

"Booker! What are you doing?" cried Tatum.

"We meet again, Arabella," he said. "I should've dropped a pin in you on the James River."

"Hold it!" yelled Marshall. Everyone froze. "Let's all just calm down."

"Marshall!" whispered Tatum. Is that...is she..."

"Delilah? It's me, in the flesh. Marshall's real wife. And who are you, tomboy?"

Tatum made steps toward Delilah with her hands extended like claws. Marshall hooked her arm. Tatum struggled to free herself from his powerful grip. "I'm his *real* wife you baby-murdering *bitch!* You had your chance back in Tennessee and you blew it! You corrupt, profane piece of..."

"Marshall," said Delilah. She spoke calmly, evenly. "We were captured and held here as prisoners against our will to serve as slaves of Hostis Dei. Thank God you came to rescue us." Her tone resonated in Marshall like an echo inside a bottomless cavern; to him it sounded unnatural: as if something else was speaking through her.

"Hah!" said Arabella. "Hostis Dei and the god Hubal will rescue us. You'll see, Delilah. Hostis will come and waste the two boogers and lezzie and—"

"Marshall," said Booker. "Sorry, but I must sink an arrow into this race-hating filth…"

"Hey Arabella: how come you four don't have any crescent moon brands on your fronts like those in the basement?" yelled Tatum. "Are you special or something? So very pregnant, too. You married the devil? Looking pretty plump: what have you been eating, Bella? Or should I ask *whom* it is you've been eating?"

Arabella's eyes narrowed on Tatum. "Eating skinny little lezbos like you, Tatesy, mmm mm mm. And yeah, I am pregnant; Delilah, too. He's no devil; the one true god, Hubal, runs Hostis Dei. You people are the devils."

"Where is Hostis Dei now, Arabella?" asked Marshall.

"At war. Taking apart those stupid Bible-bangers to make way for our new home. He'll return, and when he finds you here, well. See those skeletons outside the Breeder Pen? That was a Sunday picnic compared to what Hostis Dei will do to each of you with his own two hands."

Marshall could not tear his gaze away from Delilah's face. *Eyes of a corpse. How did I overlook this terrible feature? Like a doll's eyes.* He also noticed no crescent moon brands on their exposed skin like that of Mary Mills, or other marks. Gabriel's whispered words returned to him. *'As for the woman with whom you had carnal knowledge, she is now a bride of Satan. Also know that any woman you find inside the chapel not bearing the mark of the crescent moon must never be allowed near the Church of the Elect. If any have conceived, the children are also unclean and may never commingle with the Elect. It may be a mercy to end their lives, but this was not given to me from above. When the time comes, pray to the Father in Yeshua's name for guidance in the moment. Under no circumstances are you to bring any of these here.'*

Marshall closed his eyes. *Father in Heaven, please give me y'all's Spirit without measure. Guide me, please. And quickly. In Yeshua's name I pray. Amen.*

Marshall lifted his arm. Gently, he laid his hand on Booker's right shoulder. "Gabriel said it was my choice to kill 'em or leave 'em here to die. We just won a war, and we ain't had to tap the spirit 'a hate to do it. Let's just go. Let 'em rot. They can't survive long with no food source."

Marshall started walking toward the door. Booker's left arm trembled from intense frustration. "I was born without one shred of your purgation gene, Marshall" Booker said. Nevertheless, Booker followed Marshall and Tatum toward the front door of the church.

Never had Marshall or Tatum seen Booker's untroubled face so replete with indifference, with stone ataraxy, as he spoke. "Please accept the fact that some of us are wired differently, Marshall," said Booker. Whatever happens next is a result of all forces that you can neither feel, nor see, nor relate to." They also noticed his flat tone of voice, now as suddenly deep and tuneless as a large, cracked bell. "But you do perfectly understand the paradoxical nature of God. Thou Shall Not Kill. Then he creates malware programs like that hate-consumed piece of shit, Arabella, and every other

Golgoth."

"Yes, Booker," Marshall said. "He gave every soul complete free will. Love and hate are spirits. They present us all with a binary choice. Decide to be ruled by one, or by the other. Arabella chose poorly. But Booker, it is never too late for her, or for any sinner to repent. And y'all should know as a student 'a languages, in old Aramaic, Greek, Hebrew, and others of the region, words for 'kill' and 'murder' were often used interchangeably by the ancients. Thou Shall Not Murder. Killing is different, as when defending the innocent. See? Snap! No more paradox."

Booker's expression was of one unconvinced. "Sometimes killing in combat or to protect lives is necessary, sanctioned by God. I do not feel that shooting a non-combatant is murder when we all know she'll seize any opportunity to come around and kill me and mine, and you and yours, if I give her the chance. I cannot in good conscience give her that chance, Marshall."

"Y'all's a good man, Booker Bailey," said Marshall. "Not a killer of unarmed women. I'm sure y'all's parents would be proud of the brave man y'all have become. Please reconsider this cold-blooded execution. Actions like this weigh down a man's conscience for life, draggin' it around like a bag of heavy stones around the heart."

Booker advanced with Tatum beside him, arrow aimed at the heart of Arabella from mere feet away. Still, both Arabella and Delilah, along with two pregnant strangers across the aisle from them, stood defiantly.

Tatum stopped. In the brides of Hostis Dei, Tatum perceived their misplaced overconfidence. "Your infernal master is *dead*," she said. "They're all dead, every demon. Repent; be washed clean by the blood of Jesus Christ; and live."

Tatum's eyes flamed with fresh mental images of Arabella knocking out Marshall behind the cabin. She glanced at the famous Delilah. For a moment Tatum wondered if Delilah were prettier than she. She decided yes, Delilah is truly beautiful, which inflamed her all the more.

Booker joined Marshall and Tatum at the door. Three hearts raced like never before swamped by a flood of dark emotions. Marshall's love for Tatum was absolute. But the sight of Delilah again tugged at pieces of himself he never knew existed. His head throbbed. Murder hornets in his head and heart, bolts of lightning in his glands. *"Lord, Lord. My dear sweet Lord."*

Booker tried to suppress his fury against the inconceivably hateful creature who attempted to murder him and the love of his life; he could not fathom how Arabella could have survived the James River rapids. Seeing her now fanned flames of fury not felt since seeing his parents roasting in Five Points South, Birmingham.

Tatum struggled against what she knew was an unhealthy jealousy of

Delilah, and deep loathing for these willing, complicit cannibals. *What if they have male baby cannibals gestating inside them that will grow up to kill Elect? Should we really leave these hateful, murderous bitches here? What if they somehow find stashed food and survive: then they can lie in wait along the Trail to pick off the Elect one by one for years to come. Maybe they'd start a new society to oppose us, repeating the cycle ad infinitum.*

"Take us with you, Marshall. Please?" Delilah had somehow resurrected the voice of her twelve-year-old self, strident and helplessly innocent, the one she had used on him inside the Gatlinburg pharmacy; the voice that had melted his self-serving resistance like butter on a stove. No longer did Marshall's mind see the nude, pregnant ghostly white adult, out of place in God's house who regarded him with fisheyes and a malevolent slit of a grin. Once again she appeared to Marshall as the frightened little orphan sitting on the floor hiding from torture and death, like an innocent dove in a snare.

But then another image flashed to mind, foreign and repugnant: Hostis Dei thrusting his infernal seed into Delilah. She was smiling. Moaning. Pregnant with his satanic seed. Marshall wondered from where the image came. *The Spirit? Gabriel spoke 'a short movin' pictures delivered at decision points exactly when needed. Was that disgustin' little pornographic scene one 'a them signs?*

"Can't do it, Delilah. Can't take you back with us," he said. "Goes against God. Tatum; Booker: I'm walkin' outside through this big front door. Follow me." They did.

Just as Marshall had put forty feet between him and Delilah and once again breathed welcome fresh air, he heard her sardonic laughter. He turned to look back. Delilah held up both middle fingers exactly like the last moments they had been together back on Mount LeConte. "Here's to your God, Marshall." She reached down to the pew seat, as did Arabella, as did the two pregnant women now standing beside them.

Marshall could not tear his eyes from Delilah's homicidal face; his cognitive brain barely acknowledged the four long daggers pointed at him.

Shoulder to shoulder the four women mounted a full-sprint charge at him.

Signs and Wonders

Booker raised his arrow at the four hostile women charging at them now fewer than twenty feet away. They picked up momentum. Booker refused to give Marshall time to intervene; Booker respected Marshall but something inside decided the question for him. Taking hasty aim, he let the razor-tipped arrow fly. It hit low. As he reached back to grab a second arrow, Booker watched Arabella's face. On it he read agony, that she felt every sensation when his arrow pierced her lower abdomen and sliced through her intestine, and uterus, and whatever unclean life was developing inside it. The projectile advanced with a slowness that seemed implacable, yet somehow grand. The actual time until the point protruded from her back was a fraction of second. To her, it felt far longer. Adrenaline and endorphin-fueled, the arrow managed to slow her, but only momentarily.

Delilah and the other two pregnant brides paused in surprise, but only for a moment. Arabella, Delilah, and the two unknown brides of Hostis Dei resumed their knife attack charge.

The arrow in Arabella's belly jiggled up and down in rhythm with her milk-enlarged breasts like unhallowed tom-tom drums. *Obscene fruit,* Booker thought. He nocked another arrow, fired, and hit one of the women left of Arabella straight through the heart. She crumpled instantly. A few twitches and she moved no more."

"Booker— stop!" shouted Marshall.

Booker gauged about five seconds before Arabella, Delilah, and the other bride would each plunge knives into him, Tatum, and Marshall. His muscles remembered the prior night on the tower deck, high-speed firing: he drew the string and released. The arrow pierced the second unknown woman's throat. Both hands flew up to her neck. *Threat neutralized,* he thought.

Arabella and Delilah both aimed knives straight at Marshall. Just as Booker's arrow deprived one woman of her ability to breathe, Tatum darted behind Marshall. She unsheathed both machetes and, quicker than either Booker or Marshall had ever seen a person move, she whipped around in front, putting herself between the two charging brides and Marshall, one second before Arabella and Delilah's dagger points would pierce him.

Tatum's growl turned to a fierce screech. Like lightning, she thrust one machete at Arabella and one at Delilah. Tatum's speed and strength met their forward-charging kinetic energy. The long blades had become serrated in places from Marshall's kisses against tens of thousands of skulls and bones the prior night.

In Tatum's hands, Marshall's machetes ripped through skin just below Arabella and Delilah's breastbones. The serrated steel sawed and sliced through major arteries and organs. "Try to kill my husband—devils!" Tatum screamed at the two now on their backs, blood erupting from their cleaved middles like fountains. She pushed against the blades with every ounce of strength. "This is what you get! Die-die-DIE! And go to *Hell!*"

Tatum's narrowed eyes appeared wolfen to Marshall; her small, even teeth were exposed through lips drawn back in a snarl.

Arabella and Delilah's legs kicked as their daggers pinged against the tile. Tatum soaked in their expressions of mortal shock. "Dieeeeeeeeee!" she screamed, sawing in and out, her full weight pressing down, sawing through lungs and other organs. The damage Tatum wrought made it physiologically impossible for them to scream. Tatum sensed it. "Screams of inconceivable pain: I trapped those inside…left you devils with no way to vent the worst agony anyone can feel. Wish I could rewind this scene and kill you again!"

Tatum withdrew the machetes to a wet sucking sound then kicked both women in the head. As her breathing normalized, she closed her lips. She turned to Marshall; eyes ablaze.

"They're still alive but not for long. They'll bleed out in minutes and awaken to Judgement," Tatum said, breathing hard.

Marshall's throat constricted. He looked at Tatum in a way that she had never seen. Disappointment and mistrust.

A guilty twinge of regret crept down Tatum's spine.

"They were going to kill you! They left me no choice. Please don't hate me, Marshall."

He went back to staring at Delilah, his face inscrutable. The next few minutes drew out like a bloodletting, for Tatum.

Tatum watched Marshall's expression soften. He turned his back on the abominable scene upon the tiles.

"Thanks, wife" he whispered. "I could never hate y'all. God knows it's true." The machetes tinkled loudly against the tiles as she threw herself against him. He held her.

Marshall stole another glance at Delilah. *Our baby, the one I made with y'all will see the face of God. Y'all won't ever see it. Not ever.*

"Tatum I—I just couldn't do it," his high-pitched, emotional words muffled against her scalp. "I felt many things for her once back there in another life far from this place. There was attraction, sure, but not to the insane levels I feel for y'all."

"Did you ever love her?" Tatum held him tighter.

"I'm Christian. I suppose I love every person. My feelins' for her seemed more…protective. At first it felt like I had adopted her, like a daughter or kid sister. It wasn't until much later that she developed romantic designs on me. I gave in to it…succumbed to her charms. What happened up there didn't break my heart, but it squeezed it a little. So, no.

What I feel for y'all is universes different."

"It's okay, shhh. I know, my love. I know. Really, I promise, it's okay," Tatum whispered. She pulled away a little to watch his eyes. Again, he could not help steal glances as Delilah's life pumped out of her, at eyes once brighter than all the stars now slowly going dim, like a lit candle placed in a big glass jar with a lid.

"I rescued 'er from Golgoths," he said. "She thanked me by murderin' my baby and reject'n my Lord…and reject'n *me*. She made herself the enemy of everythin' that I am. And there wasn't one gall-darned thing I could do or say to change that truth. She dreamed 'a the Antichrist and ended up wedded to it. That's exactly what Hostis Dei was."

Together they looked at the dying Delilah and Arabella. "Behold, the wages of sin," he said. "But I couldn't kill no woman."

"Because you still love her a little, some part of you does."

He spoke into Tatum's cobalt blue eyes. "Pity. That's all I feel for her. I imagine God feels this multiplied by a trillion. But his judgement is righteous. No exceptions. She made 'er bed. I couldn't bring myself to do what y'all did even though I should've. Gabriel said it would be better; said that endin' whatever lives we found inside the chapel unmarked by the brands of the beast would be righteous killin' ordained by God."

"Thank you, Marshall," said Tatum through her tears. "Gabriel washed me clean of past sins. I had no intention of sinning further. Thank you for absolving me of sin, for what I just did."

"Gimme your hands," Marshall said. Tatum did. "Booker, please. Join us." Booker laid his dark hands atop theirs. Marshall bowed his head, closed his eyes. Booker and Tatum imitated. "Heavenly Father, we pray that if it pleases y'all, save Delilah's immortal spirit, and Arabella's, and them other two as y'all saved us. Please forgive us for these kills and wash these stains from our spirits. Thy will be done. In the name of y'all's Son, Jesus—I mean Yeshua—we pray…amen."

"Amen," muttered Tatum.

Booker stood like a statue. His all-the-way-open eyes then narrowed on Arabella. He sensed Marshall and Tatum studying him. He turned and met their gaze. "Amen," he muttered, distantly.

Fully absorbed by Arabella's last moments, nothing could tear Booker away. "The wounds I inflicted would have killed Arabella slowly and miserably from infection and internal bleeding, had it not been for Tatum's more catastrophic blade-work. I claim this kill, Tatum. My arrow cooked this turkey. You only sliced it up."

Tatum looked at Marshall, who nodded. "Truth, Booker."

Marshall turned to see who was running toward them. Jayden's amiable expression sagged when he saw their faces. Then he looked down. All three heard his deep, startled inhale. "Oh my God. Arabella. How in the hell did she—"

"Golgoths probably picked 'er up along a waterway on their way back here and beat us by days or weeks," said Marshall.

"Who's the one beside her? And what about those two lying just outside the door?" Jayden asked.

Marshall spoke through gritted teeth. "She ain't nobody. An apostate of Hell like Arabella and them other two. Four brides 'a Satan."

"Dear Lord. No other victims inside?" Jayden asked.

"Yes but not alive," said Booker. "We walked all the way through. Hey Marshall. What do we do with the bodies?"

Marshall momentarily considered dragging them back inside the greatest chapel he had ever seen which had been built to endure two great Floods and Golgoth habitation. "They stay where they lay. Let the birds and insects have 'em, which is what Gabriel told me to do with any Golgoths we find. Jayden, how many rescued Elect 'r we takin' back with us?"

"Ten who can walk," said Jayden. "Whether Mary Mills makes it is in God's hands. We filled a wheelbarrow with straw and extra robes; she's curled up inside, nursing a water bottle and nibbling at some little cakes. Maybe she'll live. There's another who refused to eat human meat who wasted away like Mary. She's in the other wheelbarrow. Which leaves ten fit enough to walk, barely. They must've eaten grass and straw to remain alive, but there isn't much physical mass left to any of these girls, Marshall. They wasted away from lack of protein. Aliyah and Dodie did their best to clean them up a little. They gave each a robe but they're all shoeless."

"Great news!" said Marshall.

"That they're shoeless?"

Marshall frowned at Jayden. "The King will reply, 'Truly I tell you, whatever you did for one of the least of these brothers and sisters of mine, you did for me.'"

"Matthew 25:40," said Booker.

"Don't know how y'all do that, remember so much, Booker Bailey, but I'm just sure glad y'all do it. Jayden, any robes left?"

"Three."

"Go tear 'em into long rags and bind their feet. The Trail is long and harsh. Smooth pink skin ain't no match for it. Then we go home," said Marshall. He took one last glance at dying Delilah and started walking.

Quietly, certain no one could see, Booker spit on Arabella's corpse.

Marshall and Tatum took up their familiar positions in front. He pushed the wheelbarrow containing Mary Mills, who remained asleep despite the jostling. Twilight rapidly descended into darkness. Marshall turned and could just barely spot Jayden and Dodie in the rear. He felt no need for goggles given the brightness of the zodiac supernova starlight. The festering red moon regarded him like a conjunctivitis infected evil eye floating in pus. Marshall knew that the blood moon may have been one of the Biblical signs of the Second Coming of Christ, but that night on the Trail, it looked and felt to him like the angry, bleeding, and defeated moon god. He continually glanced up at it.

Y'all lose, Hubal. Or Lucifer, Ba'al, Beelzebub, Satan, or whatever men have named y'all. We destroyed y'all's seed upon the earth, we who are only men, just men. But soon, one far more powerful than we all's gonna come, the straps of whose sandals I ain't worthy to untie. He will bind y'all for a thousand years.

"How y'all feelin'?" Marshall asked Tatum, as he took the first steps toward home.

"Kinda lousy, actually."

"Wait, what? How?"

"Sick to my stomach," Tatum said. "My boobs hurt."

Marshall searched his memory banks. "Are y'all peein' a lot? More than usual?"

"Mm hmm, yes. You see all the stops I keep making to squirt. Way more. Why?"

He thought some more. "I know we all been losin' sleep 'n carryin' a ton 'a stress in the last thirty hours, but have y'all been feelin' super-fatigued? Like all y'all's wantin' to do is lie in bed?"

"God, yes, for a week now… like I have half the energy of usual."

"Breasts feelin' a bit more tender than usual? Swollen, maybe?"

"Marshall, yes. Why, what's going on?"

"Shouldn't y'all be on y'all's period right now? It's been over thirty days since I last heard y'all talk 'bout a pom-pom."

"Tampon. And you should know, animal. Can't get you to stop poking and sniffing around down there."

Wearing a guilty dog grin, he stopped, and so everyone behind him stopped. "Well then. Y'all got your wish."

"I—I what?"

"You're pregnant!" he shouted. "Y'all's gonna have a baby!"

Exuberant cheers and claps erupted behind them. Tatum's entire skin incandesced with embarrassment. "Are you sure?"

Marshall nodded. He whispered, "Seen it before. Only this time, Satan won't be stealin' my future from me. This time it's our future, wife." He released the wheelbarrow, kissed her, and spun her around. More cheers, even from the exhausted, emaciated rescued women.

Tatum's eyes held his. She cupped his bearded cheeks. "Not today, Satan. Not ever. Praise Jesus, Marshall. Glory be to God in the highest," Tatum spoke through her ceaseless grin. Marshall kissed her, smiled back, and turned behind him to address the followers.

"Everyone, listen up: y'all newcomers 'bout to be welcomed into the

Church of the Elect with more love, safety, smiles, and open arms than anyone could imagine! No more tears, ever again! Five more hours 'a hikin' separates us from the community of y'all's dreams. Follow me and Tatum, or Booker and Aliyah, or Jayden and Dodie. Try to keep up. If y'all 'r feelin' completely beat, like y'all can't go on, let us know. We'll take short breaks, but I need y'all to find energy inside yourselves, somehow. Really tasty hot food and hot showers, clean clothes, and pretty log cabin homes await. But only if y'all make it there. Got it? Let me hear y'all say, thank you Jesus!"

"Thank you Jesus!" said all.

"Praise God! Hallelujah!" he said. They all answered in kind.

Eighteen hearts beat free and light along the wooded Trail outside of Valley Forge National Park. Each pondered a future without evil forces grinding them down to a horrific, painful death. Rescued teen girls and young adult women wept incessant tears of deep relief; of freedom; and for the first time since being captured: hope.

"How many Golgoths did you ghost last night do ya think?" Aliyah asked.

"Thousands, baby. Thousands," said Booker.

Her arm around his waist, she pulled herself close. "So proud of you, husband. You may be younger than I am, but you are a thousand years older in your heart and soul. Love you so much." He reached behind her and squeezed the back of her neck. "Did you really spit on Arabella?"

"You saw that?"

"Remember this, Burl 'Booker' Bailey: I have eyes in the back of my head. You can't get anything past me. How did it feel to sink that arrow into her antebellum plantation guts?"

Booker remained silent. "I thought that maybe after killing thousands of Golgoths, my hate would die with them, for what they did to my parents. It didn't. My hate died with her. It wasn't that she tried to kill me. My parents are my past, but you are my future. She tried to kill *you* and almost succeeded—you who grew up under the same roof, raised by the same man. She knew you and yet *still* wanted you dead, simply for being Black. Ripping into her gut was…well. Sorry, Lord, but it was the single most deeply satisfying act of violence in the history of mankind. It felt so good, and righteous, and true, Aliyah. Now I feel as though I can never hate again. From now on it's all love. Love for God, love for you. Love for everyone, so help me God." Aliyah tapped Booker's right shoulder with her temple.

"So, you gave away the song you keep promising to sing to me in front of the entire Church to Mary, the sixty-pound teenager. Feeling a little cheated here, Jayden," said Dodie.

Jayden snickered. "I've spent a few hundred hours lately trapped inside my own head. Recall weeks of not making noise because of Golgoths? I thought about God. Thought about him a lot. I thought about Jupiter and the stars, and about super-volcanoes. About war. About my parents. But I thought about you more than you know, Dolores."

She backhanded his groin. "Do tell. Confess all."

He shrugged. "All these other thoughts vexed me to the marrow. I guess you could say that even before our first kiss, I used you. Well, thoughts of you, anyway. Used you to regain a sense of normalcy, of peace, hope, and love. I speculated about us coming together. Then, after my dream became real, I used the quiet time to compose the greatest love song in history.

"After some food and a hot shower, a few hours of you giving me a massage because I damned-well-earned it," he said with a smirk, "and a good night's sleep that lasts thirty-six hours, I'm gonna pick it out on my guitar and sing it for you. Then, I'll sing it into Gabriel's microphone, I'll sing it to the entire Elect Church, but first dedicate it to my wife, the love of my life. Still feel cheated?"

Knowing no one could see, she grabbed where she had backhanded. "You belong to me, husband. 'Til death does us part, you are mine." He smiled into the darkness.

"Besides, the lyrics I sang to Mary now seems less like a love song, more like a paeon, a requiem. Poor kid is barely clinging to life. If she dies, I will never sing that song again. If she lives, I'll name it God Delivered Mary and sing it in his honor."

The climb up the trail connecting Gravel Pike and Perkiomen Creek to the top of Spring Mount Road ended just before midnight. Thirsty, Marshall called for their fifth break. All but Mary sat on the crumbling old asphalt of the road. Some of the newcomers sipped water. Others lay flat and fell asleep immediately. Marshall and friends, well-conditioned from weeks of night-hiking across mountain ranges required no break. The road ahead was plainly visible under sanguine moonlight and supernova starlight.

"Marshall," Tatum whispered. "Do you feel something weird?"

He looked at her. He opened his ears and eyes to their maximum sensitivities. "Like a low thrummin' from somewhere deep underneath?"

"That, and a change in the air."

He nodded. The vibration was steady and disquieting. It smelled as though all oxygen had gotten ionized away, replaced with ozone. "Gabriel told us all from the Bible that before the Lord comes, the moon will turn to blood, and—"

Lightning flashes exploded silently in the sky from one end to the other. The shocking brightness of the hard, persistent, shadowless light—and the incessance of it—penetrated every eyelid. Sleepers awakened. A low rumbling bass sound replaced what under normal conditions would have been thunder and filled every cubic foot of air with vibration.

"Jayden, why are we seeing lightning and hearing thunder when there isn't even one cloud in the sky?" Dodie asked. Her voice trembled.

Jayden recognized a deep, rumbling bass clef from low G to high G, with a brassy shrill high G note sustained throughout, like pairing a tuba with a French horn or trumpet. He covered his ears to save his eardrums from ripping. All clapped hands to ears as the volume increased.

"That isn't thunder. What the—that's at least a hundred-fifty decibels," he shouted from the rear. The same blast of sound again. To Jayden, it seemed to come from above and below at the same time. He counted off seconds. *Again, the identical sound. Precise nine-second intervals,* he thought. "We should all be deaf by now. This level of sound destroys hearing. Yet we're fine."

"What is it?" screamed Aliyah.

Booker smiled. "It is he, wife."

"Who is he?"

"Marshall, look!" Tatum shouted and pointed skyward. "Watch the lighting! Watch it!"

"I...I am." Bolts of light silently touched down somewhere high on the Spring Mountain slope. They could see the electricity travel down from where they stood on the other side of trees but could not see where it came to ground. The lightning kept going to ground in the exact same spot somewhere on the long, green Spring Mountain slope.

"Watch it, Marshall," Tatum yelled. "Do not take your eyes off the lighting." The din of bizarre sounds now rendered human conversation impossible.

None could avoid seeing the pure white energy, enormous preternaturally bright bolts of it. The energy of lightning but far wider, intense, and vertical, stretching up through a cloudless sky seemingly deep into outer space. Those with focus spotted something dark, possibly solid, travel down through the opaque energy at the speed of electricity.

"My God, Marshall. What was that?" Tatum screamed into his ear.

He closed his unhinged jaw and blinked. He smiled.

"I think y'all mean who."

Marshall leapt up and turned back to the group. "Break's over!"

He abandoned his backpack on the road. He grabbed Tatum's hand and ran toward the light.

ABOUT THE AUTHOR

John James Minster was born in Norristown, Pennsylvania. He commenced a successful international business career since the 1980s in the technology sector while publishing horror short stories in anthologies. In July 2018, his first middle-grade full-length horror novel, Dreamjacker, was born of nightmares. Hellbender Books published The Undertaker's Daughter, disruptive religious horror for mature audiences on Halloween, 2022, to acclaim from authors, critics, and genre fans. In May 2023, his short story collection, The Vengeful Dead, was published, winning the attention of Hollywood and other horror movie producers. All three of John's publications have generated mostly five-star reader reviews from international horror fans.

As a child, John walked in his sleep. His parents found him at the top of the stairs about to leap down, dreaming that he could fly. He still talks and punches walls in his sleep during nightmares, which he describes as "Nightly mini horror movies—so, no writer's block on the horizon; no chance that I'll run out of stories." Learn more at JohnJamesMinster.com.